ALBANY COUNTY
PUBLIC LIBRARY
Serving the Laramie Plains since 1887

Laramie, Wyoming 82070

PRESENTED BY

A Friend

Murder on the Menu

Murder on the Menu

Edited by Peter Haining

Carroll & Graf Publishers, Inc.
New York

Published by arrangement with Souvenir Press Ltd., London.

Carroll & Graf Publishers, Inc.
260 Fifth Avenue
New York, NY 10001

ISBN: 0-88184-859-X

Manufactured in the United States of America

For
PHILIPPA and SUE
Anglo-Oz Caterers
Fiendishly Good Food!

CONTENTS

INTRODUCTION

The scene is a small dinner party. Three couples are sitting round a table, and the sound of chinking cutlery and the gentle buzz of conversation create an atmosphere of enjoyment and general well-being. One of the guests, the rather effusive man on the left of the hostess, takes another mouthful of food, swallows it, and then, suddenly, clutching his throat, makes a horrible choking sound. Before any of the other five diners has a chance to move, the man slumps forward onto the table . . . dead.

It is not only in crime fiction that stories such as this are to be found. History, too, can provide similar instances in which poison has brought a dramatic end to some unsuspecting diner's meal.

The ways in which mealtime killers, whether real or fictional, have dispatched their victims are many and varied, and the place of death may have been a restaurant, café, club or inn as often as a private home. But truth is always stranger than fiction, and I doubt if any author could possibly have matched the fiendish ingenuity of Cardinal Ferdinando de' Medici, one of the hugely wealthy Florentine dynasty, some four hundred years ago.

It appears that the Cardinal was anxious to rid himself of his elder brother and had hit upon the idea of poisoning him with a peach which he would share. Using a golden knife, he sliced the fruit precisely down the middle, then passed one half to his brother, proceeding to munch the rest contentedly himself. A moment later, the elder man sank dying to the floor.

How had the Cardinal survived the poisoned peach? The blade of the knife had been carefully smeared with poison on only *one* side—and the half *it* had cut de' Medici handed to his unsuspecting brother.

Of course, poisoning men and women through their palates was much easier in the past when food was often over-salted, over-spiced or rancid; and even in the earlier part of this century, when there seemed to be something of a vogue for killing people with toxic doses, forensic science was still in its infancy and there were plenty of substances extremely difficult to trace in a corpse.

Where a dose of poison has always had the advantage over other forms of murder is that the victim has no time to duck as he or she may do when confronted by a gun, or to ward off the lunge of a knife thrust. And getting the person to take the bait is simplicity itself if it is served up in a favourite dish.

Looking through the crime novels of the genre's 'Golden Age', between the two World Wars, it is interesting to draw up a list of the poisons that were used. Naturally enough, arsenic, cyanide, hemlock, nitrobenzene and strychnine were essential ingredients in many killers' pharmacopoeias. Weed killer was a very popular choice in country house murders, while botulism in tinned foods was ideal for use in the city. Some of the cleverer criminals even managed to come up with arcane poisons from far-off places like South America.

Equally interesting are the dishes in which the poison was served. Porridge and eggs (unless they were hard-boiled) were breakfast favourites; Dover sole, either baked or poached, was the ideal lunchtime killer; while for the evening meal, a meat dish or any cream sauce seemed to avoid suspicion until it was too late. Spirits, too, were easy to doctor, as were boxes of chocolates. And the glass of warm milk (or cocoa) taken before going to bed probably killed off more victims in these novels than all the rest put together!

Of course, not all mealtime murders have been committed with the aid of poison. The good old-fashioned blunt instrument has cropped up on a number of occasions, as have the gun and the knife, all striking down diners when they least expected it. Nor does the list end there, as the reader will find in this book.

For the gourmet of crime stories, the composition of the fateful meal often holds as much interest as trying to solve the cause of death. The more exotic the dishes, and the more succulently they are described, the greater the sensation of pleasure experienced by the reader. Even the finest *cordon bleu* cookbook cannot offer quite the same *frisson* as some of these mixtures of crime and culinary delights.

In this anthology the reader will find a wide variety of short stories mixing food and murder—not to mention some mystery and horror—and because they fall neatly into categories I have divided them into three main 'courses'. Firstly, some outstanding stories by famous writers like P. D. James, Ruth Rendell and Patricia Highsmith, set mainly in fine restaurants, clubs, and cafés; then a selection of historical culinary tales ranging from the activities of the infamous Borgias to a modern variation on the Last Supper; and, finally, a group of detective cases featuring such famous gourmet sleuths as Hercule Poirot, Nero Wolfe and Inspector Maigret. All the stories are written with the same skill that one would expect from a master chef, and it is no surprise to learn that most of the authors were gourmets and proud of it. Some of them were excellent cooks, too.

One of my favourite stories about food and death was told some years ago by Lord Dunsany, that larger-than-life Irish nobleman who was known around the clubs and restaurants of London and Dublin as 'the worst dressed man in Ireland'. One of Dunsany's pet hates was the adulteration of food, and he recounted a parable concerning Death and what happened when he became ill and his followers set about curing him with modern nutriments.

'One day,' Dunsany said, 'they carried Death into the dining-room of a great hotel and brought him bread such as the modern bakers make, whitened with alum, and the tinned meats of Chicago, with a pinch of our modern substitute for salt. They brought him a bottle of wine that they called champagne and gave him their cheap Indian tea. They also bought a newspaper and looked up the patient medicines and gave him the foods that it recommended for invalids. And after a while, Death arose ravening and strong and strode once again through the cities.'

Having survived thanks to those adulterated foods, Death will be found stalking the following pages where the dishes are rather richer and certainly more exotic. The menu is ready for the reader's selection. Dine well!

Peter Haining
Boxford, Suffolk
February 1991.

Murder on the Menu

I

SPECIALITÉS DE LA MAISON

Stories by Some Famous Authors

THE SPECIALITY OF THE HOUSE

Stanley Ellin

Every major city in the world has a little restaurant that looks like Sbirro's in this opening story by Stanley Ellin (1916–1986): inconspicuous, but highly regarded by its gourmet clientele. Appearances, however, can be deceptive, especially in the hands of a writer whom The Times *described as 'a master of the thriller, a man in the tradition of great storytellers'. Some readers may well have seen the films from his works, including* Nothing but the Best *(1964, starring Alan Bates) and* House of Cards *(1968, with Orson Welles). 'The Speciality of the House' was Stanley Ellin's first published story, written in 1948, and it has been widely praised. Alfred Hitchcock presented a brilliant television adaptation some years ago, claiming that he had had to overcome strong resistance from the TV network. After reading the denouement the reader will undoubtedly understand why!*

'And this,' said Laffler, 'is Sbirro's.' Costain saw a square brownstone façade identical with the others that extended from either side into the clammy darkness of the deserted street. From the barred windows of the basement at his feet a glimmer of light showed behind heavy curtains.

'Lord,' he observed, 'it's a dismal hole, isn't it?'

'I beg you to understand,' said Laffler stiffly, 'that Sbirro's is the restaurant without pretensions. Besieged by these ghastly, neurotic times, it has refused to compromise. It is perhaps the last important establishment in this city lit by gas jets. Here you will find the same honest furnishing, the same magnificent Sheffield service, and possibly, in a far corner, the very same spider webs that were remarked by the patrons of a half-century ago!'

'A doubtful recommendation,' said Costain, 'and hardly sanitary.'

'When you enter,' Laffler continued, 'you leave the insanity of this year, this day, and this hour, and you find yourself for a brief span restored in spirit, not by opulence, but by dignity, which is the lost quality of our time.'

Costain laughed uncomfortably. 'You make it sound more like a cathedral than a restaurant,' he said.

In the pale reflection of the street lamp overhead, Laffler peered at his companion's face. 'I wonder,' he said abruptly, 'whether I have not made a mistake in extending this invitation to you.'

Costain was hurt. Despite an impressive title and large salary, he was no more than clerk to this pompous little man, but he was impelled to make some display of his feelings. 'If you wish,' he said coldly, 'I can make other plans for my evening with no trouble.'

With his large, cowlike eyes turned up to Costain, the mist drifting into the ruddy, full moon of his face, Laffler seemed strangely ill at ease. Then 'No, no,' he said at last, 'absolutely not. It's important that you dine at Sbirro's with me.' He grasped Costain's arm firmly and led the way to the wrought-iron gate of the basement. 'You see, you're the sole person in my office who seems to know anything at all about good food. And on my part, knowing about Sbirro's but not having some appreciative friend to share it, is like having a unique piece of art locked in a room where no one else can enjoy it.'

Costain was considerably mollified by this. 'I understand there are a great many people who relish that situation.'

'I'm one of that kind!' Laffler said sharply. 'And having the secret of Sbirro's locked in myself for years has finally become unendurable.' He fumbled at the side of the gate and from within could be heard the small, discordant jangle of an ancient pull-bell. An interior door opened with a groan, and Costain found himself peering into a dark face whose only discernible feature was a row of gleaming teeth.

'Sair?' said the face.

'Mr Laffler and a guest.'

'Sair,' the face said again, this time in what was clearly an invitation. It moved aside and Costain stumbled down a single step behind his host. The door and gate creaked behind him, and he stood blinking in a small foyer. It took him a moment to realise that the figure he now stared at was his own reflection in a gigantic pier glass that extended from floor to ceiling. 'Atmosphere,' he said under his breath and chuckled as he followed his guide to a seat.

He faced Laffler across a small table for two and peered curiously around the dining-room. It was no size at all, but the half-dozen guttering gas jets which provided the only illumination threw such a deceptive light that the walls flickered and faded into uncertain distance.

There were no more than eight or ten tables about, arranged to ensure the maximum privacy. All were occupied, and the few waiters serving them moved with quiet efficiency. In the air was a soft clash and scrape of cutlery and a soothing murmur of talk. Costain nodded appreciatively.

Laffler breathed an audible sigh of gratification. 'I knew you would share my enthusiasm,' he said. 'Have you noticed, by the way, that there are no women present?'

Costain raised inquiring eyebrows.

'Sbirro,' said Laffler, 'does not encourage members of the fair sex to enter the premises. And, I can tell you, his method is decidedly effective. I had the experience of seeing a woman get a taste of it not long ago. She sat at a table for not less than an hour waiting for service which was never forthcoming.'

'Didn't she make a scene?'

'She did.' Laffler smiled at the recollection. 'She succeeded in annoying the customers, embarrassing her partner, and nothing more.'

'And what about Mr Sbirro?'

'He did not make an appearance. Whether he directed affairs from behind the scenes, or was not even present during the episode, I don't know. Whichever it was, he won a complete victory. The woman never reappeared nor, for that matter, did the witless gentleman who by bringing her was really the cause of the entire contretemps.'

'A fair warning to all present,' laughed Costain.

A waiter now appeared at the table. The chocolate-dark skin, the thin, beautifully moulded nose and lips, the large liquid eyes, heavily lashed, and the silver white hair so heavy and silken that it lay on the skull like a cap, all marked him definitely as an East Indian. The man arranged the stiff table linen, filled two tumblers from a huge, cut glass pitcher, and set them in their proper places.

'Tell me,' Laffler said eagerly, 'is the special being served this evening?'

The waiter smiled regretfully and showed teeth as spectacular as those of the majordomo. 'I am so sorry, sair. There is no special this evening.'

Laffler's face fell into lines of heavy disappointment. 'After waiting so long. It's been a month already, and I hoped to show my friend here . . .'

'You understand the difficulties, sair.'

'Of course, of course.' Laffler looked at Costain sadly and

shrugged. 'You see, I had in mind to introduce you to the greatest treat that Sbirro's offers, but unfortunately it isn't on the menu this evening.'

The waiter said: 'Do you wish to be served now, sair?' and Laffler nodded. To Costain's surprise the waiter made his way off without waiting for any instructions.

'Have you ordered in advance?' he asked.

'Ah,' said Laffler, 'I really should have explained. Sbirro's offers no choice whatsoever. You will eat the same meal as everyone else in this room. Tomorrow evening you would eat an entirely different meal, but again without designating a single preference.'

'Very unusual,' said Costain, 'and certainly unsatisfactory at times. What if one doesn't have a taste for the particular dish set before him?'

'On that score,' said Laffler solemnly, 'you need have no fears. I give you my word that, no matter how exacting your tastes, you will relish every mouthful you eat in Sbirro's.'

Costain looked doubtful, and Laffler smiled. 'And consider the subtle advantages of the system,' he said. 'When you pick up the menu of a popular restaurant, you find yourself confronted with innumerable choices. You are forced to weigh, to evaluate, to make uneasy decisions which you may instantly regret. The effect of all this is a tension which, however slight, must make for discomfort.

'And consider the mechanics of the process. Instead of a hurly-burly of sweating cooks rushing about a kitchen in a frenzy to prepare a hundred varying items, we have a chef who stands serenely alone, bringing all his talents to bear on one task, with all the assurance of a complete triumph!'

'Then you have seen the kitchen?'

'Unfortunately, no,' said Laffler sadly. 'The picture I offer is hypothetical, made of conversational fragments I have pieced together over the years. I must admit, though, that my desire to see the functioning of the kitchen here comes very close to being my sole obsession nowadays.'

'But have you mentioned this to Sbirro?'

'A dozen times. He shrugs the suggestion away.'

'Isn't that a rather curious foible on his part?'

'No, no,' Laffler said hastily, 'a master artist is never under the compulsion of petty courtesies. Still,' he sighed, 'I have never given up hope.'

The waiter now reappeared bearing two soup bowls which he set in place with mathematical exactitude, and a small tureen from which he slowly ladled a measure of clear, thin broth. Costain dipped his spoon into the broth and tasted it with some curiosity. It was delicately flavoured, bland to the verge of tastelessness. Costain frowned, tentatively reached for the salt and pepper cellars, and discovered there were none on the table. He looked up, saw Laffler's eyes on him, and although unwilling to compromise with his own tastes, he hesitated to act as a damper on Laffler's enthusiasm. Therefore he smiled and indicated the broth.

'Excellent,' he said.

Laffler returned his smile. 'You do not find it excellent at all,' he said coolly. 'You find it flat and badly in need of condiments. I know this,' he continued as Costain's eyebrows shot upward, 'because it was my own reaction many years ago, and because like yourself I found myself reaching for salt and pepper after the first mouthful. I also learned with surprise that condiments are not available in Sbirro's.'

Costain was shocked. 'Not even salt!' he exclaimed.

'Not even salt. The very fact that you require it for your soup stands as evidence that your taste is unduly jaded. I am confident that you will now make the same discovery that I did: by the time you have nearly finished your soup your desire for salt will be nonexistent.'

Laffler was right; before Costain had reached the bottom of his plate he was relishing the nuances of the broth with steadily increasing delight. Laffler thrust aside his own empty bowl and rested his elbows on the table. 'Do you agree with me now?'

'To my surprise,' said Costain, 'I do.'

As the waiter busied himself clearing the table, Laffler lowered his voice significantly. 'You will find,' he said, 'that the absence of condiments is but one of several noteworthy characteristics which mark Sbirro's. I may as well prepare you for these. For example, no alcoholic beverages of any sort are served here, nor for that matter any beverage except clear, cold water, the first and only drink necessary for a human being.'

'Outside of mother's milk,' suggested Costain dryly.

'I can answer that in like vein by pointing out that the average patron of Sbirro's has passed that primal stage of his development.'

Costain laughed. 'Granted,' he said.

'Very well. There is also a ban of the use of tobacco in any form.'

'But, good heavens,' said Costain, 'doesn't that make Sbirro's more a teetotaller's retreat than a gourmet's sanctuary?'

'I fear,' said Laffler solemnly, 'that you confuse the words, *gourmet* and *gourmand*. The gourmand, through glutting himself, requires a wider and wider latitude of experience to stir his surfeited senses, but the very nature of the gourmet is simplicity.

The ancient Greek in his coarse chiton savouring the ripe olive; the Japanese in his bare room contemplating the curve of a single flower stem—these are the true gourmets.'

'But an occasional drop of brandy, or pipeful of tobacco,' said Costain dubiously, 'are hardly over-indulgences.'

'By alternating stimulant and narcotic,' said Laffler, 'you seesaw the delicate balance of your taste so violently that it loses its most precious quality: the appreciation of fine food. During my years as a patron of Sbirro's I have proved this to my satisfaction.'

'May I ask,' said Costain, 'why you regard the ban on these things as having such deep aesthetic motives? What about such mundane reasons as the high cost of a liquor licence, or the possibility that patrons would object to the smell of tobacco in such confined quarters?'

Laffler shook his head violently. 'If and when you meet Sbirro,' he said, 'you will understand at once that he is not the man to make decisions on a mundane basis. As a matter of fact, it was Sbirro himself who first made me cognisant of what you call "aesthetic" motives.'

'An amazing man,' said Costain, as the waiter prepared to serve the entrée.

Laffler's next words were not spoken until he had savoured and swallowed a large portion of meat. 'I hesitate to use superlatives,' he said, 'but to may way of thinking Sbirro represents man at the apex of his civilisation!'

Costain cocked an eyebrow and applied himself to his roast which rested in a pool of stiff gravy ungarnished by green or vegetable. The thin steam rising from it carried to his nostrils a subtle, tantalising odour which made his mouth water. He chewed a piece as slowly and thoughtfully as if he were analysing the intricacies of a Mozart symphony. The range of taste he discovered was really extraordinary, from the pungent nip of the crisp outer edge to the peculiarly flat yet soul-satisfying ooze of blood which the pressure of his jaws forced from the half-raw interior.

Upon swallowing, he found himself ferociously hungry for another piece, and then another, and it was only with an effort that he prevented himself from wolfing down all his share of the meat and gravy without waiting to get the full voluptuous satisfaction from each mouthful. When he had scraped his platter clean, he realised that both he and Laffler had completed the entire course without exchanging a single word. He commented on this, and Laffler said: 'Can you see any need for words in the presence of such food?'

Costain looked round at the shabby, dimly lit room, the quiet diners, with a new perception. 'No,' he said humbly, 'I cannot. For any doubts I had I apologise unreservedly. In all your praise of Sbirro's there was not a single word of exaggeration.'

'Ah,' said Laffler delightedly. 'And that is only part of the story. You heard me mention the special which unfortunately was not on the menu tonight. What you have just eaten is as nothing when compared to the absolute delights of that special!'

'Good Lord!' cried Costain; 'What is it? Nightingales' tongues? Fillet of unicorn?'

'Neither,' said Laffler. 'It is lamb.'

'Lamb?'

Laffler remained lost in thought for a minute. 'If,' he said at last, 'I were to give you in my own unstinted words my opinion of this dish you would judge me completely insane. That is how deeply the mere thought of it affects me. It is neither the fatty chop, nor the too solid leg; it is, instead, a select portion of the rarest sheep in existence and is named after the species—lamb Amirstan.'

Costain knit his brows. 'Amirstan?'

'A fragment of desolation almost lost on the border which separates Afghanistan and Russia. From chance remarks dropped by Sbirro, I gather it is no more than a plateau which grazes the pitiful remnants of a flock of superb sheep. Sbirro, through some means or other, obtained rights to the traffic in this flock and is, therefore, the sole restaurateur ever to have lamb Amirstan on his bill of fare. I can tell you that the appearance of this dish is a rare occurrence indeed, and luck is the only guide in determining for the clientele the exact date when it will be served.'

'But surely,' said Costain, 'Sbirro could provide some advance knowledge of this event.'

'The objection to that is simply stated,' said Laffler. 'There exists in this city a huge number of professional gluttons. Should advance information slip out, it is quite likely that they will, out of curiosity, become familiar with the dish and thenceforth supplant the regular patrons at these tables.'

'But you don't mean to say,' objected Costain, 'that these few people present are the only ones in the entire city, or for that matter, in the whole wide world, who know of the existence of Sbirro's!'

'Very nearly. There may be one or two regular patrons who, for some reason, are not present at the moment.'

'That's incredible.'

'It is done,' said Laffler, the slightest shade of menace in his voice, 'by every patron making it his solemn obligation to keep the secret. By accepting my invitation this evening, you automatically assume that obligation. I hope you can be trusted with it.'

Costain flushed. 'My position in your employ should vouch for me. I only question the wisdom of a policy which keeps such magnificent food away from so many who would enjoy it.'

'Do you know the inevitable result of the policy *you* favour?' asked Laffler bitterly. 'An influx of idiots who would nightly complain that they are never served roast duck with chocolate sauce. Is that picture tolerable to you?'

'No,' admitted Costain, 'I am forced to agree with you.'

Laffler leaned back in his chair wearily and passed his hand over his eyes in an uncertain gesture. 'I am a solitary man,' he said quietly, 'and not by choice alone. It may sound strange to you, it may border on eccentricity, but I feel to my depths that this restaurant, this warm haven in a coldly insane world, is both family and friend to me.'

And Costain, who to this moment had never viewed his companion as other than tyrannical employer or officious host, now felt an overwhelming pity twist inside his comfortably expanded stomach.

By the end of two weeks the invitations to join Laffler at Sbirro's had become something of a ritual. Every day, at a few minutes after five, Costain would step out into the office corridor and lock his cubicle behind him; he would drape his overcoat neatly over his left arm, and peer into the glass of the door to make sure his Homburg was set at the proper angle. At one time he would have followed this by lighting a cigarette, but under Laffler's prodding he had decided to give abstinence a fair trial. Then he would start down the corridor, and Laffler would fall in step at his elbow, clearing his throat. 'Ah, Costain. No plans for this evening, I hope.'

'No,' Costain would say, 'I'm foot-loose and fancy-free,' or 'At your service,' or something equally inane. He wondered at times whether it would not be more tactful to vary the ritual with an occasional refusal, but the glow with which Laffler received his answer, and the rough friendliness of Laffler's grip on his arm, forestalled him.

Among the treacherous crags of the business world, reflected Costain, what better way to secure your footing than friendship with one's employer. Already, a secretary close to the workings of the inner office had commented publicly on Laffler's highly favourable opinion of Costain. That was all to the good.

And the food! The incomparable food at Sbirro's! For the first time in his life, Costain, ordinarily a lean and bony man, noted with gratification that he was certainly gaining weight; within two weeks his bones had disappeared under a layer of sleek firm flesh, and here and there were even signs of incipient plumpness. It struck Costain one night, while surveying himself in his bath, that the rotund Laffler himself might have been a spare and bony man before discovering Sbirro's.

So there was obviously everything to be gained and nothing to be lost by accepting Laffler's invitations. Perhaps after testing the heralded wonders of lamb Amirstan and meeting Sbirro, who thus far had not made an appearance, a refusal or two night be in order. But certainly not until then.

That evening, two weeks to a day after his first visit to Sbirro's, Costain had both desires fulfilled: he dined on lamb Amirstan, and he met Sbirro. Both exceeded all his expectations.

When the waiter leaned over their table immediately after seating them and gravely announced: 'Tonight is special, sair,' Costain was shocked to find his heart pounding with expectation. On the table before him he saw Laffler's hands trembling violently. 'But it isn't natural,' he thought suddenly: 'Two full-grown men, presumably intelligent and in the full possession of their senses, as jumpy as a pair of cats waiting to have their meat flung to them!'

'This is it!' Laffler's voice startled him so that he almost leaped from his seat. 'The culinary triumph of all times! And faced by it you are embarrassed by the very emotions it distils.'

'How did you know that?' Costain asked faintly.

'How? Because a decade ago I underwent your embarrassment. Add to that your air of revulsion and it's easy to see how affronted you are by the knowledge that man has not yet forgotten how to slaver over his meat.'

'And these others,' whispered Costain, 'do they all feel the same thing?'

'Judge for yourself.'

Costain looked furtively around at the nearby tables. 'You are right,' he finally said. 'At any rate, there's comfort in numbers.'

Laffler inclined his head slightly to the side. 'One of the numbers,' he remarked, 'appears to be in for a disappointment.'

Costain followed the gesture. At the table indicated a grey-haired man sat conspicuously alone, and Costain frowned at the empty chair opposite him.

'Why, yes,' he recalled, 'that very stout, bald man, isn't it? I believe it's the first dinner he's missed here in two weeks.'

'The entire decade more likely,' said Laffler sympathetically. 'Rain or shine, crisis or calamity, I don't think he's missed an evening at Sbirro's since the first time I dined here. Imagine his expression when he's told that on his very first defection lamb Amirstan was the *plat du jour.*'

Costain looked at the empty chair again with a dim discomfort. 'His very first?' he murmured.

'Mr Laffler! And friend! I am so pleased. So very, very pleased. No, do not stand; I will have a place made.' Miraculously a seat appeared under the figure standing there at the table. 'The lamb Amirstan will be an unqualified success, hurr? I myself have been stewing in the miserable kitchen all the day, prodding the foolish chef to do everything just so. The just so is the important part, hurr? But I see your friend does not know me. An introduction, perhaps?'

The words ran in a smooth, fluid eddy. They rippled, they purred, they hypnotised Costain so that he could do no more than stare. The mouth that uncoiled this sinuous monologue was alarmingly wide, with thin mobile lips that curled and twisted with every syllable. There was a flat nose with a straggling line of hair under it; wide-set eyes, almost oriental in appearance, that glittered in the unsteady flare of gaslight; and long, sleek hair that swept back from high on the unwrinkled forehead—hair so pale that it might have been bleached of all colour. An amazing face surely, and the sight of it tortured Costain with the conviction that it was somehow familiar. His brain twitched and prodded but could not stir up solid recollection.

Laffler's voice jerked Costain out of his study. 'Mr Sbirro. Mr Costain, a good friend and associate.' Costain rose and shook the proffered hand. It was warm and dry, flint-hard against his palm.

'I am so very pleased, Mr Costain. So very, very pleased,' purred the voice. 'You like my little establishment, hurr? You have a great treat in store, I assure you.'

Laffler chuckled. 'Oh, Costain's been dining here regularly for two weeks,' he said. 'He's by way of becoming a great admirer of yours, Sbirro.'

The eyes were turned on Costain. 'A very great compliment. You compliment me with your presence and I return same with my food, hurr? But the lamb Amirstan is far superior to anything of your past experience, I assure you. All the trouble of obtaining it, all the difficulty of preparation, is truly merited.'

Costain strove to put aside the exasperating problem of that face. 'I have wondered,' he said, 'why with all these difficulties you mention, you even bother to present lamb Amirstan to the public. Surely your dishes are excellent enough to uphold your reputation.'

Sbirro smiled so broadly that his face became perfectly round.

'Perhaps it is a matter of the psychology, hurr? Someone discovers a wonder and must share it with others. He must fill his cup to the brim, perhaps, by observing the so evident pleasure of those who explore it with him. Or,' he shrugged, 'perhaps it is just a matter of good business.'

'Then in the light of all this,' Costain persisted, 'and considering all the conventions you have imposed on your customers, why do you open the restaurant to the public instead of operating it as a private club?'

The eyes abruptly glinted into Costain's, then turned away. 'So perspicacious, hurr? Then I will tell you. Because there is more privacy in a public eating place than in the most exclusive club in existence! Here no one inquires of your affairs; no one desires to know the intimacies of your life. Here the business is eating. We are not curious about names and address or the reasons for the coming and going of our guests. We welcome you when you are here; we have no regrets when you are here no longer. That is the answer, hurr?'

Costain was startled by this vehemence. 'I had no intention of prying,' he stammered.

Sbirro ran the tip of his tongue over his thin lips. 'No, no,' he reassured, 'you are not prying. Do not let me give you that impression. On the contrary, I invite your questions.'

'Oh, come, Costain,' said Laffler. 'Don't let Sbirro intimidate you. I've known him for years and I guarantee that his bark is worse than his bite. Before you know it, he'll be showing you all the privileges of the house—outside of inviting you to visit his precious kitchen, of course.'

'Ah,' smiled Sbirro, 'for that, Mr Costain may have to wait a little while. For everything else I am at his beck and call.'

Laffler slapped his hand jovially on the table. 'What did I tell you!' he said. 'Now let's have the truth, Sbirro. Has anyone, outside of your staff, ever stepped into the sanctum sanctorum?'

Sbirro looked up. 'You see on the wall above you,' he said earnestly, 'the portrait of one to whom I did the honour. A very dear friend and a patron of most long standing, he is evidence that my kitchen is not inviolate.'

Costain studied the picture and started with recognition. 'Why,' he said excitedly, 'that's the famous writer—you know the one, Laffler—he used to do such wonderful short stories and cynical bits and then suddenly took himself off and disappeared in Mexico!'

'Of course!' cried Laffler, 'and to think I've been sitting under his portrait for years without even realising it!' He turned to Sbirro. 'A dear friend, you say? His disappearance must have been a blow to you.'

Sbirro's face lengthened. 'It was, it was, I assure you. But think of it this way, gentlemen: he was probably greater in his death than in his life, hurr? A most tragic man, he often told me that his only happy hours were spent here at this very table. Pathetic, is it not? And to think the only favour I could ever show him was to let him witness the mysteries of my kitchen, which is, when all is said and done, no more than a plain, ordinary kitchen.'

'You seem very certain of his death,' commented Costain. 'After all, no evidence has ever turned up to substantiate it.'

Sbirro contemplated the picture. 'None at all,' he said softly. 'Remarkable, hurr?'

With the arrival of the entrée Sbirro leaped to his feet and set about serving them himself. With his eyes alight he lifted the casserole from the tray and sniffed at the fragrance from within with sensual relish. Then, taking great care not to lose a single drop of gravy, he filled two platters with chunks of dripping meat. As if exhausted by this task, he sat back in his chair, breathing heavily. 'Gentlemen,' he said, 'to your good appetite.'

Costain chewed his first mouthful with great deliberation and swallowed it. Then he looked at the empty tines of his fork with glazed eyes.

'Good God!' he breathed.

'It is good, hurr? Better than you imagined?'

Costain shook his head dazedly. 'It is as impossible,' he said slowly, 'for the uninitiated to conceive the delights of lamb Amirstan as for mortal man to look into his own soul.'

'Perhaps,' Sbirro thrust his head so close that Costain could feel the warm, fetid breath tickle his nostrils, 'perhaps you have just had a glimpse into your soul, hurr?'

Costain tried to draw back slightly without giving offence. 'Perhaps,' he laughed, 'and a gratifying picture it made: all fang and claw. But without intending any disrespect, I should hardly like to build my church on *lamb en casserole*.'

Sbirro rose and laid a hand gently on his shoulder. 'So perspicacious,' he said. 'Sometimes when you have nothing to do, nothing, perhaps, but sit for a very little while in a dark room and think of this world—what it is and what it is going to be—then you must turn your thoughts a little to the signifiance of the Lamb in religion. It will be so interesting. And now,' he bowed deeply to both men, 'I have held you long enough from your dinner. I was most happy'—he nodded to Costain—'and I am sure we will meet again.' The teeth gleamed, the eyes glittered, and Sbirro was gone down the aisle of tables.

Costain twisted around to stare after the retreating figure. 'Have I offended him in some way?' he asked.

Laffler looked up from his plate. 'Offended him? He loves that kind of talk. Lamb Amirstan is a ritual with him; get him started and he'll be back at you a dozen times worse than a priest making a conversion.'

Costain turned to his meal with the face still hovering before him. 'Interesting man,' he reflected. 'Very.'

It took him a month to discover the tantalising familiarity of that face, and when he did, he laughed aloud in his bed. Why, of course! Sbirro might have sat as the model for the Cheshire cat in *Alice*!

He passed this thought on to Laffler the very next evening as they pushed their way down the street to the restaurant against a chill, blustering wind. Laffler only looked blank.

'You may be right,' he said, 'but I'm not a fit judge. It's a far cry back to the days when I read the book. A far cry, indeed.'

As if taking up his words, a piercing howl came ringing down the street and stopped both men short in their tracks. 'Someone's in trouble there,' said Laffler. 'Look!'

Not far from the entrance to Sbirro's two figures could be seen struggling in the near darkness. They swayed back and forth and suddenly tumbled into a writhing heap on the sidewalk. The piteous howl went up again, and Laffler, despite his girth, ran toward it at a fair speed with Costain tagging cautiously behind.

Stretched out full length on the pavement was a slender figure with the dusky complexion and white hair of one of Sbirro's servitors. His fingers were futilely plucking at the huge hands which encircled his throat, and his knees pushed weakly up at the gigantic bulk of a man who brutally bore down with his full weight.

Laffler came up panting. 'Stop this!' he shouted. 'What's going on here?'

The pleading eyes almost bulging from their sockets turned towards Laffler. 'Help, sair. This man—drunk—'

'Drunk am I, ya dirty—' Costain saw now that the man was a sailor in a badly soiled uniform. The air around him reeked with the stench of liquor. 'Pick me pocket and then call me drunk, will ya!' He dug his fingers in harder, and his victim groaned.

Laffler seized the sailor's shoulder. 'Let go of him, do you hear! Let go of him at once!' he cried, and the next instant was sent careening into Costain, who staggered back under the force of the blow.

The attack on his own person sent Laffler into immediate and berserk action. Without a sound he leaped at the sailor, striking and kicking furiously at the unprotected face and flanks. Stunned at first, the man came to his feet with a rush and turned on Laffler. For a moment they stood locked together, and then as Costain joined the attack, all three went sprawling to the ground. Slowly Laffler and Costain got to their feet and looked down at the body before them.

'He's either out cold from liquor,' said Costain, 'or he struck his head going down. In any case, it's a job for the police.'

'No, no, sair!' The waiter crawled weakly to his feet, and stood swaying. 'No police, sair. Mr Sbirro do not want such. You understand, sair.' He caught hold of Costain with a pleading hand, and Costain looked at Laffler.

'Of course not,' said Laffler. 'We won't have to bother with the police. They'll pick him up soon enough, the murderous sot. But what in the world started all this?'

'That man, sir. He make most erratic way while walking, and with no meaning I push against him. Then he attack me, accusing me to rob him.'

'As I thought.' Laffler pushed the waiter gently along. 'Now go on in and get yourself attended to.'

The man seemed ready to burst into tears. 'To you, sair, I owe my life. If there is anything I can do—'

Laffler turned into the areaway that led to Sbirro's door. 'No, no, it was nothing. You go along, and if Sbirro has any questions send him to me. I'll straighten it out.'

'My life, sair,' were the last words they heard as the inner door closed behind them.

'There you are, Costain,' said Laffler, as a few minutes later he drew his chair under the table: 'civilised man in all his glory. Reeking with alcohol, strangling to death some miserable innocent who came too close.'

Costain made an effort to gloss over the nerve-shattering memory of the episode. 'It's the neurotic cat that takes to alcohol,' he said. 'Surely there's a reason for that sailor's condition.'

'Reason? Of course there is. Plain atavistic savagery!' Laffler swept his arm in an all-embracing gesture. 'Why do we all sit here at our meat? Not only to appease physical demands, but because our atavistic selves cry for release. Think back, Costain. Do you remember that I once described Sbirro as the epitome of civilisation? Can you now we see why? A brilliant man, he fully understands the nature of human beings. But unlike lesser men he bends all his efforts to the satisfaction of our innate natures without resultant harm to some innocent bystander.'

'When I think back on the wonders of lamb Amirstan,' said Costain, 'I quite understand what you're driving at. And, by the way, isn't it nearly due to appear on the bill of fare? It must have been over a month ago that it was last served.'

The waiter, filling the tumblers, hesitated. 'I am so sorry, sair. No special this evening.'

'There's your answer,' Laffler grunted, 'and probably just my luck to miss out on it altogether the next time.'

Costain stared at him. 'Oh, come, that's impossible.'

'No, blast it.' Laffler drank off half his water at a gulp and the waiter immediately refilled the glass. 'I'm off to South America for a surprise tour of inspection. One month, two months, Lord knows how long.'

'Are things that bad down there?'

'They could be better.' Laffler suddenly grinned. 'Mustn't forget it takes very mundane dollars and cents to pay the tariff at Sbirro's.'

'I haven't heard a word of this around the office.'

'Wouldn't be a surprise tour if you had. Nobody knows about this except myself—and now you. I want to walk in on them completely unsuspected. Find out what flimflammery they're up to down there. As far as the office is concerned, I'm off on a jaunt somewhere. Maybe recuperating in some sanatorium from my hard work. Anyhow, the business will be in good hands. Yours, among them.'

'Mine?' said Costain, surprised.

'When you go in tomorrow you'll find yourself in receipt of a promotion, even if I'm not there to hand it to you personally. Mind you, it has nothing to do with our friendship either; you've done fine work, and I'm immensely grateful for it.'

Costain reddened under the praise. 'You don't expect to be in tomorrow. Then you're leaving tonight?'

Laffler nodded. 'I've been trying to wangle some reservations. If they come through, well, this will be in the nature of a farewell celebration.'

'You know,' said Costain slowly, 'I devoutly hope that your reservations don't come through. I believe our dinners here have come to mean more to me than I ever dared imagine.'

The waiter's voice broke in. 'Do you wish to be served now, sair?' and they both started.

'Of course, of course,' said Laffler sharply, 'I didn't realise you were waiting.'

'What bothers me,' he told Costain as the waiter turned away, 'is the thought of the lamb Amirstan I'm bound to miss. To tell you the truth, I've already put off my departure a week, hoping to hit a lucky night, and now I simply can't delay any more. I do hope that when you're sitting over your share of lamb Amirstan, you'll think of me with suitable regrets.'

Costain laughed. 'I will indeed,' he said as he turned to his dinner.

Hardly had he cleared the plate when a waiter silently reached for it. It was not their usual waiter, he observed; it was none other than the victim of the assault.

'Well,' Costain said, 'how do you feel now? Still under the weather?'

The waiter paid no attention to him. Instead, with the air of a man under great strain, he turned to Laffler. 'Sair,' he whispered. 'My life. I owe it to you. I can repay you!'

Laffler looked up in amazement, then shook his head firmly. 'No,' he said; 'I want nothing from you, understand? You have repaid me sufficiently with your thanks. Now get on with your work and let's hear no more about it.'

The waiter did not stir an inch, but his voice rose slightly. 'By the body and blood of your God, sair, I will help you even if you do not want! *Do not go into the kitchen, sair.* I trade you my life for yours, sair, when I speak this. Tonight or any night of your life, do not go into the kitchen at Sbirro's!'

Laffler sat back, completely dumbfounded. 'Not go into the kitchen? Why shouldn't I go into the kitchen if Mr. Sbirro ever took it into his head to invite me there. What's all this about?'

A hard hand was laid on Costain's back, and another gripped the waiter's arm. The waiter remained frozen to the spot, his lips compressed, his eyes downcast.

'What is all *what* about, gentlemen?' purred the voice. 'So opportune an arrival. In time as ever, I see, to answer all the questions, hurr?'

Laffler breathed a sigh of relief. 'Ah, Sbirro, thank heaven you're here. This man is saying something about my not going into your kitchen. Do you know what he means?'

The teeth showed in a broad grin. 'But of course. This good man was giving you advice in all amiability. It so happens that my too emotional chef heard some rumour that I might have a guest into his precious kitchen, and he flew into a fearful rage. Such a rage, gentlemen! He even threatened to give notice on the spot, and you can understand what that should mean to Sbirro's, hurr? Fortunately, I succeeded in showing him what a signal honour it is to have an esteemed patron and true connoisseur observe him at his work first hand, and now he is quite amenable. Quite, hurr?'

He released the waiter's arm. 'You are at the wrong table,' he said softly. 'See that it does not happen again.'

The waiter slipped off without daring to raise his eyes and Sbirro drew a chair to the table. He seated himself and brushed his hand lightly over his hair. 'Now I am afraid that the cat is out of the bag, hurr? This invitation to you, Mr Laffler, was to be a surprise; but the surprise is gone, and all that is left is the invitation.'

Laffler mopped beads of perspiration from his forehead. 'Are you serious?' he said huskily. 'Do you mean that we are really to witness the preparation of your food tonight?'

Sbirro drew a sharp fingernail along the tablecloth, leaving a thin, straight line printed in the linen. 'Ah,' he said, 'I am faced with a dilemma of great proportions.' He studied the line soberly. 'You, Mr Laffler, have been my guest for ten long years. But our friend here—'

Costain raised his hand in protest. 'I understand perfectly. This invitation is solely to Mr Laffler, and naturally my presence is embarrassing. As it happens, I have an early engagement for this evening and must be on my way anyhow. So you see there's no dilemma at all, really.'

'No,' said Laffler, 'absolutely not. That wouldn't be fair at all. We've been sharing this until now, Costain, and I won't enjoy this experience half as much if you're not along. Surely Sbirro can make his conditions flexible, this one occasion.'

They both looked at Sbirro, who shrugged his shoulders regretfully.

Costain rose abruptly. 'I'm not going to sit here, Laffler, and spoil your great adventure. And then too,' he bantered, 'think of that ferocious chef waiting to get his cleaver on you. I prefer not to be at the scene. I'll just say good-bye,' he went on, to cover Laffler's guilty silence, 'and leave you to Sbirro. I'm sure he'll take pains to give you a good show.' He held out his hand and Laffler squeezed it painfully hard.

'You're being very decent, Costain,' he said. 'I hope you'll continue to dine here until we meet again. It shouldn't be too long.'

Sbirro made way for Costain to pass. 'I will expect you,' he said. 'Au 'voir.'

Costain stopped briefly in the dim foyer to adjust his scarf and fix his Homburg at the proper angle. When he turned away from the mirror, satisfied at last, he saw with a final glance that Laffler and Sbirro were already at the kitchen door; Sbirro holding the door invitingly wide with one hand, while the other rested, almost tenderly, on Laffler's meaty shoulders.

BRIBERY AND CORRUPTION

Ruth Rendell

The setting for this next story is very different from Sbirro's. It is a grand and imposing place—one of the most expensive in London—and certainly does not hide the same kind of dark secrets in its kitchen. There is, however, a surprise awaiting Nicholas Hawthorne when he takes a friend to dine there and finds himself thrust into a situation fraught with danger—the kind of danger and intrigue for which the author, Ruth Rendell (1930–), has become internationally famous. Described as 'a natural storyteller' and the winner of innumerable literary prizes on both sides of the Atlantic, she always provides a chilling finale to her short stories. This is precisely what awaits Nicholas after his night out at Potters . . .

Everyone who makes a habit of dining out in London knows that Potters in Marylebone High Street is one of the most expensive of eating places. Nicholas Hawthorne, who usually dined in his rented room or in a steak house, was deceived by the humble-sounding name. When Annabel said, 'Let's go to Potters,' he agreed quite happily.

It was the first time he had taken her out. She was a small pretty girl with very little to say for herself. In her little face her eyes looked huge and appealing—a flying fox face, Nicholas thought. She suggested they take a taxi to Potters 'because it's difficult to find'. Seeing that it was a large building and right in the middle of Marylebone High Street, Nicholas didn't think it would have been more difficult to find on foot than in a taxi but he said nothing.

He was already wondering what this meal was going to cost. Potters was a grand and imposing restaurant. The windows were of that very clear but slightly warped glass that bespeaks age, and the doors of a dark red wood that looked as if it had been polished evey day for fifty years. Because the curtains were drawn and the interior not visible, it appeared as if they were approaching some private residence, perhaps a rich man's town house.

Immediately inside the doors was a bar where three couples sat about in black leather chairs. A waiter took Annabel's coat and they were conducted to a table in the restaurant. Nicholas, though young, was perceptive. He had expected Annabel to be made as shy and awkward by this place as he was himself but she seemed to have shed her diffidence with her coat. And when waiters approached with menus and the wine list she said boldly that she would start with a Pernod.

What was it all going to cost? Nicholas looked unhappily at the prices and was thankful he had his newly acquired credit card with him. Live now, pay later—but, oh God, he would still have to pay.

Annabel chose asparagus for her first course and roast grouse for her second. The grouse was the most expensive item on the menu. Nicholas selected vegetable soup and a pork chop. He asked her if she would like red or white wine and she said one bottle wouldn't be enough, would it, so why not have one of each?

She didn't speak at all while they ate. He remembered reading in some poem or other how the poet marvelled of a schoolmaster that one small head could carry all he knew. Nicholas wondered how one small body could carry all Annabel ate. She devoured roast potatoes with her grouse and red cabbage and runner beans, and when she heard the waiter recommending braised artichokes to the people at the next table she said she would have some of those too. He prayed she wouldn't want another course. But that fawning insinuating waiter had to come up with the sweet trolley.

'We have fresh strawberries, madam.'

'In November?' said Annabel, breaking her silence. 'How lovely.'

Naturally she would have them. Drinking the dregs of his wine, Nicholas watched her eat the strawberries and cream and then call for a slice of chocolate roulade. He ordered coffee. Did sir and madam wish for a liqueur? Nicholas shook his head vehemently. Annabel said she would have a green chartreuse. Nicholas knew that this was of all liqueurs the pearl—and necessarily the most expensive.

By now he was so frightened about the bill and so repelled by her concentrated guzzling that he needed briefly to get away from her. It was plain she had come out with him only to stuff and drink herself into a stupor. He excused himself and went off in the direction of the men's room.

In order to reach it he had to pass across one end of the bar. The place was still half-empty but during the past hour—it was now nine o'clock—another couple had come in and were sitting at a table in the centre of the floor. The man was middle-aged with thick silver hair and a lightly tanned taut-skinned face. His right arm was round the shoulder of his companion, a very young, very pretty blonde girl, and he was whispering something in her ear. Nicholas recognised him at once as the chairman of the company for which his own father has been sales manager until two years before when he had been made redundant on some specious pretext. The company was called Sorensen-McGill and the silver-haired man was Julius Sorensen.

With all the fervour of a young man loyal to a beloved parent, Nicholas hated him. But Nicholas was a very young man and it was beyond his strength to cut Sorensen. He muttered a stiff good evening and plunged for the men's room where he turned out his pockets, counted the notes in his wallet and tried to calculate what he already owed to the credit card company. If necessary he would have to borrow from his father, though he would hate to do that, knowing as he did that his father had been living on a reduced income ever since that beast Sorensen fired him. Borrow from his father, try and put off paying the rent for a month if he could, cut down on his smoking, maybe give up altogether . . .

When he came out, feeling almost sick, Sorensen and the girl had moved farther apart from each other. They didn't look at him and Nicholas too looked the other way. Annabel was on her second green chartreuse and gobbling up *petit fours*. He had thought her face was like that of a flying fox and now he remembered that flying fox is only a pretty name for a fruit bat. Eating a marzipan orange, she looked just like a rapacious little fruit bat. And she was very drunk.

'I feel ever so sleepy and strange,' she said. 'Maybe I've got one of those viruses. Could you pay the bill?'

It took Nicholas a long time to catch the waiter's eye. When he did the man merely homed in on them with the coffee pot. Nicholas surprised himself with his own firmness.

'I'd like the bill,' he said in the tone of one who declares to higher authority that he who is about to die salutes thee.

In half a minute the waiter was back. Would Nicholas be so good as to come with him and speak to the maître d'hôtel? Nicholas nodded, dumbfounded. What had happened? What had he done wrong? Annabel was slouching back in her chair, her big eyes half-closed, a trickle of something orange dribbling out of the corner of her mouth. They were going to tell him to remove her, that she had disgraced the place, not to come here again. He followed the waiter, his hands clenched.

A huge man spoke to him, a man with the beak and plumage of a king penguin. 'Your bill has been paid, sir.'

Nicholas stared. 'I don't know what you mean.'

'Your father paid it, sir. Those were my instructions, to tell you your father had settled your bill.'

The relief was tremendous. He seemed to grow tall again and light and free. It was as if someone had made him a present of— well, what would it have been? Sixty pounds? Seventy? And he understood at once. Sorensen had paid his bill and said he was his father. It was a little bit of compensation for what Sorensen had done in dismissing his father. He had paid out sixty pounds to show he meant well, to show that he wanted, in a small way, to make up for injustice.

Tall and free and masterful, Nicholas said, 'Call me a cab, please,' and then he went and shook Annabel awake in quite a lordly way.

His euphoria lasted for nearly an hour, long after he had pushed the somnolent Annabel through her own front door, then climbed the stairs up to the furnished room he rented and settled down to the crossword in the evening paper. Things would have turned out very differently if he hadn't started that crossword. 'Twelve across: Bone in mixed byre goes with corruption. (7 letters)' The I and the Y were already in. He got the answer after a few seconds—'Bribery'. 'Rib' in an anagram of 'byre'. 'Bribery'.

He laid down the paper and looked at the opposite wall. That which goes with corruption. How could he ever have been such a fool, such a naive innocent fool, as to suppose a man like Sorensen cared about injustice or ever gave a thought to wrongful dismissal or even believed for a moment he *could* have been wrong? Of course Sorensen hadn't been trying to make restitution, of course he hadn't paid that bill out of kindness and remorse. He had paid it as a bribe.

He had paid the bribe to shut Nicholas's mouth because he didn't want anyone to know he had been out drinking with a girl, embracing a girl, who wasn't his wife. It was bribery, the bribery that went with corruption.

Once, about three years before, Nicholas had been with his parents to a party Sorensen had given for his staff and Mrs Sorensen had been the hostess. A brown-haired mousey little woman, he remembered her, and all of forty-five which seemed like old age to Nicholas. Sorensen had paid that bill because he didn't want his wife to find out he had a girlfriend young enough to be his daughter.

He had bought him, Nicholas thought, bribed and corrupted him—or tried to. Because he wasn't going to succeed. He needn't think he could kick the Hawthorne family around any more. Once was enough.

It had been nice thinking that he hadn't after all wasted more than half a week's wages on that horrible girl but honour was more important. Honour, surely, meant sacrificing material things for a principle. Nicholas had a bad night because he kept waking up and thinking of all the material things he would have to go short of during the next few weeks on account of his honour. Nevertheless, by the morning his resolve was fixed. Making sure he had his cheque book with him, he went off to work.

Several hours passed before he could get the courage together to phone Sorensen-McGill. What was he going to do if Sorensen refused to see him? If only he had a nice fat bank account with five hundred pounds in it he could make the grand gesture and send Sorensen a blank cheque accompanied by a curt and contemptuous letter.

The telephonist who used to answer in the days when he sometimes phoned his father at work answered now.

'Sorensen-McGill. Can I help you?'

His voice rather hoarse, Nicholas asked if he could have an appointment with Mr Sorensen that day on a matter of urgency. He was put through to Sorensen's secretary. There was a delay. Bells rang and switches clicked. The girl came back to the phone and Nicholas was sure she was going to say no.

'Mr Sorensen asks if one o'clock will suit you?'

In his lunch hour? Of course it would. But what on earth could have induced Sorensen to have sacrificed one of those fat expense account lunches just to see him? Nicholas set off for Berkeley Square, wondering what had made the man so forthcoming. A weak hopeful little voice inside him began once again putting up those arguments which on the previous evening the voice of a common sense had so decisively refuted.

Perhaps Sorensen really meant well and when Nicholas got there would tell him the paying of the bill had been no bribery but a way of making a present to the son of a once-valued employee. The pretty girl could have been Sorensen's daughter. Nicholas had no idea if the man had children. It was possible he had a daughter. No corruption then, no betrayal of his honour, no need to give up cigarettes or abase himself before his landlord.

They knew him at Sorensen-McGill. He had been there with his father and, besides, he looked like his father. The pretty blonde girl hadn't looked in the least like Sorensen. A secretary showed him into the chairman's office. Sorensen was sitting in a yellow leather chair behind a rosewood desk with an inlaid yellow leather top.

There were Modigliani-like murals on the wall behind him and on the desk a dark green jade ashtray, stacked with stubs, which the secretary replaced with a clean one of pale green jade.

'Hallo, Nicholas,' said Sorensen. He didn't smile. 'Sit down.' The only other chair in the room was one of those hi-tech low-slung affairs made of leather hung on a metal frame. Beside it was a black glass coffee table with a black leather padded rim and on the glass lay a magazine open at the centrefold of a nude girl. There are some people who know how to put others at their ease and there are those who know how to put others in difficulties. Nicholas sat down, right down—about three inches from the floor.

Sorensen lit a cigarette. He didn't offer the box. He looked at Nicholas and moved his head slowly from side to side. At last he said:

'I suppose I should have expected this.'

Nicholas opened his mouth to speak but Sorensen held up his hand. 'No, you can have your say in a minute.' His tone became hard and brisk. 'The girl you saw me with last night was someone—not to put too fine a point on it—I picked up in a bar. I have never seen her before, I shall never see her again. She is not, in any sense of the words, a girlfriend or mistress. Wait,' he said as Nicholas again tried to interrupt. 'Let me finish. My wife is not a well woman. Were she to find out where I was last night and whom I was with she would doubtless be very distressed. She would very likely become ill again. I refer, of course, to mental illness, to an emotional sickness, but . . .'

He drew deeply on his cigarette. 'But all this being so and whatever the consequences, I shall not on any account allow myself to be blackmailed. Is that understood? I paid for your dinner last night and that is enough. I do not want my wife told what you saw, but you may tell her and publish it to the world before I pay you another penny.'

At the word blackmail Nicholas's heart had begun to pound. The blood rushed into his face. He had come to vindicate his honour and his motive had been foully misunderstood. In a choked voice he stuttered:

'You've no business—it wasn't—why do you say things like that to me?'

'It's not a nice word, is it? But to call it anything else would merely be semantics. You came, didn't you, to ask for more?'

Nicholas jumped up. 'I came to give you your money back!'

'Aah!' It was a strange sound Sorensen made, old and urbane, cynical yet wondering. He crushed out his cigarette. 'I see. Youth is moralistic. Inexperience is puritanical. You'll tell her anyway because you can't be bought, is that it?'

'No, I can't be bought.' Nicholas was trembling. He put his hands down flat on Sorensen's desk but still they shook. 'I shall never tell anyone what I saw, I promise you that. But I can't let you pay for my dinner—and pretend to be my father!' Tears were pricking the backs of his eyes.

'Oh, sit down, sit down. If you aren't trying to blackmail me and your lips are sealed, what the hell did you come here for? A social call? A man-to-man chat about the ladies you and I took out last night? Your family aren't exactly my favourite companions, you know.'

Nicholas retreated a little. He felt the man's power. It was the power of money and the power that is achieved by always having had money. There was something he hadn't ever before noticed about Sorensen but which he noticed now. Sorensen looked as if he were made of metal, his skin of copper, his hair of silver, his suit of pewter.

And then the mist in Nicholas's eyes stopped him seeing anything but a blur. 'How much was my bill?' he managed to say.

'Oh, for God's sake.'

'How much?'

'Sixty-seven pounds,' said Sorensen, 'give or take a little.' He sounded amused.

To Nicholas it was a small fortune. He got out his cheque book and wrote the cheque to J. Sorensen and passed it across the desk and said, 'There's your money. But you needn't worry. I won't say I saw you. I promise I won't.'

Uttering those words made him feel noble, heroic. The threatening tears receded. Sorensen looked at the cheque and tore it in two. 'You're a very tiresome boy. I don't want you on my premises. Get out.'

Nicholas got out. He walked out of the building with his head in the air. He was still considering sending Sorensen another cheque when, two mornings later, reading his paper in the train, his eye caught the hated name. At first he didn't think the story referred to 'his' Sorensen—and then he knew it did. The headline read: 'Woman Found Dead in Forest. Murder of Tycoon's Wife.'

'The body of a woman,' ran the story beneath,

> was found last night in an abandoned car in Hatfield Forest in Hertfordshire. She had been strangled. The woman was today identified as Mrs Winifred Sorensen, 45, of Eaton Place, Belgravia. She was the wife of Julius Sorensen, chairman of Sorensen-McGill, manufacturers of office equipment.

Mrs Sorensen had been staying with her mother, Mrs Mary Clifford, at Mrs Clifford's home in Much Hadham. Mrs Clifford said, 'My daughter had intended to stay with me for a further two days. I was surprised when she said she would drive home to London on Tuesday evening.'

'I was not expecting my wife home on Tuesday,' said Mr Sorensen. 'I had no idea she had left her mother's house until I phoned there yesterday. When I realised she was missing I immediately informed the police.'

Police are treating the case as murder.

That poor woman, thought Nicholas. While she had been driving home to her husband, longing for him probably, needing his company and his comfort, he had been philandering with a girl he had picked up, a girl whose surname he didn't even know. He must now be overcome with remorse. Nicholas hoped it was biting agonised remorse. The contrast was what was so shocking, Sorensen cheek to cheek with that girl, drinking with her, no doubt later sleeping with her; his wife alone, struggling with an attacker in a lonely place in the dark.

Nicholas, of course, wouldn't have been surprised if Sorensen had done it himself. Nothing Sorensen could do would have surprised him. The man was capable of any iniquity. Only this he couldn't have done, which none knew better than Nicholas. So it was a bit of a shock to be accosted by two policemen when he arrived home that evening. They were waiting in a car outside his gate and they got out as he approached.

'Nothing to worry about, Mr Hawthorne,' said the older of them who introduced himself as a Detective Inspector. 'Just a matter of routine. Perhaps you read about the death of Mrs Winifred Sorensen in your paper today?'

'Yes.'

'May we come in?'

They followed him upstairs. What could they want of him? Nicholas sometimes read detective stories and it occurred to him that, knowing perhaps of his tenuous connection with Sorensen-McGill, they would want to ask him questions about Sorensen's character and domestic life. In that case they had come to the right witness.

He could tell them all right. He could tell them why poor Mrs Sorensen, jealous and suspicious as she must have been, had taken it into her head to leave her mother's house two days early and drive home. Because she had intended to catch her husband in the act. And she would have caught him, found him absent or maybe entertaining that girl in their home, only she had never got home.

Some maniac had hitched a lift from her first. Oh yes, he'd tell them!

In his room they sat down. They had to sit on the bed for there was only one chair.

'It has been established,' said the Inspector, 'that Mrs Sorensen was killed between eight and ten p.m. on Tuesday.'

Nicholas nodded. He could hardly contain his excitement. What a shock it was going to be for them when he told them about this supposedly respectable businessman's private life! A split second later Nicholas was left deflated and staring.

'At nine that evening Mr Julius Sorensen, her husband, was in a restaurant called Potters in Marylebone High Street accompanied by a young lady. He has made a statement to us to that effect.'

Sorensen had told them. He had confessed. The disappointment was acute.

'I believe you were also in the restaurant at that time?' In a small voice Nicholas said, 'Oh yes. Yes, I was.'

'On the following day, Mr Hawthorne, you went to the offices of Sorensen-McGill where a conversation took place between you and Mr Sorensen. Will you tell me what that conversation was about, please?'

'It was about my seeing him in Potters the night before. He wanted me to . . .' Nicholas stopped. He blushed.

'Just a moment, sir. I think I can guess why you're so obviously uneasy about this. If I may say so without giving offence you're a very young man as yet and young people are often a bit confused when it comes to questions of loyalty. Am I right?'

Mystified now, Nicholas nodded.

'Your duty is plain. It's to tell the truth. Will you do that?'

'Yes, of course.'

'Good. Did Mr Sorensen try to bribe you?'

'Yes.' Nicholas took a deep breath. 'I made him a promise.'

'Which must carry no weight, Mr Hawthorne. Let me repeat. Mrs Sorensen was killed between eight and ten. Mr Sorensen has told us he was in Potters at nine, in the bar. The bar staff can't remember him. The surname of the lady he says he was with is unknown to him. According to him you were there and you saw him.' The Inspector glanced at his companion, then back to Nicholas. 'Well, Mr Hawthorne? This is a matter of the utmost seriousness.'

Nicholas understood. Excitement welled in him once more but he didn't show it. They would realise why he hesitated. At last he said:

'I was in Potters from eight till about nine-thirty.' Carefully he kept to the exact truth. 'Mr Sorensen and I discussed my being there and seeing him when I kept my appointment with him in his office on Wednesday and he—he paid the bill for my dinner.'

'I see.' How sharp were the Inspector's eyes! How much he thought he knew of youth and age, wisdom and naivety, innocence and corruption! 'Now then—did you in fact see Mr Sorensen in Potters on Tuesday evening?'

'I can't forget my promise,' said Nicholas.

Of course he couldn't. He had only to keep his promise and the police would charge Sorensen with murder. He looked down. He spoke in a guilty troubled voice.

'I didn't see him. Of course I didn't.'

CHEF D'OEUVRE

Paul Gallico

Many readers will be familiar with those superior French country res-
taurants to be found along the River Loire, havens of gourmet excellence
and with a far-flung reputation. But times have suddenly become hard for
Monsieur Armand Bonneval, the proprietor of the auberge in the following
story, and he is in desperate need of money to avoid financial ruin—when a
most unexpected customer calls in. Paul Gallico (1897–1976), novelist,
journalist and bon vivant, whose classic novels like The Snow Goose
(1941), The Small Miracle *(1951) and the series featuring the irrepress-*
ible Mrs Harris have been read all over the world, reveals in 'Chef
D'Oeuvre' both his knowledge of French cuisine and his skill at weaving a
murder story full of suspense and surprises . . .

You who recall the tale of the secret ingredient added to the recipe
for Chicken Royal Surprise by means of which Monsieur Armand
Bonneval, proprietor of the Auberge Château Loiret on the Loire,
won his two-star rating in the famous Guide Michelin, bible of the
touring gastronome, will be astonished to learn that this was not an
unmixed blessing.

   In ordinary circumstances this designation would have guaran-
teed Monsieur Bonneval, retired Chef of the Cordon Bleu, and
Madame, his faithful partner through life's vicissitudes, an old age
of ease if not of affluence. But considering what, weatherwise, the
previous season had been like abroad, the circumstances were not
ordinary at all.

   In fact, so miserable had it been—wet, cold, and stormy—that it
drove all the visitors away from France, southwards to Italy and
Spain in search of sun, bringing Bonneval to the brink of bank-
ruptcy, the loss of the Auberge Château Loiret, and of his life-
savings which it represented.

   The five crossed spoons and forks and two stars that Monsieur

Bonneval had won for his great dish meant that his was a superior restaurant with an excellent cuisine, 'worthy of a detour,' and a 'must' stop for lunch or dinner en route past the châteaux.

But it also required the proprietor always to have on hand an adequate supply of the delicious but expensive Loire salmon, prohibitively-priced lobsters and langoustes, sweet water crayfish, legs of lamb, poulets de Bresse, duck from Nantes, truffles from Perigord, goose-livers from Strasbourg . . .

When the customers came, the profit was adequate if not handsome. But when they did not, as happened during that disastrous season, the spoilage was catastrophic. Now Monsieur Bonneval found himself unable to meet the interest payment on the mortgage due on the auberge, and likewise lacking money to discharge his obligations to the provisioners.

Thus, on one of those wretched end-of-October days, with the rain pouring down in torrents after a severe all-night gale, Monsieur Bonneval sat with Madame in the little office where she kept the cash accounts and sought for some means of evading the ruin that stared them both in the face.

'If we could only win the lottery,' sighed Madame Bonneval. She was a stout, red–cheeked woman with fine eyes, who believed in God and her husband.

'Or receive a small unexpected legacy,' brooded Bonneval.

Short, rotund, clad in classic light-blue trousers, white coat, napkin about his neck, and high stiffly-starched chef's toque on his head, he looked exactly like what he was, a kind man and one of the great cooks of France.

But alas, the letters which Madame Bonneval was engaged in opening consisted of accounts pressing for payment, circulars, and a police handbill warning of a dangerous criminal at large.

There had been an unhappy spate of such notices recently, with the usual ugly rogues'-gallery photograph of some desperate character wanted for murder, kidnapping, or bank robbery, and more often than not the warning: *Dangerous! May be armed! Notify the police at once if you encounter this man*.

Such notices were sent regularly to Monsieur Bonneval in his capacity as innkeeper, and he was supposed to display them prominently, which however he did not do, considering such a spectacle depressing to the appetites of his clientele.

'Oh, là là,' murmured Madame Bonneval, 'but here is a wicked one indeed!' as she drew forth the police handbill with a photograph of a lean man with a fierce, beaked nose. But Bonneval had eyes only for the black type topping the sheet:

500,000 FRANCS REWARD!
HAVE YOU SEEN THIS MAN?
IF SO, NOTIFY THE POLICE IMMEDIATELY!

'Five hundred thousand francs!' he cried. 'Exactly the sum we are lacking to save us. Ah ah, it is unkind of Fate to remind us so violently of our insoluble dilemma.'

'He must have done something fearful for them to offer so much,' his wife remarked. 'I read of a frightful murder in Paris a week ago. A fellow cut the throat of his mistress, and placed the corpse in a cistern. This one looks quite capable of it.'

Together they read the description: *Goes under the name of Henri Blanchard; six feet four inches tall; extremely powerful physique; age between fifty and fifty-five; slight cast in left eye; old scar running from right eyebrow to jawbone . . .*

Madame Bonneval shuddered. 'The poor girl! The paper said that she was nearly decapitated.'

'I don't doubt it,' Bonneval commented. 'Hah! If it were only our good fortune to have him appear here, our troubles would soon be over.'

'You mean he would quickly murder us both,' shrieked Madame Bonneval. 'Heuh! Do not ask for such a thing.'

But Monsieur Bonneval, it seems, *had* asked and Fate was already organising the reply. For at that very moment, no more than a kilometre away, up the road leading from Blois there trudged a tall man with a beaked nose under a battered hat, his worn clothes and knapsack soaked by the driving downpour.

It was the custom of Monsieur Bonneval, when a client or party arrived at his inn, to make a brief appearance at the service door of the dining-room to appraise them. For when he went to work on a dish he liked to have a mental image of the person who was going to enjoy it, to know whether he was lean and hungry or fat and well-fed, whether he looked like a bon viveur or gourmet, a bourgeois, a tourist, or a gentleman. He felt that this knowledge aided him in his creations.

Thus, on this rainy autumn day when Monsieur Bonneval heard the scrape of a chair in the dining-room and saw Odette, the waitress, give her hair a pat before going in, he stepped as usual into the doorway for reconnaissance.

What he saw caused him to turn as white as his coat. For he recognised immediately, seated, menu in hand, at a side table in the empty room, Henri Blanchard, murderer.

Certainly he answered every descriptive detail of the man Madame Bonneval decided had brutally slain a young girl in a Left Bank Paris attic. There was the great size, the powerful frame, the beaked nose, greying hair, the cast in one eye, and the sinister disfiguring scar from temple to jaw. There could be no mistaking him.

A frisson of terror ran through Monsieur Bonneval's portly frame as he contemplated the formidable customer, but along with the shudder a wave of joy, also. For seated likewise at the table, in the person of Henri Blanchard, were 500,000 sorely-needed francs.

A man of rapid decisions, Bonneval quickly signalled the waitress back, whispered in the ear of Brazon, the man-of-all-work—so as not to alarm Céleste, the kitchenmaid—setting him to watch the front door, and then nipped round through the passage that ran behind the dining-room to the front of the house and joined Madame Bonneval in her office.

There he slid back a small panel in the wall, permitting a glimpse into the dining-room. 'Maman,' he cried, 'look there. Tell me what you see.'

Madame Bonneval applied her eye, gave a shriek, and seizing the black-japanned cashbox, proceeded to conceal it beneath her many black petticoats. 'Armand! It is he, the murderer!' She appeared about to faint as, remembering the handbill, she quaked, 'He may be armed. We shall all be slaughtered.'

'Pssst, woman! Keep quiet!' the chef hissed. 'Do you not realise it is the opportunity of a lifetime? I will telephone the police. They will come to arrest him. We shall collect the reward and pay the interest as well as our bills.'

Strangely, Madame Bonneval did not react to this as Bonneval expected. 'Oh, Armand,' she said, 'do you think that is right? He is a human being after all. Blood money is never lucky.'

'Are you out of your senses?' Bonneval whispered. 'This is the answer to our prayers. Keep your eye on him. Brazon is watching at the other door.'

He seized the telephone to connect with the gendarmerie at Blois, thirty kilometres distant, and the nearest police post capable of coping with so dangerous and valuable a customer. The sorely-needed 500,000 francs was practically in the till.

Yet, not quite. For no sooner had Bonneval picked up the receiver to listen for the buzzes, clicks, wails, hums, and cracklings which would indicate that the machine was activating itself than he realised that on this of all days, the telephone—never a fully developed invention in France at any time—was silent. As a matter of fact, the great windstorm during the night had taken down the lines between Loiret and Chaumont, and the instrument contained not so much as a whisper.

The only alternative then was for him to leap swiftly into his ancient shooting brake, and drive to Blois to alert the authorities. Yet, even as he rushed into the courtyard where the vehicle stood, he was aware of a serious dilemma. If he went himself, he exposed Madame Bonneval to a dangerous killer. And if he sent Brazon to break the news, he risked losing the reward or a substantial share of it.

The car solved this impasse for him as Monsieur Bonneval trod on the starter. Water from the torrential rain had managed to intrude itself into a sensitive chamber in the engine reserved to petrol. The resulting dilution caused the ignition to respond with a splutter and a sigh, after which it went as dead as the telephone. With 500,000 francs and a dangerous man at large in the dining-room, Monsieur Bonneval found himself with neither means of communication nor transport.

It was enough to try the stoutest heart. Yet stout-hearted was an exact description of Monsieur Bonneval when the survival of Madame Bonneval and himself was threatened. The telephone, it developed, when Brazon nipped over to the tiny exchange nearby, might be a matter of two or three hours, one could not say exactly.

The garage men fetched in haste estimated the same time to mobilise the vehicle. But by that time, Henri Blanchard would be many kilometres away, and the reward for his apprehension lost to them for ever.

Unless . . . Unless . . . A plan formed itself.

Shaking, inwardly, Monsieur Bonneval entered the dining-room, presented himself at the table occupied by the fugitive, and said, 'Bonjour, monsieur. I am sorry you have been kept waiting. What may I serve you?'

The stranger replied amiably enough, 'Waiting does not matter. It is good to be out of the rain. A plate of soup, a little bread, a glass of wine.'

Monsieur Bonneval thought, Ha, playing the innocent, eh? You do not realise that I know all. The cast in Blanchard's left eye made him look shifty, the nose gave him an aspect of ferocity, the scar an appearance of evil.

'Eh, now,' said the host in his most seductive voice, 'soup, a crust, and a glass of wine? Impossible at the Auberge Loiret. You must permit me to create a meal for you.'

Had Blanchard not appeared so sinister, his smile might have seemed wistful. 'You are good,' he said, 'but forgive me, I am poor and a stranger here. I cannot afford more.'

Monsieur Bonneval thought, Ho ho, you smooth villain. And your wallet probably bulging with stolen notes.

Aloud he said, 'No, no! I will not hear of it. I was about to prepare something special for Madame and myself, to keep my hand in. With this wretched weather we have not had a customer for days. You will see, it will cost you no more than you can afford.'

'If you are so kind then,' the huge man replied, his eyes lighting up, his voice slightly hoarse.

'To begin with,' temporised Monsieur Bonneval, racking his brains for dishes that would be not only succulent but a long time in preparation, since it was his bold and ingenious plan to keep Blanchard there by the art of his cookery until either the wretched telephone or the miserable vehicle should be restored to him. 'But, of course. Mousseline de Saumon de Loire Dijonnaise, a recipe of my old friend, host of a famous restaurant in Dijon.'

The formula for preparing this superb creation was unreeling through his head. Pound in a mortar a half-kilo of magnificent fresh salmon. Force the pounded flesh through a strainer, and work it again lovingly in the mortar, incorporating little by little three to four cups of pure sweet butter, two fresh eggs, two egg yolks, a delicate head of lettuce parboiled and forced through a sieve, a tablespoon chopped chervil, two tablespoons chopped parsley, one and a half teaspoons salt, freshly-ground pepper, and a pinch of nutmeg.

Work for thirty minutes with a wooden spatula in a bowl placed in ice. Stir in two cups whipped cream.

An attractive three-quarters of an hour would be occupied by this step.

And this, the chef recalled with immense satisfaction, was but the beginning.

Turn this delectable mixture, the recipe continued, into a buttered ring mould, and poach it over hot water for forty minutes.

In an hour and a half, that wretched shooting brake might have composed itself.

Unmould the Mousseline on a round platter and place in the centre the twenty-five finest cooked crayfish tails or shrimps, and thirty small mushroom caps sauté'd in butter.

Then occupy yourself with the following sauce: to two cups warm stock made of the bones, head, and trimmings of the salmon, add one cup cream combined with four beaten egg yolks. Heat gradually, stirring. Do not let the sauce boil. Add five tablespoons butter, a little at a time, and the crayfish or shrimp shells in butter, adding a little hot water and reducing. Serve over and with the Mousseline.

By this time life could have returned to that salaud telephone.
'If you think . . .' said Henri Blanchard.

'But of course. First, however, an appetiser. Ha! Œufs Meurette
will be just the thing. After the Mousseline, I suggest a dish from
the Auvergnat made famous by my old colleague Monsieur
Laronde—Escalope de Veau à la Brune et à la Blonde. Then, to
finish, an Omelette Norvégienne.'

'A meal fit for a king!' said Henri Blanchard.

Or the last dinner of a condemned murderer, thought Monsieur
Bonneval, but aloud said, 'Of course, it will take a little time.
Everything is freshly cooked.'

The wanted man smiled. 'I have nothing but time,' he said.

Time! Ha ha, Bonneval thought to himself, that is what you
think, my villainous-looking friend. But it is the guillotine that
awaits just round the corner.

He returned to the kitchen through the pantry, but then quickly
scuttled via the passage to the front office where he cautioned
Madame Bonneval. 'Signal to me immediately the telephone
functions again. I will deal with him in the meantime.'

'Oh, Armand! I am terrified for your life.'

'Never fear. I will tame him with my cooking. For, once he has
tasted my first dish, he will never leave.'

And this indeed proved to be the case.

When the Œufs Meurette appeared, afloat in a sauce com-
pounded of bacon, garlic, onion, and red wine, Blanchard sniffed,
passed a hand over his brow as though he was in a dream, fell to,
and in a short time put away the entire quantity of the recipe of
eight eggs intended for four persons, causing Monsieur Bonneval
to gape, for the chef had a true admiration for big eaters, holding
with regret that they were a vanishing species. But the Mousseline,
when at last Monsieur Bonneval brought it in triumphantly and set
it before his unsuspecting victim, had an even more outstanding
effect.

Henri Blanchard regarded the composition for an instant, the
delicate pink mould, the tantalising parade of crayfish tails, the
exquisite sauce, and a tear ran down his cheek and fell on to the
plate. Then he tasted the first mouthful, and turned upon Monsieur Bonneval a smile which, to the host's horror, transfigured his
face most astonishingly. 'Oh, mon cher chef!' he murmured,
deeply moved.

The horror was that, for an instant, the smile seemed to wipe all
the evil from his countenance, leaving Monsieur Bonneval badly
shaken as he watched the man again devour the portion for four

with undiminished appetite. For, Monsieur Bonneval found himself suddenly asking in his mind, what really was an evil face. A flaw in a retina, a misfortune of birth, a beak nose, a family inheritance, a scar caused by an accident? The smile had nullified them all.

Was it not easy to find a wicked gleam in the eye of almost anyone, a smirk, a baring of the teeth, a disarrangement of the hair, an irregularity in the walk, a twitching of the fingers, leading one to imagine one is to be butchered on the spot? But then Bonneval's mind returned to the police notice which left no room for doubt. He went into the kitchen to complete the weaving of the culinary net about the man he intended to betray.

But, truth to tell, his conscience was far from easy as he set about pounding six thin escalopes of veal quite flat, and cooked them slowly in butter a fine golden brown on both sides. For the words of his wife were weighing upon him: 'He is a human being after all. Blood money is never lucky.'

True, the 500,000 francs was desperately needed. Yet the sum was to obtained at the price of the life of a man who had shed a tear over his Mousseline and called him, 'My dear chef.'

Thoughtfully Monsieur Bonneval removed the meat, adding a half cup of white wine to the pan, stirring, then adding another half cup of strong veal stock flavoured with a tablespoon of meat glaze. He reduced and thickened the brown sauce slightly with a teaspoonful of potato starch.

A drastic idea came to him. Madame Bonneval suffered from migraine and frequently took a sleeping powder. Two of these added to the sauce would guarantee the presence of Henri Blanchard until the police came, as well as spare Bonneval the reproachful look at the betrayal. When Blanchard woke up he would be in goal.

Bonneval the archconspirator actually held the powder in his fingers. But Bonneval the master chef found himself unable to add them to the mixture, for who could tell what undesirable alteration in flavour might result?

Disposing of it in the waste bucket, he stuffed a pound of cooked white mushroom caps with chopped ham and pâté-de-fois-gras; then with the mushroom stock, heavy cream, and egg yolks he confected one and three-quarter cupfuls of cream sauce. A sudden vision of Blanchard's head laid upon the block of the guillotine assailed him, inducing in Monsieur Bonneval a shudder that almost caused a fatality to the sauce.

Now, with care, he heated in butter six slices of Normandy ham on both sides just long enough, and then arranged the escalopes of veal and ham slices alternately on the serving platter. Glancing at the clock he noted that it was four in the afternoon, three hours since his dangerous guest had arrived. It did not make him happy.

Filling in the centre of the veal and ham ring with the stuffed mushrooms, he carefully spooned the aromatic brunette gravy over the meat and the magnificent blonde sauce over the fungi. Then he carried it in to Henri Blanchard.

The reaction was spontaneous and startling.

A look, a sniff, a taste! Then the man rose to his feet and folded Monsieur Bonneval to his breast with his enormous and powerful arms. A good thing that Madame Bonneval was engaged on the telephone at that moment, and not applying her eye to the panel in the wall, for she would have thought certainly that Bonneval's last moment had come.

'Maître!' exclaimed Blanchard, and then he cried, 'Magus!' or magician.

To his surprise, Monsieur Bonneval found himself with his eyes quite moist, returning the pressure. 'Friend,' he said, 'Grand gourmet! Connoisseur! Bon appétit! Enjoy yourself. I go to prepare the Omelette Norvegiénne for you.'

It was only when he was delicately folding the ten stiffly-beaten eggwhites into the soufflé mixture of four yolks, mixed with a cup of sugar, almonds, and a glass of 1901 Armagnac, that it came to him he had been wrapped in the embrace of a murderer.

The next instant, a lightning bolt smote him as he clapped his hand to his sweating brow; he was riven by the thought that Henri Blanchard must be innocent. For no man who loved good food and cooking, and so appreciatively filled his belly with it, could be a murderer. In all the history of crime there was no record of a hungry or even starving gourmet having slain anyone. The two were incompatible.

Have you ever, Monsieur Bonneval would have asked you, after a satisfying repast, when you sat half drowsy, hands folded over paunch, the fragrance of the good cigar still lingering, re-memorising the tastes, flavours, aromas, the blends and clashes of spices, colour and texture of meat, fish, or fowl, the subtleties of the sauces, the airiness of the soufflé, contemplated murder?

But when the mind is not on food . . . you might suggest.

The mind of a great gourmet, Monsieur Bonneval would assure you, is always on food.

At this moment, the startled chef became aware that Madame was signalling frantically to him from the passage. When he went to her she whispered, 'The telephone is restored. I have been through to the police at Blois a short while ago. They will arrive in less than ten minutes now.'

'Woman,' Bonneval cried, 'what have you done? You yourself declared that it was wrong to accept blood money—'

'But, Armand! It was only because I feared for your life!'

There was not a moment to be lost. Frantically, Bonneval burst into the dining-room where sat Henri Blanchard, the last vestige of Escalope Brune et Blonde scraped from the platter, an expression of ineffable bliss upon a face that now appeared not only handsome but even somewhat noble.

'You must fly!' Bonneval shouted. 'All is known. The police will be here at any moment!'

The violence of Bonneval's entrance brought Henri Blanchard to his feet, and for an instant he looked stupefied.

'Fly?' he said. 'Where to? Why?'

'You are accused of murder. There is a reward of 500,000 francs offered for your apprehension; but only I, Armand Bonneval, know that you are innocent. Go now, while there is still time. You must leave the country at once.'

'But I have no money with which to leave the country. And I have never murdered anything but a little white paper.'

'Ah ah, but once the police have captured you they will see that you go to the block. Wait here an instant.'

Bonneval rushed into the little office and, opening the cashbox, extracted eighty thousand francs. It was their last reserve, but his conscience was very bad for he knew that he had come close to selling the life of a fellow man.

Returning to the dining-room he thrust the notes into the hands of Henri Blanchard.

'Here,' he said, 'take this. It is all I have. It will get you across the border.'

But it was already too late.

From without came the wailing of sirens, the squealing of brakes, the slamming of car doors, the running of feet. Monsieur Bonneval had time only to leap to the sideboard and seize a carving-knife and fork with which he ranged himself fiercely before Henri Blanchard as the gendarmes, led by a lieutenant, burst into the room.

'You shall not take him. He is innocent. Advance at your peril!' Bonneval challenged.

But the gendarmes made no attempt to advance, and only ranged themselves opposite the tall man and his stout little protector, while the lieutenant consulted a copy of the handbill he had brought with him.

Finally the police officer spoke. 'Monsieur le Duc,' he said.

'Oh,' said the tall man softly. 'So that is how it is.'

'Forgive this means of tracing you,' the lieutenant continued, 'but the word from Paris is that the lawyers are frantic. They know you never see newspapers or listen to the radio when you are abroad. I have to inform you that His Grace, your uncle, died some months ago. The message is that if you do not immediately assume the title and its responsibilities his entire fortune will be devoted to the propagation of the giant grasshoppers that were the subject of his lifelong research.'

Blanchard said, 'I am happier to remain poor, and a poet, roaming the highways and byways of France as I have done in the past.'

There was a moment of silence broken uncomfortably by Monsieur Bonneval, who suddenly felt slightly ridiculous brandishing his massive knife and fork. 'But the handbill: the charge of murder of that unfortunate girl!' he said.

The lieutenant turned to him with some amusement. 'What are you talking about, little puff-pigeon? There is nothing here about murder, only that we wished to be put in touch with Henri Blanchard, here pictured.'

Seizing the handbill, Monsieur Bonneval examined it closely as Madame Bonneval, Odette, and the others crowded into the room. It was true. The overheated imaginations of his wife and himself had supplied all the rest.

'Oh,' he cried in such anguish that Madame at once rushed to his side and slipped her arm through his, 'I am the greatest fool alive!'

Henri Blanchard said gravely, 'Not the greatest fool but, surely, the greatest chef.' He asked the officer, 'How much time is there left to decide?'

'Only eight hours, under the terms of the will, Your Grace. We must drive you to Paris at once.'

Henri Blanchard went to the window and gazed down the rain-swept road for a moment. Then he said to Bonneval, 'If it had not been for you and your magnificent cookery, I should long have been down that road and free for ever, for tomorrow it would have been too late. So you took me for a murderer, and kept me here that you might gain the reward?'

Bonneval turned a brilliant scarlet.

'But when you became convinced of my innocence you thrust upon me your last sou to help me to escape. You have taught me that people may yet be generous, noble, and kind, Monsieur Bonneval.'

He came over and placed his hands on the shoulder of the chef, saying, 'But you have also taught me something else by the artistry of your creations; namely, that there is another kind of good life besides that of a wandering vagabond. The beauties of art of every kind await me. A rich man can support and perpetuate these beauties. I believe I shall essay this kind of life for a time.

'Besides—' he smiled suddenly—'I do not very much care for those giant grasshoppers . . .'

Henri Blanchard fingered the banknotes Bonneval had thrust upon him and, smiling, patted the little chef on the shoulder. 'I shall need these when I arrive in Paris. But they will be returned to you manifold, along with the reward for my—ah—apprehension. Come, lieutenant, we had better hasten.'

He strode from the room, followed by the gendarmes, leaving Monsieur Bonneval feeling a little ashamed, yet also deeply touched and extraordinarily happy.

LA SPÉCIALITÉ DE M. DUCLOS

Oliver La Farge

Pierre Duclos is also a maître de cuisine, *although he has chosen to practise his art across the Atlantic, in America. He, too, has his own restaurant and sets a standard of excellence that seems to please all his customers—all, that is, except one. The result is murder, and the subsequent trial is reported hereunder in 'La Spécialité de M. Duclos' by Oliver La Farge (1901–1963). La Farge, who was best-known as an anthropologist and led archaeological expeditions in Mexico and Guatemala, as well as being a Pulitzer Prize winner for his novel* Laughing Boy *(1929), here created a most ingenious tale of a courtroom drama where the question being debated is whether homicide might be justifiable on the grounds of culinary interference!*

The jurists of Paris were surprised when Maître Béchamil, the famous advocate, undertook the defence of Pierre Duclos. The United States had asked for Duclos's extradition to the province of Connecticut to be tried for a homicide that he himself admitted he had committed. His extradition seemed certain. Moreover, Duclos was an Auvergnat, and Maître Béchamil, a Norman, had often and openly expressed his dislike for the people of Auvergne. He detested their accent. He distrusted their smallness, their darkness, their ferocity. He said that they were emotional primitives in a country founded upon civilisation and pure reason, more Spanish than French, more Latin than Gallic, and that they used too much garlic.

Maître Béchamil was an effective trial lawyer, a brilliant legal thinker, a gourmet, and a man of sound common sense. His taking of the case attracted attention that was further heightened when he exercised great ingenuity to have the case put over from the winter to the spring sessions. He did nothing without cause. The delay was essential, for the whole matter hung upon a proper understanding of the *haute cuisine française*. The later sessions would insure that the presiding judge would be no less a person than the president of the Société Gastronomique des Légistes, that famous organisation of jurist-connoisseurs, with two other members of the society as his associates. The winter sessions, Béchamil confided to his client, would be presided over by a man who had been seen— here he lowered his voice—sprinkling vinegar upon *rognons sautés madère*. They shuddered together.

Maître Béchamil had equally good reasons for taking the case to begin with. In the privacy of the advocate's bachelor apartment Duclos had amply proven that he was a *maître chef*. Above all, his amazing variation upon ordinary *sauce blanche*, which was the very heart of the case, was one of the those great innovations that enshrine an artist's name in history. The advocate saw a good chance of success. He also thought he saw the means of at last winning membership in the Société Gastronomique, which was not only a constellation of gourmets but the controlling inner circle of his profession.

Duclos planned, if he was set free, to proceed immediately to Auvergne, where he would visit his relatives and marry his fiancée. With her and her dowry he would return to Paris and open a restaurant. Maître Béchamil found this plan commendable. He asked how long the master chef would stay in Auvergne. Duclos said about a month. The advocate nodded. Inwardly, he smiled. A month would do nicely, he thought.

The case was heard by the panel of three judges for which Béchamil had hoped. The courtroom was well filled, and the presence of an American attaché testified to the importance of the matter. The prosecution put its case bluntly. The evidence was inescapable. The accused had run a restaurant in Connecticut. One evening he invited a group of his patrons to a dinner. In the course of the meal, for no apparent reason, the accused stabbed one of them, a M. Hathaway, through the heart with a carving knife. (The pronunciation of the names 'Hathaway' and 'Connecticut' caused the prosecutor no slight difficulty.) It was not for the present court to find the named Duclos innocent or guilty, but merely to determine, as it could not help but determine, that there existed a sufficient shadow of guilt to require him to return to the suburb or province of Connecticut where he would receive a fair trial under American law.

When Maître Béchamil rose, the audience felt that his case was already lost. The great advocate surveyed the bench. He shook back the sleeves of his robe and adjusted his cravat. He would not, he said, deny the facts set forth by his learned colleague. His client had indeed stabbed one of his guests and patrons through the heart as he sat at the table. He would, however, show the court that this act had been honourable and completely justified. He would further show that it would be a travesty upon justice to deliver a man who was in effect a hero to the jurisdiction of a people incapable of grasping the principles involved.

'I must give you,' he said, 'some little idea of the populace of that province of Connecticut, adjoining the metropolis of New York. I must describe them from the point of view of a *maître de cuisine*, a gastronome, and an artist, such as my client.'

He described how these people daily wolfed a hurried breakfast, sped to New York by train or automobile, and, after a day of the intensely sustained work characteristic of American energy, hastened home, to arrive exhausted, in time only to numb themselves against their fatigue with an excess of cocktails before approaching the pleasures of the table. From this point, by an interesting transition, he reached the subject of clam chowder.

Maître Béchamil described that bivalve, paler than a mussel, tougher than a scallop, less succulent than an oyster, mere leather when cooked. He described the process of the chowder from the crude salt pork smoking in the pan to the completed dish with spots of grease floating in the milk. The bench was impressed, but it was apparent that the judges were wondering what this description of monstrosities had to do with the case.

'Among these people,' he went on, 'there is a certain affectation of epicureanism. There is also an affectation of the *cuisine*, with a creditable desire to emulate *la cuisine française*. But the mastery of great art requires generations. Just as that great nation leads all others in questions of the machine, so has it a long way to go before its members have absorbed a true sense of gastronomy. Many among them have formed some palate—enough so that they patronised my client's little restaurant. They have not, however, learned to cook. They may produce their chowders, and they are fairly good with a simple beef-steak, but when they step beyond that point, they err.

'It is impossible to persuade them that very little of anything is enough. If one pinch of sweet basil is good, they think, then two are better. In their cooking they seek to taste not the influence of the ingredients but the ingredients themselves. One of those gentlemen concocting a dish in his kitchen and finding that the recipe calls for a teaspoonful of dry Sauternes will unhesitatingly substitute for it a tablespoon of one of their wines of California.'

Maître Béchamil paused dramatically. The judges looked profoundly shocked. Everyone glanced toward the representative of the American Embassy, who was staring at his clasped hands and blushing. Nothing had yet been brought out to prevent Duclos's extradition, but the atmosphere in the court was now strongly in his favour.

'Among my client's patrons was that M. Hathaway,' the advocate resumed, 'a man blindly pleased with his own cookery. A man who prided himself upon his omelettes, and yet insisted publicly that oleo-margarine was just as good as butter.' His eyes flickered toward the judge on the right, who was internationally famous for his omelettes.

'Now, Messieurs, I have set the stage. We approach the day and hour of the act, an act far more deserving of reward than of punishment. My client, ever improving his art, discovered an amazing variation upon one of the simplest of all elements of cookery—white sauce—that elevated it to a celestial plane. I shall not elaborate, as the court will have the opportunity to judge for itself the deliciousness of this compound, a product of the purest essentials of French cookery, of simplicity, perfect timing, and restraint.

'This sauce, my client realised, would become his chiefest *specialité de la maison*. It would become famous as *sauce blanche Duclos*. It assured at last his successful return to his native land. Launched in Connecticut, then transferred to France, where it belonged, it would be a magnet to Americans, a source of dollar exchange, an aid to his country in her restoration of herself under the Marshall Plan. To introduce this sauce, he invited a select group of patrons to dinner. Among them was the individual Hathaway, included not for his personal character or for his palate but because of his wealth and position, which dictated even that he be seated upon my client's left.

'The sauce was served with the *entrée* exactly as it will shortly be served to the court. Everyone exclaimed over it. The guests toasted their host and *sauce blanche Duclos*. They asked for the recipe, but my client only smiled. They tasted, they guessed, but the new elements—the secret—were beyond them.

'Supremely happy, my client went into the kitchen to supervise the final moments of the *piéce de résistance*. This man named Hathaway, pretending good-fellowship, followed him. Before my client knew what was happening, the man had stepped quickly to the small stove at which my client prepared his personal creations. There was the saucepan with remnants of *sauce blanche Duclos* in it, and there, on the shelf, were all the ingredients. Hathaway scanned the shelf, chuckled, and returned to the table. Shaken, but ever courtly, my client saw the main course made ready and returned to his seat.

'The individual Hathaway sat at his left. He had prepared himself for the feast in the usual manner, with an excess of cocktails. Now he leaned over and in my client's ear he said these terrible words: 'Come to dinner next Wednesday, old boy'. And then he named three names, the secret of *sauce blanche Duclos*, and again he chuckled.'

Maître Béchamil was silent long enough to let the full horror of the situation sink in. 'My client's years in the Resistance had taught him speed of thought and action. Instantly, as fast as ever in a crisis confronting the Gestapo, he grasped the situation. With heavy hand, this individual would prepare a travesty that from then on he would serve under the name of *sauce blanche Duclos*. Before ever the creation was launched, a counterfeit would be in circulation, its reputation would be destroyed, and not only its creator but the French Republic would have been robbed.

'What could be done? How can knowledge be removed from a mind? There was only one thing to do, and my client did it, knowing full well that thus once more he offered the sacrifice of his life if the Good God so willed. The essence of what followed you already know. He miraculously made good his escape. I shall not waste the court's time with details of his voyage to Mexico or of his embarkation from there. Suffice in that, having set foot once more upon the soil of his beloved France, this patriot openly assumed his own name, conscious of the correctness of his position, desiring only his vindication.'

Maître Béchamil fell silent. The President of the Court said that it was indeed essential that the court examine this *spécialité de M. Duclos*. A table was wheeled in, bearing cooking equipment and ingredients. M. Duclos stepped forward, bowed to the court, and went to work without speaking.

While he made his preparations, the advocate explained that the *entrée* consisted simply of slices of breast of chicken, broiled, and seethed in white Burgundy. That the court might be sure what was the contribution of the sauce to the whole, a plate with slices of the meat was passed to them. The judges entertained themselves determining the wine and vintage used.

At a certain point the little chef took three phials from an envelope and emptied them into his saucepan. He then dropped the phials into the trash receptacle. The sauce was poured over the warmed meat. The combination was allowed to simmer briefly. Then it was placed on dishes and served, with thin slices of good bread and a well-chosen Graves. As the judges tasted, it could be

seen that the effect upon them was electric. It began to seem that
Maître Béchamil was winning.

The judges withdrew to consider. Maître Béchamil waited
calmly. He was sure he had made and sustained all his points. He
was confident, too, that no member of the Société Gastronomique
could permit the secret of such a sauce to be eliminated from the
world. He was inwardly pleased, in addition, because he had
obtained possession of the three phials as the table had been
wheeled out, and already had identified the contents of one of
them.

The judges returned. The President of the Court spoke well of
the Marshall Plan, and with deep feeling of the liberation of France.
He pointed out that these matters, however, were not on trial in his
court. It was the specific act of the defendant, which must be
considered in its context. There was a man's inherent right to
protect his livelihood. There was the sacredness of art. There were
questions of national interest. There was the matter of delivering a
man for trial under circumstances such that, with all admiration for
American jurisprudence, it must be assumed that true justice
would not be done, because of a fundamental conflict of mores and
of cultures. One must doubt that any court in a land of chowder
and oleomargarine could understand the values involved.

'Finally,' he said, ' the theft of a recipe of this order, aggravated
by the incompetence of the thief, is an especially despicable form of
larceny. The killing of the thief in the very act is legally identical
with, but far more noble than, the shooting of a common burglar as
he enters one's window. Extradition is denied.'

The courtroom cheered. The American attaché departed furtively. M. Duclos embraced Maître Béchamil. The victory was
tremendous.

At 11 o'clock the following morning the advocate told his staff
that he would be absent for several hours on personal business. He
then repaired to his apartment, proceeding directly to the kitchen.
With precise, delicate motions he laid out the publicly known
ingredients of *sauce blanche Duclos*. From a locked drawer he took
out the three secret elements, identified by him the night before.
The crucial question now was: How much of each?

He did not expect truly to duplicate the sauce. Connoisseur that
he was, he knew he was a mediocre cook. Duclos would be a
month in Auvergne. Time enough to come so close to the real thing
that even the fine palate of the president of the society, after the
lapse of a few weeks, would believe that he had indeed duplicated
sauce blanche Duclos simply from having tasted it once before the

trial. Election to the Société Gastronomique would then be certain.

He removed his frock coat, put on a large apron, and went to work. A very little of this, he suspected, rather more of that, and of the third—barely a drop? Or was that merely his timidity? Perhaps, in his greatness, M. Duclos had dared use as much as half a teaspoonful. One must experiment, that was all. This time, one-quarter of a teaspoonful.

The result was not right. It missed being very good—probably by some indefinable yet disagreeable imbalance of the elements. Béchamil sighed and started again. As he stirred and meditated, lost to the world, he was startled into dropping the spoon with a clatter by the sound of a step behind him and a familiar Auvergnat voice saying, 'Good day, Maître Béchamil.'

He whirled about. Duclos, who should have been in Auvergne by now, walked toward him. He wore a black suit, a white shirt with stiff collar, and a sober tie. Maître Béchamil noticed that his shoes squeaked slightly. He laid his bowler hat on a chair, and took from under his arm a case about half a metre long, covered with purplish plush.

'I am on my way to the station,' he said. 'I just stopped by to show you the bargain I picked up. Look.' He opened the case. In it lay a carving knife of fine steel, moderately worn and very sharp. M. Duclos placed the case on the table and took out the knife. 'Believe you, Monsier, this is almost the exact duplicate of the fine knife I sacrificed when I eliminated the individual Hathaway.'

Maître Béchamil said something vague.

The little man glanced at the articles on the table. 'You experiment, Monsieur l'Avocat? You encounter trouble?' The Auvergnat accent was stronger than ever. 'Incompetence, I fear. No good cook would think that I ever put that'—he pointed at one ingredient—'in a sauce. I had a phial of it along as a blind. Incompetent.'

He smiled. He was dark, small, ferocious, the light in his eyes was primitive, he was more Spanish than French, more Latin than Gallic. He caressed the blade of the knife with the fingers of his left hand. Softly, in that detestable accent, he quoted, '"The killing of the thief in the very act is legally identical with, but far more noble than . . ."'

THREE, OR FOUR, FOR DINNER

L. P. Hartley

The Italians, like the French, enjoy a cuisine unmistakably their own, and there are restaurants and hotels to be found all over Italy which can provide the setting for meals that please the eye as well as the appetite. Few cities, however, can match the places to choose from in Venice, the location of this unnerving story by L. P. Hartley (1895–1972), author of those two remarkable novels The Go-Between *(1953) and* The Hireling *(1957). Hartley was a sedate man of letters with a devotion to Italy which took him to the country on numerous occasions. The Hotel San Giorgio in Venice, in which he sets his grim story of an unexpected dinner guest, was, apparently, among his favourite places to eat . . .*

It was late July in Venice, suffocatingly hot. The windows of the bar in the Hotel San Giorgio stood open to the Canal. But no air came through. At six o'clock a little breeze had sprung up, a feebler repetition of the mid-day sirocco, but in an hour it had blown itself out.

One of the men got off his high stool and walked somewhat unsteadily to the window.

'It's going to be calm all right,' he said. 'I think we'll go in the gondola. I see it's there, tied up at the usual post.'

'As you please, Dickie,' said his friend from the other stool.

Their voices proclaimed them Englishmen; proclaimed also the fact that they were good clients of the barman.

'Giuseppe!' called the man at the window, turning his eyes from the Salute with its broad steps, its mighty portal and its soaring dome back to the counter with the multi-coloured bottles behind it. 'How long does it take to row to the Lido?'

'Sir?'

'Didn't you say you'd lived in England, Giuseppe?'

'Yes, sir, eight years at the Hôtel Métropole.'

'Then why—?'

His friend intervened, pacifically, in Italian.

'He wants to know how long it takes to row to the Lido.'

Relief in his voice, the barman answered, 'That depends if you've got one oar or two.'

'Two.'

'If you ask me,' said Dickie, returning to his stool, 'I don't think Angelino, or whatever his damned name is, counts for much. It's the chap in front who does the work.'

'Yes, sir,' said the barman, solicitously. 'But the man at the back he guide the boat, he give the direction.'

'Well,' said Dickie, 'as long as he manages to hit the Lido. . . . We want to be at the Splendide by eight. Can we do it?'

'Easily, sir, you have got an hour.'

'Barring accidents.'

'We never have accidents in Venice,' said the barman, with true Italian optimism.

'Time for another, Phil?'

'Three's my limit, Dickie.'

'Oh, come on, be a man.'

They drank.

'You seem to know a lot,' said Dickie more amiably to the barman. 'Can you tell us anything about this chap who's dining with us—Joe O'Kelly, or whatever his name is?'

The barman pondered. He did not want to be called over the coals a second time. 'That would be an English name, sir?'

'English! Good Lord!' exploded Dickie. 'Does it sound like English?'

'Well, now, as you say it, it does,' remonstrated his companion. 'Or rather Irish. But wait—here's his card. Does that convey anything to you, Giuseppe?'

The barman turned the card over in his fingers. 'Oh, now I see, sir—Giacomelli—il Conte Giacomelli.'

'Well, do you know him?'

'Oh yes, sir. I know him very well.'

'What's he like?'

'He's a nice gentleman, sir, very rich . . .'

'Then he must be different from the rest of your aristocracy,' said Dickie, rather rudely. 'I hear they haven't two penny pieces to rub together.'

'Perhaps he's not so rich now,' the barman admitted, mournfully. 'None of us are. Business is bad. He is *grand azionista*—how do you say?' he stopped, distressed.

'Shareholder?' suggested Philip.

'Good Lord!' exclaimed Dickie, 'I didn't know you were so well up in this infernal language. You're a regular Wop!'

The barman did not notice the interruption.

'Yes, shareholder, that's it,' he was saying delightedly. 'He is a great shareholder in a *fabbrica di zucchero*—'

'Sugar-factory,' explained Philip, not without complacence.

The barman lowered his voice. 'But I hear they are . . .' He made a curious rocking movement with his hand.

'Not very flourishing?' said Philip.

The barman shrugged his shoulders. 'That's what they say.'

'So we mustn't mention sugar,' said Dickie, with a yawn. 'Come on, Phil, you're always so damned abstemious. Have another.'

'No, no, really not.'

'Then I will.'

Philip and even the barman watched him drink with awe on their faces.

'But,' said Philip as Dickie set down his glass, 'Count Giacomelli lives in Venice, doesn't he?'

'Oh yes, sir. Usually he comes in here every night. But it's four—five days now I do not see him.'

'Pity,' said Philip, 'we might have given him a lift. But perhaps he has a launch?'

'I don't think he's using his launch now, sir.'

'Oh well, he'll find some way of getting there, you may be sure,' said Dickie. 'How shall we know him, Giuseppe?'

'I expect you'll see him double, my poor Dickie,' remarked his friend.

The barman, with his usual courtesy, began replying to Dickie's question.

'Oh, he's a common-looking gentleman like yourself, sir. . . .'

'I, common?'

'No,' said the barman, confused. 'I mean *grande come lei*—as tall as you.'

'That's nothing to go by. Has he a beard and whiskers and a moustache?'

'No, he's clean-shaven.'

'Come on, come on,' said Philip. 'We shall be late, and perhaps he won't wait for us.'

But his friend was in combative mood. 'Damn it! how are we to dine with the chap if we don't recognise him? Now, Giuseppe, hurry up; think of the Duce and set your great Italian mind working. Isn't there anything odd about him? Is he cross-eyed?'

'No, sir.'

'Does he wear spectacles?'

'Oh no, sir.'

'Is he minus an arm?'

'*Nossignore*,' cried the barman, more and more agitated.

'Can't you tell us anything about him, except that he's common-looking, like me?'

The barman glanced helplessly round the room. Suddenly his face brightened. 'Ah, *ecco*! He limps a little.'

'That's better,' said Dickie. 'Come on, Philip, you lazy hound, you always keep me waiting.' He got down from the stool. 'See you later,' he said over his shoulder to the barman. 'Mind you have the whisky pronto. I shall need it after this trip.'

The barman, gradually recovering his composure, gazed after Dickie's receding, slightly lurching figure with intense respect.

The gondola glided smoothly over the water towards the island of San Giorgio Maggiore, the slender campanile of which was orange with the light of the setting sun. On the left lay the Piazzetta, the two columns, the rich intricate stonework of St Mark's, the immense façade of the Ducal Palace, still perfectly distinct for all the pearly pallor in the air about them. But, as San Giorgio began to slide past them on the right, it was the view at the back of the gondola which engrossed Philip's attention. There, in the entrance of the Grand Canal, the atmosphere was deepening into violet while the sky around the dome of the Salute was of that clear deep blue which, one knows instinctively, may at any moment be pierced by the first star. Philip, who was sitting on his companion's left, kept twisting round to see the view, and the gondolier, whose figure blocked it to some extent, smiled each time he did so, saying '*Bello, non è vero?*' almost as though from habit. Dickie, however, was less tolerant of his friend's aesthetic preoccupations.

'I wish to goodness you wouldn't keep wriggling about,' he muttered, sprawling laxly in the depths of the more comfortable seat. 'You make me feel seasick.'

'All right, old chap,' said Philip, soothingly. 'You go to sleep.'

Dickie hauled himself up by the silk rope which was supported by the brass silhouette of a horse at one end and by a small but solid brass lion at the other.

He said combatively: 'I don't want to go to sleep. I want to know what we're to say to this sugar-refining friend of yours. Supposing he doesn't talk English? Shall we sit silent through the meal?'

'Oh, I think all foreigners do.' Philip spoke lightly; his reply was directed to the first of Dickie's questions; it would have been obviously untrue as an answer to the second. 'Jackson didn't tell me; he only gave me that letter and said he was a nice fellow and could get us into palaces and so on that ordinary people don't see.'

'There are too many that ordinary people do see, as it is, if you ask me,' groaned Dickie. 'For God's sake don't let him show us any more sights.'

'He seems to be a well-known character,' said Philip. 'He'll count as a sight himself.'

'If you call a limping dago a sight, I'm inclined to agree with you,' Dickie took him up crossly.

But Philip was unruffled.

'I'm sorry, Dickie, but I had to do it—couldn't ignore the letter, you know. We shall get through the evening somehow. Now, sit up and look at the lovely scenery. *Cosa è questa isola?*' he asked the gondolier, indicating an island to the right that looked if it might be a monastery.

'*Il manicomio,*' said the gondolier, with a grin. Then, as Philip looked uncomprehending, he tapped his forehead and smiled still more broadly.

'Oh,' said Philip, 'it's the lunatic asylum.'

'I do wish,' said Dickie, plaintively, 'if you must show me things, you'd direct my attention to something more cheerful.'

'Well, then,' said Philip, 'look at these jolly old boats. They're more in your line.'

A couple of tramp-steamers, moored stern to stern, and, even in the fading twilight, visibly out of repair—great gangrenous patches of rust extending over their flanks—hove up on the left. Under the shadow of their steep sides the water looked oily and almost black.

Dickie suddenly became animated. 'This reminds me of Hull,' he exclaimed. 'Good old Hull! Civilisation at last! Nothing picturesque and old-world. Two ugly useful old ships, nice oily water and lots of foreign bodies floating about in it. At least,' he said, rising unsteadily to his feet, 'I take that to be a foreign body.'

'*Signore, signore!*' cried the first gondolier, warningly.

A slight swell, caused perhaps by some distant motor-boat, made the gondola rock alarmingly. Dickie subsided—fortunately, into his seat; but his hand was still stretched out, pointing, and as the water was suddenly scooped into a hollow, they all saw what he meant: a dark object showed up for an instant in the trough of the wave.

'Looks like an old boot,' said Philip, straining his eyes. '*Cosa è, Angelino?*'

The gondolier shrugged his shoulders.

'*Io non so. Forsè qualche gatto,*' he said, with the light-heartedness with which Italians are wont to treat the death of animals.

'Good God, does the fellow think I don't know a cat when I see one?' cried Dickie, who had tumbled to the gondolier's meaning. 'Unless it's a cat that has been in the water a damned long time. No, it's—it's . . .'

The gondoliers exchanged glances and, as though by mutual consent, straightened themselves to row. '*E meglio andare, signori,*' said Angelino firmly.

'What does he say?'

'He says we'd better be going.'

'I'm not going till I've found out what that is,' said Dickie obstinately. 'Tell him to row up to it, Phil.'

Philip gave the order, but Angelino seemed not to understand. '*Non è niente interessante, niente interessante,*' he kept repeating stubbornly.

'But it is interesting to me,' said Dickie, who like many people could understand a foreign language directly his own wishes were involved. 'Go to it! There!' he commanded.

Reluctantly the men set themselves to row. As the boat drew up alongside, the black patch slid under the water and there appeared in its place a gleam of whiteness, then features—a forehead, a nose, a mouth. . . . They constituted a face, but not a recognisable one.

'Ah, *povero annegato,*' murmured Angelino, and crossed himself.

The two friends looked at each other blankly.

'Well, this has torn it,' said Dickie, at last. 'What are we going to do now?'

The gondoliers had already decided. They were moving on.

'Stop! Stop!' cried Philip. We can't leave him like this.' He appealed to the men. '*Non si può lasciarlo così.*'

Angelino spread his hands in protest. The drowned man would be found by those whose business it was to patrol the waters. Who knew what he had died of? Perhaps some dreadful disease which the signori would catch. There would be difficulties with the police; official visits. Finally, as the Englishmen still seemed unconvinced, he added, '*Anche fa sporca la gondola. Questo tappeto, signori, m'ha costato più che mille duecento lire.*'

Somewhat grimly Philip explained to Dickie this last, unanswerable reason for not taking the drowned man on board. 'He will dirty the gondola and spoil the carpet, which cost twelve hundred lire.'

'Carpet be damned! exclaimed Dickie. 'I always told you dagoes were no good. Here, catch hold of him.'

Together they pulled the dead man into the boat, though not before Angelino had rolled back his precious carpet. And when the dead man was lying in the bottom of the boat, decently covered with a piece of brown water-proof sheeting, he went round with sponge and wash-leather and carefully wiped away every drop of water from the gunwale and its brass fittings.

Ten minutes sufficed to take them to the Lido. The little *passeggiata* that had started so pleasantly had become a funeral cortège. The friends hardly spoke. Then, when they were nearing the landing-stage and the ugly white hotel, an eyesore all the way across the lagoon, impended over them with its blazing lights and its distressing symmery, Dickie said:

'By Jove, we shall be late for that fellow.'

'He'll understand,' said Philip. 'It'll be something to talk to him about.'

He regretted the words the moment they were out of his mouth: they sounded so heartless.

The landing-stage was almost deserted when the gondola drew up at the steps, but the aged, tottering and dirty *rampino* who hooked it in and held out his skinny hand for *soldi*, soon spread the news. While Philip was conferring with the gondoliers upon the proper course to be taken, a small crowd collected and gazed, expressionlessly but persistently, at the shapeless mound in the gondola. The *rampino* professed himself capable of keeping watch; the gondoliers declared they could not find a *vigile* unless they went together; they hinted that it might take some time. At last Dickie and Philip were free. They walked along the avenue under acacia trees stridently lighted by arc-lamps, towards the sea and the Hotel Splendide. As they looked back they saw that the little knot of spectators was already dispersing.

No, they were told: Count Giacomelli had not yet arrived. But that is nothing, smiled the *maître d'hôtel*; the Signor Conte is often late. Would the gentlemen take a cocktail while they waited?

Dickie agreed with enthusiasm. 'I think we've earned it,' he said. 'Think of it, but for us that poor chap would be floated about the lagoons till Doomsday and none of his dusky offspring know what had happened to him.'

'Do you think they will now?' asked Philip.

'You mean . . . ? Oh, I think anyone who really knew him could tell.'

They were sitting at a table under the trees. The air was fresh and pleasant; the absence of mosquitoes almost miraculous. Dickie's spirits began to rise.

'I say,' he said. 'It's damned dull waiting. He's twenty minutes late. Where's that boy?'

When a second round had been served, Dickie motioned the page to stay. Philip looked at him in surprise.

'Listen,' said Dickie, in a thick, excited undertone. 'Wouldn't it be a lark if we sent this lad down to the gondola and told him to ask the chap that's resting inside to come and dine with us?'

'A charming idea, Dickie, but I doubt whether they understand practical jokes in this country.'

'Nonsense, Phil, that's a joke that anyone could understand. Now, put on your thinking-cap and find the appropriate words. I'm no good; you must do it.'

Philip smiled.

'We don't want to be four at dinner, do we? I'm sure the Count wouldn't like having to sit down with a—a drowned rat.'

'That's absurd; he may be a man of excellent family; it's generally the rich who commit suicide.'

'We don't know that he did.'

'No, but all that's beside the point. Now just tell this boy to run down to the jetty, or whatever it is called, give our message and bring us back the answer. It won't take him ten minutes. I'll give him five lire to soothe his shattered nerves.'

Philip appeared to be considering it. 'Dick, I really don't think— a foreign country and all, you know. . . .'

The boy looked interrogatively from one to the other.

'It's a good idea,' repeated Philip, 'and I don't want to be a spoil-sport. But really, Dickie, I should give it up. The boy would be very scared, perhaps tell his parents, and then we might be mobbed and thrown into the Canal. It's the kind of thing that gives us a bad name abroad,' he concluded, somewhat pompously.

Dickie rose unsteadily to his feet.

'Bad name be hanged!' he said. 'What does it matter what we do in this tuppeny ha'penny hole? If you won't tell the boy I'll arrange it with the concierge. He understands English.'

'All right,' agreed Philip, for Dickie was already lurching away, the light of battle in his eye. 'I don't expect it'd do any harm, really. *Senta, piccolo!*' He began to explain the errand.

'Don't forget,' admonished Dickie, 'we expect the gentleman *subito*. He needn't bother to dress or wash or brush up or any-thing.'

Philip smiled in spite of himself.

'*Dica al signore,*' he said, '*di non vestirsi nero.*'

'Not "smoking"?' said the boy, pertly, delighted to display his English.

'No, not "smoking".'

The boy was off like a streak.

It must be boring waiting for a bomb to go off; it is almost equally tedious waiting for a practical joke to take effect. Dickie and Philip found the minutes drag interminably and they could think of nothing to say.

'He must be there now,' said Dickie, at last, taking out his watch.

'What's the time?'

'Half-past eight. He's been gone seven minutes.'

'How dark it is,' said Philip. 'Partly the trees, I suppose. But it wouldn't be dark in England now.'

'I've told you, much better stick to the Old Country. More daylight, fewer corpses, guests turn up to dinner at the proper time. . . .'

'Giacomelli's certainly very late. Over half an hour.'

'I wonder if he ever got your message.'

'Oh yes, he answered it.'

'You never told me. How long ago was that?'

'Last Wednesday. I wanted to give him plenty of time.'

'Did he write?'

'No, he telephoned. I couldn't understand very well. The servant said the Count was away but he would be delighted to dine with us. He was sorry he couldn't write, but he had been called away on business.'

'The sugar factory, perhaps?'

'Very likely.'

'It's bloody quiet, as the navvy said,' remarked Dickie.

'Yes, they are all dining in that glass place. You can see it through the leaves.'

'I suppose they'll know to bring him here.'

'Oh, yes.'

Silence fell, broken a moment later by Philip's exclamation, 'Ah, here's the boy!'

With no little excitement they watched his small figure approaching over the wilderness of small grey pebbles which serve the Venetians in lieu of gravel. They noticed at once that his bearing was erect and important; if he had had a shock he bore no traces of it. He stopped by them, smiling and breathing hard.

'Ho fatto un corso,' he said, swelling with pride.

'What's that?'

'He says he ran.'

'I expect he did.'

The friends exchanged amused glances.

'I must say he's got a good pluck,' remarked Dickie, ruefully admiring. Their joke had fallen flat. 'But I expect these Italian kids see corpses every day. Anyhow, ask him what the gentleman said.'

'*Che cosa ha detto il signore?*' asked Philip.

Still panting, the boy replied:

'*Accetta con molto piacere. Fra pochi minuti sarà qui.*'

Philip stared at the page in amazement.

'*Si, si, signore,*' repeated the boy. '*Così ha detto, "vengo con molto piacere".*'

'What does he say?' asked Dickie irritably.

'He says that the gentleman accepts our invitation with great pleasure and will be here in a few minutes.'

'Of course,' said Dickie, when the boy had gone off with his *mancia*, 'he's having us on. But he's a tough youngster. Can't be more than twelve years old.'

Philip was looking all around him, clenching and unclenching his fingers.

'I don't believe he invented that.'

'But if he didn't?'

Philip did not answer.

'How like a cemetery the place looks,' he said, suddenly, 'with all the cypresses and this horrible monumental mason's road-repairing stuff all round.'

'The scene would look better for a few fairy-lights,' rejoined Dickie. 'But your morbid fancies don't help us to solve the problem of our friend in the boat. Are we being made fools of by this whippersnapper, or are we not?'

'Time will show,' said Philip. 'He said a few minutes.'

They both sat listening.

'This waiting gives me the jim-jams,' said Dickie at last. 'Let's call the little rascal back and make him tell us what really did happen.'

'No, no, Dickie, that would be too mortifying. Let's try to think it out; let's proceed from the known to the unknown, as they do in detective stories. The boy goes off. He arrives at the landing stage. He finds some ghoulish loafers hanging about . . .'

'He might not,' said Dickie. 'There were only two or three corpse-gazers when we left.'

'Anyhow, he finds the *rampino* who swore to mount guard.'

'He might have slipped in for a drink,' said Dickie. 'You gave him the wherewithal, and he has to live like others.'

'Well, in that case, the boy would see—what?'

'Just that bit of tarpaulin stuff, humped up in the middle.'

'What would he do, then? Put yourself in his place, Dickie.'

Dickie grimaced slightly.

'I suppose he'd think the man was resting under the water-proof and he'd say, "Hullo, there!" in that ear-splitting voice Italians have, fit to wake. . . .'

'Yes, yes. And then?'

'Then perhaps, as he seems an enterprising child, he'd descend into the hold and give the tarpaulin a tweak and—well, I suppose he'd stop shouting,' concluded Dickie lamely. 'He'd see it was no good. You must own,' he added, 'it's simpler to assume that half way down the street he met a pal who told him he was being ragged: then he hung about and smoked a cigarette and returned puffing with this cock-and-bull story—simply to get his own back on us.'

'That is the most rational explanation,' said Philip. 'But just for fun, let's suppose that when he called, the tarpaulin began to move and rear itself up and a hand came round the edge, and—'

There was a sound of feet scrunching on the stones, and the friends heard a respectful voice saying, 'Per qui, signor Conte.'

At first they could only see the robust, white-waistcoated figure of the concierge advancing with a large air and steam-roller tread; behind him they presently descried another figure, a tall man dressed in dark clothes, who walked with a limp. After the concierge's glorious effulgence, he seemed almost invisible.

'Il Conte Giacomelli,' announced the concierge, impressively.

The two Englishmen advanced with outstretched hands, but their guest fell back half a pace and raised his arm in the Roman salute.

'How do you do?' he said. His English accent was excellent. 'I'm afraid I am a little late, no?'

'Just a minute or two, perhaps,' said Philip. 'Nothing to speak of.' Furtively, he stared at the Count. A branch of the overhanging ilex tree nearly touched his hat; he stood so straight and still in the darkness that one could fancy he was suspended from the tree.

'To tell you the truth,' said Dickie bluntly, 'we had almost given you up.'

'Given me up?' The Count seemed mystified. 'How do you mean, given me up?'

'Don't be alarmed,' Philip laughingly reassured him. 'He didn't mean give you up to the police. To give up, you know, can mean so many things. That's the worst of our language.'

'You can give up hope, isn't it?' inquired the Count.

'Yes,' replied Philip cheerfully. 'You can certainly give up hope. That's what my friend meant: we'd almost given up hope of seeing you. We couldn't give *you* up—that's only an idiom—because, you see, we hadn't got you.'

'I see,' said the Count. 'You hadn't got me.' He pondered.

The silence was broken by Dickie.

'You may be a good grammarian, Phil,' he said, 'but you're a damned bad host. The Count must be famished. Let's have some cocktails here and then go in to dinner.'

'All right, you order them. I hope you don't mind,' he went on when Dickie had gone, 'but we may be four at dinner.'

'Four?' echoed the Count.

'I mean,' said Philip, finding it absurdly difficult to explain, 'we asked someone else as well. I—I think he's coming.'

'But that will be delightful,' the Count said, raising his eyebrows slightly. 'Why should I mind? Perhaps he is a friend of mine, too—your—your other guest?'

'I don't think he would be,' said Philip, feeling more than ever at a loss. 'He—he . . .'

'He is not *de notre monde*, perhaps?' the Count suggested, indulgently.

Philip knew that foreigners refer to distinctions of class more openly than we do, but all the same, he found it very difficult to reply.

'I don't know whether he belongs to our world or not,' he began, and realising the ludicrous appropriateness of the words, stopped suddenly. 'Look here,' he said, 'I can't imagine why my friend is staying so long. Shall we sit down? Take care!' he cried as the Count was moving towards a chair. 'It's got a game leg—it won't hold you.'

He spoke too late; the Count had already seated himself. Smiling, he said: 'You see, she carries me all right.'

Philip marvelled.

'You must be a magician.'

The Count shook his head. 'No, not a magician, a—a . . .' he searched for the word. 'I cannot explain myself in English. Your friend who is coming—does he speak Italian?'

Inwardly Philip groaned.

'I—I really don't know.'

The Count tilted his chair back.

'I don't want to be curious, but is he an Englishman, your friend?'

Oh God, thought Philip. Why on earth did I start this subject? Aloud he said: 'To tell you the truth I don't know much about him. That's what I wanted to explain to you. We only saw him once and we invited him through a third person.'

'As you did me?' said the Count, smiling.

'Yes, yes, but the circumstances were different. We came on him by accident and gave him a lift.'

'A lift?' queried the Count. 'You were in a hotel, perhaps?'

'No,' said Philip, laughing awkwardly. 'We gave him a lift—a ride—in the gondola. How did you come?' he added, thankful at last to have changed the subject.

'I was given a lift, too,' said the Count.

'In a gondola?'

'Yes, in a gondola.'

'What an odd coincidence,' said Philip.

'So, you see,' said the Count, 'your friend and I will have a good deal in common.'

There was a pause. Philip felt a growing uneasiness which he couldn't define or account for. He wished Dickie would come back: he would be able to divert the conversation into pleasanter channels. He heard the Count's voice saying:

'I'm glad you told me about your friend. I always like to know something about a person before I make his acquaintance.'

Philip felt he must make an end of all this. 'Oh, but I don't think you will make his acquaintance,' he cried. 'You see, I don't think he exists. It's all a silly joke.'

'A joke?' asked the Count.

'Yes, a practical joke. Don't you in Italy have a game on the first of April making people believe or do silly things? April Fools, we call them.'

'Yes, we have that custom,' said the Count, gravely, 'only we call them *pesci d'Aprile*—April Fish.'

'Ah,' said Philip, 'that's because you are a nation of fishermen. An April fish is a kind of fish you don't expect—something you pull out of the water and—'

'What's that?' said the Count. 'I heard a voice.'

Philip listened.

'Perhaps it's your other guest.'

'It can't be him. It can't be!'

The sound was repeated: it was only just audible, but it was Philip's name. But why did Dickie call so softly?

'Will you excuse me?' said Philip. 'I think I'm wanted.'

The Count inclined his head.

'But it's the most amazing thing,' Dickie was saying, 'I think I must have got it all wrong. But here they are and perhaps you will be able to convince them. I think they're mad myself—I told them so.'

He led Philip into the hall of the hotel. The concierge was there and two *vigili*. They were talking in whispers.

'*Ma è scritto sul fazzoletto*,' one of them was saying.

'What's that?' asked Dickie.

'He says it's written on his handkerchief,' said Philip.

'Besides, we both know him,' chimed in the other policeman.

'What *is* this all about?' cried Philip. 'Know whom?'

'Il Conte Giacomelli,' chanted the *vigili* in chorus.

'Well, do you want him?' asked Philip.

'We *did* want him three days ago,' said one of the men. 'But now it's too late.'

'Too late? But he's . . .' Philip stopped suddenly and looked across at Dickie.

'I tell them so,' shouted the concierge, who seemed in no way disposed to save Count Giacomelli from the hands of justice. 'Many times, many times, I say: "The Count is in the garden with the English gentlemen." But they do not believe me.'

'But it's true!' cried Philip. 'I've only just left him. What do the *vigili* say?'

'They say that he is dead,' said the concierge. 'They say he is dead and his body is in your boat.'

There was a moment of silence. The *vigili*, like men exhausted by argument, stood apart, moody and indifferent. At last one of them spoke.

'It is true, *signori*. *Si è suicidato*. His affairs went badly. He was a great swindler—and knew he would be arrested and condemned. *Così si è salvato*.'

'He may be a swindler,' said Philip, 'but I'm certain he's alive. Come into the garden and see.'

Shaking their heads and shrugging their shoulders, the *vigili* followed him out of the hotel. In a small group they trooped across the stony waste towards the tree. There was no one there.

'You see, *signori*,' said one of the vigili, with an air of subdued triumph, 'it's as we said.'

'Well, he must have gone away,' said Philip, obstinately. 'He was sitting on this chair—so . . .' But his effort to give point to his contention failed. The chair gave way under him and he sprawled rather ludicrously and painfully on the stony floor. When he had picked himself up one of the policemen took the chair, ran his hand over it, and remarked:

'It's damp.'

'Is it?' said Philip expressionlessly.

'I don't think anyone could have sat on this chair,' pursued the policeman.

He is telling me I am a liar, thought Philip, and blushed. But the other *vigile*, anxious to spare his feelings, said:

'Perhaps it was an impostor whom you saw—a confidence man. There are many such, even in Italy. He hoped to get money out of the *signori*.' He looked round for confirmation; the concierge nodded.

'Yes,' said Philip, wearily. 'No doubt that explains it. Will you want us again?' he asked the *vigili*. 'Have you a card, Dickie?'

The *vigili*, having collected the information they required, saluted and walked off.

Dickie turned to the concierge.

'Where's that young whippersnapper who took a message for us?'

'Whippersnapper?' repeated the concierge.

'Well, page-boy?'

'Oh, the *piccolo*? He's gone off duty, sir, for the night.'

'Good thing for him,' said Dickie. 'Hullo, who's this? My poor nerves won't stand any more of this Maskelyne and Devant business.'

It was the *maître d'hôtel*, bowing obsequiously.

'Will there be three gentlemen, or four, for dinner?' he asked.

Philip and Dickie exchanged glances and Dickie lit a cigarette.

'Only two gentlemen,' he said.

A TERRIBLE TALE

Gaston Leroux

*There are several surprising guests who come to dinner in the following
story by Gaston Leroux (1868–1927), the famous author of* The Phantom
of the Opera. *A journalist and gourmet, Leroux found the inspiration for
many of his tales in the bistros of Paris and Toulon which he loved to visit.
Among his short stories is a series about a quartet of old sailors who gather
to recount their experiences in a typical French café in Toulon. 'A Terrible
Tale' is one of the best of these, but the reader should be warned that it is no
tale for those with weak stomachs!*

Captain Michel had but one arm, which he found useful when he
lit his pipe. He was an old sea dog whose acquaintance, with that of
four other old salts, I made one evening on the open front of a café
in the Vieille Darse, Toulon, where I was taking an appetiser. And
in this way we fell into the habit of foregathering over a glass
within a stone's throw of the rippling waves and the swinging
dinghys, about the hour when the sun sinks behind Tamaris.

The four old marines were known as Zinzin, Dorat—Captain
Dorat—Bagatelle, and Chanlieu—that old fellow Chanlieu. They
had, of course, sailed every sea and met with a thousand adventures; and now that they were retired on their pensions, they spent
their time telling each other terrible tales.

Captain Michel alone never indulged in any reminiscences. And
as he seemed in no way surprised by anything he heard, his old
comrades in the end grew exasperated with him.

'Look here, Captain Michel, hasn't anything out of the way ever
happened to you?'

'Oh yes,' the captain made answer, taking his pipe from his
mouth. 'Yes, something happened to me once—just once.'

'Well, let's have it.'

'No.'

'Why not?'

'Because it's too awful. You might not be able to stand it. I've often tried to tell the story but people have slipped away before I finished it.'

The four sea dogs vied with each other in the loudness of their guffaws, declaring that Captain Michel was trying to find some excuse, because in reality, nothing extraordinary had ever happened to him.

The old fellow stared at them a moment, and then suddenly accepting the situation, laid his pipe on the table. This unusual gesture was in itself startling!

'Messieurs, I'll tell you how I lost my arm,' he began.

'In those days—some twenty years ago—I owned a small villa, in the suburb of Le Mourillon, which had been left to me, for my family were long settled in these parts and I myself was born here.

'It suited me to take a little rest after a long voyage and before setting sail again. For that matter, I rather liked the place, and lived quite peaceably among sea-faring men and colonials who troubled me very little, and whom I rarely saw, occupied as they were as a rule in opium-smoking with their lady friends, or with other business which did not concern me. Of course there is no accounting for tastes, but as long as they didn't interfere with me, I was satisfied . . .

'It so happened that one night they did interfere with my habit of going to sleep. I was awakened with a start by an extraordinary uproar, the meaning of which I couldn't possibly make out. I had left my window open as usual. I listened in a state of bewilderment to a tremendous din, which was a cross between the rumbling of thunder and the roll of a drum, but such a drum! It was as though a couple of hundred drumsticks were being madly beaten, not on ordinary drum-skin, but on a wooden drum.

'The disturbance came from the villa opposite, which had been empty for some five years, and on which I had noticed, the previous evening, a board bearing the announcement: "To be sold."

'I let my gaze stray from the window of my bedroom, on the first floor, beyond the small garden in which the house stood, and my eye took in every door and window, even the doors and windows on the ground floor. They were still closed as I had seen them during the day; but I caught sight of gleams of light through the chinks in the shutters on the ground floor. Who and what were these people? How had they found their way into this solitary house at the far end of Le Mourillon? What sort of company was it that had obtained admission into this deserted dwelling, and why were they kicking up such a shindy?

'The extraordinary din, like the thunderous beating of a wooden drum, continued. It went on for another hour, and then as dawn was breaking, the front door opened, and there appeared in the doorway the most radiant creature that I have ever beheld. She was clad in a low-necked dress, and held with perfect grace a lamp whose beams fell over the shoulders of a goddess. I distinctly heard her say in the echoing night, while a kind and quiet smile flickered across her face:

'"Good-bye, dear friend, till next year."

'To whom was she speaking? It was impossible for me to tell for I could see no one standing beside her. She remained at the entrance holding the lamp for some minutes, until the garden gate opened by itself and closed by itself. Then the front door of the house was shut in its turn, and I saw nothing more.

'It seemed to me that I was either losing my head or was the sport of a dream, for I knew that it was out of the question for anyone to pass through the garden without my perceiving him.

'I was still planted at the window, incapable of the least movement or thought, when the door of the house opened a second time, and the same vision of beauty appeared still carrying a lamp and still alone.

'"Hush," she said, "Don't make a noise any of you. We mustn't disturb our neighbour opposite. I'll come with you."

'And silently and alone she crossed the garden and stopped at the gate on which the full rays of the lamp shone; so much so, indeed, that I clearly saw the knob of the gate turn of its own accord without any hand being placed upon it. And the gate opened once again by itself in the presence of this woman who, moreover, did not evince any surprise. Need I explain that from where I was posted, I could see both in front and behind the gate; in other words, that I saw it sideways?

'This "splendid apparition" made a charming movement of her head towards the empty darkness which the glare of the lamp made visible; then she smiled and said:

'"Well, good-bye until next year. My husband is very pleased. Not a single one of you failed to answer the call. Good-bye, messieurs."

'And I heard several voices in unison:

'"Good-bye, madame, good-bye, dear madame, until next year."

'And as the mysterious hostess was preparing to close the door herself, I heard a voice:

'"Oh, please, don't trouble."

'And the door was once more closed.

'The next moment the air was filled with a curious sound; it was like the chirping of a flock of birds, and it seemed as if this beautiful woman had opened the cage of a whole brood of house sparrows.

'She quietly walked back to the house. The lights on the ground floor were then out, but I noticed a glimmer in the windows of the first floor.

'When she reached the house she said:

'"Are you upstairs, Gérard?"

'I could not hear the answer, but the front door was again closed, and a few minutes later the light on the first floor went out.

'I was still standing at my window at eight o'clock in the morning, staring in blank amazement at the house and garden which had revealed such strange happenings in darkness, and which now in the full light of day assumed their familiar aspect. The garden was a waste, and the house itself seemed as desolate as it was the day before.

'So much so, indeed, that when I told my old charwoman who had just come, of the queer events which I had witnessed, she tapped my forehead with her dirty forefinger and muttered that I had smoked one pipe too many. Now I have never been a smoker of opium, and her answer gave me a good opportunity of sacking the old sloven whom I had for some time wanted to get rid of, and who came for a couple of hours each day to "clean up" the place for me. For that matter I did not need any one, as I was setting sail again next day.

'I barely had time to put my things together, make a few purchases, say farewell to my friends, and catch the train for Havre. I had fixed up an appointment with the Transatlantic company which would keep me away from Toulon for some eleven or twelve months.

'In due course I returned to Toulon, but though I had refrained from mentioning my adventure to a soul, I still continued to think of it. The vision of the lady of the lamp obsessed me wherever I went, and the last words which she uttered to her unseen friends still rang in my ears:

'"Well, good-bye until next year."

'And I never ceased to think of the meeting. I, too, was determined to be there and to discover, at whatever cost, the solution of a mystery which was intensely perplexing to a sensible man like myself, who did not believe in ghosts or phantom vessels.

'Unfortunately I was soon to learn that neither heaven nor hell were concerned in the terrible story.

'It was six o'clock in the evening when I set foot again in my house at Toulon; and it was two days before the anniversary of the wonderful night.

'The first thing that I did on going inside was to run up to my room and open the window. It was summer and broad daylight, and my eyes at once fell upon a lady of great beauty who was placidly walking about gathering flowers in the garden of the house opposite. At the noise made by the opening window she looked up.

'It was the lady of the lamp. I recognised her, and she seemed not less beautiful by day than by night. Her skin was as white as the teeth of an African, her eyes bluer than the waters at Tamaris, her hair as soft and fair as the finest flax.

'Why should I not make the confession? When I beheld this woman of whom I had been dreaming for a year, a strange feeling came over me. She was no illusion of a diseased imagination. She stood before me in the flesh; and every window of the house was open and flower-bedecked by her hands. There was nothing fantastic in all this.

'She caught sight of me and at once displayed some degree of annoyance. She walked a few steps farther in the centre path of the garden, and then shrugging her shoulders as though she were disconcerted said:

'"Let's go in, Gérard. I'm beginning to feel the coolness of the night."

'I let my gaze stray round the garden. I could perceive no one. To whom was she speaking? . . . Nobody there!

'Then was she mad? It scarcely seemed so.

'I watched her return to the house. She passed into it, the door was closed, and she at once shut the windows.

'I did not see or hear anything worth noticing that night. Next morning at ten o'clock I observed my neighbour leaving the garden attired as if for a walk. She locked the gate after her and set out in the direction of Toulon.

'I started off in my turn. Pointing to the fashionably dressed figure in front of me I asked the first tradesman whom I met if he knew the lady's name.

'"Why, of course. She's your neighbour. She is living with her husband at the Villa Makoko. They moved in about a year ago, just as you went away. They are regular boors. They never speak to anybody, unless it's absolutely necessary, but every one in Le Mourillon, as you know, goes his own way, and is never surprised at anything. The captain for one . . ."

'"What captain?"

'"Captain Gérard. It seems he is an ex-captain of marines. Well, no one ever sees him . . . Sometimes when food has to be delivered at the house, and the lady is not in, some person shouts out an order from behind the door to leave the stuff on the step, and waits until you are a good distance away before taking it in."

'You can imagine that I was growing more and more puzzled. I went to Toulon in order to ask the agent who let the villa a few questions about these people. He, likewise, had never seen the husband, but he told me that his name was Gérard Beauvisage.

'When I heard the name I uttered a cry: "Gérard Beauvisage! Why I know him!"

'I had an old friend of that name whom I had not seen for twenty-five years. He was an officer in the marines and had left Toulon for Tonkin about that period. How could I doubt that it was he? At all events, I had a straightforward reason for calling on him, that very evening, though he was expecting a visit from his friends, for it was the anniversary of the famous night. I made up my mind to renew my old friendship with him.

'When I got back to Le Mourillon I espied in front of me, in the sunk road leading to the Villa Makoko, the figure of my neighbour. I did not hesitate, but hastened to overtake her.

'"Have I the honour of speaking to Madame Beauvisage, the wife of Captain Gérard Beauvisage?" I asked with a bow.

'She coloured and tried to pass on without answering me.

'"Madame, I am your neighbour, Captain Michel Alban," I persisted.

'"Oh please forgive me, monsieur," she returned, "my husband has often spoken of you . . . Captain Michel Alban . . ."

'She seemed terribly ill at ease, and yet in her confusion, she was more beautiful than ever, if that were possible. In spite of her obvious desire to elude me I went on:

'"How comes it that Captain Beauvisage has returned to France without letting his old friend know? I shall be particularly obliged if you will tell Gérard that I'm coming to shake hands with him this very evening."

'And observing that she was hastening her steps, I bowed, but as I was speaking she turned round, betraying an agitation which was more and more difficult to comprehend.

'"Impossible to-night . . . I promise to tell Gérard of our meeting. That's the most I can do. Gérard doesn't wish to see anyone—anyone. He lives alone . . . We live alone . . . And we took the house because we were told that the next house was occupied only for a few days once or twice a year by someone who is never seen! . . ."

'And she added in a voice tinged with sadness:

'"You must forgive Gérard, monsieur. We do not receive anyone—anyone. Good day, monsieur."

'"Madame, the Captain and you receive friends occasionally," I returned with some impatience. "For instance, tonight you are expecting friends with whom you made an appointment a year ago."

'She flushed scarlet.

'"Oh, but that's an exceptional case . . . that's an absolutely exceptional case . . . They are our very particular friends."

'Having said which she made her escape, but at once stopped her retreat and turned back.

'"Whatever you do, don't call tonight", she entreated, and disappeared into the garden.

'I returned to my house and began to keep watch on my neighbours. They did not show themselves, and long before it was dark I saw the shutters being closed and lights gleaming through the openings, such as I had seen on that amazing night a year ago. But I did not hear the same extraordinary din like the thunderous beating of a wooden drum.

'At seven o'clock I began to dress for I called to mind the low-necked robe worn by the lady of the lamp. Madame Beauvisage's last words had but strengthened my determination. The captain was seeing some of his friends that evening; he dared not refuse me admission. After dressing it crossed my mind, before I went downstairs, to put my revolver in my pocket, but in the end I left it in its place, considering that to take it would be an act of stupidity.

'The stupidity lay in not taking it with me.

'On reaching the entrance to the Villa Makoko I turned the handle of the gate on the off chance—the handle which last year I had seen turn by itself. And to my intense surprise the door opened. Therefore my neighbours were expecting visitors. I walked up to the house and knocked at the door.

'"Come in!" a voice cried.

'I recognised Gérard's voice. I walked gaily into the house. I passed first through the hall, and then as the door of a small drawing-room stood open, and the room was lit up, I entered it.

'"Gérard it's me," I exclaimed, "your old pal Michel Alban."

'"Oh, really, so you made up your mind to come, my dear old Michel! I told my wife only just now that you would come and I should be glad to see you . . . But you are the only one, apart from our particular friends . . . Do you know, my dear Michel, you haven't altered much . . ."

'It would be impossible for me to describe my stupefaction. I heard Gérard, but I could not see him. His voice rang in my ears, but no one was near me, no one was in the drawing-room. The Voice went on:

'"Sit down, won't you? My wife will soon be here, for she will remember that she left me on the mantelpiece!"

'I looked up, and then discovered above me . . . above me resting on a high mantelpiece—a bust.

'It was this bust which had been speaking. It resembled Gérard. It was Gérard's body. It had been placed there as people are wont to place busts on mantelpieces. It was a bust like those carved by sculptors, that is to say, it was without arms.

'"I can't shake hands with you, my dear Michel," the voice went on, "for as you see I have no hands, but if you raise yourself on tiptoe you will be able to take me in your arms and place me on the table. My wife put me up here in a moment of temper, because she said I was in the way when she swept the room. She's a funny thing is my wife."

'And the bust burst out laughing.

'It seemed to me that I was the victim of an optical illusion as happens in those entertainments where you behold living heads and shoulders suspended in mid-air, the result of tricks with mirrors; but after setting down my friend on the table, as he requested, I had to admit that this head and body without arms or legs was indeed all that remained of the excellent officer whom I had known in days gone by. His body was resting on a small wheeled platform, such as are used by cripples without legs, but Gérard did not possess even the stumps of legs which can be seen in the case of most cripples. To think that my old friend was nothing but a bust!

'Small hooks took the place of arms, and language fails me to describe how, leaning for support on a hook here, or on another there, he set to work to hop, skip and jump and perform a hundred swift movements which shot him from the table to a chair, from a chair to the floor, and then suddenly made him appear on the table once more, where he indulged in the gayest chatter.

'Myself, I was in a state of consternation. I was rendered speechless. I watched this freak perform his antics and say with a chuckle which alarmed me:

'"I have greatly changed I daresay. You must admit, my dear Michel, that you hardly recognise me. You did quite right to call this evening. We shall see some sport. We have a few very special friends, and, you know, apart from them I don't care to meet anyone—merely as a matter of pride. We don't even keep a servant. Wait for me here. I must get into my smoking jacket."

'He went off, and almost at once the lady of the lamp appeared.

She wore the same low-necked dress of the year before. As soon as her eyes fell upon me, she seemed strangely perturbed, and said in a strained voice:

'"Oh, so you are here! You've made a mistake, Captain Michel. I gave your message to my husband, but I forbade you to call this evening. I may tell you that when he learnt that you were in this place, he asked me to invite you this evening, but I did no such thing because," she went on, ill at ease, "I had good reasons. We have certain very particular friends who are rather a worry—they are very fond of noise—uproar. You must have heard them last year," she added, giving me a look out of the corner of her eye. "Well, promise me to leave early."

'"I promise to leave early, madame," I returned, and yet a vague misgiving took possession of me at this conversation the meaning of which I was far from understanding. "I promise you faithfully, but can you tell me how it is that I find my old friend in such a state? What terrible accident happened to him?"

'"None at all, monsieur, none."

'"What do you mean, 'none at all'? Don't you know anything about the accident which deprived him of arms and legs. Yet he must have met with it since your marriage."

'"No, monsieur, no. I married the captain as he is now . . . But excuse me, our guests will be here presently, and I must help my husband to put on his smoking jacket."

'She left me to myself, dazed by the one stupefying thought: "She married the captain as he is now!" and almost at once I heard sounds in the hall, the curious sounds which had accompanied the lady of the lamp to the garden gate and baffled me last year. This noise was followed by the appearance, on their wheeled platforms, of four cripples without arms or legs who stared at me in wonder. They were all attired in perfectly-fitting evening dress with snow-white shirt fronts.

'One wore gold-rimmed pince-nez, another, an old man, spectacles, the third a single eye-glass, and the fourth was content to gaze at me out of his own proud, shrewd eyes with an expression of boredom. All four, however, saluted me with their little hooks, and asked after Captain Beauvisage. I told them that he was dressing, and Madame Beauvisage was quite well. When I took the liberty of speaking of Madame Beauvisage, I caught an exchange of glances between them which seemed to embody a certain raillery.

'"Haw, haw, I presume you are a great friend of our good old captain," drawled the cripple with the monocle.

'The others smiled with a look which was by no means pleasant, and then they all started to talk in the same breath:

'"Sorry, sorry, monsieur . . . We are quite naturally surprised to meet you at the house of the good old captain, who swore on his wedding day to shut himself up in the country with his wife, and not to receive anyone—anyone but his very special friends, you understand. When one is so thoroughly a cripple as the captain consented to be, and is married to such a beautiful woman, it is quite natural—quite natural. But, after all, if in the course of his life he met a man of honour who does not happen to be a cripple, we're glad of it . . . We congratulate you."

'And they repeated: "We're glad of it . . . We congratulate you."

'Lord how odd they were, these dwarfs! I watched them and held my peace. Others arrived in twos and threes and so on. And they all contemplated me with a look of surprise or uneasiness or irony. For my part I was rendered speechless by the spectacle of so many cripples without arms or legs; for after all I was beginning to see through most of the extraordinary happenings which had so greatly stirred my mind; and though the cripples, by their presence, explained many things, the presence of the cripples still required explanation, as also did the monstrous union of that splendid woman with that awful shred of humanity.

'True, I realised now that these little ambulating trunks were bound to pass unperceived by me in the narrow garden path lined with verbena, and the road running between two low hedges; and, truth to tell, when at the time I said to myself that it was impossible to avoid seeing any person going down those paths, I had in mind persons who would be standing upright on their two legs.

'The handle of the garden gate itself no longer puzzled me, and in my mind's eye I saw the invisible hook which had turned it.

'The peculiar noise which I heard was but the creaking made by the small badly oiled wheels of these cars for freaks. Finally, the extraordinary sound like the thunderous beating of a wooden drum, was obviously caused by the many cars and hooks striking the floor when, after an excellent dinner, our friends the cripples indulged in a dance.

'Yes all this was capable of explanation but I was conscious as I caught a curious eager gleam in their eyes, and heard the peculiar sound of their nippers, that something terrible still remained to be cleared up, and that all else which had surprised me was of no account.

'Meanwhile Madame Beauvisage promptly appeared, accompanied by her husband. They were greeted with shouts of delight. The little hooks "applauded" them with an infernal din. I was deafened by it. Then I was introduced. Cripples were all over the place: on the tables, chairs, stools, on stands usually occupied by vases, on the sideboard. One of them sat on the shelf of a dresser like a Buddha in his recess. And each one politely held out his hook to me. They seemed for the most part people of good position, with titles and names indicating their relationship to aristocratic families, but I learned afterwards that these were false names given to me for reasons which will be obvious. Lord Wilmer certainly maintained the best front of them all, with his fine golden beard and no less fine moustache which he continually stroked with his hook. He did not leap from chair to table like the others, nor did he have the air of a huge bat taking wing from wall to wall.

'"We are only waiting for the doctor," said the mistress of the house, who every now and then gave me a look of obvious gloom, but quickly resumed her smile for her guests.

'The doctor arrived. He was a cripple but he possessed both arms.

'He offered one of them to Madame Beauvisage and led her to the dining-room. I mean that she touched his arm with the tips of her fingers.

'Covers were laid in the room with the closed shutters. The table, which was laden with flowers and *hors d'œuvre*, was illuminated by a large candelabrum. There was no fruit. The dozen cripples at once leapt upon their chairs and began to pick greedily from the dishes with their hooks. It was not a pleasant sight, and I marvelled at the voracity with which these trunks of men, who seemed just before so well-mannered, devoured their food.

'And then suddenly they quietened down; their hooks kept still, and it seemed to me that they lapsed into what is usually described as a "painful silence."

'Every eye was turned on Madame Beauvisage, whose husband sat by her side, and I noticed that she buried her face in her napkin, looking very uncomfortable. Then my friend Gérard, clapping one hook against the other with a flourish, said:

'"Well, my dear old friends, it can't be helped. One doesn't meet the luck of last year every day. But don't distress yourselves. With the exercise of a little imagination we shall succeed in being as merry as we were then . . ."

'And turning to me as he lifted the small handle of the glass which stood on the table before him:

'"Your health my dear Michel. To us all!"

'And each man raised his glass by its handle with the end of his hook. The glasses swung over the table in the quaintest fashion.

'My host went on:

'"You don't seem to be equal to the occasion, my dear Michel. I have known you in merrier mood, more up to the mark. Is it because we are 'like this' that you are so gloomy? What do you expect? We are what we are. But let us have some amusement. We are met together here, all of us very special friends, to celebrate the time when we became 'like this.' Is that not true my friends of the *Daphné?* . . ."

'Then my old comrade,' Captain Michel went on to explain, heaving a deep sigh, 'told us how the *Daphné*, which sailed between France and the Far East, was wrecked; how the crew escaped in the boats, and how these miserable people took refuge on a chance raft.

'Miss Madge, a beautiful young girl who lost her parents in the catastrophe, was also picked up by the raft. Some thirteen persons in all were on it, and at the end of three days the victuals were consumed, and at the end of a week the survivors were dying of hunger. It was then that, as the old song says, they agreed to draw lots as to "which should be eaten."

'Messieurs,' added Captain Michel, in a serious voice, 'such things have happened more often perhaps than they have been talked about, for the great blue waters close over these peculiar feats of digestion.

'They were on the point, therefore, of drawing lots on the raft when the doctor's voice was heard: "Mesdames and Messieurs," said the doctor, "You have lost all your belongings in the wreck of the ship, but I have saved my case of instruments and my forceps for arresting haemorrhage. This is my suggestion: There is no object in any one of us running the risk of being eaten as a whole. Let us, to begin with, draw lots of an arm or leg at will, and we will then see tomorrow what the day brings forth, and perhaps a sail may appear on the horizon."'

At this point in Captain Michel's story the four old salts, who up to this had not interrupted, cried:

'Well done!'

'What do you mean "well done"?' asked Captain Michel with a frown.

'Yes, "well done!" Your story is a good joke. These people were ready to lose an arm or leg in turn . . . That's a good joke, but there's nothing frightful about it.'

'So you really find it a good joke!' growled the Captain, bristling with annoyance. 'Well, I swear that if you had been seated among all those cripples whose eyes were bulging like live coal, and heard the story, you wouldn't have found it such a good joke . . . And if you had noticed how restless they were in their chairs! And how vigorously they clasped hooks across the table with an obvious delight which I couldn't make out, but which was none the less frightful for all that.'

'No, no,' broke in Chanlieu once more—that old fellow Chanlieu—'your story is not in the least frightful. It is funny simply because it is logical. Would you like me to tell you the end of the story? You shall say whether I am right or not. The people on the raft drew lots. The lot fell to Miss Madge who was to lose one of her beautiful limbs. Your friend the captain, who is a gentleman, offered his own instead, and he had his four limbs amputated so that Miss Madge should remain unscathed.'

'Yes, old man, you've got it. That is so,' exclaimed Captain Michel who felt a longing to break the heads of these imbeciles who treated his story as a good joke. 'Yes, and what's more, when it was a question of cutting off Miss Madge's limbs after the survivors, except the young lady and the doctor—who had been left with both arms because they were wanted—had lost all their limbs, Captain Beauvisage had the pluck to have the poor stumps left from the first operation, cut off on a level with his body.'

'And the young lady could do no other than offer the Captain her hand which he had so heroically saved,' interposed Zinzin.

'Why, of course,' growled the Captain in his beard. 'And you consider it a good joke!'

'Did they eat all those limbs quite raw?' enquired that ass of a Bagatelle.

Captain Michel struck the table such a resounding blow that the glasses danced like rubber balls.

'That'll do, shut up,' he exclaimed. 'All that I've told you is nothing. Now comes the frightful part of it.'

The four friends looked at each other smiling, and Captain Michel grew pale, whereupon seeing that they had carried matters too far they hung their heads.

'Yes, the frightful part of it,' went on Michel with his gloomiest air, 'was that these people who were only rescued a month later by a Chinese sailing vessel which landed them somewhere on the Yang-Tse-Kiang where they separated—the frightful part of it was that these people retained a taste for human flesh, and when they returned to Europe arranged to meet together once a year to renew as far as possible the abominable banquet. Well, messieurs, it did not take me long to find that out! First of all there was the scarcely enthusiastic reception accorded to certain dishes, which Madame Beauvisage herself brought to the table. Though she ventured to claim, but with no great assurance, that they were pretty nearly the same thing, the guests were of one mind in abstaining from congratulating her. Only certain slices of tunny-fish were received with any sort of favour, because they were, to use the doctor's terrible expression, "well cut," and, "if the flavour was not entirely satisfactory at all events the eye was deceived." But the cripple with the spectacles met with general approval when he declared that "it was not equal to the plumber."

'When I heard those words I felt my blood run cold,' growled Captain Michel huskily, 'for I remembered that about this time the year before a plumber had fallen from a roof near the Arsenal and was killed, and his body was picked up minus an arm.

'Then . . . O then . . . I could not help thinking of the part which my beautiful neighbour must, of necessity, have played in this horrible, culinary drama. I turned my eyes to her and I noticed that she had put on her gloves again, gloves which covered her arms to the shoulder, and also hastily thrown a wrap over her shoulders which wholly concealed them. The guest on my right, who was the doctor, and, as I have said, was the only man among the cripples with both arms intact, had also put on his gloves.

'Instead of bothering my head in vain to discover the reason of this fresh eccentricity, I should have done better to follow the advice which Madame Beauvisage gave me at the beginning of this infernal party, namely, to leave the place early—advice which she did not repeat.'

'After showing an interest in me during the first part of this amazing feast in which I seemed to discern—I don't know why—a sort of pity, Madame Beauvisage now avoided looking at me and took a part which greatly grieved me in the most frightful conversation which I have ever heard. These little people with a vigorous clatter of nippers and clinking of glasses indulged in bitter recriminations or warm congratulations with regard to their peculiar appetite.

'To my horror Lord Wilmer who until then had been most correct, nearly 'came to hooks' with the cripple with the monocle, because the latter had once on the raft complained of the former being tough, and the mistress of the house had the greatest difficulty in putting things in their true light by retorting to the monocled bust, who was obviously at the time of the shipwreck a good-looking stripling, that neither was it particularly agreeable to have to put up with "an animal that was too young."'

'That's also funny,' the old salt Dorat could not help interjecting.

It looked as if Captain Michel would fly at his throat, particularly as the three other mariners seemed to be shaking with inward joy and gave vent to queer little clucks. It was as much as the Captain could do to control himself. After puffing like a seal he turned to the foolhardy Dorat:

'Monsieur you have two arms still, and I have no wish for you to
lose one of them, as I did on that particular night, to make you see
the frightful part of the story. The cripples had drunk a great deal.
Some of them jumped on the table round me, and were gazing at
my arms in a very embarrassing manner and I ended by hiding
them from sight as far as possible by thrusting my hands deep into
my pockets.

'I realised then, and it was a startling thought, why Madame
Beauvisage and the doctor, the two persons who still had arms and
hands, did not show them. I grasped the meaning of the sudden
ferocity which blazed in the eyes of some of them. And at that very
moment, as luck would have it, I wanted to use my pocket
handkerchief, and instinctively I made a movement which revealed the whiteness of my skin under my sleeve, and three
terrible hooks swooped down at once on my wrist and entered my
flesh. I uttered a fearful shriek.'

'That'll do, Captain, that'll do,' I exclaimed, interrupting Captain Michel's story. 'You were quite right. I'm off. I can't stand any
more.'

'Stay, monsieur,' said the Captain in a peremptory tone. 'Stay,
monsieur, for I shall soon finish this frightful story which has made
four imbeciles laugh. When a man has Phocean blood in his veins,'
he added with an accent of unspeakable contempt turning to the
four ancient mariners who were obviously choking in their efforts
to keep back their laughter, 'when a man has Phocean blood in his
veins, he can't get over it.

'And when a man lives in Marseilles he is doomed never to
believe in anything. So it is for you, for you alone, monsieur, that I
am telling this story, and, be assured, I will pass over the most
loathsome details, knowing as I do how much the mind of a
gentleman can bear. The tragedy of my martyrdom proceeded so
quickly that I can call to mind only their inhuman cries, the protests
of some and the rush of others while Madame Beauvisage stood up
and murmured:

'"Be careful not to hurt him!"

'I tried to leap to my feet, but by this time a posse of mad cripples
was round me who tripped me up and I crashed to the floor. And I
felt their awful hooks hold my flesh captive just as the meat in a
butcher's shop is held captive on its hooks.

'Yes, monsieur, I will spare you the details. I pledged you my
word; all the more so as I couldn't give them to you, for I did not see
the operation. The doctor clapped a plug of cotton wool steeped in
chloroform on my mouth by way of a gag.

'When I came to myself I was in the kitchen, and I had lost an arm. The cripples were all around me. They had ceased their wrangling. They seemed to be united in the most touching harmony; in reality they were in a state of dazed intoxication which caused them to sway their heads like children who feel the need to go and lie down after eating their fill, and I had not a doubt but that they were beginning, alas! to digest me . . . I was stretched at full length on the floor, securely bound, and deprived of all power of movement, but I could both see and hear them. My old comrade, Gérard Beauvisage, had tears of joy in his eyes as he exclaimed:

'"I should never have thought you would be so tender!"

'Madame Beauvisage was not present, but she, too, must have taken part in the feast, for I heard someone ask Gérard how "she liked her share."

'Yes, monsieur, I have finished my story. I have finished my story. Those loathsome cripples having satisfied their weakness, must have at last realised the full extent of their iniquity. They made themselves scarce, and Madame Beauvisage, of course, escaped with them. They left the doors wide open but no one came to set me free until four days afterwards, when I was pretty well dead with hunger . . .

'Those miserable wretches had not even left the bone behind!'

SO YOU WON'T TALK!

Damon Runyon

On New York's Broadway, not far from where The Phantom of the
Opera *has been playing to full houses, can be found one of America's best
known restaurants—Lindy's. It is famous not only for its food and for the
stars who have dined there (the faces of many of them smiling down from
photographs on the walls), but also because it has been immortalised in the
stories of Damon Runyon (1884–1946). In his racy tales of underworld
characters, written in a mixture of American slang and jargon, Runyon
referred to the restaurant as Mindy's. His interest in the juxtaposition of
food and crime is to be found in several of these stories—as well as in his
play,* A Slight Case of Murder, *co-authored with Howard Lindsay
(1935)—but most particularly in this next tale, 'So You Won't Talk!'
about a silent parrot and a millionaire's death over dinner.*

It is along about two o'clock of a nippy Tuesday morning, and I am
sitting in Mindy's Restaurant on Broadway with Regret, the horse
player, speaking of this and that, when who comes in but Ambrose
Hammer, the newspaper scribe, and what is he carrying in one
hand but a big bird cage, and what is in this bird cage but a green
parrot.

Well, if anybody sits around Mindy's Restaurant long enough,
they are bound to see some interesting and unusual scenes, but
this is undoubtedly the first time that anybody cold sober ever
witnesses a green parrot in there, and Mindy himself is by no
means enthusiastic about this spectacle. In fact, as Ambrose Hammer places the cage on our table, and sits down beside me, Mindy
approaches us and says to Ambrose:

'Horse players, yes,' Mindy says. 'Wrong bettors, yes. Dogs and
song writers and actors, yes. But parrots,' Mindy says, 'no. Take it
away,' he says.

But Ambrose Hammer pays no attention to Mindy and starts
ordering a few delicacies of the season from Schmalz, the waiter,

and Mindy finally sticks his finger in the cage to scratch the parrot's head, and goes cootch-cootch-cootch, and the next thing anybody knows, Mindy is sucking his finger and yelling bloody murder, as it seems the parrot starts munching on the finger as if it is a pretzel.

Mindy is quite vexed indeed, and he says he will go out and borrow a Betsy off of Officer Gloon and blow the parrot's brains out, and he also says that if anybody will make it worth his while, he may blow Ambrose Hammer's brains out, too.

'If you commit such a deed,' Ambrose says, 'you will be arrested. I mean, blowing this parrot's brains out. This parrot is a material witness in a murder case.'

Well, this statement puts a different phase on the matter, and Mindy goes away speaking to himself, but it is plain to be seen that his feelings are hurt as well as his finger, and personally, if I am Ambrose Hammer, I will not eat anything in Mindy's again unless I have somebody taste it first.

Naturally, I am very curious to know where Ambrose Hammer gets the parrot, as he is not such a character as makes a practice of associating with the birds and beasts of the forest, but of course I do not ask any questions, as the best you can get from asking questions along Broadway is a reputation for asking questions. And of course I am wondering what Ambrose Hammer means by saying this parrot is a material witness in a murder case, although I know that Ambrose is always mixing himself up in murder cases, even when they are really none of his put-in. In fact, Ambrose's hobby is murder cases.

He is a short, pudgy character, of maybe thirty, with a round face and googly eyes, and he is what is called a dramatic critic on one of the morning blatters, and his dodge is to observe new plays such as people are always putting on in the theatres and to tell his readers what he thinks of these plays, although generally what Ambrose Hammer really thinks of them is unfit for publication.

In fact, Ambrose claims the new plays are what drive him to an interest in murder for relief. So he is always looking into crimes of this nature, especially if they are mysterious cases, and trying to solve these mysteries, and between doing this and telling what he thinks of the new plays, Ambrose finds his time occupied no little, and quite some.

He is a well-known character along Broadway, because he is always in and out, and up and down, and around and about, but to tell the truth, Ambrose is not so popular with the citizens around Mindy's, because they figure that a character who likes to solve murder mysteries must have a slight touch of copper in him which will cause him to start investigating other mysteries at any minute.

Furthermore, there is a strong knockout on Ambrose in many quarters because he is in love with Miss Dawn Astra, a very beautiful young Judy who is playing the part of a strip dancer in a musical show at the Summer Garden, and it is well known to one and all that Miss Dawn Astra is the sweet pea of a character by the name of Julius Smung, until Ambrose comes into her life, and that Julius' heart is slowly breaking over her.

This Julius Smung is a sterling young character of maybe twenty-two, who is in the taxicab business as a driver. He is the son of the late Wingy Smung, who has his taxi stand in front of Mindy's from 1922 down to the night in 1936 that he is checking up the pockets of a sailor in Central Park to see if the sailor has the right change for his taxi fare, and the sailor wakes up and strikes Wingy on the head with Wingy's own jack handle, producing concussion of the brain.

Well, when Wingy passes away, leaving behind him many sorrowing friends, his son Julius takes his old stand, and naturally all who know Wingy in life are anxious to see his son carry on his name, so they throw all the taxicab business they can to him, and Julius gets along very nicely.

He is a good-looking young character and quite energetic, and he is most courteous to one and all; except maybe sailors, consequently public sentiment is on his side when Ambrose Hammer moves in on him with Miss Dawn Astra, especially as Miss Dawn Astra is Julius Smung's sweet pea since they are children together over on Tenth Avenue.

Their romance is regarded as one of the most beautiful little romances ever seen in this town. In fact, there is some talk that Julius Smung and Miss Dawn Astra will one day get married, although it is agreed along Broadway that this may be carrying romances a little too far.

Then Ambrose Hammer observes Miss Dawn Astra playing the part of a strip dancer, and it is undoubtedly love at first sight on Ambrose's part, and he expresses his love by giving Miss Dawn Astra better write-ups in the blatter he works for than he ever gives Miss Katharine Cornell, or even Mr Noel Coward. In fact, to read what Ambrose Hammer says about Miss Dawn Astra, you will think that she is a wonderful artist indeed, and maybe she is, at that.

Naturally, Miss Dawn Astra reciprocates Ambrose Hammer's love, because all the time she is Julius Smung's sweet pea, the best she ever gets is a free taxi ride now and then, and Julius seldom speaks of her as an artist. To tell the truth, Julius is always beefing about her playing the part of a strip dancer, as he claims it takes her too long to get her clothes back on when he is waiting outside the

Summer Garden for her, and the chances are Ambrose Hammer is a pleasant change to Miss Dawn Astra as Ambrose does not care if she never gets her clothes on.

Anyway, Miss Dawn Astra starts going around and about with Ambrose Hammer, and Julius Smung is so downcast over this matter that he scarcely knows what he is doing. In fact, inside of three weeks, he runs through traffic lights twice on Fifth Avenue, and once he almost drives his taxi off the Queensboro Bridge with three passengers in it, although it comes out afterwards that Julius thinks the passengers may be newspaper scribes, and nobody has the heart to blame him for this incident.

There is much severe criticism of Ambrose Hammer among the citizens around Mindy' Restaurant, as they feel he is away out of line in moving in on Julius Smung's sweet pea, when any one of a hundred other Judys in this town will do him just as well and cause no suffering to anybody, but Ambrose pays no attention to this criticism.

Ambrose says he is very much in love with Miss Dawn Astra, and he says that, besides, taxicab drivers get enough the best of it in this town as it is, although it is no secret that Ambrose never gets into a taxi after he moves in on Julius Smung without first taking a good look at the driver to make sure that he is not Julius.

Well, by the time it takes me to explain all this, Miss Dawn Astra comes into Mindy's, and I can see at once that Ambrose Hammer is not to blame for being in love with her, and neither is Julius Smung, for she is undoubtedly very choice indeed. She is one of these tall, limber Judys, with a nice expression in her eyes and a figure such as is bound to make anybody dearly love to see Miss Dawn Astra play the part of a strip dancer.

Naturally, the first thing that attracts Miss Dawn Astra's attention when she sits down at the table with us is the parrot in the cage, and she says to Ambrose, 'Why, Ambrose,' she says, 'where does the parrot come from?'

'This parrot is a material witness,' Ambrose says. 'Through this parrot I will solve the mystery of the murder of the late Mr Grafton Wilton.'

Well, at this, Miss Dawn Astra seems to turn a trifle pale around the gills, and she lets out a small gasp and says, 'Grafton Wilton?' she says. 'Murdered?' she says. 'When and where and how?'

'Just a few hours ago,' Ambrose says. 'In his apartment on Park Avenue. With a blunt instrument. This parrot is in the room at the time. I arrive ten minutes after the police. There is a small leopard there, too, also a raccoon and a couple of monkeys and several dogs.

'The officers leave one of their number to take care of these creatures,' Ambrose says. 'He is glad to let me remove the parrot, because he does not care for birds. He does not realise the importance of this parrot. In fact,' Ambrose says, 'this officer is in favour of me removing all the livestock except the monkeys, which he plans to take home to his children, but,' Ambrose says, 'this parrot is all I require.'

Well, I am somewhat surprised to hear this statement, as I am acquainted with Grafton Wilton, and in fact, he is well known to one and all along Broadway as a young character who likes to go about spending the money his papa makes out of manufacturing soap back down the years.

This Grafton Wilton is by no means an odious character, but he is considered somewhat unusual in many respects, and in fact, if his family does not happen to have about twenty million dollars, there is no doubt but what Grafton will be placed under observation long ago. But of course nobody in this town is going to place anybody with a piece of twenty million under observation.

This Grafton Wilton is quite a nature lover, and he is fond of walking into spots leading a wild animal of some description on a chain, or with a baboon sitting on his shoulder, and once he appears in the 9-9 Club carrying a young skunk in his arms, which creates some ado among the customers.

In fact, many citizens are inclined to censure Grafton for the skunk, but the way I look at it, a character who spends his money the way he does is entitled to come around with a boa constrictor in his pocket if he feels like it.

I am really somewhat depressed to hear of Grafton Wilton being murdered, and I am sitting there wondering who will replace him in the community, when all of a sudden Miss Dawn Astra says:

'I hate parrots,' she says.

'So do I,' I say. 'Ambrose,' I say, 'why do you not bring us the leopard? I am very fond of leopards.'

'Anyway,' Miss Dawn Astra says, 'how can a parrot be a material witness to anything, especially such a thing as a murder?'

'Look,' Ambrose says. 'Whoever kills Grafton Wilton must be on very friendly terms with him, because every indication is that Grafton and the murderer sit around the apartment all evening, eating and drinking. And,' Ambrose says, 'anybody knows that Grafton is always a very solitary character, and he seldom has anybody around him under any circumstances. So it is a cinch he is not entertaining a stranger in his apartment for hours.

'Grafton has two servants,' Ambrose says. 'A butler, and his wife. He permits them to take the day off to go to Jersey to visit relatives. Grafton and his visitor wait on themselves. A private elevator that the passenger operates runs to Grafton's apartment. No one around the building sees the visitor arrive or depart.

'In the course of the evening,' Ambrose says, 'the visitor strikes Grafton down with a terrific blow from some blunt instrument and leaves him on the floor, dead. The deceased has two black eyes and a badly lacerated nose. The servants find the body when they arrive home late tonight. The weapon is missing. There are no strange fingerprints anywhere around the apartment.'

'It sounds like a very mysterious mystery, to be sure,' I say. 'Maybe it is a stick-up, and Grafton Wilton resists.'

'No,' Ambrose says, 'there is no chance that robbery is the motive. There is a large sum of money in Grafton's pockets, and thousands of dollars' worth of valuables scattered around, and nothing is touched.'

'But where does the parrot come in?' Miss Dawn Astra says.

'Well,' Ambrose says, 'if the murderer is well known to Grafton Wilton, the chances are his name is frequently mentioned by Grafton during the evening, in the presence of this parrot. Maybe it is Sam. Maybe it is Bill or Frank or Joe. It is bound to be the name of some male character,' Ambrose says, 'because no female can possibly strike such a powerful blow as causes the death of Grafton Wilton.

'Now then,' Ambrose says, 'parrots pick up names very quickly, and the chances are this parrot will speak the name he hears so often in the apartment, and then we will have a clue to the murderer.

'Maybe Grafton Wilton makes an outcry when he is struck down, such as "Oh, Henry," or, "Oh, George." This is bound to impress the name on the parrot's mind,' Ambrose says.

Naturally, after hearing Ambrose's statement, the parrot becomes of more interest to me, and I examine the bird in the cage closely, but as far as I can see, it is like any other green parrot in the world, except that it strikes me as rather stupid.

It just sits there on the perch in the cage, rolling its eyes this way and that and now and then going awk-awk-awk, as parrots will do, in a low tone of voice, and of course nobody can make anything of these subdued remarks. Sometimes the parrot closes its eyes and seems to be sleeping, but it is only playing possum, and any time anybody gets close to the cage, it opens its eyes and makes ready for another finger, and it is plain to be seen that this is really a most sinister fowl.

'The poor thing is sleepy,' Ambrose says. 'I will now take it home with me. I must never let it out of my sight or hearing,' he says, 'as it may utter the name at any moment out of a clear sky, and I must be present when this comes off.'

'But you promise to take me to the Ossified Club,' Miss Dawn Astra says.

'Tut-tut!' Ambrose says. 'Tut-tut-tut,' he says. 'My goodness, how can you think of frivolity when I have a big murder mystery to solve? Besides, I cannot go to the Ossified Club unless I take the parrot, and I am sure it will be greatly bored there. Come to think of it,' Ambrose says, 'I will be greatly bored myself. You run along home, and I will see you some other night.'

Personally, I feel that Ambrose speaks rather crisply to Miss Dawn Astra, and I can see that she is somewhat offended as she departs, and I am by no means surprised the next day when Regret, the horse player, tells me that he sees somebody that looks very much like Miss Dawn Astra riding on the front seat of Julius Smung's taxicab as the sun is coming up over Fiftieth Street.

Naturally, all the blatters make quite a fuss over the murder of Grafton Wilton, because it is without doubt one of the best murders for them that takes place in this town in a long time, what with the animals in the apartment, and all this and that, and the police are also somewhat excited about the matter until they discover there is no clue, and as far as they can discover, no motive.

Then the police suggest that maybe Grafton Wilton cools himself off somehow in a fit of despondency, although nobody can see how such a thing is possible, and anyway, nobody will believe that a character with an interest in twenty million is ever despondent.

Well, the next night Ambrose Hammer has to go to a theatre to see the opening of another new play, and nothing will do but he must take the parrot in the cage to the theatre with him, and as nobody is expecting a dramatic critic to bring a parrot with him to an opening, Ambrose escapes notice going in.

It seems that it is such an opening as always draws the best people, and furthermore it is a very serious play, and Ambrose sets the cage with the parrot in it on the floor between his legs, and everything is all right until the acting begins on the stage. Then all of a sudden the parrot starts going awk-awk-awk in a very loud tone of voice indeed, and flapping its wings and attracting general attention to Ambrose Hammer.

Well, Ambrose tries to soothe the parrot by saying shush-shush to it, but the parrot will not shush, and in fact, it keeps on going awk-awk louder than ever, and presently there are slight complaints from the people around Ambrose, and finally the leading character in the play comes down off the stage and says he can see that Ambrose is trying to give him the bird in a subtle manner, and that he has a notion to punch Ambrose's nose for him.

The ushers request Ambrose to either check the parrot in the cloakroom or leave the theatre, and Ambrose says he will leave. Ambrose says he already sees enough of the play to convince him that it is unworthy of his further attention, and he claims afterwards that as he goes up the aisle with the birdcage in his hand he is stopped by ten different theatregoers, male and female, who all whisper to him that they are sorry they do not bring parrots.

This incident attracts some little attention, and it seems that the editor of the blatter that Ambrose works for tells him that it is undignified for a dramatic critic to go to the theatre with a parrot, so Ambrose comes into Mindy's with the parrot again and informs me that I must take charge of the parrot on nights when he has to go to the theatre.

Ambrose says he will pay me well for this service, and as I am always willing to pick up a few dibbs, I do not object, although personally, I am by no means a parrot fan. Ambrose says I am to keep a notebook, so I can jot down anything the parrot says when it is with me, and when I ask Ambrose what it says to date, Ambrose admits that so far it does not say a thing but awk.

'In fact,' Ambrose says, 'I am commencing to wonder if the cat has got its tongue. It is the most noncommittal parrot I ever see in all my life.'

So now I am the custodian of the parrot the next night Ambrose has to go to the theatre, and every time the parrot opens its trap, I out with my notebook and jot down its remarks, but I only wind up with four pages of awks, and when I suggest to Ambrose that maybe the murderer's name is something that begins with awk, such as 'Awkins, he claims that I am nothing but a fool.

I can see Ambrose is somewhat on edge to make a comment of this nature, and I forgive him because I figure it may be because he is not seeing as much of Miss Dawn Astra as formerly, as it seems Miss Dawn Astra will not go around with the parrot, and Ambrose will not go around without it, so it is quite a situation.

I run into Miss Dawn Astra in the street a couple of times, and she always asks me if the parrot says anything as yet, and when I tell her nothing but awk, it seems to make her quite happy, so I judge the figures that Ambrose is bound to get tired of listening to nothing but awk and will return to her. I can see that Miss Dawn Astra is looking thin and worried, and thinks I, love is too sacred a proposition to let a parrot disturb it.

Well, the third night I am in charge of the parrot I leave it in my room in the hotel where I reside in West Forty-ninth Street, as I learn from Big Nig, the crap shooter, that a small game is in progress in a garage in Fifty-fourth Street, and the parrot does not act as if it is liable to say anything important in the next hour.

But when I return to the room after winning a sawbuck in two passes in the game, I am horrified to find that the parrot is absent.

The cage is still there, but the gate is open, and so is a window in the room, and it is plain to be seen that the parrot manages to unhook the fastening of the gate and make its escape, and personally I will be very much pleased if I do not remember about Ambrose Hammer and think how bad he will feel over losing the parrot.

So I hasten at once to a little bird store over in Eighth Avenue, where they have parrots by the peck, and I am fortunate to find the proprietor just closing up for the night and willing to sell me a green parrot for twelve dollars, which takes in the tenner I win in the crap game and my night's salary from Ambrose Hammer for looking after his parrot.

Personally, I do not see much difference between the parrot I buy and the one that gets away, and the proprietor of the bird store tells me that the new parrot is a pretty good talker when it feels like it and that, to tell the truth, it generally feels like it.

Well, I carry the new parrot back to my room in a little wooden cage that the proprietor says goes with it and put it in the big cage, and then I meet Ambrose Hammer at Mindy's Restaurant and tell him that the parrot says nothing worthy of note during the evening.

I am afraid Ambrose may notice that this is not the same old parrot, but he does not even glance at the bird, and I can see that Ambrose is lost in thought, and there is no doubt but what he is thinking of Miss Dawn Astra.

Up to this time the new parrot does not say as much as awk. It is sitting in the little swing in the cage rocking back and forth, and the chances are it is doing some thinking, too, because all of a sudden it lets out a yell and speaks as follows:

'Big heel! Big heel! Big heel!'

Well, at this, three characters at tables in different parts of the room approach Ambrose and wish to know what he means by letting his parrot insult them, and it takes Ambrose several minutes to chill these beefs. In the meantime, he is trying to think which one of Grafton Wilton's acquaintances the parrot may have reference to, though he finally comes to the conclusion that there is no use trying to single out anyone, as Grafton Wilton has a great many acquaintances in his life.

But Ambrose is greatly pleased that the parrot at last displays a disposition to talk, and he says it will not be long now before the truth comes out, and that he is glad of it, because he wishes to renew his companionship with Miss Dawn Astra. He no sooner says this than the parrot lets go with a string of language that is by no means pure, and causes Ambrose Hammer himself to blush.

From now on, Ambrose is around and about with the parrot every night, and the parrot talks a blue streak at all times, though it never mentions any names, except bad names. In fact, it mentions so many bad names that the female characters who frequent the restaurants and night clubs where Ambrose takes the parrot commence complaining to the managements that they may as well stay home and listen to their husbands.

Of course I never tell Ambrose that the parrot he is taking around with him is not the parrot he thinks it is, because the way I look at it, he is getting more out of my parrot than he does out of the original, although I am willing to bet plenty that my parrot does not solve any murder mysteries. But I never consider Ambrose's theory sound from the beginning, anyway, and the chances are nobody else does, either. In fact, many citizens are commencing to speak of Ambrose Hammer as a cracky, and they do not like to see him come around with his parrot.

Now one night when Ambrose is to go to a theatre to witness another new play, and I am to have charge of the parrot for a while, he takes me to dinner with him at the 9-9 Club, which is a restaurant that is patronised by some of the highest-class parties, male and female, in this town.

As usual, Ambrose has the parrot with him in its cage, and although it is plain to be seen that the headwaiter does not welcome the parrot, he does not care to offend Ambrose, so he gives us a nice table against the wall, and as we sit down, Ambrose seems to notice a strange-looking young Judy who is at the next table all by herself.

She is all in black, and she has cold-looking black hair slicked down tight on her head and parted in the middle, and a cold eye, and a cold-looking, dead-white face, and Ambrose seems to think he knows her and half bows to her, but she never gives him a blow.

So Ambrose puts the birdcage on the settee between him and the cold-looking Judy and orders our dinner, and we sit there speaking of this and that, but I observe that now and then Ambrose takes a sneak-peak at her as if he is trying to remember who she is. She pays no attention to him whatever, and she does not pay any attention to the parrot alongside her, either, although everybody else in the 9-9 Club is looking our way and, the chances are, making remarks about the parrot.

Well, now what happens but the headwaiter brings a messenger boy over to our table, and this messenger boy has a note which is addressed to Ambrose Hammer, and Ambrose opens this note and reads it and then lets out a low moan and hands the note to me, and I also read it, as follows:

Dear Ambrose:
    When you receive this Julius and I will be on our way to South America where we will be married and raise up a family. Ambrose I love Julius and will never be happy with anybody else. We are leaving so suddenly because we are afraid it may come out about Julius calling on Mr Grafton the night of the murder to demand an apology from him for insulting me which I never tell you about Ambrose because I do not wish you to know about me often going to Mr Grafton's place as you are funny that way. They have a big fight and Ambrose Julius is sorry he kills Mr Wilton but it is really an accident as Julius does not know his own strength when he hits anybody.
    Ambrose pardon me for taking your parrot but I tell Julius what you say about the parrot speaking the name of the murderer some day and it worries Julius. He says he hears parrots have long memories, and he is afraid it may remember his name although Julius only mentions it once when he is introducing himself to Mr Wilton to demand the apology. I tell him he is thinking of elephants but he says it is best to be on the safe side so I take the parrot out of the hotel and you will find your parrot in the bottom of the East River Ambrose and thanks for everything.
                                                                                          Dawn
    P.S.   Ambrose kindly do not tell it around about Julius killing Mr Wilton as we do not wish any publicity about this. D.

Well, Ambrose is sitting there as if he is practically stunned, and shaking his head this way and that, and I am feeling very sorry for him indeed, because I can understand what a shock it is to anybody to lose somebody they dearly love without notice.

Furthermore, I can see that presently Ambrose will be seeking explanations about the parrot matter, but for maybe five minutes Ambrose does not say a word, and then he speaks as follows:

'What really hurts,' Ambrose says, 'is to see my theory go wrong. Here I am going around thinking it is somebody in Grafton Wilton's own circle that commits this crime, and the murderer turns out to be nothing but a taxicab driver.

'Furthermore, I make a laughing-stock of myself thinking a parrot will one day utter the name of the murderer. By the way,' Ambrose says, 'what does this note say about the parrot?'

Well, I can see that this is where it all comes out, but just as I am about to hand him the note and start my own story, all of a sudden the parrot in the cage begins speaking in a loud tone of voice as follows:

'Hello, Polly,' the parrot says. 'Hello, Pretty Polly.'

Now I often hear the parrot make these remarks and I pay no attention to it, but Ambrose Hammer turns at once to the cold-looking Judy at the table next to him and bows to her most politely, and says to her like this:

'Of course,' he says. 'To be sure,' he says. 'Pretty Polly. Pretty Polly Oligant,' he says. 'I am not certain at first, but now I remember. Well, well, well,' Ambrose says. 'Two years in Auburn, if I recall, for trying to put the shake on Grafton Wilton on a phony breach-of-promise matter in 1932, when he is still under age.

'Strange I forget it for a while,' Ambrose says. 'Strange I do not connect you with this thing marked *P*, that I pick up in the apartment the night of the murder. I think maybe I am protecting some female character of good repute.'

And with this, Ambrose pulls a small gold cigarette case out of his pocket that he never mentions to me before and shows it to her.

'He ruins my life,' the cold-looking Judy says. 'The breach-of-promise suit is on the level, no matter what the jury says. How can you beat millions of dollars? There is no justice in this world,' she says.

Her voice is so low that no one but Ambrose and me can hear her, and her cold eyes have a very strange expression to be sure as she says:

'I kill Grafton Wilton, all right,' she says. 'I am glad of it, too. I am just getting ready to go to the police and give myself up, anyway, so I may as well tell you. I am sick and tired of living with this thing hanging over me.'

'I never figure a Judy,' Ambrose says. 'I do not see how a female can strike a blow hard enough to kill such a sturdy character as Grafton Wilton.'

'Oh, that,' she says. 'I do not strike him a blow. I get into his apartment with a duplicate key that I have made from his lock, and I find him lying on the floor half conscious. I revive him, and he tells me a taxicab driver comes to his apartment and smashes him between the eyes with his fist when he opens the door, and Grafton claims he does not know why. Anyway,' she says, 'the blow does not do anything more serious to him than skin his nose a little and give him a couple of black eyes.

'Grafton is glad to see me,' she says. 'We sit around talking and eating and listening to the radio all evening. In fact,' she says, 'we have such an enjoyable time that it is five hours later before I have the heart and the opportunity to slip a little cyanide in a glass of wine on him.'

'Well,' I say, 'the first thing we must do is to look up Miss Dawn Astra's address and notify her that she is all wrong about Julius doing the job. Maybe,' I say, 'she will feel so relieved that she will return to you, Ambrose.'

'No,' Ambrose says. 'I can see that Miss Dawn Astra is not the one for me. If there is anything I cannot stand it is a female character who does not state the truth at all times, and Miss Dawn Astra utters a prevarication in this note when she says my parrot is at the bottom of the East River, for here it is right here in this cage, and a wonderful bird it is, to be sure. Let us all now proceed to the police station, and I will then hasten to the office and write my story of this transaction, and never mind about the new play.'

'Hello, Polly,' the parrot says. 'Pretty Polly.'

SAUCE FOR THE GOOSE

Patricia Highsmith

Any meal can take on a very different flavour when a husband and wife begin to wonder if the other partner might be trying to kill them. Such suspicions arise in 'Sauce for the Goose' by Patricia Highsmith (1921–   ), a writer much admired by Graham Greene for her exposures of the darker side of the human psyche. Her novel, Strangers on a Train *(1951) was brilliantly filmed by Alfred Hitchcock. Here, though, it is two people very well known to each other who become entangled in a web of intrigue culminating in the most chilling finale to any story in this collection . . .*

The incident in the garage was the third near-catastrophe in the Amory household, and it put a horrible thought into Loren Amory's head: his darling wife Olivia was trying to kill herself.

Loren had pulled at a plastic clothesline dangling from a high shelf in the garage—his idea had been to tidy up, to coil the clothesline properly—and at that first tug an avalanche of suitcases, an old lawnmower, and a sewing machine weighing God-knows-how-much crashed down on the spot that he barely had time to leap from.

Loren walked slowly back to the house, his heart pounding at his awful discovery. He entered the kitchen and made his way to the stairs. Olivia was in bed, propped against pillows, a magazine in her lap. 'What was that terrible noise, dear?'

Loren cleared his throat and settled his black-rimmed glasses more firmly on his nose. 'A lot of stuff in the garage. I pulled just a little bit on a clothesline—' He explained what had happened.

She blinked calmly as if to say, 'Well, so what? Things like that do happen.'

'Have you been up to that shelf for anything lately?'

'Why, no. Why?'

'Because—well, everything was just poised to fall, darling.'

'Are you blaming me?' she asked in a small voice.

'Blaming your carelessness, yes. I arranged those suitcases up there and I'd never have put them so they'd fall at a mere touch. And I didn't put the sewing machine on top of the heap. Now, I'm not saying—'

'Blaming my carelessness,' she repeated, affronted.

He knelt quickly beside the bed. 'Darling, let's not hide things any more. Last week there was the carpet sweeper on the cellar stairs. And that ladder! You were going to climb it to knock down that wasps' nest! What I'm getting at, darling, is that you *want* something to happen to you, whether you realise it or not. You've got to be more careful, Olivia—Oh, darling, please don't cry. I'm trying to help you. I'm not criticising.'

'I know, Loren. You're good. But my life—it doesn't seem worth living any more, I suppose. I don't mean I'm *trying* to end my life, but—'

'You're still thinking—of Stephen?' Loren hated the name and hated saying it.

She took her hands down from her pinkened eyes. 'You made me promise you not to think of him, so I haven't. I swear it, Loren.'

'Good, darling. That's my little girl.' He took her hands in his. 'What do you say to a cruise soon? Maybe in February? Myers is coming back from the coast and he can take over for me for a couple of weeks. What about Haiti or Bermuda?'

She seemed to think about it for a moment, but at last shook her head and said she knew he was only doing it for her, not because he really wanted to go. Loren remonstrated briefly, then gave it up. If Olivia didn't take to an idea at once, she never took to it. There had been one triumph—his convincing her that it made sense not to see Stephen Castle for a period of three months.

Olivia had met Stephen Castle at a party given by one of Loren's colleagues on the Stock Exchange. Stephen was thirty-five, was ten years younger than Loren and one year older than Olivia, and Stephen was an actor. Loren had no idea how Toohey, their host that evening, had met him, or why he had invited him to a party at which every other man was either in banking or on the Exchange; but there he'd been, like an evil alien spirit, and he'd concentrated on Olivia the entire evening, and she'd responded with her charming smiles that had captured Loren in a single evening eight years ago.

Afterwards, when they were driving back to Old Greenwich, Olivia had said, 'It's such fun to talk to somebody who's not in the stock-market for a change! He told me he's rehearsing in a play now—*The Frequent Guest*. We've got to see it, Loren.'

They saw it. Stephen Castle was on for perhaps five minutes in

Act One. They visited Stephen backstage, and Olivia invited him to a cocktail party they were giving the following weekend. He came, and spent that night in their guest room. In the next weeks Olivia drove her car into New York at least twice a week on shopping expeditions, but she made no secret of the fact she saw Stephen for lunch on those days and sometimes for cocktails too. At last she told Loren she was in love with Stephen and wanted a divorce.

Loren was speechless at first, even inclined to grant her a divorce by way of being sportsmanlike; but forty-eight hours after her announcement he came to what he considered his senses. By that time he had measured himself against his rival—not merely physically (Loren did not come off so well there, being no taller than Olivia, with a receding hairline and a small paunch) but morally and financially as well. In the last two categories he had it all over Stephen Castle, and modestly he pointed this out to Olivia.

'I'd never marry a man for his money,' she retorted.

'I didn't mean you married me for my money, dear. I just happened to have it. But what's Stephen Castle ever going to have? Nothing much, from what I can see of his acting. You're used to more than he can give you. And you've known him only six weeks. How can you be sure his love for you is going to last?'

That last thought made Olivia pause. She said she would see Stephen just once more—'to talk it over'. She drove to New York one morning and did not return until midnight. It was a Sunday, when Stephen had no performance. Loren sat up waiting for her. In tears Olivia told him that she and Stephen had come to an understanding. They would not see each other for a month, and if at the end of that time they did not feel the same way about each other, they would agree to forget the whole thing.

'But of course you'll feel the same,' Loren said. 'What's a month in the life of an adult? If you'd try it for three months—'

She looked at him through tears. 'Three months?'

'Against the eight years we've been married? Is that unfair? Our marriage deserves at least a three-month chance, too, doesn't it?'

'All right, it's a bargain. Three months. I'll call Stephen tomorrow and tell him. We won't see each other or telephone for three months.'

From that day Olivia had gone into a decline. She lost interest in gardening, in her bridge club, even in clothes. Her appetite fell off, though she did not lose much weight, perhaps because she was proportionately inactive. They had never had a servant. Olivia took pride in the fact that she had been a working girl, a saleswoman in the gift department of a large store in Manhattan, when

Loren met her. She liked to say that she knew how to do things for herself. The big house in Old Greenwich was enough to keep any woman busy, though Loren had bought every conceivable labour-saving device. They also had a walk-in deep freeze, the size of a large closet, in the basement, so that their marketing was done less often than usual, and all food was delivered, anyway. Now that Olivia seemed low in energy, Loren suggested getting a maid, but Olivia refused.

Seven weeks went by, and Olivia kept her word about not seeing Stephen. But she was obviously so depressed, so ready to burst into tears, that Loren lived constantly on the brink of weakening and telling her that if she loved Stephen that much, she had a right to see him. Perhaps, Loren thought, Stephen Castle was feeling the same way, also counting off the weeks until he could see Olivia again. If so, Loren had already lost.

But it was hard for Loren to give Stephen credit for feeling anything. He was a lanky, rather stupid chap with oat-coloured hair, and Loren had never seen him without a sickly smile on his mouth—as if he were a human billboard of himself, perpetually displaying what he must have thought was his most flattering expression.

Loren, a bachelor until at thirty-seven he married Olivia, often sighed in dismay at the ways of women. For instance, Olivia: if he had felt so strongly about another woman, he would have set about promptly to extricate himself from his marriage. But here was Olivia hanging on, in a way. What did she expect to gain from it, he wondered. Did she think, or hope, that her infatuation for Stephen might disappear? Or did she want to spite Loren and prove that it wouldn't? Or did she know unconsciously that her love for Stephen Castle was all fantasy, and that her present depression represented to her and to Loren a fitting period of mourning for a love she didn't have the courage to go out and take?

But the Saturday of the garage incident made Loren doubt that Olivia was indulging in fantasy. He did not want to admit that Olivia was attempting to take her own life, but logic compelled him to. He had read about such people. They were different from the accident-prone, who might live to die a natural death, whatever that was. The others were the suicide-prone, and into this category he was sure Olivia fell.

A perfect example was the ladder episode. Olivia had been on the fourth or fifth rung when Loren noticed the crack in the left side of the ladder, and she had been quite unconcerned, even when he pointed it out to her. If it hadn't been for her saying she suddenly felt a little dizzy looking up at the wasps' nest, he never would have started to do the chore himself, and therefore wouldn't have seen the crack.

Loren noticed in the newspaper that Stephen's play was closing, and it seemed to him that Olivia's gloom deepened. Now there were dark circles under her eyes. She claimed she could not fall asleep before dawn.

'Call him if you want to, darling,' Loren finally said. 'See him once again and find out if you both—'

'No, I made a promise to you. Three months, Loren. I'll keep my promise,' she said with a trembling lip.

Loren turned away from her, wretched and hating himself.

Olivia grew physically weaker. Once she stumbled coming down the stairs and barely caught herself on the banister. Loren suggested, not for the first time, that she see a doctor, but she refused to.

'The three months are nearly up, dear. I'll survive them,' she said, smiling sadly.

It was true. Only two more weeks remained until 15 March, the three months' deadline. The Ides of March, Loren realised for the first time. A most ominous coincidence.

On Sunday afternoon Loren was looking over some office reports in his study when he heard a long scream, followed by a clattering crash. In an instant he was on his feet and running. It had come from the cellar, he thought, and if so, he knew what had happened. That damned carpet sweeper again!

'Olivia?'

From the dark cellar he heard a groan. Loren plunged down the steps. There was a little whirr of wheels, his feet flew up in front of him, and in the few seconds before his head smashed against the cement floor he understood everything: Olivia had not fallen down the cellar steps, she had only lured him here; all this time she had been trying to kill *him*, Loren Amory—and all for Stephen Castle.

'I was upstairs in bed reading,' Olivia told the police, her hands shaking as she clutched her dressing gown around her. 'I heard a terrible crash and then—I came down—' She gestured helplessly toward Loren's dead body.

The police took down what she told them and commiserated with her. People ought to be more carful, they said, about things like carpet sweepers on dark stairways. There were fatalities like this every day in the United States. Then the body was taken away, and on Tuesday Loren Amory was buried.

Olivia rang Stephen on Wednesday. She had been telephoning him every day except Saturdays and Sundays, but she had not rung him since the previous Friday. They had agreed that any weekday she did not call him at his apartment at 11 a.m. would be a signal that their mission had been accomplished. Also, Loren Amory had got quite a lot of space on the obituary page Monday. He had left nearly a million dollars to his widow, and houses in Florida, Connecticut and Maine.

'Dearest! You look so tired!' were Stephen's first words to her when they met in an out-of-the-way bar in New York on Wednesday.

'Nonsense! It's all make-up,' Olivia said gaily. 'And you an actor!' She laughed. 'I have to look properly gloomy for my neighbours, you know. And I'm never sure when I'll run into someone I know in New York.'

Stephen looked around him nervously, then said with his habitual smile, 'Darling Olivia, how soon can we be together?'

'Very soon,' she said promptly. 'Not up at the house, of course, but remember we talked about a cruise? Maybe Trinidad? I've got the money with me. I want you to buy the tickets.'

They took separate staterooms, and the local Connecticut paper, without a hint of suspicion, reported that Mrs Amory's voyage was for reasons of health.

Back in the United States in April, suntanned and looking much improved Olivia confessed to her friends that she had met someone she was 'interested in'. Her friends assured her that was normal, and that she shouldn't be alone for the rest of her life. The curious thing was that when Olivia invited Stephen to a dinner party at her house, none of her friends remembered him, though several had met him at that cocktail party a few months before. Stephen was much more sure of himself now, and he behaved like an angel, Olivia thought.

In August they were married. Stephen had been getting nibbles in the way of work, but nothing materialised. Olivia told him not to worry, that things would surely pick up after the summer. Stephen did not seem to worry very much, though he protested he ought to work, and said if necessary he would try for some television parts. He developed an interest in gardening, planted some young blue spruces, and generally made the place look alive again.

Olivia was delighted that Stephen liked the house, because she did. Neither of them ever referred to the cellar stairs, but they had a light switch put at the top landing, so that a similar thing could not occur again. Also, the carpet sweeper was kept in its proper place, in the broom closet in the kitchen.

They entertained more often than Olivia and Loren had done. Stephen had many friends in New York, and Olivia found them amusing. But Stephen, Olivia thought, was drinking just a little too much. At one party, when they were all out on the terrace, Stephen nearly fell over the parapet. Two of the guests had to grab him.

'Better watch out for yourself in this house, Steve,' said Parker Barnes, an actor friend of Stephen's. 'It just might be jinxed.'

'What d'ya mean?' Stephen asked. 'I don't believe that for a minute. I may be an actor, but I haven't got a single superstition.'

'Oh, so you're an actor, Mr Castle!' a woman's voice said out of the darkness.

After the guests had gone, Stephen asked Olivia to come out again on the terrace.

'Maybe the air'll clear my head,' Stephen said, smiling. 'Sorry I was tipsy tonight. There's old Orion. See him?' He put his arm around Olivia and drew her close. 'Brightest constellation in the heavens.'

'You're hurting me, Stephen! Not so—' Then she screamed and squirmed, fighting for her life.

'Damn you!' Stephen gasped, astounded at her strength.

She twisted away from him and was standing near the bedroom door, facing him now. 'You were going to push me over.'

'No! Good God, Olivia!—I lost my balance, that's all. I thought I was going over myself!'

'That's a fine thing to do, then, hold on to a woman and pull her over too.'

'I didn't realise. I'm drunk, darling. And I'm sorry.'

They lay as usual in the same bed that night, but both of them were only pretending to sleep. Until, for Olivia at least, just as she had used to tell Loren, sleep came around dawn.

The next day, casually and surreptitiously, each of them looked over the house from attic to cellar—Olivia with a view to protecting herself from possible death traps, Stephen with a view to setting them. He had already decided that the cellar steps offered the best possibility, in spite of the duplication, because he thought no one would believe anyone would dare to use the same means twice—if the intention was murder.

Olivia happened to be thinking the same thing.

The cellar steps had never before been so free of impediments or so well lighted. Neither of them took the initiative to turn the light out at night. Outwardly each professed love and faith in the other.

'I'm sorry I ever said such a thing to you, Stephen,' she whispered in his ear as she embraced him. 'I was afraid on the terrace that night, that's all. When you said "Damn you"—'

'I know, angel. You *couldn't* have thought I meant to hurt you. I said "Damn you" just because you were there, and I thought I might be pulling you over.'

They talked about another cruise. They wanted to go to Europe next spring. But at meals they cautiously tasted every item of food before beginning to eat.

How could I have done anything to the food, Stephen thought to himself, since you never leave the kitchen while you're cooking it.

And Olivia: I don't put anything past you. There's only one direction you seem to be bright in, Stephen.

Her humiliation in having lost a lover was hidden by a dark resentment. She realised she had been victimised. The last bit of Stephen's charm had vanished. Yet now, Olivia thought, he was doing the best job of acting in his life—and a twenty-four-hour-a-day acting job at that. She congratulated herself that it did not fool her, and she weighed one plan against another, knowing that this 'accident' had to be even more convincing than the one that had freed her from Loren.

Stephen realised he was not in quite so awkward a position. Everyone who knew him and Olivia, even slightly, thought he adored her. An accident would be assumed to be just that, an accident, if he said so. He was now toying with the idea of the closet-sized deep freeze in the cellar. There was no inside handle on the door, and once in a while Olivia went into the farthest corner of the deep freeze to get steaks or frozen asparagus. But would she dare to go into it, now that her suspicions were aroused, if he happened to be in the cellar at the same time? He doubted it.

While Olivia was breakfasting in bed one morning—she had taken to her own bedroom again, and Stephen brought her breakfast as Loren had always done—Stephen experimented with the door of the deep freeze. If it so much as touched a solid object in swinging open, he discovered, it would slowly but surely swing shut on its rebound. There was no solid object near the door now, and on the contrary the door was intended to be swung fully open, so that a catch on the outside of the door would lock in a grip set in the wall for just that purpose, and thus keep the door open. Olivia, he had noticed, always swung the door wide when she went in, and it latched on to the wall automatically. But if he put something in its way, even the corner of the box of kindling wood, the door would strike it and swing shut again, before Olivia had time to realise what had happened.

However, that particular moment did not seem the right one to put the kindling box in position, so Stephen did not set his trap. Olivia had said something about their going out to a restaurant tonight. She would not be taking anything out to thaw today.

They took a little walk at three in the afternoon—through the woods behind the house, then back home again—and they almost started holding hands, in a mutually distasteful and insulting pretence of affection; but their fingers only brushed and separated.

'A cup of tea would taste good, wouldn't it, darling?' said Olivia.

'Um-m.' He smiled. Poison in the tea? Poison in the cookies? She'd made them herself that morning.

He remembered how they had plotted Loren's sad demise—her tender whispers of murder over their luncheons, her infinite patience as the weeks went by and plan after plan failed. It was he who had suggested the carpet sweeper on the cellar steps and the lure of a scream from her. What could *her* bird-brain ever plan?

Shortly after their tea—everything had tasted fine—Stephen strolled out of the living room as if with no special purpose. He felt compelled to try out the kindling box again to see if it could really be depended on. He felt inspired, too, to set the trap now and leave it. The light at the head of the cellar stairs was on. He went carefully down the steps.

He listened for a moment to see if Olivia was possibly following him. Then he pulled the kindling box into position, not parallel to the front of the deep freeze, of course, but a little to one side, as if someone had dragged it out of the shadow to see into it better and left it there. He opened the deep-freeze door with exactly the speed and force Olivia might use, flinging the door from him as he stepped in with one foot, his right hand outstretched to catch the door on the rebound. But the foot that bore his weight slid several inches forward just as the door bumped against the kindling box.

Stephen was down on his right knee, his left leg straight out in front of him, and behind him the door shut. He got to his feet instantly and faced the closed door wide-eyed. It was dark, and he groped for the auxiliary switch to the left of the door, which put a light on at the back of the deep freeze.

How had it happened? The damned glaze of frost on the floor! But it wasn't only the frost, he saw. What he had slipped on was a little piece of suet that he now saw in the middle of the floor, at the end of the greasy streak his slide had made.

Stephen stared at the suet neutrally, blankly, for an instant, then faced the door again, pushed it, felt along its firm rubber-sealed crack. He could call Olivia, of course. Eventually she'd hear him, or at least *miss* him, before he had time to freeze. She'd come down to the cellar, and she'd be able to hear him there even if she couldn't hear him in the living room. Then she'd open the door, of course.

He smiled weakly, and tried to convince himself she *would* open the door.

'Olivia?—*Olivia*! I'm down in the *cellar*!'

It was nearly a half hour later when Olivia called to Stephen to ask him which restaurant he preferred, a matter that would influence what she wore. She looked for him in his bedroom, in the library, on the terrace, and finally called out the front door, thinking he might be somewhere on the lawn.

At last she tried the cellar.

By this time, hunched in his tweed jacket, his arms crossed, Stephen was walking up and down in the deep freeze, giving out distress signals at intervals of thirty seconds and using the rest of his breath to blow into his shirt in an effort to warm himself. Olivia was just about to leave the cellar when she heard her name called faintly.

'Stephen?—Stephen, where are you?'

'In the deep freeze!' he called as loudly as he could.

Olivia looked at the deep freeze with an incredulous smile.

'Open it, can't you? I'm in the *deep freeze*!' came his muffled voice.

Olivia threw her head back and laughed, not even caring if Stephen heard her. Then still laughing so hard that she had to bend over, she climbed the cellar stairs.

What amused her was that she had thought of the deep freeze as a fine place to dispose of Stephen, but she hadn't worked out how to get him into it. His being there now, she realised, was owing to some funny accident—maybe he'd been trying to set a trap for her. It was all too comical. And lucky!

Or, maybe, she thought, cagily, his intention even now was to trick her into opening the deep-freeze door, then to yank her inside and close the door on her. She was certainly not going to let *that* happen!

Olivia took her car and drove nearly twenty miles northward, had a sandwich at a roadside café, then went to a movie. When she got home at midnight she found she had not the courage to call 'Stephen' to the deep freeze, or even to go down to the cellar. She wasn't sure he'd be dead by now, and even if he were silent it might mean he was only pretending to be dead or unconscious.

But tomorrow, she thought, there wouldn't be any doubt he'd be dead. The very lack of air, for one thing, ought to finish him by that time.

She went to bed and assured herself a night's sleep with a light sedative. She would have a strenuous day tomorrow. Her story of the mild quarrel with Stephen—over which restaurant they'd go to, nothing more—and his storming out of the living room to take a walk, she thought, would have to be very convincing.

At ten the next morning, after orange juice and coffee, Olivia felt ready for her role of the horrified, grief-stricken widow. After all, she told herself, she had practised the role—it would be the second time she had played the part. She decided to face the police in her dressing gown, as before.

To be quite natural about the whole thing she went down to the cellar to make the 'discovery' before she called the police.

'Stephen? Stephen?' she called out with confidence.

No answer.

She opened the deep freeze with apprehension, gasped at the curled-up, frost-covered figure on the floor, then walked the few feet toward him—aware that her footprints on the floor would be visible to corroborate her story that she had come in to try to revive Stephen.

Ka-*bloom* went the door—as if someone standing outside had given it a good hard push.

Now Olivia gasped in earnest, and her mouth stayed open. She'd flung the door wide. It should have latched on to the outside wall. 'Hello! Is anybody out there? Open this door, please! At once!'

But she knew there was no one out there. It was just some damnable accident. Maybe an accident that Stephen had arranged.

She looked at his face. His eyes were open, and on his white lips was his familiar little smile, triumphant now, and utterly nasty. Olivia did not look at him again. She drew her flimsy dressing gown as closely about her as she could and began to yell.

'Help! Someone!—*police*!'

She kept it up for what seemed like hours, until she grew hoarse and until she did not really feel very cold any more, only a little sleepy.

A VERY COMMONPLACE MURDER

P. D. James

A public restaurant or a secret rendezvous can serve equally well as the setting for a lovers' meal, and it is such a meeting that provides the catalyst to the last story in this section, 'A Very Commonplace Murder' by P. D. James (1920–   ), described recently by The Times *as the 'Queen of the English detective story who has helped turn it into a respectable literary genre'. On being made a Life Peer in the 1991 New Year Honours list, Baroness James said of her interest in crime fiction, 'I do not see why one cannot say something very true about people and relations, and particularly about how people behave under the ultimate stress of death, while using a form that is obviously popular.' This conviction will be found brilliantly expounded in the following story of what happens when death interrupts a lovers' weekly feast of food and lovemaking . . .*

'We close at twelve on Saturday,' said the blonde in the estate office. 'So if you keep the key after then, please drop it back through the letter box. It's the only key we have, and there may be other people wanting to view on Monday. Sign here, please, sir.'

The 'sir' was grudging, an afterthought. Her tone was reproving. She didn't really think he would buy the flat, this seedy old man with his air of spurious gentility, with his harsh voice. In her job you soon got a nose for the genuine inquirer. Ernest Gabriel. An odd name, half-common, half-fancy.

But he took the key politely enough and thanked her for her trouble. No trouble, she thought. God knew there were few enough people interested in that sordid little dump, not at the price they were asking. He could keep the key a week, for all she cared.

She was right. Gabriel hadn't come to buy, only to view. It was the first time he had been back since it all happened sixteen years ago. He came neither as a pilgrim nor a penitent. He had returned under some compulsion which he hadn't even bothered to analyse. He had been on his way to visit his only living relative, an elderly aunt, who had recently been admitted to a geriatic ward. He hadn't even realised the bus would pass the flat.

But suddenly they were lurching through Camden Town, and the road became familiar, like a photograph springing into focus; and with a *frisson* of surprise he recognised the double-fronted shop and the flat above. There was an estate agent's notice in the window. Almost without thinking, he had got off at the next stop, gone back to verify the name, and walked the half-mile to the office. It had seemed as natural and inevitable as his daily bus journey to work.

Twenty minutes later he fitted the key into the lock of the front door and passed into the stuffy emptiness of the flat. The grimy walls still held the smell of cooking. There was a spatter of envelopes on the worn linoleum, dirtied and trampled by the feet of previous viewers. The light bulb swung naked in the hall, and the door into the sitting room stood open. To his right was the staircase, to his left the kitchen.

Gabriel paused for a moment, then went into the kitchen. From the windows, half-curtained with grubby gingham, he looked upward to the great black building at the rear of the flat, eyeless except for the one small square of window high on the fifth floor. It was from this window, sixteen years ago, that he had watched Denis Speller and Eileen Morrisey play out their commonplace little tragedy to its end.

He had no right to be watching them, no right to be in the building at all after six o'clock. That had been the nub of his awful dilemma. It had happened by chance. Mr Maurice Bootman had instructed him, as the firm's filing clerk, to go through the papers in the late Mr Bootman's upstairs den in case there were any which should be in the files. They weren't confidential or important papers—those had been dealt with by the family and the firm's solicitors months before. They were just a miscellaneous, yellowing collection of out-of-date memoranda, old accounts, receipts, and fading press clippings which had been bundled together into old Mr Bootman's desk. He had been a great hoarder of trivia.

But at the back of the left-hand bottom drawer Gabriel had found a key. It was by chance that he tried it in the lock of the corner cupboard. It fitted. And in the cupboard Gabriel found the late Mr Bootman's small but choice collection of pornography.

He knew that he had to read the books; not just to snatch surreptitious minutes with one ear listening for a footstep on the stairs or the whine of the approaching elevator, and fearful always that his absence from his filing room would be noticed. No, he had to read them in privacy and in peace. So he devised his plan.

It wasn't difficult. As a trusted member of the staff, he had one of the Yale keys to the side door at which goods were delivered. It was locked on the inside at night by the porter before he went off duty. It wasn't difficult for Gabriel, always among the last to leave, to find the opportunity of shooting back the bolts before leaving with the porter by the main door. He dared risk it only once a week, and the day he chose was Friday.

He would hurry home, eat his solitary meal beside the gas fire in his bed-sitting-room, then make his way back to the building and let himself in by the side door. All that was necessary was to make sure he was waiting for the office to open on Monday morning so that, among the first in, he could lock the side door before the porter made his ritual visit to unlock it for the day's deliveries.

These Friday nights became a desperate but shameful joy to Gabriel. Their pattern was always the same. He would sit crouched in old Mr Bootman's low leather chair in front of the fireplace, his shoulders hunched over the book in his lap, his eyes following the pool of light from his torch as it moved over each page. He never dared to switch on the room light, and even on the coldest night he never lit the gas fire. He was fearful that its hiss might mask the sound of approaching feet, that its glow might shine through the thick curtains at the window, or that, somehow, the smell of gas would linger in the room next Monday morning to betray him. He was morbidly afraid of discovery, yet even this fear added to the excitement of his secret pleasure.

It was on the third Friday in January that he first saw them. It was a mild evening, but heavy and starless. An early rain had slimed the pavements and bled the scribbled headlines from the newspaper placards. Gabriel wiped his feet carefully before climbing to the fifth floor. The claustrophobic room smelled sour and dusty, the air struck colder than the night outside. He wondered whether he dared open the window and let in some of the sweetness of the rain-cleansed sky.

It was then that he saw the woman. Below him were the back entrances of the two shops, each with a flat above. One flat had boarded windows, but the other looked lived in. It was approached by a flight of iron steps leading to an asphalt yard. He saw the woman in the glow of a street lamp as she paused at the foot of the steps, fumbling in her handbag. Then, as if gaining resolution, she came swiftly up the steps and almost ran across the asphalt to the flat door.

He watched as she pressed herself into the shadow of the doorway, then swiftly turned the key in the lock and slid out of his sight. He had time only to notice that she was wearing a pale mackintosh buttoned high under a mane of fairish hair and that she carried a string bag of what looked like groceries. It seemed an oddly furtive and solitary homecoming.

Gabriel waited. Almost immediately he saw the light go on in the room to the left of the door. Perhaps she was in the kitchen. He could see her faint shadow passing to and fro, bending and then lengthening. He guessed that she was unpacking the groceries. Then the light in the room went out.

For a few moments the flat was in darkness. Then the light in the upstairs window went on, brighter this time, so that he could see the woman more plainly. She could not know how plainly. The curtains were drawn, but they were thin. Perhaps the owners, confident that they were not overlooked, had grown careless. Although the woman's silhouette was only a faint blur, Gabriel could see that she was carrying a tray. Perhaps she was intending to eat her supper in bed. She was undressing now.

He could see her lifting the garments over her head and twisting down to release stockings and take off her shoes. Suddenly she came very close to the window, and he saw the outline of her body plainly. She seemed to be watching and listening. Gabriel found that he was holding his breath. Then she moved away, and the light dimmed. He guessed that she had switched off the central bulb and was using the bedside lamp. The room was now lit with a softer, pinkish glow within which the woman moved, insubstantial as a dream.

Gabriel stood with his face pressed against the cold window, still watching. Shortly after eight o'clock the boy arrived. Gabriel always thought of him as 'the boy'. Even from that distance his youth, his vulnerability, were apparent. He approached the flat with more confidence than the woman, but still swiftly, pausing at the top of the steps as if to assess the width of the rain-washed yard.

She must have been waiting for his knock. She let him in at once, the door barely opening. Gabriel knew that she had come naked to let him in. And then there were two shadows in the upstairs room, shadows that met and parted and came together again before they moved, joined, to the bed and out of Gabriel's sight.

The next Friday he watched to see if they would come again. They did, and at the same times, the woman first, at twenty minutes past seven, the boy forty minutes later. Again Gabriel stood, rigidly intent at his watching post, as the light in the upstairs window sprang on and then was lowered. The two naked figures, seen dimly behind the curtains, moved to and fro, joined and parted, fused and swayed together in a ritualistic parody of a dance.

This Friday Gabriel waited until they left. The boy came out first, sidling quickly from the half-open door and almost leaping down the steps, as if in exultant joy. The woman followed five minutes later, locking the door behind her and darting across the asphalt, her head bent.

After that he watched for them every Friday. They held a fascination for him even greater than Mr Bootman's books. Their routine hardly varied. Sometimes the boy arrived a little late, and Gabriel would see the woman watching motionless for him behind the bedroom curtains. He too would stand with held breath, sharing her agony of impatience, willing the boy to come. Usually the boy carried a bottle under his arm, but one week it was in a wine basket, and he bore it with great care. Perhaps it was an anniversary, a special evening for them. Always the woman had the bag of groceries. Always they ate together in the bedroom.

Friday after Friday Gabriel stood in the darkness, his eyes fixed on that upstairs window, straining to decipher the outlines of their naked bodies, picturing what they were doing to each other.

They had been meeting for seven weeks when it happened. Gabriel was late at the building that night. His usual bus did not run, and the first to arrive was full. By the time he reached his watching post, there was already a light in the bedroom. He pressed his face to the window, his hot breath smearing the pane. Hastily rubbing it clear with the cuff of his coat, he looked again. For a moment he thought that there were two figures in the bedroom. But that must surely be a freak of the light. The boy wasn't due for thirty minutes yet. But the woman, as always, was on time.

Twenty minutes later he went into the washroom on the floor below. He had become much more confident during the last few weeks and now moved about the building, silently, and using only his torch for light, but with almost as much assurance as during the day. He spent nearly ten minutes in the washroom. His watch showed that it was just after eight by the time he was back at the window, and, at first, he thought that he had missed the boy. But no, the slight figure was even now running up the steps and across the asphalt to the shelter of the doorway.

Gabriel watched as he knocked and waited for the door to open. But it didn't open. She didn't come. There was a light in the bedroom, but no shadow moved on the curtains. The boy knocked again. Gabriel could just detect the quivering of his knuckles against the door. Again he waited. Then the boy drew back and looked up at the lighted window. Perhaps he was risking a low-pitched call. Gabriel could hear nothing, but he could sense the tension in that waiting figure.

Again the boy knocked. Again there was no response. Gabriel watched and suffered with him until, at twenty past eight, the boy finally gave up and turned away. Then Gabriel too stretched his cramped limbs and made his way into the night. The wind was rising and a young moon reeled through the torn clouds. It was getting colder. He wore no coat and missed its comfort. Hunching his shoulders against the bite of the wind, he knew that this was the last Friday he would come late to the building. For him, as for that desolate boy, it was the end of a chapter.

He first read about the murder in his morning paper on his way to work the following Monday. He recognised the picture of the flat at once, although it looked oddly unfamiliar with the bunch of plainclothes detectives conferring at the door and the stolid uniformed policeman at the top of the steps.

The story so far was slight. A Mrs Eileen Morrisey, aged thirty-four, had been found stabbed to death in a flat in Camden Town late on Sunday night. The discovery was made by the tenants, Mr and Mrs Kealy, who had returned late on Sunday from a visit to Mr Kealy's parents. The dead woman, who was the mother of twin daughters aged twelve, was a friend of Mrs Kealy. Detective Chief-Inspector William Holbrook was in charge of the investigation. It was understood that the dead woman had been sexually assaulted.

Gabriel folded his paper with the same precise care as he did on any ordinary day. Of course, he would have to tell the police what he had seen. He couldn't let an innocent man suffer, no matter what the inconvenience to himself. The knowledge of his intention, of his public-spirited devotion to justice, was warmly satisfying. For the rest of the day he crept around his filing cabinets with the secret complacency of a man dedicated to sacrifice.

But somehow his first plan of calling at a police station on his way home from work came to nothing. There was no point in acting hastily. If the boy were arrested, he would speak. But it would be ridiculous to prejudice his reputation and endanger his job before he even knew whether the boy was a suspect. The police might never learn of the boy's existence. To speak up now might only focus suspicion on the innocent. A prudent man would wait. Gabriel decided to be prudent.

The boy was arrested three days later. Again Gabriel read about it in his morning paper. There was no picture this time, and few details. The news had to compete with a society elopement and a major air crash and did not make the first page. The inch of newsprint stared briefly: 'Denis John Speller, a butcher's assistant, aged nineteen, who gave an address at Muswell Hill, was today charged with the murder of Mrs Eileen Morrisey, the mother of twelve-year-old twins, who was stabbed to death last Friday in a flat in Camden Town.'

So the police now knew more precisely the time of death. Perhaps it was time for him to see them. But how could he be sure that this Denis Speller was the young lover he had been watching these past Friday nights? A woman like that—well, she might have had any number of men. No photograph of the accused would be published in any paper until after the trial. But more information would come out at the preliminary hearing. He would wait for that. After all, the accused might not even be committed for trial.

Besides, he had himself to consider. There had been time to think of his own position. If young Speller's life were in danger, then, of course, Gabriel would tell what he had seen. But it would mean the end of his job with Bootman's. Worse, he would never get another. Mr Maurice Bootman would see to that. He, Gabriel, would be branded as a dirty-minded, sneaking little voyeur, a Peeping Tom who was willing to jeopardise his livelihood for an hour or two with a naughty book and a chance to pry into other people's happiness. Mr Maurice would be too angry at the publicity to forgive the man who had caused it.

And the rest of the firm would laugh. It would be the best joke in years, funny and pathetic and futile. The pedantic, respectable, censorious Ernest Gabriel found out at last! And they wouldn't even give him credit for speaking up. It simply wouldn't occur to them that he could have kept silent.

If only he could think of a good reason for being in the building that night. But there was none. He could hardly say that he had stayed behind to work late, when he had taken such care to leave with the porter. And it wouldn't do to say that he had returned later to catch up with his filing. His filing was always up-to-date, as he was fond of pointing out. His very efficiency was against him.

Besides, he was a poor liar. The police wouldn't accept his story without probing. After they had spent so much time on the case they would hardly welcome his tardy revelation of new evidence. He pictured the circle of grim, accusing faces, the official civility barely concealing their dislike and contempt. There was no sense in inviting such an ordeal before he was sure of the facts.

But after the preliminary hearing, at which Denis Speller was sent up for trial, the same arguments seemed equally valid. By now he knew that Speller was the lover he had seen. There had never really been much room for doubt. By now, too, the outlines of the case for the Crown were apparent. The Prosecution would seek to prove that this was a crime of passion, that the boy, tormented by her threat to leave him, had killed in jealousy or revenge. The accused would deny that he had entered the flat that night, would state again and again that he had knocked and gone away. Only Gabriel could support his story. But it would still be premature to speak.

He decided to attend the trial. In that way he would hear the strength of the Crown's case. If it appeared likely that the verdict would be 'Not Guilty,' he could remain silent. And if things went badly, there was an excitement, a fearful fascination, in the thought of rising to his feet in the silence of that crowded court and speaking out his evidence before all the world. The questioning, the criticism, the notoriety would come later. But he would have had his moment of glory.

He was surprised and a little disappointed by the court. He had expected a more imposing, more dramatic setting for justice than this modern, clean-smiling, businesslike room. Everything was quiet and orderly. There was no crowd at the door jostling for seats. It wasn't even a popular trial.

Sliding into his seat at the back of the court, Gabriel looked round, at first apprehensively and then with more confidence. But he needn't have worried. There was no one there he knew. It was really a very dull collection of people, hardly worthy, he thought, of the drama that was to be played out before them. Some of them looked as if they might have worked with Speller or lived in the same street. All looked ill-at-ease, with the slightly furtive air of people who find themselves in unusual or intimidating surroundings. There was a thin woman in black crying softly into a handkerchief. No one took any notice of her; no one comforted her.

From time to time one of the doors at the back of the court would open silently, and a newcomer would sidle almost furtively into his seat. When this happened, the row of faces would turn momentarily to him without interest, without recognition, before turning their eyes again to the slight figure in the dock.

Gabriel stared too. At first he dared to cast only fleeting glances, averting his eyes suddenly, as if each glance were a desperate risk. It was unthinkable that the prisoner's eyes should meet his, should somehow know that here was the man who could save him and should signal a desperate appeal. But when he had risked two or three glances, he realised that there was nothing to fear. That solitary figure was seeing no one, caring about no one except himself. He was only a bewildered and terrified boy, his eyes turned inward to some private hell. He looked like a trapped animal, beyond hope and beyond fight.

The judge was rotund, red-faced, his chins sunk into the bands at his neck. He had small hands, which he rested on the desk before him except when he was making notes. Then counsel would stop talking for a moment before continuing more slowly, as if anxious not to hurry his Lordship, watching him like a worried father explaining with slow deliberation to a not very bright child.

But Gabriel knew where lay the power. The judge's chubby hands, folded on the desk like a parody of a child in prayer, held a man's life in their grasp. There was only one person in the court with more power than that scarlet-sashed figure high under the carved coat-of-arms. And that was he, Gabriel. The realisation came to him in a spurt of exultation, at once intoxicating and satisfying. He hugged his knowledge to himself gloatingly. This was a new sensation, terrifyingly sweet.

He looked round at the solemn watching faces and wondered how they would change if he got suddenly to his feet and called out what he knew. He would say it firmly, confidently. They wouldn't be able to frighten him. He would say, 'My Lord. The accused is innocent. He did knock and go away. I, Gabriel, saw him.'

And then what would happen? It was impossible to guess. Would the judge stop the trial so that they could all adjourn to his chambers and hear his evidence in private? Or would Gabriel be called now to take his stand in the witness box? One thing was certain—there would be no fuss, no hysteria.

But suppose the judge merely ordered him out of the court. Suppose he was too surprised to take in what Gabriel had said. Gabriel could picture him leaning forward irritably, hand to his ear, while the police at the back of the court came silently forward to drag out the offender. Surely in this calm, aseptic atmosphere, where justice itself seemed an academic ritual, the voice of truth would be merely a vulgar intrusion. No one would believe him. No one would listen. They had set this elaborate scene to play out their drama to the end. They wouldn't thank him for spoiling it now. The time to speak had passed.

Even if they did believe him, he wouldn't get any credit now for coming forward. He would be blamed for leaving it so late, for letting an innocent man get so close to the gallows. If Speller were innocent, of course. And who could tell that? They would say that he might have knocked and gone away, only to return later and gain access to kill. He, Gabriel, hadn't waited at the window to see. So his sacrifice would have been for nothing.

And he could hear those taunting office voices: 'Trust old Gabriel to leave it to the last minute. Bloody coward. Read any naughty books lately, Archangel?' He would be sacked from Bootman's without even the consolation of standing well in the public eye.

Oh, he would make the headlines, all right. He could imagine them: *Outburst in Old Bailey. Man Upholds Accused's Alibi.* Only it wasn't an alibi. What did it really prove? He would be regarded as a public nuisance, the pathetic little voyeur who was too much of a coward to go to the police earlier. And Denis Speller would still hang.

Once the moment of temptation had passed and he knew with absolute certainty that he wasn't going to speak, Gabriel began almost to enjoy himself. After all, it wasn't every day that one could watch British justice at work. He listened, noted, appreciated. It was a formidable case which the prosecution unfolded. Gabriel approved of the prosecuting counsel. With his high forehead, beaked nose, and bony, intelligent face, he looked so much more distinguished than the judge. This was how a famous lawyer should look. He made his case without passion, almost without interest. But that, Gabriel knew, was how the law worked. It wasn't the duty of prosecuting counsel to work for a conviction. His job was to state with fairness and accuracy the case for the Crown.

He called his witnesses. Mrs Brenda Kealy, the wife of the tenant of the flat. A blonde, smartly dressed, common little slut if ever Gabriel saw one. Oh, he knew her type, all right. He could guess what his mother would have said about her. Anyone could see what she was interested in. And by the look of her, she was getting it regularly, too. Dressed up for a wedding. A tart if ever he saw one.

Snivelling into her handkerchief and answering counsel's questions in a voice so low that the judge had to ask her to speak up. Yes, she had agreed to lend Eileen the flat on Friday nights. She and her husband went every Friday to visit his parents at Southend. They always left as soon as he shut the shop. No, her husband didn't know of the arrangement. She had given Mrs Morrisey the spare key without consulting him. There wasn't any other spare key that she knew of. Why had she done it? She was sorry for Eileen. Eileen had pressed her. She didn't think the Morriseys had much of a life together.

Here the judge interposed gently that the witness should confine herself to answering counsel's questions. She turned to him. 'I was only trying to help Eileen, my Lord.'

Then there was the letter. It was passed to the snivelling woman in the box, and she confirmed that it had been written to her by Mrs Morrisey. Slowly it was collected by the clerk and borne majestically across to counsel, who proceeded to read it aloud:

Dear Brenda,
    We shall be at the flat on Friday after all. I thought I'd better let you
know in case you and Ted changed your plans. But it will definitely be
for the last time. George is getting suspicious, and I must think of the
children. I always knew it would have to end. Thank you for being such
a pal.

                                                                        Eileen

The measured, upper-class voice ceased. Looking across at the
jury, counsel laid the letter slowly down. The judge bent his head
and made another notation. There was a moment of silence in the
court. Then the witness was dismissed.

And so it went on. There was the paper-seller at the end of
Moulton Street who remembered Speller buying an *Evening Standard* just before eight o'clock. The accused was carrying a bottle
under his arm and seemed very cheerful. He had no doubt his
customer was the accused.

There was the publican's wife from the Rising Sun at the junction
of Moulton Mews and High Street who testified that she served the
prisoner with a whisky shortly before half-past eight. He hadn't
stayed long. Just long enough to drink it down. He had seemed
very upset. Yes, she was quite sure it was the accused. There was a
motley collection of customers to confirm her evidence. Gabriel
wondered why the prosecution had bothered to call them, until he
realised that Speller had denied visiting the Rising Sun, had denied
that he had needed a drink.

There was George Edward Morrisey, described as an estate
agent's clerk, thin-faced, tight-lipped, standing rigidly in his best
blue serge suit. He testified that his marriage had been happy, that
he had known nothing. His wife had told him that she spent Friday
evenings learning to make pottery at LCC evening classes. The
court tittered. The judge frowned.

In reply to counsel's questions, Morrisey said that he had stayed
at home to look after the children. They were still a little young to
be left alone at night. Yes, he had been at home the night his wife
was killed. Her death was a great grief to him. Her liaison with the
accused had come as a terrible shock. He spoke the word 'liaison'
with an angry contempt, as if it were bitter on his tongue. Never
once did he look at the prisoner.

There was the medical evidence—sordid, specific, but mer-
cifully clinical and brief. The deceased had been raped, then
stabbed three times through the jugular vein. There was the
evidence of the accused's employer, who contributed a vague and

imperfectly substantiated story about a missing meat-skewer. There was the prisoner's landlady, who testified that he had arrived home on the night of the murder in a distressed state and that he had not got up to go to work next morning. Some of the threads were thin. Some, like the evidence of the butcher, obviously bore little weight even in the eyes of the prosecution. But together they were weaving a rope strong enough to hang a man.

The defending counsel did his best, but he had the desperate air of a man who knows that he is foredoomed to lose. He called witnesses to testify that Speller was a gentle, kindly boy, a generous friend, a good son and brother. The jury believed them. They also believed that he had killed his mistress. He called the accused. Speller was a poor witness, unconvincing, inarticulate. It would have helped, thought Gabriel, if the boy had shown some sign of pity for the dead woman. But he was too absorbed in his own danger to spare a thought for anyone else. Perfect fear casteth out love, thought Gabriel. The aphorism pleased him.

The judge summed up with scrupulous impartiality, treating the jury to an exposition on the nature and value of circumstantial evidence and an interpretation of the expression 'reasonable doubt'. The jury listened with respectful attention. It was impossible to guess what went on behind those twelve pairs of watchful, anonymous eyes. But they weren't out long.

Within forty minutes of the court rising, they were back, the prisoner reappeared in the dock, the judge asked the formal question. The foreman gave the expected answer, loud and clear. 'Guilty, my Lord.' No one seemed surprised.

The judge explained to the prisoner that he had been found guilty of the horrible and merciless killing of the woman who had loved him. The prisoner, his face taut and ashen, stared wild-eyed at the judge, as if only half hearing. The sentence was pronounced, sounding doubly horrible spoken in those soft judicial tones. Gabriel looked with interest for the black cap and saw with surprise and some disappointment that it was merely a square of some black material perched incongruously atop the judge's wig. The jury was thanked. The judge collected his notes like a businessman clearing his desk at the end of a busy day. The court rose. The prisoner was taken below. It was over.

The trial caused little comment at the office. No one knew that Gabriel had attended. His day's leave 'for personal reasons' was accepted with as little interest as any previous absence. He was too solitary, too unpopular, to be included in office gossip. In his dusty and ill-lit office, insulated by tiers of filing cabinets, he was the object of vague dislike or, at best, of a pitying tolerance. The filing room had never been a centre for cosy office chat. But he did hear the opinion of one member of the firm.

On the day after the trial, Mr Bootman, newspaper in hand, came into the general office while Gabriel was distributing the morning mail. 'I see they've disposed of our little local trouble,' Mr Bootman said. 'Apparently the fellow is to hang. A good thing too. It seems to have been the usual sordid story of illicit passion and general stupidity. A very commonplace murder.'

No one replied. The office staff stood silent, then stirred into life. Perhaps they felt that there was nothing more to be said.

It was shortly after the trial that Gabriel began to dream. The dream, which occurred about three times a week, was always the same. He was struggling across a desert under a blood-red sun, trying to reach a distant fort. He could sometimes see the fort clearly, although it never got any closer. There was an inner courtyard crowded with people, a silent black-clad multitude whose faces were all turned toward a central platform. On the platform was a gallows. It was a curiously elegant gallows, with two sturdy posts at either side and a delicately curved crosspiece from which the noose dangled.

The people, like the gallows, were not of this age. It was a Victorian crowd, the women in shawls and bonnets, the men in tophats or narrow-brimmed bowlers. He could see his mother there, her thin face peaked under the widow's veil. Suddenly she began to cry, and as she cried, her face changed and became the face of the weeping woman at the trial. Gabriel longed desperately to reach her, to comfort her. But with every step he sank deeper into the sand.

There were people on the platform now. One, he knew, must be the prison governor, tophatted, frockcoated, bewhiskered, and grave. His clothes were those of a Victorian gentleman, but his face, under that luxuriant beard was the face of Mr Bootman. Beside him stood the chaplain, in gown and bands, and, on either side, were two warders, their dark jackets buttoned high to their necks.

Under the noose stood the prisoner. He was wearing breeches and an open-necked shirt, and his neck was as white and delicate as a woman's. It might have been that other neck, so slender it looked. The prisoner was gazing across the desert toward Gabriel, not with desperate appeal but with great sadness in his eyes. And, this time, Gabriel knew that he had to save him, had to get there in time.

But the sand dragged at his aching ankles, and although he called that he was coming, coming, the wind, like a furnace blast, tore the words from his parched throat. His back, bent almost double, was blistered by the sun. He wasn't wearing a coat. Somehow, irrationally, he was worried that his coat was missing, that something had happened to it that he ought to remember.

As he lurched forward, floundering through the gritty morass, he could see the fort shimmering in the heat haze. Then it began to recede, getting fainter and farther, until at last it was only a blur among the distant sandhills. He heard a high, despairing scream from the courtyard—then awoke to know that it was his voice and that the damp heat on his brow was sweat, not blood.

In the comparative sanity of the morning, he analysed the dream and realised that the scene was one pictured in a Victorian news-sheet which he had once seen in the window of an antiquarian bookshop. As he remembered, it showed the execution of William Corder for the murder of Maria Marten in the red barn. The remembrance comforted him. At least he was still in touch with the tangible and sane world.

But the strain was obviously getting him down. It was time to put his mind to his problem. He had always had a good mind, too good for his job. That, of course, was why the other staff resented him. Now was the time to use it. What, exactly, was he worrying about? A woman had been murdered. Whose fault had it been? Weren't there a number of people who shared the responsibility?

That blonde tart, for one, who had lent them the flat. The husband, who had been so easily fooled. The boy, who had enticed her away from her duty to husband and children. The victim herself—particularly the victim. The wages of sin are death. Well, she had taken her wages now. One man hadn't been enough for her.

Gabriel pictured again that dim shadow against the bedroom curtains, the raised arms as she drew Speller's head down to her breast. Filthy. Disgusting. Dirty. The adjectives smeared his mind. Well, she and her lover had taken their fun. It was right that both of them should pay for it. He, Ernest Gabriel, wasn't concerned. It had only been by the merest chance that he had seen them from that upper window, only by chance that he had seen Speller knock and go away again.

Justice was being served. He had sensed its majesty, the beauty of its essential rightness, at Speller's trial. And he, Gabriel, was a part of it. If he spoke now, an adulterer might even go free. His duty was clear. The temptation to speak had gone forever.

It was in this mood that he stood with the small silent crowd outside the prison on the morning of Speller's execution. At the first stroke of eight, he, like the other men present, took off his hat.

Staring up at the sky high above the prison walls, he felt again the warm exultation of his authority and power. It was on his behalf, it was at his, Gabriel's, bidding that the nameless hangman inside was exercising his dreadful craft. . .

But that was sixteen years ago. Four months after the trial the firm, expanding and conscious of the need for a better address, had moved from Camden Town to north London. Gabriel had moved with it. He was one of the few people on the staff who remembered the old building. Clerks came and went so quickly nowadays; there was no sense of loyalty to the job.

When Gabriel retired at the end of the year, only Mr Bootman and the porter would remain from the old Camden Town days. Sixteen years. Sixteen years of the same job, the same bed-sitting-room, the same half-tolerant dislike on the part of the staff. But he had had his moment of power. He recalled it now, looking round the small sordid sitting room with its peeling wallpaper, its stained boards. It had looked different sixteen years ago.

He remembered where the sofa had stood, the very spot where she had died. He remembered other things—the pounding of his heart as he made his way across the asphalt; the quick knock; the sidling through the half-opened door before she could realise it wasn't her lover; the naked body cowering back into the sitting room; the taut white throat; the thrust with his filing bodkin that was as smooth as puncturing soft rubber. The steel had gone in so easily, so sweetly.

And there was something else which he had done to her. But that was something it was better not to remember. And afterwards he had taken the bodkin back to the office, holding it under the tap in the washroom until no spot of blood could have remained. Then he had replaced it in his desk drawer with half a dozen identical others. There had been nothing to distinguish it any more, even to his eyes.

It had all been so easy. The only blood had been a gush on his right cuff as he withdrew the bodkin. And he had burned the coat in the office furnace. He still recalled the blast on his face as he thrust it in, and the spilled cinders like sand under his feet.

There had been nothing left to him but the key of the flat. He had seen it on the sitting-room table and had taken it away with him. He drew it now from his pocket and compared it with the key from the estate agent, laying them side by side on his outstretched palm. Yes, they were identical. They had had another one cut, but no one had bothered to change the lock.

He stared at the key, trying to recall the excitement of those weeks when he had been both judge and executioner. But he could feel nothing. It was all so long ago. He had been fifty then; now he was sixty-six. It was too old for feeling. And then he recalled the words of Mr Bootman. It was, after all, a very commonplace murder.

On Monday morning the girl in the estate office, clearing the mail from the letter box, called to the manager.

'That's funny! The old chap who took the key to the Camden Town flat has returned the wrong one. This hasn't got our label on it. Unless he pulled it off. Cheek! But why would he do that?'

She took the key over to the manager's desk, dumping his pile of letters in front of him. He glanced at it casually.

'That's the right key, anyway—it's the only one of that type we still have. Probably the label worked loose and fell off. You should put them on more carefully.'

'But I did!' Outraged, the girl wailed her protest. The manager winced.

'Then label it again, put it back on the board, and for God's sake don't fuss, that's a good girl.'

She glanced at him again, ready to argue. Then she shrugged. Come to think of it, he had always been a bit odd about that Camden Town flat.

'Okay, Mr Morrisey,' she said.

II

ENTRÉES HISTORIQUES

Tales from the Culinary Past

A DINNER AT IMOLA

August Derleth

History reveals that quite a number of famous men and women perished while eating—some, no doubt, because the food was contaminated, but others just as clearly poisoned. No one is quite sure, for instance, how many Egyptian pharaohs died in this way, but the Emperor Claudius was certainly poisoned, as were Charles the Bald, Louis V of France and Pope Leo X. Among the ladies, Gabriella d'Estrées, Henry IV's mistress, and Henrietta of England, Louis XIV's sister-in-law, met similar fates. With such a list to draw upon it is hardly surprising that a number of writers have produced historical stories of death brought about by culinary means. No name is more widely associated with the poisoning of food than that of the Italian family, the Borgias, in particular the ambitious Cesare Borgia (who himself survived a poisoning attempt at a banquet in 1499) and his sister, Lucrezia, who became synonymous with wantonness, vice and crime. The American writer August Derleth (1909–1971) was fascinated by the legends surrounding the Borgias and drew them together for 'A Dinner at Imola' which also introduces another of the sinister figures of the period, Niccolo Machiavelli . . .

Messer Niccolo Machiavelli had just signed his name to a letter to the Ten, when the flap of his tent swung wide in the hand of a lackey, permitting His Highness, the Prince Cesare Borgia, to enter.

'Ah! Excellency.' Machiavelli half turned.

'Another letter to the Ten, Messer Machiavelli?' Cesare Borgia shrugged his shoulders. 'You keep them well informed as to my movements.'

Niccolo Machiavelli made a deprecating gesture. The Borgia prince smiled.

'You had best warn them against guile in their dealings with me, Messer Machiavelli. Florence holds no interest for me—but let them once deceive me, and the Medici rule no longer.'

Messer Machiavelli bowed his head. 'Florence has no intention, Highness, of going against your wishes. Indeed, she is most anxious to preserve your friendship.'

'That will remain as it is, Messer Machiavelli. For the present I have come to ask you to dine with my company on the third night hence. The dinner is in honour of the young Duke Paolo di Colonna.'

Messer Machiavelli started. He looked at his host with raised eyebrows. Only yesterday his trusted lackey had informed him of the rumour of a plot against the Borgias, the headquarters of which were in Rome, at the palaces of the Cardinals Orsini and della Rovere. It was rumoured, too, that the young Paolo di Colonna was in alliance with this secret revolt, and that he was furthering the cause by sowing the seeds of revolt among the troops in camp at Imola, while at the same time the Duke Giovanni di Orsini was seeking to stir up the Borgia soldiers at Forli. As yet Machiavelli had no knowledge that the prince knew of the affair.

Messer Machiavelli nodded his head. 'You honour me,' he murmured.

'You will come?'

'With pleasure.'

'Very well. We will meet at table, if not before.'

The prince signalled to his lackey, who raised the tent flap for his master to take leave of the Florentine envoy. But hardly had the Borgia prince left the tent than Machiavelli gave a quick, short call. 'Giulio!'

From somewhere in the rear of the tent a small, stooped figure arose and stood before Niccolo Machiavelli.

'You called me, Messer Machiavelli?'

'You heard the Borgia?' The figure nodded. 'It is well. You will follow him continually until the third night hence.' The lackey laughed silently. He nodded. 'At the third night, report here before dinner.'

The lackey nodded quickly again, and without a word vanished into the interior of the tent, to emerge in the gathering darkness at its back within the minute. Messer Niccolo Machiavelli yawned, and gazed speculatively at the hour-glass on his table.

At the hour before dinner on the third night, Messer Machiavelli was startled out of his reverie by the sudden appearance of his lackey, Giulio.

'He visited at Luigi Reni's,' said Giulio abruptly.

'And this Reni?' queried Machiavelli with arched brows.

'Is a magician,' answered Giulio suggestively.

'Ah! And what did the Borgia there?'

'He brought with him and left at Reni's a small portrait of the Duke Paolo di Colonna. That was yesterday. Today he went again, and the portrait was returned to him, together with a large package. This package contained, I have made certain, numerous curiously wrought candles for the table tonight.'

'That is all?'

'Other than that is of no account. The Borgia prince attended to the usual matters of his troops.'

Messer Machiavelli toyed with a quill on his table. 'What make you of the candles, Giulio?' he asked.

The lackey smiled suggestively. He hunched his shoulders and spread his hands in an empty gesture.

'Who knows?' he said. 'The Borgia takes a portrait of his enemy to a magician, and receives at its return a packet of wax candles. It is said that if one burns a wax effigy of one's foe, made according to certain secret formulas, or if one pierces it to the heart, the model dies.'

Messer Machiavelli pondered a space. 'How many figures are needed? How many must be burned to rid oneself of an enemy?'

'But one, Excellency. But Cesare is a true Borgia. His resources know no end.'

Messer Machiavelli nodded. 'It is good work, Giulio; I shall not forget it.'

The lackey bowed and vanished in the shadows at the rear of the tent. Messer Machiavelli rose and donned a great cloak. He raised the flap of his tent and looked out at the cloudless sky. Far away, on the horizon toward the east, the full moon was just rising above the hills, and from the marshlands to the west thin wisps of vapour were moving towards the camp. Messer Machiavelli glanced dubiously at the hour-glass on the table, saw that the sand had passed the half-hour, and slipped out of his tent.

At the banquet hall the young Paolo di Colonna was the centre of a boisterous crowd. Cesare Borgia stood some distance away from him, and was the first to greet the Florentine envoy at his arrival. Messer Machiavelli sought vainly for some trace, some premonition on the inscrutable face of his host; there was naught save a sardonic smile. Messer Machiavelli was uneasy; he bethought himself of the pending alliance between the Council of Ten and di Colonna. He resolved to keep a watchful eye on the Borgia ring, which he knew served as a container for the white powder that Cesare had once shown him. He had often been told that for the Borgia prince to open this ring meant instant death for someone.

Messer Machiavelli moved somewhat closer to the table, the better to observe what Cesare Borgia was occupied with. He gave an involuntary start when he noticed that the prince himself was distributing before the places at table the carven candles that he had received from the magician, Reni. He sought out the place reserved for the prince, and found it quickly by the banner of the Bull draped over the back of the chair. Directly opposite this chair stood one marked with the arms of di Colonna. Messer Machiavelli's eyes strayed unconsciously to the wax figure before his own plate, set at the arms of the Medici. The figure was merely a replica of a trooper, and so, Messer Machiavelli saw, were many of the others. Some were copies of kings or princes, others of dukes or barons. As his eyes stole down the line of figures, Messer Machiavelli found himself curiously attracted by one, slightly larger than the rest, that bore a suspicious resemblance to someone he knew. He looked at the chair; it was the chair of Paolo di Colonna, and the figure was an exact replica of the young duke.

The strident voice of Cesare Borgia interrupted Messer Machiavelli's thoughts, calling him to table. Some of the young officers were already seated. Smiling inwardly, Machiavelli noticed that the Duke Paolo di Colonna had brought his taster with him; so, he saw, had several of the noblemen who were known to be in sympathy with Borgia enemies.

The dinner progressed smoothly—much too smoothly, Messer Machiavelli thought. Cesare Borgia, as host, discoursed volubly on many subjects, and he did not lack those to argue with him.

During the entire meal the prince had not once touched his ring. Now, towards the end of the meal, the prince indicated by example that his guests were to light the candles at their plates with tapers that had been furnished. Hardly had this been done, than, to the amazement of all present, Cesare Borgia abruptly changed the conversation.

'It is generally know, I believe, that there is a conspiracy now stirring in Rome.' The prince looked casually over at the Duke Paolo di Colonna; the duke paled. 'Its leaders have been determined, and unless all plans are immediately surrendered to the papal government, they and their estates will be seized and confiscated by His Holiness, Alexander VI. The Cardinals Orsini and della Rovere are heading this move, and there is talk of allying the rebellious Colonna faction—'

The prince was interrupted by a hoarse scream from the Duke Paolo di Colonna, who had half risen from his chair and was clawing at his collar.

'I am burning,' he shrieked, and fell towards the table.

A lackey hastily ran to aid him, and in a loud voice Cesare Borgia summoned his physician. Then he crossed around the table and supported the young duke until the doctor came. When at last he entered, the prince gave an order for the duke's removal to his own chamber, aiding the physician and two lackeys to carry the duke to the door of the hall.

Cesare Borgia returned to the table outwardly calm; all about him hummed excited whispers. Many of the soldiers looked questioningly at the duke's taster standing unharmed behind the empty chair. The prince reopened the conversation, and continued to speak until he saw that the flame of di Colonna's candle had burned out. Then he stopped abruptly, and Messer Machiavelli caught him glancing towards the door. At the same moment the curtains at the end of the hall were thrust aside, and the prince's physician ran into the room. He bowed and spoke.

'Highness,' he said simply, 'the Duke Paolo di Colonna is dead of an unknown illness.'

The prince nodded his head and opened his lips. 'It is unfortunate; but as God wills, so shall it be.'

Without further comment he again opened the subject of the Orsini conspiracy.

THE FEAST IN THE ABBEY

Robert Bloch

Eating in the Middle Ages was one long banquet for the nobility, the landowners and the Church, but little more than subsistence for the greater mass of the population. Many of the clergy, in particular, looked after their stomachs well, a factor that Robert Bloch (1917–) draws upon for his story, 'The Feast in the Abbey'. Bloch, who is famous as the author of Psycho, *that terrifying story of a maniac in a motel which was brilliantly filmed by Alfred Hitchcock in 1960, is also one of the best after-dinner speakers in his home town, Los Angeles, with a nice line in ghoulish humour. It may come as no surprise to the reader, after reading this story, to learn that its theme created quite a stir when it was first published, even in such a repository of horror as* Weird Tales.

A clap of thunder in the sullen west heralded the approach of night and storm together, and the sky deepned to a sorcerous black. Rain fell, the wind droned dolefully, and the forest pathway through which I rode became a muddy, treacherous bog that threatened momentarily to ensnare both my steed and myself in its unwelcome embrace. A journey under such conditions is most inauspicious; in consequence I was greatly heartened when shortly through the storm-tossed branches I discerned a flicker of hospitable light glimmering through mists of rain.

Five minutes later I drew rein before the massive doors of a goodly-sized, venerable building of grey, moss-covered stone, which, from its extreme size and sanctified aspect, I rightly took to be a monastery. Even as I gazed thus perfunctorily upon it, I could see that it was a place of some importance, for it loomed most imposingly above the crumbled foundations of many smaller buildings which had evidently once surrounded it.

The force of the elements, however, was such as to preclude all further inspection or speculation, and I was only too pleased when, in reply to my continued knocking, the great oaken door was thrown open and I stood face to face with a cowled man who courteously ushered me past the rain-swept portals into a well-lighted and spacious hallway.

My benefactor was short and fat, garbed in voluminous gabardine, and from his ruddy, beaming aspect, seemed a very pleasant and affable host. He introduced himself as the abbot Henricus, head of the monkish fraternity in whose headquarters I now found myself, and begged me to accept the hospitality of the brethren until the inclemencies of the weather had somewhat abated.

In reply I informed him of my name and station, and told him that I was journeying to keep tryst with my brother in Vironne, beyond the forest, but had been arrested in my journey by the storm.

These civilities having been concluded, he ushered me past the panelled ante-chamber to the foot of a great staircase set in stone, hewn out of the very wall itself. Here he called out sharply in an uncomprehended tongue, and in a moment I was startled by the sudden appearance of two blackamoors, who seemed to have materialised out of nowhere, so swiftly silent had been their coming. Their stern ebony faces, kinky hair and rolling eyes, set off by a most outlandish garb—great, baggy trousers of red velvet and waists of cloth-of-gold, in Eastern fashion—intrigued me greatly, though they seemed curiously out of place in a Christian monastery.

The abbot Henricus addressed them now in fluent Latin, bidding one to go without and care for my horse, and ordering the other to show me to an apartment above, where, he informed me, I could change my rain-bedraggled garments for a more suitable raiment, while awaiting the evening meal.

I thanked my courteous host and followed the silent black automaton up the great stone staircase. The flickering torch of the giant servitor cast arabesque shadows upon bare stone walls of great age and advanced decrepitude; clearly the structure was very old. Indeed, the massive walls that rose outside must have been constructed in bygone day, for the other buildings that presumably were contemporaneously erected beside this had long since fallen into irremediable, unrecognisable decay.

Upon reaching the landing, my guide led me along a richly carpeted expanse of tessellated floor, between lofty walls tapestried and bedizened with draperies of black. Such velvet finery was most unseemly for a place of worship, to my mind.

Nor was my opinion shaken by the sight of the chamber which was indicated as my own. It was fully as large as my father's study at Nimes—its walls hung in Spanish velvets of maroon, of an elegance surpassed only by their bad taste in such a place. There was a bed such as would grace the palace of a king; furniture and other appurtenances were of truly regal magnificence. The black-amoor lighted a dozen mammoth candles in the silver candelabra that stood about the room, and then bowed and withdrew.

Upon inspecting the bed I found thereupon the garments the abbot had designated for my use during the evening meal. These consisted of a suit of black velveteen with satin breeches and hose of a corresponding hue, and a sable surplice. Upon doffing my travel-worn apparel I found that they fitted perfectly, albeit most sombrely.

During this time I engaged myself in observing the room more closely. I wondered greatly at the lavishness, display and ostentation, and more greatly still at the complete absence of any religious paraphernalia—not even a simple crucifix was visible. Surely this order must be a rich and powerful one; albeit a trifle worldly; perchance akin to those societies of Malta and Cyprus whose licentiousness and extravagance is the scandal of the world.

As I thus mused there fell upon my ears the sounds of sonorous chanting that swelled symphonically from somewhere far below. Its measured cadence rose and fell solemnly as if it were borne from a distance incredible to human ears. It was subtly disturbing; I could distinguish neither words nor phrases that I knew, but the potent rhythm bewildered me. It welled, a malefic rune, fraught with insidious, strange suggestion. Abruptly it ceased, and I breathed unconsciously a sigh of relief. But not an instant during the remainder of my sojourn was I wholly free from the spark of unease generated by the far-distant sound of that nameless, measured chanting from below.

Never have I eaten a stranger meal than that which I partook of at the monastery of the abbot Henricus. The banquet hall was a triumph of ostentatious adornment. The meal took place in a vast chamber whose lofty eminence rose the entire height of the building to the arched and vaulted roof. The walls were hung with tapestries of purple and blood-royal, emblazoned with devices and escutcheons of noble, albeit to me unknown, significance. The banquet table itself extended the length of the chamber—at one end unto the double doors through which I had entered from the stairs; the other end was beneath a hanging balcony under which was the scullery entrance. About this vast festal board were seated some two-score churchmen in cowls and gabardines of black, who were already eagerly assailing the multitudinous array of foodstuffs with which the table was weighted. They scarcely ceased their gorging to nod a greeting when the abbot and I entered to take our place at the head of table, but continued to devour rapaciously the wonderful array of victuals set before them, accomplishing this task in a most unseemly fashion. The abbot neither paused to motion me to my seat nor to intone a blessing, but immediately followed the example of his flock and proceeded directly to stuff his belly with choice titbits before my astounded eyes. It was certain that these Flemish barbarians were far from fastidious in their table habits. The meal was accompanied by uncouth noises from the mouths of the feasters; the food was taken up in fingers and the untasted remains cast upon the floor; the common decencies were often ignored. For a moment I was dumbfounded, but natural politeness came to my rescue, so that I fell to without further ado.

Half a dozen of the black servants glided silently about the board, replenishing the dishes or bearing platters filled with new and still more exotic viands. My eyes beheld marvels of cuisine upon golden platters—verily, but pearls were cast before swine! For these cowled and hooded brethren, monks though they were, behaved like abominable boors. They wallowed in every kind of fruit—great luscious cherries, honeyed melons, pomegranates and grapes, huge plums, exotic apricots, rare figs and dates. There were huge cheeses, fragrant and mellow; tempting soups; raisins, nuts, vegetables, and great smoking trays of fish, all served with ales and cordials that were as potent as the nectar of nepenthe.

During the meal we were regaled with music from unseen lutes, wafted from the balconies above; music that triumphantly swelled in an ultimate crescendo as six servitors marched solemnly in, bearing an enormous platter of massy, beaten gold, in which reposed a single haunch of some smoking meat, garnished with and redolent of aromatic spices. In profound silence they advanced and set down their burden in the centre of the board, clearing away the giant candelabra and smaller dishes. Then the abbot rose, knife in hand, and carved the roast, the while muttering a sonorous invocation in an alien tongue. Slices of meat were apportioned to the monks of the assemblage on silver plates. A marked and definite interest was apparent in this ceremony; only politeness restrained me from questioning the abbot as to the significance of the company's behaviour. I ate a portion of my meat and said nothing.

To find such barbaric dalliance and kingly pomp in a monastic order was indeed curious, but my curiosity was regrettably dulled by copious imbibing of the potent wines set before me at the table, in beaker, bumper, flask, flagon, and bejewelled cup. There were vintages of every age and distillation; curious fragrant potions of marvellous headiness and giddy sweetness that affected me strangely.

The meat was peculiarly rich and sweet. I washed it down with great draughts from the wine-vessels that were now freely circulating about the table. The music ceased and the candle-glow dimmed imperceptibly into softer luminance. The storm still crashed against the walls without. The liquor sent fire through my veins, and queer fancies ran riot through my addled head.

I sat almost stupefied when, the company's trenchermannish appetites being at last satisfied, they proceeded, under influence of the wine, to break the silence observed during the meal by bursting into the chorus of a ribald song. Their mirth grew, and broad jests and tales were told, adding to the merriment. Lean faces were convulsed in lascivious laughter, fat paunches quivered with jollity. Some gave way to unseemly noise and gross gesture, and several collapsed beneath the table and were carried out by the silent blacks. I could not help but contrast the scene with that in which I would have figured had I reached Vironne to take my meal at the board of my brother, the good curé. There would be no such noisome ribaldry there: I wondered vaguely if he was aware of this monastic order so close to his quiet parish.

Then, abruptly, my thoughts returned to the company before me. The mirth and song had given place to less savoury things as the candles dimmed and deepening shadows wove their webs of darkness about the banquet board. Talk turned to vaguely alarming channels, and cowled faces took on a sinister aspect in the wan and flickering light. As I gazed bemused about the board, I was struck by the peculiar pallor of the assembled faces; they shone whitely in the dying light as with a distorted mockery of death. Even the atmosphere of the room seemed changed; the rustling draperies seemed moved by unseen hands; shadows marched along the walls; hobgoblin shapes pranced in weird processional over the groined arches of the ceiling. The festal board looked bare and denuded—dregs of wine besmirched the linen; half-eaten viands covered the table's expanse; the gnawed bones on the plates seemed grim reminders of mortal fate.

The conversation was ill-suited to further my peace of mind—it was far from the pious exhortations expected of such a company. Talk turned to ghosts and enchantments; old tales were told and infused with newer horror; legends recounted in broken whispers; hints of eldritch potency passed from wine-smeared lips in tones sepulchrally muted.

I sat somnolent no longer; I was nervous with an increasing

apprehension greater than I had ever known. It was almost as if I *knew* what was about to happen when at last, with a curious smile, the abbot began his tale and the monkish presences hushed their whispers and turned in their places to listen.

At the same time a black entered and deposited a small covered platter before his master, who regarded the dish for a moment before continuing his introductory remarks.

It was fortunate (he began, addressing me) that I had ventured here to stay the evening, for there had been other travellers whose nocturnal sojournings in these woods had not reached so fortunate a termination. There was, for example, the legendary 'Devil's Monastery'. (Here he paused and coughed abstractedly before continuing.)

According to the accepted folklore of the region, this curious place of which he spoke was an abandoned priory, deep in the heart of the woods, in which dwelt a strange company of the Undead, devoted to the service of Asmodeus. Often, upon the coming of darkness, the old ruins took on a preternatural semblance of their vanished glory, and the old walls were reconstructed by demon artistry to beguile the passing traveller. It was indeed fortunate that my brother had not sought me in the woods upon a night like this, for he might have blundered upon this accursed place and been bewitched into entrance; whereupon, according to the ancient chronicles, he would be seized, and his body devoured in triumph by the ghoulish acolytes that they might preserve their unnatural lives with mortal sustenance.

All this was recounted in a whisper of unspeakable dread, as if it were somehow meant to convey a message to my bewildered senses. It did. As I gazed into the leering faces all about me I realised the import of those jesting words, the ghastly mockery that lay behind the abbot's bland and cryptic smile.

The Devil's Monastery . . . subterrene chanting of the rites to Lucifer . . . blasphemous magnificence, but never the sign of the cross . . . an abandoned priory in the deep woods . . . wolfish faces glaring into my own . . .

Then, three things happened simultaneously. The abbot slowly lifted the lid of the small tray before him. ('Let us finish the meat,' I think he said.) Then I screamed. Lastly came the merciful thunderclap that precipitated me, the laughing monks, the abbot, the platter and the monastery into chaotic oblivion.

When I awoke I lay rain-drenched in a ditch beside the mired pathway, in wet garments of black. My horse grazed in the forest ways near by, but of the abbey I could see no sign.

I staggered into Vironne a half-day later, and already I was quite delirious, and when I reached my brother's home I cursed aloud beneath the windows. But my delirium lapsed into raving madness when he who found me there told me where my brother had gone, and his probable fate, and I swooned away upon the ground.

I can never forget that place, nor the chanting, nor the dreadful brethren, but I pray to God that I can forget one thing before I die; that which I saw before the thunderbolt; the thing that maddens me and torments me all the more in view of what I have since learned in Vironne. I know it is all true, now, and I can bear the knowledge, but I can never bear the menace nor the memory of what I saw when the abbot Henricus lifted up the lid of the small silver platter to disclose the rest of the meat. . . .

It was the head of my brother.

THE THREE LOW MASSES

Alphonse Daudet

There is probably no more succulent description of a seventeenth-century Christmas feast coupled with the terrible fate of a glutton than 'The Three Low Masses' by Alphonse Daudet (1840–1897). The story positively groans under the rich variety of seasonal delicacies described by Daudet whose work, not surprisingly, has been widely compared to that of Charles Dickens. Born in Nimes, he moved into the extravagant society of France as a private secretary to the Duc de Morny before turning to writing and producing a string of vivid novels like Tartarin de Tarascon *(1872) and* Sappho *(1884). The Reverend Dom Balaguere, the gourmet who commits an unforgivable sin in his desire to start the Christmas feasting, is another of Daudet's characters who remains in the memory long after the story is finished . . .*

'Two stuffed turkeys, Garrigou?'

'Yes, Father, two magnificent turkeys stuffed with truffles. And I ought to know, too, for I helped stuff them myself. One would think their skins would crack while they were roasting, they are stretched so tight.'

'Jesus and Mary! I who love truffles so much! . . . Quick, Garrigou, give me my surplice . . . And besides the turkey, what else did you see in the kitchens?'

'Oh, all sorts of good things! Ever since noon we have been plucking pheasants, hoopoes, hazel-lens and heath-cocks. The feathers filled with air. And then from the pond they brought eels, goldfish, trout, and . . .'

'How big were the trout, Garrigou?'

'So big, Father! Enormous!'

'Oh, good Lord! I can fairly see them . . . Did you put the wine in the vases?'

'Yes, Father, I put the wine in the vases. But heavens! It's nothing like the wine you will have later, when you come from the midnight mass. Oh, if you could only see the dining hall, all the decanters blazing with wines of all colours! And the silverware, the chased centrepieces, the flowers the candelabra! Never was there seen such a Christmas feast! The marquis has invited all the lords of the neighbouring estates. There will be at least forty of you at the table, without counting the bailiff or the notary. Ah! you are fortunate in being one of them, Father! Only from sniffing those wonderful turkeys, the odour of truffles follows me everywhere. Mmmm!'

'Come, come, my boy! Heaven preserve us from the sin of gluttony, above all on this eve of the Nativity! . . . Hurry off, now, and light the tapers and ring the first call for mass, for it will soon be midnight and we mustn't be late.'

This conversation took place one Christmas Eve in the year of grace sixteen hundred and something, between the Reverend Dom Balaguere, former prior of the Barnabites and present chaplain of the Sires of Trinquelage, and his little clerk Garrigou—or at least him whom he believed to be the little clerk Garrigou, for let me tell you that the devil, that evening, had assumed the round face and uncertain features of the young sacristan, the better to lead the reverend Father into temptation and make him commit the frightful sin of gluttony. So while the so-called Garrigou (hm! hm!) rang out the chimes from the seigniorial chapel, the reverend Father slipped on his chasuble in the little vestry of the castle, and, his imagination already excited by Garrigou's gastronomical descriptions, he kept muttering to himself as he got into his vestments:

'Roast turkeys . . . goldfish . . . trout, so big!'

Outside, the night wind blew and spread abroad the music of the bells. Lights began to appear in the darkness on the sides of Mount Ventoux, on whose summit the old towers of Trinquelage upreared their heads. The neighbouring farmers and their families were on their way to the castle to hear midnight mass. They climbed the mountain singing gaily, in groups of five or six, the father leading the way with his lantern, the women following, wrapped in great dark coats, under which the children snuggled to keep warm. In spite of the cold and the late hour of the night, all these good people walked along merrily, cheered by the thought that on coming from the mass they would find as usual, a great feast awaiting them downstairs in the castle kitchen. From time to time, on the rough ascent, the carriage of some lord, preceded by torch-bearers, showed its glimmering windowpanes in the moonlight; or a mule trotted along shaking its bells; or again, by the gleam of the great lanterns wrapped in mist, the farmers recognised their bailiff and hailed him as he passed:

'Good evening, good evening, Master Arnoton!'

'Good evening, good evening, my children!'

The night was clear; the stars seemed brightened by the frost; the northeast wind was nipping; and a fine sleet powdered all these cloaks without wetting them, preserving faithfully the tradition of a Christmas white with snow. On the very crest of the mountain the castle appeared as the goal, with its huge mass of towers and gables, the chapel steeple rising straight into the blue-black sky, and a crowd of little lights moving rapidly hither and thither, winking at all the windows, and looking, against the intense black of that lordly pile, like the little sparks that run through the ashes of burnt paper.

After passing the drawbridge and the postern, in order to get to the chapel one had to cross the first court, full of coaches, footmen and sedan-chairs silhouetted against the flare of the torches and the glare from the kitchens. One could hear the creaking of the turning spits, the clatter of pots, the tinkling of glassware and silver, as they were laid out for the banquet; and above it all floated a warm vapour smelling of roasted meats and the pungent herbs of elaborate sauces, which made the farmers, as well as the chaplain, the bailiff, and everybody say:

'What a wonderful midnight feast we are going to have after the mass!'

*   *   *

Ding-a-ling-ling! Ding-a-ling-ling! The midnight mass has begun. In the chapel of the castle, which is a miniature cathedral with its inter-crossed arches and oaken wainscoting up to the ceiling, all the tapestries are hung, all the tapers lighted. What a crowd of people! And what sumptuous costumes! Here, in one of the carven stalls that surround the choir, is the Sire of Trinquelage, clad in salmon-coloured silk; and around him all the noble lords, his guests. Opposite them, on velvet fall-stools, kneel the old dowager marchioness, in a gown of flame-coloured brocade, and the young lady of Trinquelage, wearing on her head a great tower of lace puffed and quilled according to the latest fashion of the French court. Farther down the aisle, all dressed in black, with vast pointed wigs and clean-shaven chins, sit Thomas Arnoton the bailiff and Master Ambroy the notary, two sombre spots among these gaudy silks and figured damasks. Then come the fat major-domos, the pages, the outriders, the stewards, and Dame Barbe, with all her keys dangling at her side on a great keyring of fine silver. On the benches in the rear is the lower service—the butlers and maids, the farmers and their families; and last of all, back by the doors, which they half open and discreetly close again, come the cooks to take a little nip of the mass between two sauces, and bring an odour of the Christmas feast into the bedecked church, which is warm with the light of so many tapers.

Can it be the sight of these little white caps that diverts the reverend Father's attention? Is it not rather Garrigou's bell?—that fiendish little bell that tinkles away at the foot of the altar with such infernal haste and seems to say all the time:

'Hurry up! Hurry up! The sooner we've finished, the sooner we shall be at the feast.'

The fact is that every time this devilish little bell peals out, the chaplain forgets his mass, and his mind wanders to the Christmas feast. Visions rise before him of the cooks running busily hither and thither, the ovens glowing like furnaces, warm vapours rising from under half-lifted lids, and through these vapours two magnificent turkeys, stuffed, crammed, mottled with truffles . . . Or then again, he sees long files of little pages carrying great dishes wrapped in their tempting fumes, and he is about to enter the dining hall with them for the feast. What ecstasy! Here stands the immense table, laden and dazzling, with peacocks dressed in their fathers, pheasants spreading their bronzed wings, ruby-coloured flagons, pyramids of luscious fruit amid the green foliage, and those wonderful fish that Garrigou spoke of (Garrigou, forsooth!) reclining on a bed of fennel, their pearly scales looking as if they were just from the pond, and a bunch of pungent herbs in their monsterlike nostrils. So vivid is the vision of these marvels that Dom Balaguere actually fancies all these glorious dishes are being served before him, on the very embroideries of the altar-cloth, and two or three times, instead of *Dominus vobiscum* he catches himself saying the *Benedicite*. But except for these slight mistakes the worthy man rattled off the service conscientiously, without skipping a line or omitting a genuflection; and all went well to the end of the first mass. For you know, you must know, that on Christmas Eve, the same officiating priest is obliged to say three masses consecutively.

'And that's one!' said the chaplain to himself with a sigh of relief; then, without losing a second, he motioned to his clerk, or him whom he believed to be his clerk, and . . .

Ding-a-ling-ling! Ding-a-ling-ling!

The second mass has begun, and with it Dom Balaguere's sin.

'Quick, quick! let us hurry!' says Garrigou's bell in its shrill, devilish voice, and this time the unfortunate priest, possessed by the demon of gluttony, pounces upon the missal and devours its pages with the avidity of his over-excited appetite. He kneels and rises frantically, barely sketches the sign of the cross and the genuflections, and shortens all his gestures in order to get through sooner. He scarcely extends his arms at the Gospel, or strikes his breast at the *Confiteor*. Between him and the clerk it is hard to tell who mumbles the faster. Verses and responses leap out and jostle each other. The words, half uttered between their teeth—for it would take too long to open their lips every time—die out into unintelligible murmurs.

'*Oremus* . . . *ps* . . . *ps* . . .'

'*Mea culpa* . . . *pa* . . . *pa* . . .'

Like hurried vintagers crushing the grapes in the vats, they both splashed about in the Latin of the service, spattering it in every direction.

'"*Dom* . . . *scum!*" says Balaguere.'

'. . . . *Stutuo!*' replies Garrigou; and all the time the accurst little bell jingles in their ears like the sleighbells that are put on stage-horses to make them gallop faster. You may well believe that at such speed a low mass is soon hurried out of the way.

'And that's two,' says the chaplain, all out of breath; then, red in the face, perspiring freely, without taking time to breathe he goes tumbling down the altar steps and . . .

Ding-a-ling-ling! Ding-a-ling-ling!

The third mass has begun. There are only a few steps between him and the dining hall; but alas! as the time approaches, the unfortunate Dom Balaguere's fever of impatience and greediness grows. His imagination waxes more vivid; the fish, the roasted turkeys, are there before him . . . he touches them . . . he—good heavens!—he breathes the perfume of the wines and the savoury fumes of the dishes, and the infernal little bell calls out frantically to him:

'Hurry, hurry! Faster, faster!'

But how on earth can he go faster?—his lips barely move; he no longer pronounces his words—unless, forsooth, he chooses to cheat the good Lord and swindle him out of His mass. And that is just what he does, the wretched man! Yielding to temptation after temptation, he begins by skipping one verse, then two; then he finds the Epistle too long, so he leaves it unfinished; he skims over the Gospel; passes the *Credo* without entering; jumps the *Pater*; salutes the preface from afar; and by leaps and bounds he plunges into eternal damnation, followed by that infamous Garrigou (*Vade retro, Satanas!*), who seconds him with marvellous sympathy, holds up his chasuble, turns the pages two at a time, jostles the lectern, upsets the vases, and constantly rings the little bell faster and louder.

It would be impossible to describe the bewildered expression of the congregation. Compelled to follow, mimicking the priest, through this mass of which they cannot make out a single word, some get up while others kneel, some sit while others stand; and all the phases of this singular service was jumbled together along the benches in confusion of varied postures. The Christmas star on its celestial road, journeying toward the little manger yonder, grows pale at seeing such a frightful confusion.

'The abbé reads too fast; one can't follow him,' murmurs the old dowager marchioness, her voluminous head-dress shaking wildly. Master Arnoton, with his great steel spectacles on his nose, hunts desperately in his prayerbook to find where on earth is the place. But at heart, all these good people, whose minds are equally bent upon the Christmas feast, are not at all disturbed at the idea of following mass at such breakneck speed; and when Dom Balaguere, his face shining, faces them and cries out in a thundering voice, '*Ite, missa est,*' the congregation answers with a '*Deo gratias*' so joyous, so enthusiastic, that one might believe they were already at the table for the first toast of the Christmas feast.

*   *   *

Five minutes later, the assembled lords, with the chaplain in their midst, had taken their seats in the great hall. The castle, brilliantly illumined from top to bottom, echoed with songs and laughter; and the venerable Dom Balaguere planted his fork in a capon's wing, drowning the remorse for his sin in floods of old wine and the savoury juice of meats. He ate and drank so heartily, this poor holy man, that he died in the night of a terrible attack of indigestion, without even having time to repent. By morning he reached heaven, his head still swimming from the odours of the feast; and I leave you to imagine how he was received.

'Get thee gone from my sight, thou wretched Christian!' said the Sovereign Judge, the Master of us all. 'Thy sin is great enough to wipe out the virtues of a lifetime! Ah, thou has stolen from me a midnight mass! Very well, then: thou shalt pay me three hundred masses in its place, and thou shalt not enter into paradise until three hundred Christmas masses have been celebrated in thine own chapel, in the presence of all those who sinned with thee and through thee.'

And this is the true legend of Dom Balaguere, as it is told in the land of the olive tree. The castle of Trinquelage has long ceased to exist; but the chapel stands erect on the crest of Mount Ventoux, in a clump of evergreen oaks. The wind sways its unhinged door, the grass grows over the threshold; there are nests in the angles of the altar and on the sills of the high ogive windows, whose jewelled panes have long ago disappeared. Still, it seems that every year, on Christmas night, a supernatural light wanders among the ruins; and the peasants, on their way to midnight mass and the Christmas feast, see this spectre of a chapel lighted by invisible tapers which burn in the open air, even in the wind and under the snow. You may laugh if you will, but a vine-dresser of the district, named Garrigue, no doubt a descendant of Garrigou, has told me that one one particular Christmas night, being somewhat in liquor, he lost his way on the mountain somewhere near Trinquelage, and this is what he saw. . . . Until 11 o'clock, nothing. Everything was silent and dark. Suddenly, towards midnight, the chimes rang out from the old steeple—old, old chimes that seemed to be ringing ten leagues away. Soon lights began to tremble along the road that climbs to the castle, and vague shadows moved about. Under the portal of the chapel there were faint footsteps, and muffled voices:

'Good evening, Master Arnoton!'

'Good evening, good evening, my children!'

When they had all gone in, the vine-dresser, who was very brave, softly approached, and, looking through the broken door, beheld a singular spectacle. All those shadows that he had seen pass were now seated around the choir in the ruined nave, just as if the old benches were still there. There were fine ladies in brocades and lace head-dresses, gaily bedecked lords, peasants in flowered coats like those our grandfathers wore; all of them old, dusty, faded, weary. Every now and then some night-bird, a habitual lodger in the chapel, awakened by all these lights, would flutter about the tapers, of which the flame rose erect and vague as if it were burning behind a strip of gauze. And what amused Garrigue most was a certain gentleman with great steel spectacles, who constantly shook his huge black wig, on which perched one of those birds, its claws entangled and its wings beating wildly.

A little old man with a childlike figure, knelt in the centre of the choir and frantically shook a tiny bell that had lost its clapper and its voice, while a priest, clad in vestments of old gold, moved hither and thither before the altar repeating orisons of which not a single syllable could be heard.

Without doubt, this was Dom Balaguere in the act of saying his third low mass.

THE COFFIN-MAKER

Alexander Pushkin

The Russians' love of gargantuan meals has been featured in any number of novels by the country's most famous writers, where lavish dishes are washed down with countless glasses of vodka, wine and champagne. Alexander Pushkin (1799–1837), the great poet whose life and death—in a duel at the age of 37—was as exotic as anything he wrote, poured his love of carousing into several stories, including the grim tale of 'The Coffin-Maker' which sets out to show that the cost of a big meal can sometimes be something far more frightening than a bout of indigestion.

The last of the effects of the coffin-maker, Adrian Prokhoroff, were placed upon the hearse, and a couple of sorry-looking jades dragged themselves along for the fourth time from Basmannaia to Nikitskaia, whither the coffin-maker was removing with all his household. After locking up the shop, he posted upon the door a placard announcing that the house was to be let or sold, and then made his way on foot to his new abode. On approaching the little yellow house, which had so long captivated his imagination, and which at last he had bought for a considerable sum, the old coffin-maker was astonished to find that his heart did not rejoice. When he crossed the unfamiliar threshold and found his new home in the greatest confusion, he sighed for his old hovel, where for eighteen years the strictest order had prevailed. He began to scold his two daughters and the servant for their slowness, and then set to work to help them himself. Order was soon established; the ark with the sacred images, the cupboard with the crockery, the table, the sofa, and the bed occupied the corners reserved for them in the back room; in the kitchen and parlour were placed the articles comprising the stock-in-trade of the master—coffins of all colours and of all sizes, together with cupboards containing mourning hats, cloaks and torches.

Over the door was placed a sign representing a fat Cupid with an inverted torch in his hand and bearing this inscription: 'Plain and coloured coffins sold and lined here; coffins also let out on hire, and old ones repaired.'

The girls retired to their bedroom; Adrian made a tour of inspection of his quarters, and then sat down by the window and ordered the tea-urn to be prepared.

The enlightened reader knows that Shakespeare and Walter Scott have both represented their grave-diggers as merry and facetious individuals, in order that the contrast might more forcibly strike our imagination. Out of respect for the truth, we cannot follow their example, and we are compelled to confess that the disposition of our coffin-maker was in perfect harmony with his gloomy occupation. Adrian Prokhoroff was usually gloomy and thoughtful. He rarely opened his mouth, except to scold his daughters when he found them standing idle and gazing out of the window at the passer-by, or to demand for his wares an exorbitant price from those who had the misfortune—and sometimes the good fortune—to need them. Hence it was that Adrian, sitting near the window and drinking his seventh cup of tea, was immersed as usual in melancholy reflections. He thought of the pouring rain which, just a week before, had commenced to beat down during the funeral of the retired brigadier. Many of the cloaks had shrunk in consequence of the downpour, and many of the hats had been put quite out of shape. He foresaw unavoidable expenses, for his old stock of funeral dresses was in a pitiable condition. He hoped to compensate himself for his losses by the burial of old Trukhina, the shopkeeper's wife, who for more than a year had been upon the point of death. But Trukhina lay dying at Rasgouliai, and Prokhoroff was afraid that her heirs, in spite of their promise, would not take the trouble to send so far for him, but would make arrangements with the nearest undertaker.

These reflections were suddenly interrupted by three masonic knocks at the door.

'Who is there?' asked the coffin-maker.

The door opened, and a man, who at the first glance could be recognised as a German artisan, entered the room, and with a jovial air advanced towards the coffin-maker.

'Pardon me, respected neighbour,' said he in that Russian dialect which to this day we cannot hear without a smile: 'Pardon me for disturbing you . . . I wished to make your acquaintance as soon as possible. I am a shoemaker, my name is Gottlieb Schultz, and I live across the street, in that little house just facing your windows. Tomorrow I am going to celebrate my silver wedding, and I have come to invite you and your daughters to dine with us.'

The invitation was cordially accepted. The coffin-maker asked the shoemaker to seat himself and take a cup of tea, and thanks to the open-hearted disposition of Gottlieb Schultz, they were soon engaged in friendly conversation.

'How is business with you?' asked Adrian.

'Just so so,' replied Schultz; 'I cannot complain. My wares are not like yours: the living can do without shoes, but the dead cannot do without coffins.'

'Very true,' observed Adrian; 'but if a living person hasn't anything to buy shoes with, you cannot find fault with him, he goes about barefooted; but a dead beggar gets his coffin for nothing.'

In this manner the conversation was carried on between them for some time; at last the shoemaker rose and took leave of the coffin-maker, renewing his invitation.

The next day, exactly at twelve o'clock, the coffin-maker and his daughters issued from the doorway of their newly-purchased residence, and directed their steps towards the abode of their neighbour. I will not stop to describe the Russian *caftan* of Adrian Prokhoroff, nor the European toilettes of Akoulina and Daria, deviating in this respect from the usual custom of modern novelists. But I do not think it superfluous to observe that they both had on the yellow cloaks and red shoes, which they were accustomed to don on solemn occasions only.

The shoemaker's little dwelling was filled with guests, consisting chiefly of German artisans with their wives and foremen. Of the Russian officials there was present but one, Yourko the Finn, a watchman, who, in spite of his humble calling, was the special object of the host's attention. For twenty-five years he had faithfully discharged the duties of postilion of Pogorelsky. The conflagration of 1812, which destroyed the ancient capital, destroyed also his little yellow watch-house. But immediately after the expulsion of the enemy, a new one appeared in its place, painted grey and with white Doric columns, and Yourko began again to pace to and fro before it, with his axe and grey coat of mail. He was known to the greater part of the Germans who lived near the Nikitskaia Gate, and some of them had even spent the night from Sunday to Monday beneath his roof.

Adrian immediately made himself acquainted with him, as with a man whom, sooner or later, he might have need of, and when the guests took their places at the table, they sat down beside each other. Herr Schultz and his wife, and their daughter Lotchen, a young girl of seventeen, did the honours of the table and helped the cook to serve. The beer flowed in streams; Yourko ate like four, and Adrian in no way yielded to him; his daughters, however, stood upon their dignity. The conversation, which was carried on in German, gradually grew more and more boisterous. Suddenly the host requested a moment's attention, and uncorking a sealed bottle, he said with a loud voice in Russian:

'To the health of my good Louise!'

The champagne foamed. The host tenderly kissed the fresh face of his partner, and the guests drank noisily to the health of the good Louise.

'To the health of my amiable guests!' exclaimed the host, uncorking a second bottle; and the guests thanked him by draining their glasses once more.

Then followed a succession of toasts. The health of each individual guest was drunk; they drank to the health of Moscow and to quite a dozen little German towns; they drank to the health of all corporations in general and of each in particular; they drank to the health of the masters and foremen. Adrian drank with enthusiasm and became so merry, that he proposed a facetious toast to himself. Suddenly one of the guests, a fat baker, raised his glass and exclaimed:

'To the health of those for whom we work, our customers!'

This proposal, like all the others, was joyously and unanimously received. The guests began to salute each other; the tailor bowed to the shoemaker, the shoemaker to the tailor, the baker to both, the whole company to the baker, and so on. In the midst of these mutual congratulations, Yourko exclaimed, turning to his neighbour:

'Come, little father! Drink to the health of your corpses!'

Everybody laughed, but the coffin-maker considered himself insulted, and frowned. Nobody noticed it, the guests continued to drink, and the bell had already rung for vespers when they rose from the table.

The guests dispersed at a late hour, the greater part of them in a very merry mood. The fat baker and the bookbinder, whose face seemed as if bound in red morocco, linked their arms in those of Yourko and conducted him back to his little watch-house, thus observing the proverb: 'One good turn deserves another.'

The coffin-maker returned home drunk and angry.

'Why is it,' he exclaimed aloud, 'why is it that my trade is not as honest as any other? Is a coffin-maker brother to the hangman? Why did those heathens laugh? Is a coffin-maker a buffoon? I wanted to invite them to my new dwelling and give them a feast, but now I'll do nothing of the kind. Instead of inviting them, I will invite those for whom I work: the orthodox dead.'

'What is the matter, little father?' said the servant, who was engaged at that moment in taking off his boots: 'why do you talk such nonsense? Make the sign of the cross! Invite the dead to your new house! What folly!'

'Yes, by the Lord! I will invite them,' continued Adrian, 'and that, too, for tomorrow! . . . Do me the favour, my benefactors, to come and feast with me tomorrow evening; I will regale you with what God has sent me.'

With these words the coffin-maker turned into bed and soon began to snore.

It was still dark when Adrian was awakened out of his sleep. Trukhina, the shopkeeper's wife, had died during the course of that very night, and a special messenger was sent off on horseback by her bailiff to carry the news to Adrian. The coffin-maker gave him ten copecks to buy brandy with, dressed himself as hastily as possible, took a *droshky* and set out for Rasgouliai. Before the door of the house in which the deceased lay, the police had already taken their stand, and the trades-people were passing backwards and forwards, like ravens that smell a dead body. The deceased lay upon a table, yellow as wax, but not yet disfigured by decomposition. Around her stood her relatives, neighbours and domestic servants. All the windows were open; tapers were burning; and the priests were reading the prayers for the dead. Adrian went up to the nephew of Trukhina, a young shopman in a fashionable surtout, and informed him that the coffin, wax candles, pall, and the other funeral accessories would be immediately delivered with all possible exactitude. The heir thanked him in an absent-minded manner, saying that he would not bargain about the price, but would rely upon him acting in everything according to his conscience. The coffin-maker, in accordance with his usual custom, vowed that he would not charge him too much, exchanged significant glances with the bailiff, and then departed to commence operations.

The whole day was spent in passing to and fro between Rasgouliai and the Nikitskaia Gate. Towards evening everything was finished, and he returned home on foot, after having dismissed his driver. It was a moonlight night. The coffin-maker reached the Nikitskaia Gate in safety. Near the Church of the Ascension he was hailed by our acquaintance Yourko, who, recognising the coffin-maker reached the Nikitskaia Gate in safety. Near the Church of the Ascension he was hailed by our acquaintance Yourko, who, recognising the coffin-maker, wished him goodnight. It was late. The coffin-maker was just approaching his house, when suddenly he fancied he saw some one approach his gate, open the wicket, and disappear within.

'What does that mean?' thought Adrian. 'Who can be wanting me again? Can it be a thief come to rob me? Or have my foolish girls got lovers coming after them? It means no good, I fear!'

And the coffin-maker thought of calling his friend Yourko to his assistance. But at that moment, another person approached the wicket and was about to enter, but seeing the master of the house hastening towards him, he stopped and took off his three-cornered hat. His face seemed familiar to Adrian, but in his hurry he had not been able to examine it closely.

'You are favouring me with a visit,' said Adrian, out of breath. 'Walk in, I beg of you.'

'Don't stand on ceremony, little father,' replied the other, in a hollow voice; 'you go first, and show your guests the way.'

Adrian had no time to spend upon ceremony. The wicket was open; he ascended the steps followed by the other. Adrian thought he could hear people walking about in his rooms.

'What the devil does all this mean!' he thought to himself, and he hastened to enter. But the sight that met his eyes caused his legs to give way beneath him.

The room was full of corpses. The moon, shining through the windows, lit up their yellow and blue faces, sunken mouths, dim, half-closed eyes, and protruding noses. Adrian, with horror, recognised in them people that he himself had buried, and in the guest who entered with him, the brigadier who had been buried during the pouring rain. They all, men and women, surrounded the coffin-maker, with bowings and salutations, except one poor fellow lately buried gratis, who, conscious and ashamed of his rags, did not venture to approach, but meekly kept aloof in a corner. All the others were decently dressed: the female corpses in caps and ribbons, the officials in uniforms, but with their beards unshaven, the tradesmen in their holiday *caftans*.

'You see, Prokhoroff,' said the brigadier in the name of all the honourable company, 'we have all risen in response to your invitation. Only those have stopped at home who were unable to come, who have crumbled to pieces and have nothing left but fleshless bones. But even of these there was one who hadn't the patience to remain behind—so much did he want to come and see you . . .'

At this moment a little skeleton pushed his way through the crowd and approached Adrian. His fleshless face smiled affably at the coffin-maker. Shreds of green and red cloth and rotten linen hung on him here and there as on a pole, and the bones of his feet rattled inside his big jackboots, like pestles in mortars.

'You do not recognise me, Prokhoroff,' said the skeleton. 'Don't you remember the retired sergeant of the Guards, Peter Petrovitch Kourilkin, the same to whom, in the year 1799, you sold your first coffin, and that, too, of deal instead of oak?'

With these words the corpse stretched out his bony arms towards him; but Adrian, collecting all his strength, shrieked and pushed him from him. Peter Petrovitch staggered, fell, and crumbled all to pieces. Among the corpses arose a murmur of indignation; all stood up for the honour of their companion, and they overwhelmed Adrian with such threats and imprecations, that the poor host, deafened by their shrieks and almost crushed to death, lost his presence of mind, fell upon the bones of the retired sergeant of the Guards, and swooned away.

For some time the sun had been shining upon the bed on which lay the coffin-maker. At last he opened his eyes and saw before him the servant attending to the tea-urn. With horror, Adrian recalled all the incidents of the previous day. Trukhina, the brigadier, and the sergeant, Kourilkin, rose vaguely before his imagination. He waited in silence for the servant to open the conversation and inform him of the events of the night.

'How you have slept, little father Adrian Prokhorovitch!' said Aksinia, handing him his dressing-gown. 'Your neighbour, the tailor, has been here, and the watchman also called to inform you that today is his name-day; but you were so sound asleep, that we did not wish to wake you.'

'Did anyone come for me from the late Trukhina?'

'The late? Is she dead, then?'

'What a fool you are! Didn't you yourself help me yesterday to prepare the things for her funeral?'

'Have you taken leave of your senses, little father, or have you not yet recovered from the effects of yesterday's drinking-bout? What funeral was there yesterday? You spent the whole day feasting at the German's, and then came home drunk and threw yourself upon the bed, and have slept till this hour, when the bells have already rung for mass.'

'Really!' said the coffin-maker, greatly relieved.

'Yes, indeed,' replied the servant.

'Well, since that is the case, make the tea as quickly as possible and call my daughters.'

GUESTS FROM GIBBET ISLAND

Washington Irving

Unexpected dinner guests are the theme of this next story by Washington Irving (1783–1859), the first American writer to gain an international literary reputation. Irving, who was the son of an Englishman, was very interested in the early history of the United States, and wrote a number of tales about the pre-Revolutionary Dutch culture along the Eastern seaboard. Pre-eminent among these was the classic 'Rip Van Winkle' and the equally evocative 'Guests From Gibbet Island'. It is a chilling story of an old pirate who, wanting to see his old shipmates again, decides to invite a group of them to a meal . . .

Whoever has visited the ancient and renowed village of Communipaw may have noticed an old stone building, of most ruinous and sinister appearance. The doors and window-shutters are ready to drop from their hinges; old clothes are stuffed in the broken panes of glass, while legions of half-starved dogs prowl about the premises, and rush out and bark at every passer-by; for your beggarly house in a village is most apt to swarm with profligate and ill-conditioned dogs. What adds to the sinister appearance of this mansion is a tall frame in front, not a little resembling a gallows, and which looks as if waiting to accommodate some of the inhabitants with a well-merited airing. It is not a gallows, however, but an ancient sign-post; for this dwelling, in the golden days of Communipaw, was one of the most orderly and peaceful of village taverns, where public affairs were talked and smoked over. In fact, it was in this very building that Oloffe the Dreamer, and his companions, concerted that great voyage of discovery and colonisation, in which they explored Buttermilk Channel, were nearly shipwrecked in the strait of Hell-gate, and finally landed on the island of Manhattan, and founded the great city of New Amsterdam.

Even after the province had been cruelly wrested from the sway of their High Mightinesses by the combined forces of the British and the Yankees, this tavern continued its ancient loyalty. It is true, the head of the Prince of Orange disappeared from the sign, a strange bird being painted over it, with the explanatory legend of 'DIE WILDE GANS,' or, The Wild Goose; but this all the world knew to be a sly riddle of the landlord's, the worthy Teunis Van Gieson, a knowing man, in a small way, who laid his finger beside his nose and winked when any one studied the signification of his sign, and observed that his goose was hatching, but would join the flock whenever they flew over the water—an enigma which was the perpetual recreation and delight of the loyal but fat-headed burghers of Communipaw.

Under the sway of this patriotic, though discreet and quiet publican, the tavern continued to flourish in primeval tranquillity, and was the resort of true-hearted Nederlanders, from all parts of Pavonia, who met here quietly and secretly, to smoke and drink the downfall of Briton and Yankee, and success to Admiral Van Tromp.

The only drawback on the comfort of the establishment was a nephew of mine host, a sister's son, Yan Yost Vanderscamp by name, and a real scamp by nature. This unlucky whipster showed an early propensity to mischief, which he gratified in a small way by playing tricks upon the frequenters of the Wild Goose: putting gunpowder in their pipes, or squibs in their pockets, and astonishing them with an explosion, while they sat nodding round the fireplace in the bar-room; and if perchance a worthy burgher from some distant part of Pavonia lingered until dark over his potation, it was odds but young Vanderscamp would slip a brier under his horse's tail as he mounted, and send him clattering along the road, in neck-or-nothing style, to the infinite astonishment and discomfiture of the rider.

It may be wondered at, that mine host of the Wild Goose did not turn such a graceless varlet out of doors; but Teunis Van Gieson was an easy-tempered man, and, having no child of his own, looked upon his nephew with almost parental indulgence. His patience and good nature were doomed to be tried by another inmate of his mansion. This was a crossgrained curmudgeon of a negro, named Pluto, who was a kind of enigma in Communipaw. Where he came from, nobody knew. He was found one morning after a storm, cast like a sea-monster on the strand, in front of the Wild Goose, and lay there, more dead than alive. The neighbours gathered round, and speculated on this production of the deep; whether it were fish or flesh, or a compound of both, commonly yclept a merman. The kind-hearted Teunis Van Gieson, seeing that he wore the human form, took him into his house, and warmed him into life. By degrees, he showed signs of intelligence, and even uttered sounds very much like language, but which no one in Communipaw could understand. Some thought him a negro just from Guinea, who had either fallen overboard, or escaped from a slave-ship. Nothing, however, could ever draw from him any account of his origin. When questioned on the subject, he merely pointed to Gibbet Island, a small rocky islet, which lies in the open bay, just opposite Communipaw, as if that were his native place, though everybody knew it had never been inhabited.

In the process of time, he acquired something of the Dutch language—that is to say, he learnt all its vocabulary of oaths and maledictions, with just words sufficient to string them together. '*Donder en blicksem!*'—thunder and lightning—was the gentlest of his ejaculations. For years he kept about the Wild Goose, more like one of those familiar spirits, or household goblins, we read of, than like a human being. He acknowledged allegiance to no one, but performed various domestic offices, when it suited his humour: waiting occasionally on the guests; grooming the horses, cutting wood, drawing water; and all this without being ordered. Lay any command on him, and the stubborn sea-urchin was sure to rebel. He was never so much at home, however, as when on the water, plying about in skiff or canoe, entirely alone, fishing, crabbing, or grabbing for oysters, and would bring home quantities for the larder of the Wild Goose, which he would throw down at the kitchen door, with a growl. No wind nor weather deterred him from launching forth on his favourite element: indeed, the wilder the weather, the more he seemed to enjoy it. If a storm was brewing, he was sure to put off from shore; and would be seen far out in the bay, his light skiff dancing like a feather on the waves, when sea and sky were in a turmoil, and the stoutest ships were fain to lower their sails. Sometimes, on such occasions, he would be absent for days together. How he weathered the tempest, and how and where he subsisted no one could divine, nor did any one venture to ask, for all had an almost superstitious awe of him. Some of the Communipaw oystermen declared they had more than once seen him suddenly disappear, canoe and all, as if plunged beneath the waves, and after a while come up again, in quite a different part of the bay; whence they concluded that he could live under water like that notable species of wild duck commonly called the hell-diver. All began to consider him in the light of a foul-weather bird, like the Mother Carey's Chicken or stormy petrel; and whenever they saw him putting far out in his skiff, in cloudy weather, made up their minds for a storm.

The only being for whom he seemed to have any liking was Yan Yost Vanderscamp, and him he liked for his very wickedness. He in a manner took the boy under his tutelage, prompted him to all kinds of mischief, aided him in every wild harum-scarum freak, until the lad became the complete scapegrace of the village; a pest to his uncle, and to every one else. Nor were his pranks confined to the land: he soon learned to accompany old Pluto on the water. Together these worthies would cruise about the broad bay, and all the neighbouring straits and rivers; poking around in skiffs and canoes; robbing the set nets of the fishermen; landing on remote coasts, and laying waste orchards and water-melon patches; in short, carrying on a complete system of piracy, on a small scale. Piloted by Pluto, the youthful Vanderscamp soon became acquainted with all the bays, rivers, creeks, and inlets of the watery world around him; could navigate from the Hook to Spitting-devil on the darkest night, and learned to set even the terrors of Hell-gate at defiance.

At length, negro and boy suddenly disappeared, and days and weeks elapsed, but without tidings of them. Some said they must have run away and gone to sea; others jocosely hinted that old Pluto, being no other than his namesake in disguise, had spirited away the boy to the nether regions. All, however, agreed in one thing—that the village was well rid of them.

In the process of time, the good Teunis Van Gieson slept with his fathers, and the tavern remained shut up, waiting for a claimant, for the next heir was Yan Yost Vanderscamp, and he had not been heard of for years. At length, one day, a boat was seen pulling for shore, from a long, black, rakish-looking schooner, that lay at anchor in the bay. The boat's crew seemed worthy of the craft from which they debarked. Never had such a set of noisy, roistering, swaggering varlets landed in peaceful Commmunipaw. They were outlandish in garb and demeanour, and were headed by a rough, burly, bully ruffian, with fiery whiskers, a copper nose, a scar across his face, and a great Flaunderish beaver slouched on one side of his head, in whom, to their dismay, the quiet inhabitants were made to recognise their early pest, Yan Yost Vanderscamp. The rear of this hopeful gang was brought up by old Pluto, who had lost an eye, grown grizzly-headed, and looked more like a devil than ever. Vanderscamp renewed his acquaintance with the old burghers, much against their will, and in a manner not at all to their taste. He slapped them familiarly on the back, gave them an iron grip of the hand, and was hail fellow well met. According to his own account, he had been all the world over; had made money by bagsful; had ships in every sea, and now meant to turn the Wild Goose into a country-seat, where he and his comrades, all rich merchants from foreign parts, might enjoy themselves in the interval of their voyages.

Sure enough, in a little while there was a complete metamorphose of the Wild Goose. From being a quiet, peaceful Dutch public-house, it became a most riotous, uproarious private dwelling; a complete rendezvous for boisterous men of the seas, who came here to have what they called a 'blow out' on dry land, and might be seen at all hours, lounging about the door, or lolling out of the windows; swearing among themselves, and cracking rough jokes on every passer-by. The house was fitted up, too, in so strange a manner: hammocks slung to the walls, instead of bedsteads; odd kinds of furniture, of foreign fashion; bamboo couches, Spanish chairs; pistols, cutlasses, and blunderbusses, suspended on every peg; silver crucifixes on the mantelpieces, silver candlesticks and porringers on the tables, contrasting oddly with the pewter and Delf ware of the original establishment. And then the strange amusements of these sea-monsters! Pitching Spanish dollars, instead of quoits; firing blunderbusses out of the window; shooting at a mark, or at any unhappy dog, or cat, or pig, or barndoor fowl, that might happen to come within reach.

The only being who seemed to relish their rough waggery was old Pluto; and yet he led but a dog's life of it; for they practised all kinds of manual jokes upon him; kicked him about like a football; shook him by his grizzly mop of wool, and never spoke to him without coupling a curse by way of adjective to his name, and consigning him to the infernal regions. The old fellow, however, seemed to like them the better the more they cursed him, though his utmost expression of pleasure never amounted to more than the growl of a petted bear, when his ears are rubbed.

Old Pluto was the ministering spirit at the orgies of the Wild Goose; and such orgies as took place there! Such drinking, singing, whooping, swearing; with an occasional interlude of quarrelling and fighting. The noisier grew the revel, the more old Pluto plied the potations, until the guests would become frantic in their merriment, smashing everything to pieces, and throwing the house out of the windows. Sometimes, after a drinking bout, they sallied forth and scoured the village, to the dismay of the worthy burghers, who gathered their women within doors, and would have shut up the house. Vanderscamp, however, was not to be rebuffed. He insisted on renewing acquaintance with his old neighbours, and on introducing his friends, the merchants, to their families; swore he was on the look-out for a wife, and meant, before he stopped, to find husbands for all their daughters. So, will-ye, nill-ye, sociable he was; swaggered about their best parlours, with his hat on one side of his head; sat on the good wife's nicely waxed mahogany table, kicking his heels against the carved and polished legs; kissed and tousled the young *vrouws*; and, if they frowned and pouted, gave them a gold rosary, or a sparkling cross, to put them in good humour again.

Sometimes nothing would satisfy him, but he must have some of his old neighbours to dinner at the Wild Goose. There was no refusing him, for he had the complete upper hand of the community, and the peaceful burghers all stood in awe of him. But what a time would the quiet, worthy men have, among these rakehells, who would delight to astound them with the most extravagant gunpowder tales, embroidered with all kinds of foreign oaths; clink the can with them; pledge them in deep potations; bawl drinking-songs in their ears; and occasionally fire pistols over their heads, or under the table, and then laugh in their faces, and ask them how they liked the smell of gunpowder.

Thus was the little village of Communipaw for a time like the unfortunate wight possessed with devils; until Vanderscamp and his brother merchants would sail on another trading voyage, when the Wild Goose would be shut up, and everything relapse into quiet, only to be disturbed by his next visitation.

The mystery of all these proceedings gradually dawned upon the tardy intellects of Communipaw. These were the times of the notorious Captain Kidd, when the American harbours were the resorts of piratical adventurers of all kinds, who, under pretext of mercantile voyages, scoured the West Indies, made plundering descents upon the Spanish Main, visited even the remote Indian Seas, and then came to dispose of their booty, have their revels, and fit out new expeditions, in the English colonies.

Vanderscamp had served in this hopeful school, and, having risen to importance among the buccaneers, had pitched upon his native village and early home as a quiet, out-of-the-way, unsuspected place, where he and his comrades, while anchored at New York, might have their feasts, and concert their plans, without molestation.

At length the attention of the British Government was called to these piratical enterprises, that were becoming so frequent and outrageous. Vigorous measures were taken to check and punish them. Several of the most noted freebooters were caught and executed, and three of Vanderscamp's chosen comrades, the most riotous swashbucklers of the Wild Goose, were hanged in chains on Gibbet Island, in full sight of their favourite resort. As to

Vanderscamp himself, he and his man Pluto again disappeared, and it was hoped by the people of Communipaw that he had fallen in some foreign brawl, or been swung on some foreign gallows.

For a time, therefore, the tranquillity of the village was restored; the worthy Dutchmen once more smoked their pipes in peace, eyeing, with peculiar complacency, their old pests and terrors, the pirates, dangling and drying in the sun, on Gibbet Island.

This perfect calm was doomed at length to be ruffled. The fiery persecution of the pirates gradually subsided. Justice was satisfied with the examples that had been made, and there was no more talk of Kidd, and the other heroes of like kidney. On a calm summer evening, a boat, somewhat heavily laden, was seen pulling into Communipaw. What was the surprise and disquiet of the inhabitants, to see Yan Yost Vanderscamp seated at the helm, and his man Pluto tugging at the oar! Vanderscamp, however, was apparently an altered man. He brought home with him a wife, who seemed to be a shrew, and to have the upper hand of him. He no longer was the swaggering, bully ruffian, but affected the regular merchant, and talked of retiring from business, and settling down quietly, to pass the rest of his days in his native place.

The Wild Goose mansion was again opened, but with diminished splendour, and no riot. It is true, Vanderscamp had frequent nautical visitors, and the sound of revelry was occasionally overheard in his house; but everything seemed to be done under the rose; and old Pluto was the only servant that officiated at these orgies. The visitors, indeed, were by no means of the turbulent stamp of their predecessors; but quiet, mysterious traders, full of nods, and winks, and hieroglyphic signs, with whom, to use their cant phrase, 'everything was smug'. Their ships came to anchor at night, in the lower bay; and, on a private signal, Vanderscamp would launch his boat, and, accompanied solely by his man Pluto, would make them mysterious visits. Sometimes boats pulled in at night, in front of the Wild Goose, and various articles of merchandise were landed in the dark, and spirited away, nobody knew whither. One of the more curious of the inhabitants kept watch, and caught a glimpse of the features of some of these night visitors, by the casual glance of a lantern, and declared that he recognised more than one of the freebooting frequenters of the Wild Goose, in former times; whence he concluded that Vanderscamp was at his old game, and that this mysterious merchandise was nothing more nor less than piratical plunder. The more charitable opinion, however, was, that Vanderscamp and his comrades, having been driven from their old line of business, by the 'oppressions of Government', had resorted to smuggling to make both ends meet.

Be that as it may: I come now to the extraordinary fact, which is the butt-end of this story. It happened late one night that Yan Yost Vanderscamp was returning across the broad bay, in his light skiff, rowed by his man Pluto. He had been carousing on board of a vessel, newly arrived, and was somewhat obfuscated in intellect by the liquor he had imbided. It was a still, sultry night; a heavy mass of lurid clouds was rising in the west, with the low muttering of distant thunder. Vanderscamp called on Pluto to pull lustily, that they might get home before the gathering storm. The old negro made no reply, but shaped his course so as to skirt the rocky shores of Gibbet Island. A faint creaking overhead caused Vanderscamp to cast up his eyes, when, to his horror, he beheld the bodies of his three pot companions and brothers in iniquity dangling in the moonlight, their rags fluttering, and their chains creaking, as they were slowly swung backward and forward by the rising breeze.

'What do you mean, you blockhead!' cried Vanderscamp, 'by pulling so close to the island?'

'I thought you'd be glad to see your old friends once more,' growled the negro. 'You were never afraid of a living man; what do you fear from the dead?'

'Who's afraid?' hiccupped Vanderscamp, partly heated by liquor, partly nettled by the jeer of the negro; 'who's afraid? Hang me, but I would be glad to see them once more, alive or dead, at the Wild Goose. Come, my lads in the wind!' continued he, taking a draught, and flourishing the bottle above his head, 'here's fair weather to you in the other world; and if you should be walking the rounds tonight, odd's fish! but I'll be happy if you will drop in to supper.'

A dismal creaking was the only reply. The wind blew loud and shrill, and, as it whistled round the gallows and among the bones, sounded as if they were laughing and gibbering in the air. Old Pluto chuckled to himself, and now pulled for home. The storm burst over the voyagers, while they were yet far from shore. The rain fell in torrents, the thunder crashed and pealed, and the lightning kept up an incessant blaze. It was stark midnight before they landed at Communipaw.

Dripping and shivering, Vanderscamp crawled homeward. He was completely sobered by the storm; the water soaked from without having diluted and cooled the liquor within. Arrived at the Wild Goose, he knocked timidly and dubiously at the door, for he dreaded the reception he was to experience from his wife. He had reason to do so. She met him at the threshold, in a precious ill-humour.

'Is this a time,' said she, 'to keep people out of their beds, and to bring home company, to turn the house upside down?'

'Company?' said Vanderscamp meekly; 'I have brought no company with me, wife.'

'No indeed! they have got here before you, but by your invitation; and blessed-looking company they are, truly!'

Vanderscamp's knees smote together. 'For the love of Heaven, where are they, wife?'

'Where?—why, in the blue room upstairs, making themselves as much at home as if the house were their own.'

Vanderscamp made a desperate effort, scrambled up to the room, and threw open the door. Sure enough, there at a table, on which burned a light as blue as brimstone, sat the three guests from Gibbet Island, with halters round their necks, and bobbing their cups together, as if they were hob-or-nobbing, and trolling the old Dutch freebooter's glee, since translated into English:

> 'For three merry lads be we,
> and three merry lads be we;
> I on the land, and thou on the sand,
> And Jack on the gallows-tree.'

Vanderscamp saw and heard no more. Starting back with horror, he missed his footing on the landing-place, and fell from the top of the stairs to the bottom. He was taken up speechless, and, either from the fall or the fright, was buried in the yard of the little Dutch church at Bergen, on the following Sunday.

From that day forward, the fate of the Wild Goose was sealed. It was pronounced a *haunted house*, and avoided accordingly. No one inhabited it but Vanderscamp's shrew of a widow, and old Pluto, and they were considered but little better than its hobgoblin visitors. Pluto grew more and more haggard and morose, and looked more like an imp of darkness than a human being. He spoke to no one, but went about muttering to himself; or, as some hinted, talking with the devil, who, though unseen, was ever at his elbow. Now and then he was seen pulling about the bay alone, in his skiff, in dark weather, or at the approach of nightfall; nobody could tell why, unless on an errand to invite more guests from the gallows. Indeed, it was affirmed that the Wild Goose still continued to be a house of entertainment for such guests, and that, on stormy nights, the blue chamber was occasionally illuminated, and sounds of diabolical merriment were overheard, mingling with the howling of the tempest. Some treated these as idle stories, until on one such night—it was about the time of the equinox—there was a horrible uproar in the Wild Goose, that could not be mistaken. It was not so much the sound of revelry, however, as strife, with two or three piercing shrieks, that pervaded every part of the village. Nevertheless, no one thought of hastening to the spot. On the contrary, the honest burghers of Communipaw drew their night-caps over their ears, and buried their heads under the bed-clothes, at the thoughts of Vanderscamp and his gallows companions.

The next morning, some of the bolder and more curious under-took to reconnoitre. All was quiet and lifeless at the Wild Goose. The door yawned wide open, and had evidently been open all night, for the storm had beaten into the house. Gathering more courage from the silence and apparent desertion, they gradually ventured over the threshold. The house had indeed the air of having been possessed by devils. Everything was topsy-turvy; trunks had been broken open, and chests of drawers and corner cupboards turned inside out, as in a time of general sack and pillage; but the most woeful sight was the widow of Yan Yost Vanderscamp, extended a corpse on the floor of the blue chamber, with the marks of a deadly gripe on the windpipe.

All now was conjecture and dismay at Communipaw; and the disappearance of old Pluto, who was nowhere to be found, gave rise to all kinds of wild surmises. Some suggested that the negro had betrayed the house to some of Vanderscamp's buccaneering associates, and that they had decamped together with the booty; others surmised that the negro was nothing more nor less than a devil incarnate, who had now accomplished his ends, and made off with his dues.

Events, however, vindicated the negro from this last imputa-tion. His skiff was picked up, drifting about the bay, bottom upward, as if wrecked in a tempest; and his body was found, shortly afterward, by some Communipaw fishermen, stranded among the rocks of Gibbet Island, near the foot of the pirates' gallows. The fishermen shook their heads, and observed that old Pluto had ventured once too often to invite Guests from Gibbet Island.

THE COMPLEAT HOUSEWIFE

Richard Dehan

American regional cookery owes a great deal to the influence of the receipes brought to the continent by the first settlers from Britain and Europe. This is the theme taken up by Richard Dehan (1863–1932) in 'The Compleat Housewife', which was originally published with the sub-heading 'The story of a Battaglio Pie'. Dehan, a playwright and novelist whose real name was Clotilde I. M. Graves, actually owned a copy of the rare eighteenth-century recipe book, The Compleat Housewife, *which plays such a sinister role in the story, and later donated it to the British Museum where it can be seen to this day!*

So many male members of the British aristocracy find their feminine complements in American social circles, that I guess I won't astonish any one that reads this when I announce myself, *née* Lydia Randolph, of Savannah—described in Glatt's *Guide to the United States* as 'the chief city and commercial metropolis of Georgia'—as a slip of Southern wild orange grafted by marriage upon one of the three-hundred-year-old citron trees that are the pride of the greenhouses at Hindsway Abbey, Deershire.

Bryan—my husband is Sir Bryan Corbryan, sixteenth baronet of that name—was travelling in the Southern States when we met at the Jasper House at Thunderbolt, a fashionable early summer resort on the Warsow River. I had seen clean-made, springy, red-and-white, handsome Englishmen before, but there was something particularly distinguished about this one, or it seemed so. We were neighbours at the *table d'hôte*, and Sir Bryan had no idea how to eat green corn until I gave him an object lesson, and was wonderfully ignorant about simple things like fried egg-plant. Chicken gumbo reminded him of Indian curries, and he thought our green oysters as good as those of Ostend, but he drew the line at raw canvas-back and roast ices. We became so friendly over the *carte de jour* that Mamie—my second sister—parodied the old rhyme about love—

> 'Oh, 'tis food, 'tis food, 'tis food
> That makes the world go round!'

she sang, as we moved towards the ladies' drawing-room.

'*Grow* round, you mean,' said I scornfully, as the elevator carried us upwards, and the coloured boy grinned.

'After all,' said Mamie thoughtfully—she is considered a very brainy girl by her school professors—'without food there would be no love. People would just pine and dwindle and die. Woudn't they, Belvidere?'

'Iss, missus,' said the lift-boy, catching and biting the quarter Mamie tossed him.

Well, next day we met Sir Bryan again. After that it was usually me. We all greatly enjoyed that June holiday in our differing ways. Marma simply drank in the restfulness of a hotel with three or four hundred guests in it, after the harassing worries of a household consisting of a husband, three daughters, and seven servants, and rocked and fanned from morning until night. For us young folks there were drives, fishing parties, walking excursions, and bathing sociables. My! the time flew, but the world stood still quite suddenly, or seemed to, when Sir Bryan asked me to be his wife. He said I was the loveliest girl on the Salts or the face of Creation, and he just burned with longing to carry me home as his bride to Deershire, and walk with me under the Tudor oaks he had told me about. Tudor oaks! And a girl whose father was making a corner in cotton on Bay Street at that very moment! But Sir Bryan appeared to see no discrepancy, and that corner in cotton made me quite an heiress, as it afterwards turned out.

Well, our wedding—Bryan's and mine—was solemnised at the Savannah Episcopal Church, fronting Madison Square. It was a jessamine and tuberose wedding, cart-loads of those blooms being employed. I had privately begged Bryan to send home for the first baronet's gold inlaid suit of tilting armour to be married in; but he begged to be excused, as wrought steel is such heavy summer-wear. Otherwise, he thought, considering the almost Presidential amount of handshaking a bridegroom usually has to go through, gauntlets would be rather an advantage than otherwise.

We spent a week of our honeymoon trip at Newport and one on the ocean, and two in that Eden of the modern Adam and Eve, Paris, and then we went home to Deershire and Hindway Abbey, driving the whole way from the station under festoons of particoloured flags, while the bells rang peals of welcome, and school-children and tenants cheered, and the guard of honour supplied by the Deershire Mounted Volunteers kept up a deafening clatter behind that made the spirited horses more spirited still: and then we turned in between old stone entrance gate-pillars crested with heraldic monsters like those on Bryan's coat-of-arms, and drove along the wide avenue under those Tudor oaks Bryan had talked about, and the Abbey, a glorious old building of ancient red brick faced with white stone, rose up before us, girt with its ancient terraced walks and clipped hedges of yew and holly, and smothered in roses and wistaria to its mossy tiled roofs and the very tips of its twisted chimneys.

'Oh,' I cried to Bryan, 'never tell *me* that gentlemen in trunks and ladies in farthingales, or *beaux* in powdered periwigs and laced brocade coats, and *belles* in hoops and furbelows don't promenade here in the witching hours of night under the glimpses of the waning moon, because I simply shan't believe you!'

'So you like it?' said my husband, looking pleased and proud.

'Like it!' was all I could say; but it seemed enough for Bryan. He took my hand and led me into our home, and the red light of the great wood fire upon the gleaming hearth-dogs of the old wainscoted hall shone upon two very happy people.

Then—I just hate to think of it!—hard upon all the cheering and curtseying welcome came the blue-enveloped cablegram from Marma, with its brief, sharp, clearly worded message of misfortune. Parpa had had a spell of hemiplegia in consequence of a slump in lumber, which he had tided through, poor dear, at the expense of his health. I cried and begged to go back to the States at any risk, but Bryan was firm. I could see that if I had owned three fathers, all lying in imminent peril, it would have been just the same. *He* would go, he declared, in my place. Parpa had two daughters on the spot, and a son ought to be an appreciated change.

I loathed to let him go, but I loved him for wanting to. I put my head right down on his dear tweed shoulder and told him so. He lifted up my face and kissed it.

'You'll be brave, little woman'—I am five feet eight—'and, Phee, I know you will take care of your mistress?' he said, looking hard at my coloured maid.

'Bless Grashus, Marsa, co'se I will!' said Phee, with a wide, brilliant smile.

And within two hours my husband had driven from the door of his ancestral dwelling, and I was a grass widow. I made this observation to Phee.

'Lor', honey,' said she, 'ain' dat heaps better dan bein' de real kin'?'

I had not regarded the situation previously from this point of view, and I could not deny that Phee was in the right. But I cried myself to sleep all the same, and woke feeling pretty cheerful, and when I had bathed and dressed, and breakfasted in the morning-room that looked upon the quaintest of old-world gardens bounded with rose-hedges and centred with a splendid four-faced dial, lifted aloft upon a twisted and carven pillar, adorned with the motto, *Nunc sol nunc umbra*, I received a respectful message from Mrs Pounds, the housekeeper, asking for an audience.

She was a handsome old lady in a lace cap and rustling black silk gown, and when she had handed me a bunch of keys similar to the bunch that dangled at her waist, she launched into many revelations concerning household affairs, to which I fear I listened absently, being mentally absorbed upon the question of the arrival or non-arrival of Bryan's letter. Joy! a guardedly expressed but distinctly affectionate telegram was handed to me before Mrs Pounds had got through. Bryan had engaged a deck cabin on the biggest of the Atlantic ferries, and would steam out of Southampton Docks precisely at two p.m. A letter was following. Dear telegram! Dear letter! Dearest Bryan! My eyes swam with tears. Oh, how I meant to try to be an ideal wife! How I—

'It being a rainy morning, and unpleasant for walking or driving,' I heard Mrs Pounds say, 'and the Abbey being one of the most interesting Tudor residences in the county, perhaps her ladyship would wish to go over the house.'

The notion was invigorating.

'Why, certainly!' I exclaimed. 'I should just adore to!'

'If her ladyship permits,' said Mrs Pounds, with refrigerating stateliness, 'I will act as her ladyship's guide!'

I thanked her and rang for Phee.

'Did her ladyship wish the young black person to attend her?' Mrs Pounds inquired, with a perfectly glacial stiffness.

'I guess so,' I said; 'since she is to live in this house, she may as well learn her way about it—the sooner, the better.'

'As her ladyship pleases,' said Mrs Pounds, and unhooked her bunch of keys with a shiver of virtuous resignation. Then she said that if her ladyship permitted, she would lead the way, and glided out of the morning-room.

What a refined and subtle pleasure there lies in going over every nook and corner of a noble, ancient house, in traversing the echoing galleries, looking from the mullioned windows upon garden, terrace, alley, pleasaunce, and park, in gazing at ancient pictures painted by inspired hands long since dust, in fingering antique china and glorious old tapestries, tapping ringing corselets and engraven helms, touching gleaming or rusty weapons, looking respectfully on chairs that have upheld historical personages, and carven, canopied beds in which they have slept! That pleasure was to me intensified a thousandfold because the house was Bryan's and mine.

Phee was as enthusiastic in her way as I was, though my way was less ebullient. Her vociferations of 'Lordy! Lawd sakes! Bless grashus!' with other kindred ejaculations, seemed to pain Mrs Pounds a good deal. But presently that rustling embodiment of respectability threw open a door on the first floor landing of what she termed the west wing, saying—

'This is called Lady Deborah's room, which, although carefully kept free from dust, as her ladyship sees, has never been occupied since the death of Lady Deborah, which occurred of quinsy in the reign of King George the Second, and the lifetime of the tenth baronet, her son. The portrait in oils by Jongmans, set in panel over the chimney-piece, is considered to be a speaking likeness. Her ladyship is wearing the very cap and gown in which she is said to haunt this house, and that book that lies upon the escritoire in the window is the identical volume she is said to carry in her hand.'

'Fo' de Lawd!' I heard Phee say gutturally behind me. As for myself, I felt no chill of awe. The triumph of being the mistress of an undeniably ancient, undoubtedly ghost-haunted abbey fired my blood and thrilled my whole being. I advanced to the escritoire, an ancient, brass-handled piece of furniture with flowers in Dutch marquetry, and opened the book—a dilapidated volume in brown leather binding—at the title-page. 'The Compleat Housewife,' I read, 'or Accomplished Gentlewoman's Companion. A Collection of Prov'd Recipys in Cookery and Confectionary, With Instructions for the Making of Wines and Cordyals, Also Above 200 Family Specificks, viz. Drinks, Syrups, Salves, Oyntments and Cures For Varyous Distempers. By Eliz. Smith; The Second Edycion. London; Printed for J. Pynkerton agaynst S'Dunstan's Church in Fleet street in the Reign of His Ma'sty King George II.'

Phee had backed nervously into the corridor. With the book in my hand, I glanced a friendly adieu towards the portrait of Lady Deborah, whose mob-cap and black silk calash encircled a wrinkled yet pleasant and placid countenance, embellished with the fine streakings of rosy red one sees on a good eating apple, and ornamented by huge round spectacles rimmed with silver.

'Thank you,' I said to the housekeeper, 'but I think I have seen enough for one while. So many stairs are fatiguing to a person accustomed to elevators.'

'Her ladyship means lifts?' said Mrs Pounds, making allowances for the foreigner.

'Not at all,' I said. 'But I guess you mean elevators.' The stout brown leather volume under my arm inspired me to ask a question: 'With regard to Lady Deborah, Mrs Pounds, you will not think it a very odd question if I ask you, Have you ever seen her?'

'I will not deceive her ladyship,' said the housekeeper. 'There have been alarms among the maids and reports circulated by guests long, long before my time, and *in* my time, but never having viewed the apparition myself, I never gave such credit for an instant. Ghostly hauntings argue unquiet consciences, I have always understood; and what should a virtuous, housekeeping lady, such as Lady Deborah was, by all accounts—and the alms-houses she built and endowed are the pride of the village to his day!—have upon her conscience? Her still-room is in the wing, though now turned into a store-room; and my jams, not to say jellies, are made after recipes in ancient writing which I believe to have been hers.'

'And this must have been the cookery-book out of which she copied them,' said I, glancing into the well-thumbed volume, 'which I am going to carry away and look over.'

'Oh, my—my lady!' exclaimed Mrs Pounds, paling slightly and forgetting the third person in her perturbation. 'I beg your lady-ship's pardon, but your ladyship had best not. They do say—'

'Ah! what do they say?' I asked.

'They say,' said Mrs Pounds, nervously smoothing her muslin apron, 'that whenever or however that book is removed from this room, it is always found in its place upon Lady Deborah's escritoire next morning. Which would argue, my lady, that she fetches it back herself!'

My Southern blood ran less warmly through my veins, but I held my head up bravely.

'Has any one put that tradition to the test, to your knowledge?' I asked.

Mrs Pounds pursed her lips and shook her head.

'Very well!' I said in my stateliest manner, and I swept down the corridor, whose ancient oaken planking creaked under my high-heeled French shoes.

It still rained. Two huge fires of apple-wood burned in my great panelled drawing-room, where tall, carved cabinets of Indian ebony, Dutch marquetry, and Chinese lacquer, crowned with lovely vases and bowls of Oriental pottery, stood sentinel on the edges of the worn but beautiful Turkey carpet. I sank into a low, deep chair near the lower hearth-place and stared up at the carvings over the bossed mantelshelf, representing Dante and Beatrice, and other personages from the *Divina Commedia*, all wearing Elizabethan ruffs, trunk hose and farthingales. The rain splashed from the leaden mouths of the lion-headed water-pipes upon the flags of the terrace. It sounded like the tap-tapping of high-heeled brodequins. There was a high-backed, narrow, black oak chair on the opposite edge of the rug, an armless, stiff, uncomfortable chair, and upholstered in gilded leather—or leather that had once been gilded, fastened on with gilt nails, or nails that were once gilt, driven through little round pieces of faded green and red felt. There are articles of furniture that irresistibly evoke in the mind fancy portraits of the people who must have owned them. As I looked at that chair, its outlines became obscure. . . . Gradually enormously hooped petticoats of strong, flowered brocade, green with a shrimp-pink pattern of roses, came into view, from the border of which peeped the ends of narrow, square-toed shoes adorned with silver buckles. Languidly and without surprise my eyes travelled from these upwards to the cobweb-lace border of a very fine Swiss—I should say muslin—apron. In the centre of the apron were a pair of withered hands adorned with antique jewelled rings, and covered to the bony knuckles with black silk mittens. I followed the mittens to the lace ruffles of the sleeves, which matched the cinnamon satin peaked bodice—so tightly laced that one could hardly credit a human body being inside—trimmed with heavy silver lace and having puffed *paniers* on either side. The neck of the bodice was cut square and filled in with soft folds of muslin, and about a withered throat I caught the gleam of a gold and amber necklace. The body I have described ended in the face I had expected. The peaked chin, the pursed-up lips, the withered rose-apple cheeks, slightly pinched nose, and huge silver-rimmed spectacles—all belonged to Lady Deborah's portrait. Almost with gladness I recognised the rolled-up, powdered hair, crowned with the enormous, lappeted mob-cap. It affected me strangely that the old lady did not wear the black silk calash or bonnet, but carried it slung over her thin arm by its wide strings, and that a tortoiseshell-headed cane not represented upon the canvas—a kit-kat—leaned against a little Indian cabinet of striped calamander wood which stood near.

Bryan's family ghost—mine, by virtue of my rights as Bryan's wife! The cold chills and crisping sensations of fear were banished by the pleasant glow of pride which stole over my being as I gazed upon the dear old lady. I had so much regretted Bryan's not having any mother or pleasant elderly women relatives living for me to be cosy and confidential with—and here was one! Not living, but still visible; not to be felt, perhaps, but possibly to be heard. All this while Lady Deborah stared piercingly in my direction. She was not looking at me, but at the open book upon my knee, which had nearly slipped off it, and just as I had made up my mind to venture on a very delicate cough, she spoke, in a dry, rasping old voice—

'Child, if you thought to persuade me you was asleep, you may spare yourself the trouble, for I have seen your eyelids blink these dozen times.'

'Oh, Lady Deborah—' I began, but the old lady caught up her cane and rapped me over the knuckles—hard, with the end of it!

'Is that the way you give greeting to your elders, Mistress Impertinence?' she cried shrilly. 'Truly, I don't know where the young women are coming to! Dry your eyes, chit!'—they were watering from the smart of my rapped knuckles—'and let me see you make a proper reverence!'

Her cane was hovering. I hastily got out of my chair and made the lowest cotillon-curtsey I had ever achieved.

'Pish!' ejaculated the Lady Deborah Corbryan, with perfectly withering contempt. She waved me aside and rose to her feet. 'Fold the arms, thus, cross the legs at the knees, bend them outwards, sink—and recover.' She sank as though the floor had opened under her, she recovered—apparently upon the point of vanishing. 'Madam,' she said, with an agreeable smile which revealed a set of boxwood teeth strung on gold wire, 'I vow I am vastly happy to see your ladyship, and venture to hope that your ladyship enjoys good health?'

'Perfectly, thank you. And—dear Lady Deborah, you can't begin to know how real glad I am to see you. I was just expiring to have you drop in!' I stopped, for the old lady's eyes were beginning to snap behind her spectacles.

'Drop in,' she said severely, 'is not a seemly expression for a young woman. But be seated, child, and tell me your name. . . . Lydia Randolph, of Georgia, d'ye say? My young descendant was travelling in the East, I presume, when he encountered you? I hoped, for the honour of the Corbryans, you was a relative of the Grand Turk, or of the Sophy, at least, for our family is very ancient and honourable, let me tell you!'

After an effort or two I gave up the task of trying to persuade Lady Deborah that the State of Georgia was located in America, which she persisted in calling 'the Virginias'. She was aware that a person named Smith had devoted his life to the exploration and colonisation of New England, and that the English, in 1664, had held possesion of New York. She approved of those commodities which came from my country. American rum, cane sugar, coffee, and tobacco, and helped herself to snuff from an amethyst-topped box as she approved.

'My young descendant will take you up to London in the family coach when he returns (I had explained why I figured as a lonely bride) and initiate you into the pleasures of the gay world of fashion,' she said. 'You must see Mr Garrick in *Hamlet*, the dear, ingenious man! and Mrs Siddons as Belvidera—Lud! how she frightened me in her frenzy. And Mr Johnson—you must see that great, if uncouth, personage—and Mr Reynolds, the painter—he must be prevailed upon to paint you, for you are not ill-looking, chit, and would be positively handsome was you dressed. Dear me, what junketings I had in my time! . . . Ranelagh, Hampstead, Vauxhall, Marybone Gardens and Totnam Farm . . . where we went for syllabubs new from the cow—and the *beaux* quarrelled among them which should have the glass I had drank out of. For I was a toast and a beauty, and a sad coquette, too, my dear!' said the old lady, complacently nodding her great cap. 'Sir George Cockerell, of Bangwood—a mon'sous rake—tried to carry me off from Bath Wells in a coach with four, in broad day, for which Sir Bryan ran him through, my dear, under the second rib on the left side—and—'You've nicked it, Corbryan,' says Sir George, 'and—and I lose!—but I don't apologise,' and swooned away. And D'Arcy D'Urfée writ a poem upon a pair of fringed gloves I wore at an assembly, and my Lord Chesterfield himself hath paid me compliments. But beauty is a passing flower, child, and so I found it when I took the smallpox and rose from my bed—hung with scarlet cloth, by orders of His Majesty's own physician—to find my face all pitted and my beautiful eyebrows and lashes gone—to a hair!'

'Oh, how dreadful!' I cried. 'And—and Sir Bryan?'

'Sir Bryan took to the claret bottle in his sorrow, and to the punch-bowl,' said Lady Deborah.

'Drank!' I cried. 'Oh, how dreadful!'

'Tush, child!' snapped the old lady. 'Don't all our men drink? And our women, too, for that matter! Liquor was made for man, we have the authority of the Ancients upon it! But Sir Bryan took to other things as well—gaming at the Grecian and White's, and other follies—and I was a very unhappy woman for a time. Then I found comfort, chit—in a book with which you are acquainted!'

'The Scriptures, madam?' I said, my lips trembling with sympathy and admiration of the simple piety of the poor, deserted wife.

'My dear mother's Cookery Book. You have it in your lap, child, and by constant study of it I became the most notable housewife in my county. . . . Let me trust you have read and pondered its pages,' said Lady Deborah, nodding solemnly. ''Tis as unseemly for a young lady to enter the world without a knowledge of the art of carving, for instance, as to appear at a ball without her sacque and paniers and hooped petticoat. Thou canst unjoint a bittern, I trust? Souse a capon, unlace a crane, dismember a heron, lift a swan and rear a bustard with elegance and discretion?'

'I—I am afraid not,' I stammered, keeping the tears back with difficulty as I realised my ignorance of English social customs. 'You see, Parpa wished me to be educated in the State where I was raised, and this is my first visit to England. Possibly I could souse a capon, but swans are such vicious things, I should never dare to lift one. And as to rearing a bustard, I've never seen one yet.'

'Lydia, I vow you horrify me! No more, child, or I shall have a fit of the spleen!' Lady Deborah fanned herself with the cunningest tortoiseshell fan, and sniffed at the silver apple pricked full of holes that hung from her *châtelaine*. 'I shall have to take a dram of gentian wine or carduus-seed bruised in old sack,' she added. 'Either is sovereign, both for spleen and the vapours. Remember that, should you happen to be attacked by these distempers.'

'I'm sure I hope I shan't be!' said I fervently.

'Rue-water is also excellent in fits,' said the old lady loftily. 'My rue-water was justly celebrated. I distributed it on Thursdays to all the poor who chose to bring bottles to contain it. The juice of the plant distilled, and mingled in the strongest brown ale, a gallon and a half to a pint. 'Twas extraordinary much sought by the labourers on Sir Bryan's estate. Even more eagerly begged for and carried away was my Palsy and Surfeit Water composed of the juice of poppies, mint, cloves, and coriander seeds, mingled with crushed loaf-sugar and the best French brandy.'

'I guess so!' I said.

'Did you suffer from dropsy, child, or gout,' said Lady Deborah, 'you would find in that volume the absolute specific.'

I said I was afraid I had never had gout, or dropsy either.

'Consumption, then, or sore throat?' said Bryan's ancestress anxiously.

I had had sore throat, and allowed as much.

'For sore throat, an excellent water is made of a peck of snails laid in hyssop, bruised and distilled in new milk,' said Lady Deborah, 'and drunk fasting. By discreet use of this cordial any sore throat can be cured.'

'Why, of course,' said I. 'The mere thought of the snails would effect the cure. One would get well directly—at least, I should!'

'Then in the treatment of jaundice I have worked absolute wonders, child, with conserve of prepared earthworms, turmeric, and rhubarb, mixed. The complaint flies before it, positively,' continued Lady Deborah.

'Or the patient does,' I said to myself, but inwardly, remembering the cane.

'You never was bit by a mad dog, was you, chit?' was the astonishing question that came next.

'Good gracious, no!' I exclaimed energetically.

'Because sage, garlic, treacle, and tin filings boiled in a quart of strong mead or clary will serve in this disorder,' said Lady Deborah. 'You pour it into the party bitten by a quarter of a pint at a time.'

'I should never pour it,' I said decidedly. 'I should be too scared the party would bite *me*, and then there'd be two of us, foaming and acting awful!'

'But supposing you was pitted after a bout of smallpox, and desired to efface the scars,' continued Lady Deborah, just as though I had not spoken, 'you would find on the hundredth page the worthy Dr Burgess's recipe for a salve, of oil of tartar, pounded docks and green goose fat, considered infallible.' She sighed meditatively.

'Did you—?' I hinted, as delicately as I could.

'The ingredients must be mingled at the time of the new moon, when Venus is in the ascendant, and Jupiter is an evening star. I fear, chit,' she sighed, 'that my knowledge of astronomics was faulty. So little result I obtained that for a while I was plunged in despair.'

'I'm real sorry, dear Lady Deborah!' I said gently.

'But I despaired not long,' resumed Bryan's ancestress. 'I shut myself in my still-room and kitchen—not to weep and lament, but to work. I had ceased to be the queen of my husband's heart, but I learned to be the goddess of his table. Men are stomach first, child, and heart afterwards. What man would not lose a lover to gain so accomplished a cook as I became?' Her lean, narrow figure dilated, her expanding hoops seemed to fill the room, her keen grey eyes flamed like burning knots of lightwood behind her glasses. 'My fame was sounded throughout the county. 'Lady Deb's battaglio pie,' the bloods toasted now, instead of Lady Deb's skin of cream and roses, and Lady Deb's salmigondin, her patty royal, her cock salmon with buttered lobster, and her tansy fritters, they raved upon, instead of her bright eyes, red lips, pearly teeth, and clustered hair. And I bore it, chit! and curtsied and thanked 'em kindly, though I wished the dishes might surfeit 'em, with all my heart!'

'Oh, poor Lady Deborah!' I said, my heart in my voice.

'I blame them not now!' She lifted her lean hand. 'There are no men that love not good eating and drinking—even the saints that denied themselves; and for the women—I'm one of 'em myself, chit, or was—and know whether they sip nectar from blossoms, as they would have the silly men believe, or have at the cold chine and apple-tart in the buttery on the sly, an hour before the dinner-bell.'

She fanned herself, and producing from a deep, swinging pocket a thin, black bone rod with a little hand carved at the end, put it to its definite purpose with an energy that made me shiver. William Blake drew the ghost of a flea, I remembered, as Lady Deborah pocketed the little black rod again.

'Please go on, madam. . . . You interested me *so* much about Sir Bryan. Did he reform and become a real devoted husband again?' I asked timidly.

'I tell thee, Lyddy—they call you Lyddy for short, don't they?' resumed Lady Deborah—'he was mine from his shoe-buckle to his wig-tie. He worshipped the tiles of my kitchen—blue-and-white Dutch, and of a pretty fancy. He took glory to himself in the envy of other men; fox-hunting lords and squires, fat-jowled justices of the peace, doctors of divinity, and doctors of law. He never wearied to his dying day of the triumphs of my cookery, especially roasted sucking-pig stuffed with farced chestnuts, and battaglio pie.'

'I guess that's good, anyhow!' I said. 'It sounds so.'

'''Tis made of young chickens, squab pigeons, quails, partridges and larks,' said the ghost of Lady Deborah, drying a shadowy tear. 'You truss them, put 'em in your dish lined with rich paste, add sweetbreads, cockscombs, a quart of oysters, sliced sheep's tongues, the marrow of a dozen bones, cloves, mace, nutmegs, the yolks of hard eggs, and forced-meat balls. . . . Cover with butter, pour in a pint of cream, and draw the paste over the pie. When done—'

'It's soon done, I guess,' said I, for the recital made me feel quite hungry. 'My! it must have been rich!'

'That is why I was left a widow, my dear,' said the poor old ghost of Lady Deborah, applying the ghost of a lace pocket-handkerchief—darned—to her eyes.

'Through—through a battaglio pie?' I gasped, appalled by the savour of tragedy that rose from the dish.

'Through a battaglio pie. Mr Pope made use of the incident in his *Moral Essays*,' said Lady Deborah, 'where 'tis a jowl of salmon and

not a pie. Alas, yes! Odious as it sounds, I was the cause of my
Bryan's too early end. Year by year he had, thanks to the perfection
of my cookery, become more and more addicted to the pleasures of
the table. Racing, gaming, hunting, had become in his eyes the
mere means to gain the appetite for fresh enjoyment. His fine
complexion had become a dusky red, his chiselled features
swelled, his eyes retired behind cushions of fat, his waist
vanished, and three chins depended upon his laced cravat.'

'Oh!' I cried in horror.

'He drank hugely, but his drinking was moderate in proportion
to his eating,' said Sir Bryan's widow. 'Too well I remember the
odious event. . . . 'Twas his name-day; he had five boon companions join him at the table, I put forth all my powers fitly to
celebrate the anniversary. There could not be a prettier supper
than that my husband sat to—not if I was to die this minute—I
crave pardon, dear Lydia, for forgetting that I am dead! The first
course was roasted pike and smelts—being June, pike was in
season. Westphalia ham and young fowls, marrow puddings,
haunch of venison roasted, ragout of lamb, sweetbreads, *fricassée*
of young rabbits, umbles, a dish of mullets, roasted ducks, and
custards.'

'And six men sat down to a supper like that?' I said, feeling my
eyes opening to their widest extent.

'Nay, child, that was only the first course,' said Lady Deborah,
sniffing at her silver pomander. 'The second course was a dish of
young pheasants, a dish of soles and eels, a potato-salad, a jowl of
sturgeon, a dish of tarts and cheese-cakes, a rock of snow with
syllabubs, *and* that fatal, that ever-to-be-regretted battaglio pie!'
She wiped her eyes and fanned herself. ''Twas the crown of the
banquet. . . . Sir Bryan and his guests called for a fresh magnum of
claret when it appeared. . . . 'Gentlemen and boon companions,'
said he, with the drops of perspiration standing on his purple
forehead, and his wig pushed back—I can see it now, for I was
peeping through the old buttery dish-slide the servants scarce ever
used—'Gentlemen, here's another bumper to the health of Lady
Deborah Corbryan, the best wife and the best cook in the Four
Kingdoms!' And the gentlemen tossed down the wine, child, but
they were full to the throats. Justice Sir Barnwell Plumptree and Sir
George Cockerell (for he and Bryan became great friends in later
years), Nainby Friswell and Mr Selwyn, and Colonel Sir Harry
Firebrace of the King's Dragoons. They could only look and water
at the chops as my dear Sir Bryan cut into the battaglio pie. He
cleared a platter full and wiped up the gravy with crust. 'Do ye
check?' says he in scorn of the others. 'Do ye balk at the best dish in

Christendom? I've supped already, but I wager ye a guinea to a tester all round that I finish the dish! They took the bet, child, and Sir Bryan put ladle to dish. The ladle dropped with a clatter . . . a surge of blackish purple rose from his chins to his crown. . . . 'Death and fire!' says he, 'you've won your money!' and fell, and never uttered word again until he had been blooded by three chirurgeons one after the other, and had had the actual cautery applied. Oh, my dear! Then he came to himself, and 'Is that thou, Deb?' says he. 'I always loved thee, lass! Tell me the truth now, do I live or die?' And the doctor shook his head. 'No hope?' says Sir Bryan. 'Why, then, I'll e'en die as I have lived. Bring me the dish here—I'll e'en finish the rest o' the battaglio pie and turn the tables on Plumptree and the others.' And he did, child—he did. And I lived to wear out my weeds and con over my cookery book but a dozen years after him, and now I'm dead'—the poor lady sobbed—'I do it still, chit—I do it still! My hapless spirit is bound up in the yellow pages of that cookery book. I know not when my bondage shall cease, and rest be mine at last!'

'Poor lady—unhappy ghost!' I cried. 'Will nothing bring you peace?'

You would have known you had been interviewing a ghost by the fading outlines of Lady Deborah's form and features, and the way in which the black oak chair upholstered with old gilt leather showed through the hooped skirts of green and pink brocade. Her vanishing lips framed but two other words . . .

'Battaglio pie,' she said, and was gone in an instant; and with a crash the cookery book fell to the floor, and I sat up, wondering whether I had been dreaming? On the whole, I guessed I had not. When I picked up the prostrate cookery book, I knew I had not, for one of the many-time dogs'-eared pages was doubled over in a perfectly fresh place, *and the page bore the famous recipe for battaglio pie.*

The post that followed brought my promised letter. The next day brought a marconigram from Bryan. Marconi is hardly the language of love, but it did at a pinch. Parpa was no worse, it said, and I was not to be anxious. Indeed, by the time the liner picked up her pilot off Sandy Hook, the bulletins were so favourable that Bryan decided to return right away, Parpa being quite out of danger. He did return—one of our great Atlantic ferryboats being on the point of starting—and I marconied a message which hit the ship 1,065 miles west of the Lizard, to say I was well and happy, and learning to cook!

That was so. I had respectfully replaced Lady Deborah's cookery book upon her escritoire, after copying the fatal and famous recipe for battaglio pie. . . . I had made friends with the ruler of the Abbey kitchen, and under her tuition was rapidly mastering the secret of flaky pastry.

June was scarcely over our heads; all the ingredients were procurable, though the heavy groan that burst from the head gamekeeper's bosom, when I demanded three young partridges, I never shall forget. He brought them, though, and I had but to amass the quail, the squab pigeon, the cockscombs, sweetbreads, oysters, sheep's tongues, and so forth, from other sources. Thus on the afternoon previous to Bryan's return, I lined a stately dish with rich pie-paste, I piled in all the good things, added the eggs, forcemeat, spices, cream and butter, and drew the cover over all, ornamenting it with devices cut with antique pewter moulds that Lady Deborah herself may have used. I glazed the outside with egg-white. And then I saw the pie slide into a gentle oven, and knew my task would soon be done. An hour later, as I lay resting in my favourite corner of the spindle-legged, tapestry-covered sofa in the long drawing-room, I had a second visit from Lady Deborah. She wore her black silk calash this time, and behind her great silver-rimmed spectacles her eyes snapped and sparkled with a joy that was—was it malign? She spread out her rustling brocade skirts as I rose up, and responded to my hesitating curtsey with the grandest cheese I had ever seen.

'I am vastly obleeged, Lydia,' she said, smiling her old cheeks into creases. 'You have behaved monstrous genteelly, child, and I feel that I shall owe my freedom to your generosity. I have taken measures that the reputation of the Abbey shall not suffer, as there is a lamentable lack of *ton* about a family residence without a ghost. Sir Umphrey, who got grant of the demesne from King Henry VIII, and, as you may have heard, murdered the abbot who took exception to the grant, has arranged to haunt the inhabited wings as well as the shut-up portion. You have also a third share in a banshee brought into the family by one of the Desmonds, who intermarried with us in 1606, and there is a hugely impressive death-watch in the wainscoting of your room. Therefore, I need have no scruples in taking the change of air so necessary for vapours.'

She took her great calash and spreading brocades away. I forgot her—forgot the pie—forgot everything an hour later, in the joy of Bryan's arrival. With the aid of the housekeeper and by the advice of the cook, I had had prepared a real traveller's dinner, and at last my battaglio pie was placed upon the table before the master of the house.

Such a pie! a mountain of golden flaky crust, exhaling delicious, tempting, savoury odours. I looked across it at Bryan, and laughed in sheer delight at his astonishment.

'So this is the joke you have been keeping to yourself all the evening. Lydia, you little witch!' said Bryan, laughing too. 'A pie—a monster pie—and a savoury pie, too, made by your own hands, what?' He sniffed the delicious steam with expanded nostrils and filled his glass with port. 'Here's to the health of Lady Lydia Corbryan,' he cried gaily, 'the best wife and the best cook in the Four Kingdoms—not to mention the Realms beyond the Seas!'

Where had I heard those words—most of them—before? I grew dizzy as Bryan seized the silver pastry-knife and spoon and plunged into the depths of the battaglio pie. . . . A change seemed to have come over him, the outlines of his face and figure seemed to waver and alter as I gazed speechlessly, waiting for something to come. . . .

'I've dined already,' my husband cried in a thick voice that frightened me, 'but I'll bet you a sovereign to a sixpence that I finish the dish!'

'Bryan!' I screamed. 'Bryan!' and barely recognised him to whom I appealed. That crimson face, with the moist shine of perspiration glossing it, the powdered wig pushed back from the swollen forehead, the piggish, twinkling eyes, gross, flabby mouth, and three chins dropping over the flowing lace cravat. . . . Strange to me . . . all strange, yet so horribly, horribly, familiar! I must have risen from my chair and rushed to him, for I found myself clinging to a man's arm and crying, 'Don't touch it! If you love me, Bryan, don't touch it!' over and over again.

'Of course not, if you don't wish it, little woman!' said the dear familiar voice. Bryan was holding me, and the face I loved was pressed comfortingly to mine. 'Look here, Pet, I didn't mean to vex you. I'll throw it out of the window if you want me to.'

'Y-yes!' I sobbed, with chattering teeth. 'Th-throw it out . . . do, please!' and Bryan heaved up the huge pie-dish in his muscular hands.

'Open the window, please,' he said, and I hurried to obey. The casement swung wide upon a square of star-jewelled darkness. . . . Did I hear a shrill, thin, eerie scream? Did I hear another casement crash open, somewhere in the west wing, as the battaglio pie was hurled into the night?

I asked Phee next morning to accompany me to Lady Deborah's room. The intrepid girl followed, only delaying to wind a thread of red marking-cotton nine times round her left thumb, and tuck her Aunt Dinah's hymn-book into what she termed 'de bosom' of her gown. As I climbed the stairs, threaded recollected passages, and with just a little qualm of nervousness opened the not-to-be-forgotten door, a blast of cold air saluted me. The casement swung open, fragments of its shattered panes still jagging in the leads, and a yellowish snow of torn papers littered the floor. They were fragments of the cookery book, torn to atoms by a force unknown. . . . What force? The portrait of Lady Deborah gazed stonily from over the fireplace and made no answer.

What would have happened had Bryan indulged the hereditary instinct that led him to hunger, even after a full meal, for battaglio pie? Would he have ended existence like the unlucky glutton, his ancestor, in stertorous coma, unrelieved by depletion? Should I have died of grief, and haunted the Abbey in Lady Deborah's stead, a disconsolate, widowed shade, continually brooding over a battered edition of the *Compleat Housewife*? Who can say?

But it smelt wonderfully good. There have been hungry moments when I have half regretted not tasting it, the sole achievement in the cookery line I am destined ever to accomplish.

I have never seen Lady Deborah since!

(The recipes quoted by the ghost of Lady Deborah have been taken from a copy of THE COMPLEAT HOUSEWIFE *in the author's possession, dated 1733.)*

THE CASE OF MR LUCRAFT

Walter Besant and James Rice

The supernatural element is also to be found in this next story, 'The Case of Mr Lucraft', which has been described by several critics as a mixture of Charles Dickens and F. Anstey at their respective bests! The story of a penniless young man who sells his one outstanding asset—an enormous appetite—and then has to suffer the excesses of the purchaser, was first published anonymously in the magazine Once A Week *in 1875, but such was its reception by readers that the authors, Sir Walter Besant (1836–1901) and James Rice (1843–1882), owned up and were acclaimed both in the national press and by that most renowned of all writers on cookery, Mrs Beeton.*

I have more than once told the story of the only remarkable thing which ever happened to me in the course of a longish life, but as no one ever believed me, I left off telling it. I wish, therefore, to leave behind me a truthful record, in which everything shall be set down, as near as I can remember it, just as it happened. I am sure I need not add a single fact. The more I consider the story, the more I realise to myself my wonderful escape and the frightful consequences which a providential accident averted from my head, the more reason I feel to be grateful and humble.

I have read of nothing similar to my own case. I have consulted books on apparitions, witchcraft, and the power of the devil as manifested in authentic history, but I have found absolutely nothing that can in any way compare with my own case. If there be any successor to my Mr Ebenezer Grumbelow, possessed of his unholy powers, endowed with his fiendish resolve and his diabolical iniquity of selfishness, this plain and simple narrative may serve as a warning to young men situated as I was in the year 1823. Except as a moral example, indeed, I see no use in telling the story at all.

I have never been a rich man, but I was once very poor, and it is of this period that I have to write.

As for my parentage, it was quite obscure. My mother died when I was still a boy; and my father, who was not a man to be proud of as a father, had long before run away from her and disappeared. He was a sailor by profession, and I have heard it rumoured that sailors of his time possessed a wife in every port, besides a few who lived, like my mother, inland; so that they could vary the surroundings when they wished. The wives were all properly married in church too, and honest women, every one of them. What became of my father I never knew, nor did I ever inquire.

I went through a pretty fair number of adventures before I settled down to my first serious profession. I was travelling companion and drudge to an itinerant tinker, who treated me as kindly as could be expected when he was sober. When he was drunk he used to throw the pots and pans at my head. Then I became a cabin-boy, but only for a single voyage, on board a collier. The ship belonged to a philanthropist, who was too much occupied with the wrongs of the West Indian niggers to think about the rights of his own sailors; so his ships, insured far above their real value, were sent to sea to sink or swim as it might please Providence. I suppose no cabin-boy ever had so many kicks and cuffs in a single voyage as I had. However, my ship carried me safely from South Shields to the port of London. There I ran away, and I heard afterwards that on her return voyage the *Spanking Sally* foundered with all hands. In the minds of those who knew the captain and his crew personally, there were doubtless, as in mine, grave fears as to their ultimate destination. After that I became steward in an Atlantic sailing packet for a couple of years; then clerk to a bogus auctioneer in New York; cashier to a store; all sorts of things, but nothing long. Then I came back to England, and not knowing what to do with myself, joined a strolling company of actors in the general utility line. It was not exactly promotion, but I liked the life; I liked the work; I liked the applause; I liked wandering about from town to town; I even liked, being young and a fool, the precarious nature of the salary. Heaven knows mine was small enough; but we were a cheery company, and one or two members subsequently rose to distinction. If we had known any history, which we did not, we might have remembered that Molière himself was once a stroller through France. Some people think it philosophical to reflect, when they are hard up, how many great men have been hard up too. It would have brought no comfort to me. Practically I felt little inconvenience from poverty, save in the matter of boots. We went share and share alike, most of us, and there was always plenty to eat even for my naturally gigantic appetite. Juliet always used to reckon me as equal to four.

Juliet was the manager's daughter—Julie Kerrans, acting as Miss Juliet Alvanley. She was eighteen and I was twenty-three, an inflammable and romantic time of life. We were thrown a good deal together too, not only off the stage but on it. I was put into parts to play up to her. I was Romeo when she played her namesake, a part sustained by her mother till even she herself was bound to own that she was too fat to play it any longer; she was Lady Teazle and I was Charles Surface; she was Rosalind and I Orlando; she was Miranda and I Ferdinand; she was Angelina and I Sir Harry Wildair. We were a pair, and looked well in love scenes. Looking back dispassionately on our performances, I suppose they must have been as bad as stage-acting could well be. At least, we had no training, and nothing but a few fixed rules to guide us; these, of course, quite stagey and conventional. Juliet had been on the stage all her life, and did not want in assurance; I, however, was nervous and uncertain. Then we were badly mounted and badly dressed; we were ambitious, we ranted, and we tore a passion to rags. But we had one or two good points—we were young and lively. Juliet had the most charming of faces and the most delicious of figures—mind you, in the year 1823, girls had a chance of showing their figures without putting on a page's costume. Then she had a soft, sweet voice, and pretty little coquettish ways, which came natural to her, and broke through the clumsy stage artificialities. She drew full houses; wherever we performed, all the men, especially all the young officers, used to come after her. They wrote her notes, they lay in wait for her, they sent her flowers; but what with old Kerrans and myself, to say nothing of the other members of the company, they might as well have tried to get at a Peri in Paradise. I drew pretty well too. I was— a man of seventy and more may say so without being accused of vanity—I was a good-looking young fellow; you would hardly believe what quantities of letters and *billets-doux* came to me. I had dozens, but Juliet found and tore them up. There they were; the note on rose-coloured note-paper with violet ink, beginning with 'Handsomest and noblest of men', and ending with 'Your fair unknown, Araminta'. There was the letter from the middle-aged widow with a taste for the drama and an income; and there was the vilely spelled note from the foolish little milliner who had fallen in love with the Romeo of a barn. Perhaps ladies are more sensible now. At all events, their letters were thrown away upon me, because I was in love already, head over ears, and with Juliet.

Juliet handed over her notes to her father, who found out their writers, and made them take boxes and bespeak plays. So that all Juliet's lovers got was the privilege of paying more than other people, for the girl was as good as she was pretty—a rarer combination of qualities on the stage fifty years ago than now. She was tall and, in those days, slender. Later on she took after her mother; but who would have thought that so graceful a girl would ever arrive at fourteen stone? Her eyes and hair were black—eyes that never lost their lustre; and hair which, though it turned grey in later years, was then like a silken net, when it was let down, to catch the hearts of lovers. Of course she knew that she was pretty; what pretty woman does not? and of course, too, she did not know and would not understand the power of her own beauty; what pretty woman does? And because it was the very worst thing she could do for herself, she fell in love with me.

Her father knew it and meant to stop it from the beginning: but he was not a man to do things in a hurry, and so we went on in a fool's paradise, enjoying the stolen kisses, and talking of the sweet time to come when we should be married. One night—I was Romeo—I was so carried away with passion that I acted for once naturally and unconventionally. There was a full house; the performance was so much out of the common that the people were astonished and forgot to applaud. Juliet caught the infection of my passion, and for once we acted well, because we acted from the heart. Never but that once, I believe, has *Romeo and Juliet* been performed by a pair who felt every word they said. It was only in a long, low room, a sort of corn exchange or town hall, in a little country town, but the memory of that night is sacred to me.

You know the words—

> See, how she leans her cheek upon her hand!
> O, that I were a glove upon that hand,
> That I might touch that cheek!

And these—

> 'O, for a falconer's voice,
> To lure this tassel-gentle back again!
> Bondage is hoarse and may not speak aloud,
> Else would I tear the cave where Echo lies,
> And make her airy tongue more hoarse than mine
> With repetition of my Romeo!'

Splendidly we gave them.

Why, even now, old as I am, the recollection of these lines and the thought of that night warm my heart still and fire my feeble pulses. I have taught them to my grandchild. She takes after my poor Juliet, and would succeed on the stage, if only her father would let her. But he is strait-laced. Ah! he should have seen the temptations which beset a girl on the stage in my time. We are Puritans now, almost—

And a good thing, too. It is time for me to own it.

Well—old Kerrans was in the front, looking after the money, as usual, and always with one eye on the stage, to see how his daughter was getting on. He was puzzled, I think, to make out the meaning of the unaccustomed fire, but he came to the conclusion that if Juliet was going to remain Miss Juliet, instead of becoming Mrs Mortimer Vavasseur (my stage name), he had better interfere at once.

So after the play, and over the domestic supper-table, he had it out with his daughter.

Juliet swore that nothing should induce her to marry another man.

'Bless the girl!' said her father; 'I don't want you to marry anybody at all.'

Juliet declared that she never, never would forget me.

'I don't want you to forget him,' Mr Kerrans replied. 'Remember him as much as you like.'

Juliet announced her intention of retiring from the stage and going into a convent. There were no convents in England in 1823, so that the threat was not so serious as it would be now.

Her father promised her that when the company passed by any respectable convent on the road, he would certainly knock at the door and inquire about the accommodation and the terms.

'Lor!' he said, caressing his weeping daughter, 'do you think I want to be cruel to you, my pretty? Not a bit. Let young Lucraft go and prove himself a man, and he shall have you. But, you see, it wouldn't do to add to the expenses of the company just now, with business so bad and all, would it, my dear? Why, you might be confined in a twelvemonth, and laid by for half the year ever after, with a troop of young children. Where should we be then?'

The next day was Saturday. As usual, I went into the treasury to draw my money, and found the old fellow with rather a red face, and a hesitation in his manner.

He told me the whole story, just as I have told it to you. And then he gave me my dismissal.

'Look here,' he said, handing me the money, 'you are a capital young fellow, Lucraft, and a likely actor. There's merit in you. But I

can't have you spoiling my Juliet for the stage. So I'm going to put
her up without you. After a bit I daresay I shall find another
Romeo. You get away to London and find another engagement—
there's a week's pay in advance—and when Juliet is married, or
when you get rich, or when anything happens to make things
different, why, you see, we shall all be glad to see you back. Go and
make your farewells to Juliet, and don't be more sentimental than
you can help. Good-bye, my boy, and good luck to you.'

Good luck! Had he known the kind of luck which awaited me!

I sought my girl, and found her crying. I remember that we
forgot all the fine verses of Shakespeare, and just put our faces
close to each other and cried together.

It did seem hard upon both of us. We were really and truly in
love, and that in a good, honest, determined way. To me there was
no other girl in the world except Juliet. To her there was no other
man besides Luke Lucraft. We had come to an understanding for
three months, and had been quietly dropping deeper and deeper
in love during all that time.

And now we were to part.

'Don't forget me, dear Luke,' she sobbed. 'There are lots of
prettier and finer girls in the world than I am, who will try to take
away your love from me. I wish I could kill the creatures!' she
added, stamping her foot.

Juliet always had a high and generous spirit. I like women to
have a high spirit.

'And will you have no admirers, Juliet?' I replied. 'Why, half the
town'—we were in Lancaster then—'half the town is at your feet
already. I intercepted two love-letters yesterday, and I kicked the
grocer's apprentice the day before for trying to get Mrs Mould to
give you a *billet-doux* from himself. Come, dear, we will trust one
another. I will try and prove myself a man—get an engagement,
make a name on the London stage, and come back with money and
an offer to act Romeo to your Juliet at Drury Lane. Think of that, my
dearest, and dry your eyes. Your father does not object to me, you
know; he only wants me to make an income. Come, Juliet, let us
say good-bye. It is only for a short time, and I shall come back with
all sorts of reasons in my pocket for persuading your father's
consent.'

So we parted, with many more promises of trust and fidelity,
and after breaking a sixpenny-bit between us. Juliet's piece is
buried with her; mine is hanging at my heart, and will be, before
long, buried with me beside her.

Oh! the weary journey to London in those days, especially
outside the coach, and for a poor man not encumbered with too

many wraps. However, I arrived at length, and found myself in the streets that are supposed to be paved with gold, with a couple of sovereigns in my pocket.

But I was brimful of hope. London was a kindly step-mother, who received adopted sons by the thousand, and led them to fame and wealth. I thought of Garrick, of Dick Whittington, and all the rest who came up to town poorer, far poorer than myself, and took comfort. I secured a lodging at a modest rent, and made my way to Drury Lane—the stage door.

I found no opening at Drury Lane; not even a vacancy for a supernumerary. There were not many London theatres in 1823, and I found the same thing everywhere—more applications than places to give.

I tried the Greenwich and the Richmond theatres with the same ill-success.

Then I endeavoured to get a country engagement, but I even failed there. I had no friends to recommend me, and my single experience with Kerrans's strolling troupe did not tell so much in my favour as I had hoped.

My ambition naturally took a town flight. I had intended to make my appearance on the metropolitan stage as Romeo, my favourite part, and at once to take the town by storm. I was prepared to give them an intelligent and novel interpretation of Hamlet. And I was not unwilling to undertake Macbeth, Othello, or even Prince Hal.

When these hopes became evidently grounded on nothing but the baseless fabrication of a dream, I resolved on beginning with second parts. Horatio, Mercutio, Paris, were, after all, characters worthy the work of a rising artist.

Again there seemed no chance.

The stage always wants young men of general utility. I would go anywhere and take anything. I offered to do so, but although hopes were held out to me by the theatrical agent, somehow he had nothing at the moment in his gift. Nothing: not even a vacancy fer a tragedian at Richardson's Show; not even a chance for Bartholomew Fair.

It took me a fortnight to run down the scale from Hamlet, say, to Francis the warder. While I passed through this descending gamut of ambition, my two sovereigns were melting away with a rapidity quite astonishing.

The rent took five shillings: that was paid in advance. Then I was extravagant in the matter of eating, and took three meals a day, finding that not enough to satisfy my vigorous appetite. Once or twice, too, I paid for admission to the pit, and saw, with a sinking heart, what real acting means. My heart failed, because I perceived that I had to begin all over again, and from the very bottom of the ladder.

Then I had to buy a new pair of boots. It was always a trouble to me, the rapid wearing out of leather.

And then there was something else; and then one morning I found myself without a sixpence in my pocket. And then I began for the first time to become seriously alarmed about the future.

I had one or two things which I could pawn—a watch, a waistcoat, a few odds and ends in the way of wardrobe, and a few books—on the proceeds of them I lived for a whole week; but at last, after spending twopence in the purchase of a penny loaf and a saveloy for breakfast, I found myself not only penniless, but also without the means of procuring another penny at all, because I had nothing left to pawn.

Many a young fellow has found himself in a similar predicament, but I doubt whether anyone ever became so desperately hungry as I did on that day. I recollect that, having rashly eaten up my sausage before eight o'clock, I felt a sinking towards twelve; it was aggravated by the savoury smell of roast meat which steamed from the cookshops and dining-rooms as I walked along the streets. About one o'clock I gazed with malignant envy on the happy clerks who could go in and order platefuls of the roast and boiled which smoked in the windows, and threw a perfume more delicious than the sweetest strains of music into the streets where I lingered and looked. And at two I observed the diners come out again, walking more slowly, but with an upright and satisfied air, while I—the sinking had been succeeded by a dull gnawing pain— was slowly doubling up. At half-past two I felt as if I could bear it no longer. I had been walking about, trying different offices for a clerkship. I might as well have asked for a partnership. But I could walk no more. I leaned against a post—it was in Bucklersbury— opposite a dining-room, where hares, fowls, and turkeys were piled in the window among a boundless prodigality and wealth of carrots, turnips, and cauliflowers, till my senses swam at the contemplation. I longed for a cauldron in which to put the whole contents of the shop front, and eat them at one Gargantuan repast. My appetite, already alluded to, was hereditary; one of the few things I can remember of my mother was a constant complaint that my father used to eat her out of house and home. To be sure, from other scraps of information handed down by tradition, I have reason to believe that the word eating was used as a figure of speech—the part for the whole—and included drinking. I was good at both, and as a trencherman I had been unsurpassed, as I said above, in the company, the dear old company among whom I have so often eaten beefsteak and fried onions with Juliet. The door of the place opened now and then to let a hungry man enter or a full man go out, and I caught a glimpse of the interior. Dining-rooms were not called restaurants in those days. They had no gilding, no bright paint, no pretty barmaids, and no silver-plated forks and spoons. Nor were they brilliant with gas. All London—that is, all working London—dined before four o'clock; the clerks from twelve to two, and the principals, except a few of the big wigs, from two to four. The cheaper rooms were like one or two places still to be found in Fleet Street. There were sanded floors; there were hard benches; you had your beer out of pewter, not plated tankards; there was no cheap claret, and the popular ideal of wine was a strong and fiery port. Also, candles stood upon the tables—not wax candles, but tallow, with long wicks which required snuffing. They dropped a good deal of mutton fat about the table, and it was not uncommon to find yourself eating a little tallow with your bread, which was not nice even to men of a strong stomach. Finally, you had steel forks, which are just as good, to my thinking, as plated silver, and more easily cleaned.

I stood by the post and watched with hungry eyes. From within I heard voices, stifled voices, as those sent up a pipe, calling for roast beef with plenty of brown—good heavens! plenty of brown; roast mutton, underdone—I loved my mutton underdone; boiled beef with suet-pudding and fat—I always took a great deal of pudding and fat with my boiled beef; roast veal and bacon with stuffing—a dish for the gods; calves' head for two—I could have eaten calves' head for a dozen; with orders pointing to things beyond my hungry imagination—hunger limits the boundaries of fancy— puddings, fish, soup, cheese, and such delicacies. Alas! I wanted the solids. I felt myself growing feebler; I became more and more doubled up; I had thoughts of entering this paradise of the hungry, and, after eating till I could eat no longer, calmly laying down my knife and fork and informing the waiter that I had no money. There was a farce in which I had once played where the comic actor sent for the landlord, after a hearty meal, and asked him what he would do in case a stranger, after ordering and eating his dinner, should declare his inability to pay. 'Do, sir?' cried the host; 'I should kick him across the street.' 'Landlord,' said the low comedian, and it always told—'Landlord,' he used to rise up slowly as he spoke, and solemnly draw aside his coat-tails, turning his face in the direction of the street-door—'landlord, I'll trouble you.' I used to play the landlord.

It struck half-past three; the dead gnawing of hunger was followed by a sharp pain, irritating and much more unpleasant.

The crowd of those who entered had been followed by the crowd of those who came out and the heaven of hungry men was nearly empty again. I gazed still upon the turkeys and the hares, but with a lack-lustre eye, for I was nearly fainting.

Presently there came down the street an elderly gentleman, bearing before him, like a Lord Mayor in a French tale, his enormous abdomen: he had white hair, white eyebrows, white whiskers, and a purple face. He walked very slowly, as if the exertion might prove apoplectic, and leaned upon a thick stick. As he passed the shop he looked in at the window and wagged his head. At that moment I groaned involuntarily. He turned round and surveyed me. I suppose I presented a strange appearance, leaning against the post, with stooping figure and tightly-buttoned coat. He had big projecting eyes flushed with red veins, which gave him a wolfish expression.

'Young man,' he said, not benignantly at all, but severely, 'you look ill. Have you been drinking?'

I shook my head.

'I am only hungry,' I said, telling the truth because I was too far gone to hide it, 'I am only hungry; that is the matter with me.'

He planted his stick on the ground, supporting both his hands upon the gold head, and wagged his head again from side to side with a grunting sound in his throat like the sawing of bones.

Grunt! 'Here's a pretty fellow for you!' Grunt! 'Hungry, and he looks miserable.' Grunt! 'Hungry, and he groans.' Grunt! 'Hungry—the most enviable position a man can be in—and he dares to repine at his lot.' Grunt! 'What are the lower classes coming to next, I wonder? Aren't you ashamed of yourself? Aren't you a model of everything that is ungrateful and'—grunt!—'and flying in the face of Providence? He lives in a land of victuals. London is a gigantic caravan, full of the most splendid things, the most glorious things to eat and drink; it only wants an appetite; and he's got that, and he laments!'

'What is the use of an appetite if you have no money to satisfy it with?'

Grunt! 'Is it a small appetite, as a rule, or is it a large appetite?'

'Large,' I replied. 'It is an awkward thing for a poor beggar like me to have such a devil of a twist. I was born with it. Very awkward just now.'

'Come with me, young man,' he grunted. 'Go before me. Don't talk, because that may interfere with the further growth of your appetite. Walk slowly, and keep your mouth shut close.'

He came behind me, walking with his chuckle and grunt.

'So. What a fine young fellow it is!' Grunt! 'What room for the development of the Alderman's Arch! What a backbone for the support of a stomach! What shoulders for a dinner-table, and what legs to put under it! Heavens! what a diner might be made of this boy if he only had money.' Grunt! 'Youth and appetite—health and hunger—and all thrown away upon a pauper! What a thing, what a thing! This way, young man.'

Turning down a court leading out of Bucklersbury, he guided me to a door, a little black portal, at which he stopped; then stooping to a keyhole of smaller size than was generally used in those days, he seemed to me to blow into it with his mouth; this was absurd, of course, but it seemed so to me. The door opened. He led the way into a passage, which, when the door shut behind us, as it did of its own accord, was pitch dark. We went up some stairs, and on the first landing the old gentleman, who was wheezing and puffing tremendously, opened another door, and led me into a room. It was a large room, resplendent with the light of at least forty wax candles. The centre was occupied by a large dining-table laid for a single person. Outside it was broad daylight, for it was not yet four o'clock.

'Sit down, young man, sit down,' puffed my host. 'Oh dear! oh dear! Sit down, do. I wish I was as hungry as you.'

I sat down in the nearest chair, and looked round the room. The first thing I remarked was that I could not see the door by which we had been admitted. The room was octagonal, and on every side stood some heavy piece of furniture; a table with glass, a case of bookshelves, a sofa, but no door. My hear began to go round as I continued my observations. There was no window either, nor was there any fireplace. Then I felt a sudden giddiness, and I suppose I fell backwards on my chair. It was partly the faintness of hunger, but partly it was the strange room, and that old man glaring at me with his great wolfish eyes.

When I recovered I was lying on a sofa, and soft cold fingers were bathing my head, and pressing a perfumed handkerchief to my lips. I opened my eyes suddenly and sat up completely recovered. At the foot of the sofa stood my entertainer.

'Easy with him, Boule-de-neige; make him rest for a moment. Perhaps his hunger has been too much for him.'

I turned to see who Boule-de-neige was. He was a negro of the blackest type, an ancient and withered as some old ourang of tropical woods; his cheeks hung in folds, and his skin seemed too much for his attenuated body; his wool was white, and his gums were almost toothless; and his nose so flattened with age as to be almost invisible, looking at him as I was looking, in profile. His hands were as soft as any woman's, but icy cold; and his eyes were red and fiery.

'Boule-de-neige, what do you think of him?'

'Him berry fine young man, massa: him beautiful young man; got lubly abbatite develoffed, I tink; him last long time, much longer time dan last oder young man. Cluck! Him poor trash, dat young man; dam poor trash; use up and go to debbel in a month. Cluck! Dis young man got lubly stumjack, strong as bull. Cluck-cluck! How much you tink him eat tonight?'

'We shall see, Boule-de-neige. We will try him with a simple dinner, and then pronounce on his performances. Young men do not always come up to their professions. But he looks well, and perhaps, Boule-de-neige—perhaps—ah!' He nodded with a deep sigh.

'What time massa dine himself?'

'I don't know,' the old gentleman answered, with another heavy sigh. 'Perhaps not till nine o'clock; perhaps not then. It all depends on this youth. Vanish, Boule-de-neige, and serve.'

There was evidently something in my host's mind by the way he sighed. Why did it depend upon me? And did Boule-de-neige go through the floor? Did the table sink when he disappeared, and come up loaded with dishes? It seemed so.

I sprang from the couch. The sight and smell of the food brought back my raging hunger.

'Let me eat!' I cried.

'You shall. One moment first—only a single moment. Young man, tell me again and explicitly the nature and extent of your appetite. Be truthful, oh, be truthful! Our little tongues should never lie for mutton-chop or apple-pie. You know the hymn. I hope you have been religiously brought up, and know that hymn.'

'I've got a devil of an appetite. What is there to lie about?'

'My dear young friend, there are many kinds of appetites. Yours may be fierce at first and promise great things, and then end in a miserably small performance. I have known such, and mourned to see them. Is it a lasting appetite, now? Is it steady through a long dinner? Is it regular in its recurrence?'

'You shall see something of my performance,' I laughed, insensate wretch. 'You shall see. I never had a long dinner in my life, because I always made short work of mine. It is steady through a good many pounds of steak, and as regular as a clock.'

'That is always something. Steak is as healthy a test as I know. Is it, secondly, an appetite that recovers itself quickly? That is very important. Is it a day-by-day or an hour-by-hour appetite? Is it good at all times of the day?'

'Alas, I wish it were not!'

'Hush, young man; do not blaspheme! Tell me, if you eat your fill now—it is half-past four—when do you think you might be ready again?' His eyes glistened like a couple of great rubies in the candlelight, and his hands trembled.

'I should say about eight. But I might do something light at seven, I daresay. Just now I feel as if I could eat a mountain.'

'He feels as if he could eat a mountain! Wonderful are the gifts of Providence! My dear young friend, I am very thankful—deeply thankful—that I met you. Sit down, and let me take the covers off for you; I long to see you eat. This is a blessed day—a truly blessed day! I will wait upon you myself. No one else. Boule-de-neige, vanish!'

As he was about to take off the covers he stopped short.

'Stay. You are without occupation?'

'I can get none.'

'You are of any trade?'

'I am an actor.'

'A bad trade—an un-Christian trade. Actors are vagabonds by Act of Parliament. Actors can never be in a state of grace. I shall be happy in being a humble instrument in removing you from a calling fatal to the Christian warrior. Why did you leave your last situation? No dishonesty? No embezzlement? No tampering with accounts?'

'Sir, I have always been an honest man. And, besides, I have never been tempted by the handling of other people's money.'

'Ha! You have got no wife?'

'No, sir; I am unmarried.'

'You have got no—I trust I am taking to my bosom no deceiver of women. You are not the father of an illegitimate offspring, I hope and pray.'

'No, sir; I am not.'

'Young man, you are about to enter upon a most serious act, perhaps the most serious act of your life, and these questions may appear to you trivial and tedious. As a Christian, and a member of the congregation of Mr—But never mind; you are hungry now, and wish to eat. We will talk after dinner.'

He took off the covers. The table was spread with a dozen different dishes, all served up together. Others I noticed, standing with bottles and decanters, on a large sideboard. As my generous benefactor removed the silver covers, his face, which had assumed during his questioning an austere gravity, suddenly lit up, and he laughed as the perfume of the hot food mounted to his nostrils. He seemed all at once a different man.

'Gently, gently, my dear young friend. Here is a dinner fit for a king; fit for *me*, if I could eat it. Oh! my dainty Boule-de-neige! Ha! is it right to waste such a dinner upon a youth whose only dreams are of a sufficiency of steak? Young man, in after years—ahem!— in after days you will remember this dinner. You will recall every item in this delicious bill of fare which Boule-de-neige has set before you. Let me teach you to eat it properly. Weigh your morsels.'

Heaven! how I cursed his delay. He kept one great hand between me and the dishes, for fear, I suppose, that I should pounce upon them and clear them off all at once.

'Patience, patience. Consider each mouthful. Try to be thankful that cooks have brought their divine art to such perfection. Carry back your thoughts to—grunt—to time when all mankind fed upon imperfectly cooked steak. Think that all the treasures of the East and West have been ransacked to furnish for me this meal, and that you will never, never, never see such a dinner again as long as you live.'

At all events, I never saw such a meal again as long as *he* lived.

'We will now,' he said, with a backward wave of his right hand, 'consider dinner as a science.'

'Oh, sir!' I exclaimed, 'I am so hungry.'

'It's beautiful to see you hungry, but I must not let you hurry. Eat as much as you like when you begin, but gently, gently—easily and gently. Think of the future. Think of ME.'

I stared at him in wonder.

'Think of you, sir?'

'Why, what would happen to me if you really destroyed your appetite, or even yourself in swallowing a bone?'

I thought he must be mad.

'Young man,' he went on, 'you will say a grace before meat, if you remember one.'

I did not.

'Then I will say one for you. Oh! wretched trade of stage acting. He does not even know a single grace before meat.'

Then he began to help me—and we went on with dinner without further interruption. He kept up a running accompaniment of comment as I devoured the meal, and his manner gradually lost all its solemnity, until before I was more than half through the dinner he was dancing about, slapping his leg with delight, and laughing till he grew almost black in the face.

Why he was so pleased I could not tell. I was soon to learn.

'These are plovers' eggs. No better thing ever discovered to begin your dinner with. Alderman Stowport says oysters are better. That is rubbish. I do not despise oysters—Why, he has eaten the whole six! Bravo! bravo! an excellent beginning. Let me take away the plate, my dear sir. Now we have turtle soup— gently, my young friend, gently. Ah, impetuous youth! More? Stay—green fat. Humour, humour your appetite; don't drive it; calipash and calipee. It's really sinful to eat so fast. He takes all down without tasting it. No—no more; you must give yourself a fair chance, and not spoil your dinner with too much turtle.' He put the soup aside, and took the cover off another dish. 'Salmon—with cucumber. Lobster-sauce—bless me, it's like a dream of fairyland! Fillet of sole—a beautiful dream to see him. Ho! ho! he's a Julius Cæsar the Conqueror. Croquet de volaille—gone like a cloud from the sky. Don't wolf the food, my friend; there is a limit to the cravings of nature imposed by the claims of art; taste it. Ris de veau—smiles of the dear little innocent, confiding calf—a little more bread with it? Mauviettes en caisse, larks in baskets—sweet, rapturous, singing larks, toothsome cockyolly larks. He eats them up, bones and all. Ha! ha! Pause, my dear sir, and drink some-thing. Here are champagne, hock, and sauterne; never touch sherry, it's a made-up wine, even the best of it. Come, a little champagne.'

'I generally take draught-beer, sir,' I replied, modestly. 'That is the drink to which I have been accustomed and—not too much of it; but, if you please, a little fizz will be acceptable.'

I drank three glasses in rapid succession, and found them good. He meanwhile nodded and winked with an ever-increasing delight which I failed to understand.

'Now, my Nero, my Paris of Troy, my Judas Maccabaeus'—he mixed up his names, but it mattered nothing—'here is saddle of mutton, with potatoes, cauliflower, currant-jelly. More cham-pagne? It's worth *sums* of money to see him. Curry? More cham-pagne? Curry of chicken? Cabob curry of chicken, young Alexander the Great? Plenty of rice? Ho, ho, ho! Plenty of rice, he said; why, he is a Goliath—a Goliath of Gath, this young man!'

He really grew so purple that I thought he would have a fit of some kind. But the flattery pleased me all the same, and I went on eating and drinking as if I was only just beginning.

'Quail or bécassine—snipe, that is? He takes both, like Pompey. More champagne? Jelly, my Heliogabalus, my modern Caracalla, apricot-jelly? Cabinet pudding? He has two helpings of the pud-ding. King Solomon in all his glory never—More champagne? A little hock to finish with? He takes his hock in a tumbler, this young Samson. Cheese—Brie—and celery. A glass of port with the cheese. He takes that in a tumbler too, like Og, King of Bashan.'

I was really overwhelmed with the splendour of the dinner, the classical and biblical flattery, and the extraordinary gratification which my really enormous hunger caused this remarkable old gentleman. He clapped his hands; he nodded his head; he slapped his legs: he winked and grinned; he smacked his lips; he evinced every sign of the most unbounded delight. When I had quite finished eating, which was not before we had got through the whole list of courses, he gave me a bottle of claret, and watched me while I rapidly disposed of it. Then he produced from a sideboard, where I certainly had not seen it a moment before, a small cup of strong black coffee with a tiny glass of liqueur. As for my own part, I hope I have made it clear that I dined extremely well; in fact, I had never even dreamed of such a dinner in my life. It was not only that I was half starved, but that the things were so good. Imagine the astonishment of a young strolling actor, whose highest dreams were of sufficient beefsteak, not of the primest part, at such a magnificent feed. I felt as if I had dropped unexpectedly into a fortune. I had.

'How do you feel now?' my host asked, a shade of anxiety crossing his brow.

*   *   *

There was still the strange look in my host's eyes—a sort of passionate and eager longing.

'I am very well, thank you, sir, and more grateful than I can tell you.'

'Hang the gratitude! Tell me if you feel any sense of repletion? Does the blood seem mounting to the head? Are you quite free from any giddiness? No thickness in the speech? It's wonderful, it's providential, my finding you. Such a windfall; and just when I most wanted it. Our blessings truly come when we least expect them.'

This was strange language, but the whole proceedings were so strange that I hardly noticed it. Besides, I was extremely comfortable after my dinner, and disposed to rest.

'Now,' he went on, 'while you are digesting—by the way, the digestion is, I trust, unimpaired by drink or excess? Quite so; and what I expected in so good and so gifted a young man. Like an ostrich, as you say. Ho, ho! ha! ha! like an ostrich! It is, indeed, too much. Tell me, now, something, gently and dispassionately, so as not to injure your digestion, about your history.'

I told him all. While I related my simple story he interrupted now and then with some fresh question on the growth, the endurance, the regularity of my appetite, to which I gave satisfactory answers. When I had quite finished he went to the table—I noticed then that all traces of the dinner had disappeared—and laid out a document, by which he placed a pen. Then he drew a chair, sat down in front of me, and assumed a serious air.

'Come,' he said, peremptorily, 'let us get now to business.'

I had not the smallest notion what the business was, but I bowed and waited. Perhaps he was going to offer me a clerkship. Visions of a large salary, to suit my expansive appetite, came across my brain.

'In your case,' he began, 'the possession of so great an appetite must be attended with serious inconveniences. You have no money, in a few hours you will be hungry again; you will endure great pain and suffering, greater than is felt by men less largely endowed with the greatest blessing—I mean with appetite.'

'Yes,' I said, 'it is a great trouble to me, this twist of mine, especially when I am hard up.'

He almost jumped out of his chair.

'Why, there,' he cried, 'what is the use of words? We are agreed already. Nothing could be more fortunate. Let us have no more beating about the bush. Young man, I will rid you of this nuisance; I will buy your appetite of you.'

I only stared. Was the old gentleman mad?

'It is a strange offer, I know,' he went on, 'a strange offer, and you have probably never heard a more remarkable one. But it is genuine. I will buy your appetite of you.'

'Buy my—buy my appetite?'

'Nothing easier. Read this.'

He gave me the paper which he had laid on the table, prepared in readiness, I suppose, for me. It was as follows:

'I, Luke Lucraft, being in sound mind and in good health, and of the mature age of twenty-four, do voluntarily and of my own free will and accord agree and promise to resign my appetite entirely and altogether for the use of Ebenezer Grumbelow from the day and hour of the execution of this deed. In return whereof I agree to accept a monthly allowance of £30, also to date from the moment of signature, with a sum of £50, to be placed in my hands. I promise also that I will carefully study to preserve by regular habits and exercise the gift of a generous appetite; that I will not work immoderately, sit up late, practise vicious courses, or do anything that may tend to impair the regular recurrence of a healthy and vigorous hunger.'

Then followed a place for the signature and one for the witnesses.

'You see,' he went on, 'I ask for no unpleasant condition. I give you a free life, coupled with the simple condition of ordinary care. Do you agree?'

'I hardly know; it is so sudden.'

'Come, come'—he spoke with a harshness quite new—'come, let us have no nonsense of that sort. Do you agree?'

I read it over again.

'Give me a little time,' I said. 'Let me reflect till tomorrow morning.'

'Reflect!' His face flushed purple, and his bloodshot eyes literally glared. 'Reflect! what the devil does the boy want to reflect about? Has he got a penny, a friend, or a chance in the whole world? I will give you five minutes—come.' He rose up and stood before me. As I looked in his face a curious dimness came over my eyes; he seemed to recede before me; he disappeared altogether. When I heard him speak again his voice sounded far, far off, but thin and clear, as if it came through some long tube. 'Luke Lucraft,' it said, 'see yourself.'

Yes; I saw myself, and though *outside* of what I saw, I felt the same emotions as if I had been the actual performer in the scenes I witnessed.

I was standing where the old gentleman met me, starving still, and suffering pangs far worse than those under which I groaned at three o'clock. The day was advanced; the diners had all gone away, and the dining-room waiters were putting up the shutters. I spoke to one of them timidly. I told him I had eaten nothing since the morning, and begged for a plate of broken victuals. He looked in my face, called a brother-servant, and they kicked me from the door. People were rougher in London fifty years ago. Then I slunk away, and wandered somewhere among the winding streets and lanes of the old city. London at night was not so empty and deserted as it is now, and the streets had people in them. Some of them were well dressed—the wealthy merchants had not, even then, all left off living in the city; some were clerks going home; some were women out for an evening's walk. The bells rang out the hours from the city clocks, and I crept along the walls wondering what would become of me, and how I should find an end of my present misery.

Then I begged. Took off my hat and held it in my hand while I asked for something—anything—the smallest coin that would get a piece of bread.

The men passed me by with pitiless and unbelieving eyes. Heavens! if they had been hungry once, only once, in all their lives, they would never again have refused the petition of a beggar, even though he was the most lying mendicant who ever disgraced the words of charity which passed his lips. But they gave me nothing.

The women edged away from me and passed on the other side if I timidly pressed my claim. They had nothing to fear from me. At last I asked a girl. She was more unfortunate than myself, but she was not hungry, and she gave me a shilling.

Then I found a shop open, and bought a plate of meat. That spent—I saw myself slinking, ashamed and wretched, again along the cold and empty street. When I could walk no more I found myself in Covent Garden Market, and threw myself under shelter of a roof at least, among the stalks and leaves and straw which littered the place.

I awoke early, and hungry again. I rose and resumed my miserable walk.

Hope by this time was dead within me; I could think of nothing but my intolerable hunger; could feel nothing but the pain which would not leave me; could look at nothing but food in the window.

I begged again, and begged all day without success.

It was a rougher time, that, than the present. More than one man laid his stick across my back with an impatient admonition to get to work, you lazy rogue. But I was too feeble to retaliate or remonstrate. Was there no charity in the world? I passed other beggars in the streets who looked fat and comfortable. People gave *them* money, but they would give me none. The time wore on, and my craving for food became irresistible.

I passed a shop which had a tray outside of baked potatoes. The owner had his back to me. I *stole* one. Yes, I stole one. No one saw me. He did not see me as I slunk past him with guilty face, and swiftly sped round the nearest corner to eat the stolen morsel.

What is the use of a single baked potato? Presently I returned to the same place with the intention of taking another. But they were all gone. I went on, looking for another provision shop. I came to a place where hot smoking sausages were bubbling in a pan over a charcoal fire. The shop stood at a corner. There was only a girl minding it. I deliberately walked in, took a sausage from the pan, hot as it was, and stepped out again before her astonishment even prompted her to cry out.

The time seemed intolerably long. All these scenes passed before me, not as the quick and steady flight of the rapidly falling moments, but as if the agony and the shame were deliberately lengthened out.

Then came a third time when I stole, maddened by the dream of hunger. This time I was detected, pursued, and apprehended. The misery and shame of the hour when I stood before the magistrate, in that horrible vision of a possible future, I cannot even yet forget. With this a constant sense of unsatisfied and craving hunger; a feeling as if hunger was the greatest evil in the whole world; a longing to get rid of it. Last scene of all, I was lying dead, starved to death with hunger and cold, in a miserable, bare, and naked garret.

By what black art did the old man delude my senses? It was a lie, and he knew it. I should have got some honest work, if only to wheel bricks or carry loads.

'There is your future, young man'—there came up from the distance the voice of the tempter—'a gloomy prospect: a miserable life: a wretched ending. Now look at the other side.'

The scene changed. I saw myself, but in another guise. My hunger had vanished; I felt it no more.

This time I was happy, light-hearted, and cheerful. I remembered scenes of misery through which I had just passed, and the recollection added more sweetness to my present enjoyment. It seemed as if I should never be hungry any more, and never feel the want of food. I was like a Greek god in my exemption from the common weakness of humanity. I was rich, too, and knew that I had the command, somehow, of all that money could buy.

I was sitting in a garden, and around me were troops of girls. I heard the rustle of their dresses, caught the laughter from their lips, watched the lustre of their eyes, saw the moonlight dance among their waving locks, as they ran and played among the trees and flowers. One of them sat by me and sang to a guitar—

> Life is made for love. Ah! why
>   Should its sweetness e'er be marred?
> List! the echoes will not die,
>   Still the sweet word 'love' to guard.
>
> Nought but love. Oh! Happy youth,
>   Free from need of baser thought,
> Stay with us, and learn this truth,
>   Set with song, with music wrought.
>
> Thine is love, an endless feast;
>   Beauty—sweeter far than wine;
> Joy, from lower cares released—
>   Never star rose bright as thine.

I knew, somehow or other, that this was allegorical, and, as if I expressed my thought, the scene changed, and I was in real life.

Chambers in London, such as I had read of, overlooking St James's Park. I sat in them in the midst of books and pictures. I had

no business to call me away from my indolent ease; I had no
anxiety about the future. I got up and strolled about the streets,
looking at the shops. If I fancied a thing I bought it. I went to
picture galleries and saw the latest works of art; I went to the
theatre and saw the performance from a comfortable box; I went
riding in the park.

Then my fancy returned to my first love, and I saw myself
walking in a country lane with Juliet. She was sweeter to look upon
than ever, and more delightful in her frank and innocent love for
me. We rambled along under the hedges while I gathered flowers
for her, and talked of the happy, happy days when we should be
one, soon now to arrive, and of the sweet, loving life which should
be ours far away from the troubles of the world.

Dreams, idle dreams; but sweet to me, after the agony of the last,
as a draught of water to a parched traveller on Sahara.

The pictures changed as fast as my fancy wandered from one
thing to another. In all I was the same—free from the downward
and earthly pressure of want and hunger, relieved from anxiety,
with plenty of money, and full of all sweet and innocent fancies.

Lies again. But by what power could this necromancer so cheat
and gull my brain?

'Very different scenes these, my dear young friend,' he said in a
winning voice, 'are they not? Now,' he went on, and his voice was
quite close to me, 'you have had your five minutes.'

The cloud passed from my eyes. I was sitting again in the
octagonal room, the old man before me, watch in hand, as if he was
counting the seconds.

'Five minutes and a quarter,' he growled. 'Now choose.'

'I have chosen,' I replied. 'I accept your offer.'

The influence of the things I had seen was too strong upon me. I
could neither reason nor reflect.

'I accept your offer.'

'Why, that's brave,' he said, with a gigantic sigh of relief. 'That's
what I expected of you. Boule-de-neige—Boule-de-neige!'

He clapped his hands.

Instantly the horrible old negro appeared behind his master's
chair, as if he had sprung up from the ground. I believe he had. He
looked more like a devil than ever, grinning from ear to ear, and his
two eyes glowing in the candlelight like two great coals. The light
fell, too, upon the seams and wrinkles of his face, bringing them
out like the hills and valleys in a raised map. Strange as it all was to
me, this ancient servitor produced the strangest effect upon me of
anything.

'Boule-de-neige is witness for us,' said the old gentleman.

'Boule-de-neige, this young gentleman, Mr Luke Lucraft, is about to sign a little deed, to which, as a matter of form, we require your signature too as witness.'

'Cluck!' said the negro. 'Dis young gegleman berry lucky—him berry lucky. What time massa take him dinner?'

'When do you think you shall be fairly hungry again?' he asked me. 'Now, no boastings—no false pretence and pride—because it will be the worse for you. Answer truthfully. It is now six.'

'I should say that at nine I should be able to take some supper, and at ten I shall certainly be hungry again. As an ordinary rule I should be ready a great deal earlier, but I have taken such an immense dinner.'

'Good.' He turned to Boule-de-neige. 'You see the young man is modest and promises fairly. I shall have supper—a plentiful supper—at ten punctually. Mr Lucraft will now sign.'

I advanced to the table and took up the pen, but there was no ink.

'Cluck!' said the infernal negro, with another grin—'cluck! Massa wait lilly bit.'

He took my left hand in his soft and cold paw. I felt a sharp prick at my wrist.

'You will dip the pen,' said the old gentleman, 'in the blood. It is a mere form.'

'Cluck!' said Boule-de-neige.

'A mere form because we have no ink handy.'

'Cluck-cluck!'

I signed my name as desired, and, following the directions of the old gentleman, placed my finger on the red wafer at the margin, saying, 'I declare this my act and deed.'

Then I gave the pen to Boule-de-neige. He signed after me, in a firm flowing hand, 'Boule-de-neige.' As I looked, the letters seemed somehow to shape themselves into 'Beezlebub.' I looked at him with a kind of terror. The creature grinned in my face as if he divined my thought, and gave utterance to one of his hideous 'clucks'.

Then I began to feel the same faintness which I had at first experienced. It mounted upwards from my feet slowly, so that I heard the old gentleman's voice, though I saw nothing. It grew gradually fainter.

'Supper at ten, Boule-de-neige,' he was saying; 'I feel getting hungry already. What shall I do with myself till ten o'clock? I am certainly getting hungry. I think I can have it served at half-past nine. Oh, blessed day! Oh, thankful, blessed day! Boule-de-neige, it must be supper for three—for four—for five. I shall have champagne—the Perrier Jouet—the curaçoa punch afterwards. Curaçoa punch—I haven't tasted it for three months and more. Oh, what a blessed—blessed—blessed—'

I heard no more because my senses failed me altogether, and his voice died away in my ears.

When I came to myself I was leaning against the post in Bucklersbury, where I had met the old man.

A whiff of stale cooked meat from the cook-shop, which caught me as I opened my eyes, produced a singular feeling of disgust. 'Pah,' I muttered, 'roast mutton!' and moved from the spot. My hunger was gone, that was quite certain. I felt a quietness about those regions, wherever they may be, which belong to appetite. I was almost dreamy in the repose which followed a morning so stormy. I walked quietly away homewards in a kind of daze, trying to make out something of what had happened. The first thing I found I could not remember was the name of the old gentleman. When that came back to me and under what circumstances I will tell you as we get along. Bit by bit I recalled the whole events of the afternoon, one after the other. I saw the old man, with his purple face and bloodshot eyes and white hair; I saw the wrinkled and seamed old negro; I saw the octagonal room without doors or windows; the splendid dinner; the host watching my every gesture; I remembered everything except the name of the man to whom I had sold—my appetite.

It was so strange that I laughed when I thought of it. I must have been drunk; he gave me a good dinner and I took too much wine; but, then, how was it that I remembered clearly every, even the smallest, detail?

On the bed in the one room which constituted my lodging I found a letter. It was from a firm of lawyers, dated that evening at half-past six—only half an hour after I signed the paper—stating that they were empowered by a client, whose name was not mentioned, to give me the sum of £30 monthly, to begin from that day, and to be paid to me personally. How did they get their instructions then? And it was all true!

I was too tired with the day's adventures to think any more; and, though it was only nine o'clock, I went to bed and fell fast asleep. In an hour I awoke again, with a choking sensation, as if I was eating too much. I knew instantly what was going on, and by a kind of prophetic insight. The old man was taking his supper, and taking more than was good—*for me.* I sprang from the bed, gasping for breath. Presently, as I gathered, he began to drink too much as well. My brain went round and round. I laughed, sang, and danced; and soon after, with a heavy fall, I rolled senseless on the carpet, and remembered nothing more.

It was early in the morning when I awoke, still lying on the floor. I had a splitting headache. I had fallen against some corner of the furniture and blackened one eye. I had broken two chairs somehow or other. I was cold, ill, and shaken. I got into bed, and tried to remember what had happened. Clearly I must have made a drunken beast of myself over the dinner, and reeled home with my head full of fancies and dreams; perhaps the dinner itself was a dream and a hallucination too; if so, the pangs of hunger would soon recommence. But they did not. Then I fell asleep, and did not awake again till the clock struck twelve. How ill and wretched I felt as I dressed! My hand shook, my eyes were red, my face swollen. Surely I must have been intoxicated. I had been, up to that day at least, a temperate man, partly, no doubt, from the very wholesome reason which keeps so many of us sober—the necessity of poverty; but of course I had not arrived at four and twenty years and seen so much of the world without recognising the signs of too much drink. I had them, every one; and, as most men know too well, they are all summed up in the simple expression, 'hot coppers'. Alas! I was destined to become only too familiar with the accursed symptoms. Involuntarily, when I had dressed myself, I put my hands in my pockets, those pockets so often empty; there was money, gold—sovereigns—my pocket was full of them. I counted them in a stupor. Forty-nine, and one rolled into the corner—fifty; it was part of the sum for which I had sold my appetite; and on the table lay the letter from Messrs Crackett and Charges, inviting me to draw thirty pounds a month.

Then it was all true!

I sat down, and, with my throbbing temples and feverish pulse, tried to make it out. Everything became plain except the name of the purchaser—Mr—Mr—I remembered Boule-de-neige, the house, the room, and the dinner, but not the name of that arch-deceiver, the whole of whose villainy I was far from realising yet; and until it was told me later on I never did remember the name.

It was strange. Men are said to have sold their souls to the devil for money, bartering away an eternity of happiness for a few years of pleasure; but as for me, I had exchanged, as it semeed at first sight, nothing but the inconvenience of a healthy appetite with nothing to eat for the means of living comfortably without it. There could be no sin in such a transaction; it was on a different level altogether from the bargain made by Faust. And there were the broad, the benevolent facts, so to speak—my pocket full of sovereigns; and the letter instructing me to call at an office for thirty pounds monthly.

Benevolent facts I thought them. You shall see. You think, as I thought, that no sin could be laid to my door for the transaction. You shall judge. You think, as I thought, that no harm could follow so simple a piece of business. You shall read. On my way out I met the landlady, who gave me notice to quit at the end of the week.

'I thought you were a quiet and a sober young man,' she said. 'Ah, never will I trust to good looks again. Me and the lodgers kept awake till two in the morning with your singing and dancing, let alone banging the floor with the chair. Not another hour after your week's up, if you was to pray on your knees, shall you stay. And next door threatening the constables; and me a quiet woman for twenty years.'

My heart sank again. But, after all, perhaps it was I myself, not the good old gentleman, my kind patron and benefactor, at all, who was the cause of this disturbance. It was undoubtedly true that I had taken a great quantity of wine with my splendid dinner. I begged her pardon humbly, and passed out.

It was now nearly one o'clock, but I felt no desire for breakfast. That was an experience quite novel to me. Still, I went to a coffee-house, according to habit, and ordered some tea and a rasher. When they came I discovered, with a horrid foreboding of worse misfortune behind, that my taste was gone. Except that one thing was solid and the other liquid, I distinguished nothing. Nor did my sense of smell assist me: as I found later, my nose was affected agreeably or disagreeably, but it lost all its discriminating and critical powers. Gunpowder, sulphuretted hydrogen gas, and tobacco offended my nose. So did certain smells belonging to cookery. On the other hand, certain flowers, tea, and claret pleased me, but I was unable to distinguish between them. Not only could I not taste them, but I had no gratification in eating them. I ate and drank mechanically, because I knew that the body must be kept going on something.

All this knowledge, however, and more, came by degrees. After making a forced breakfast I bent my steps to the lawyers', who had an office in Lincoln's Inn Fields.

The letter was received by a conceited young clerk in shiny black habiliments, a turned up nose, and a self-satisfied manner.

'Ha!' he said, 'I thought you would soon come round to us after the letter. Sign that. You haven't been long. None of them are.'

It was a receipt; and I was on the point of asking if it was to be signed in blood, when he settled the question by giving me the ink.

'There, Luke Lucraft, across the eightpenny stamp. I'm not allowed to answer any questions you may put, Mr Lucraft, nor to ask you any; so take your money, and good morning to you. I suppose, like the rest of them, you don't know the name of your benefactor, and would like to—yes; but you needn't ask *me*; and I've orders not to admit you to see either Mr Charges or Mr Crackett. They'd trouble enough with the last but one. He broke into their office once, drunk, and laid about him with the ruler.'

I burst into a cold dew of terror.

'However, Mr Lucraft, I hope you will be more fortunate than your predecessors.'

'Where are they? Who are they?'

'I do not know where they are, not for a certainty,' he replied with a grin. 'But we may guess. Dead and buried they are, all of them. Gone to kingdom come; all died of the same thing, too—DT. Delicious Trimmings killed them. Poor old gentleman! He's too good for this world, as everybody knows, and the more he's taken in the more he's deceived. Anyhow, he's very unlucky in his pensioners. He did say when the last went off that he would have no more; he wept over it, and declared that his bounty was always abused; but there never was such a benevolent old chap. I only wish he'd take a fancy to me.'

'What did you say is his name, by the way?'

The clerk looked at me with a cunning wink.

'If you don't know, I am sure I do not,' he said. 'Here is the cheque, Mr Lucraft, and I hope you will continue to come here and draw it a good deal longer than the other chaps. But there's a blight on all the pensioners. Lord, what a healthy chap Tom Kirby—he was a Monmouth man—looked when he first came for his cheques! As strong as a bull and as fresh as a lark.'

'A good appetite had he?'

'No; couldn't eat anything after a bit; said he fancied nothing. Lost his taste entirely. He pined away and died in a galloping consumption before the third month was due. Nobody ever saw him drinking, but he was drunk every night, regular, like the rest. Perhaps it's only coincidence. Better luck to *you*, Mr Lucraft.'

This conversation did not reassure me, and I determined to go over to Bucklersbury at once and see my patron. I found the post against which I was leaning when he accosted me; there was no doubt about that, for the hares and cauliflowers were still in the shop-window, only they looked disgusting to me this morning. I found the street into which he had led me, and then—then—it was the most extraordinary thing, I could not find the door by which we entered. Not only was there no door, but there seemed no place where such a door as I remembered could exist in this little narrow winding street. I went up and down twice. I looked at all the windows. I asked a policeman if he had ever seen an old gentleman about the street such as I described, or such a negro as Boule-de-neige; but he could give no information. Only as I prowled slowly along the pavement I heard distinctly—it gave me a nervous shock that I could not account for—the infernal 'Cluck-cluck!' of the negro with the cold soft hands, the wrinkled skin, and the fiery red eyes. He was chuckling at me from some hiding-place of his own, where he was safe. He had done me no harm that I knew of, but I hated him at that moment.

I was by this time not at all elated at my good fortune. I even craved to have back again what I had sold. I felt heavy at heart, and had a presentiment of fresh trouble before me. I thought of the fate of those unknown and unfortunate predecessors, all dead in consequence of drink, evil courses, and DT. Heavens! was I too to die miserably with delirium tremens, after I had sold my taste, and could only tell brandy from water, like the cask which might hold either, by the smell?

At half-past one—the luncheon time for all who have appetites—the sense of being gorged came upon me again, but this time without the giddiness. I went to a tavern in the Strand and fell sound sleep. When I awoke at six the oppression had passed away. And now I began to realise something of the consequences of my act. I say something, because worse, far worse, remained behind. I was doomed, I saw clearly, to be the victim of the old man's gluttony. He would eat and I should suffer. Already, as I guessed from the clerk's statements, he had killed four strong men before me. I was to be the fifth. I went again to Bucklersbury, and sought in every house for something that might give me a clue. I loitered in the quiet city streets in the hope of finding my tormentor, and forcing him to give me back my bond. There was no clue, and I did not meet him. But I felt him. He began dinner, as nearly as I could feel, about seven o'clock; he took his meal with deliberation, judging from the gradual nature of my sensations; but he took an amazing quantity, and by eight o'clock the weight upon me was so great that I could scarcely breathe. How I cursed my folly! How I impotently writhed under the burden I had wantonly laid upon myself! And then he began to drink. The fiend, the scoundrel! I felt the fumes mount to my head; there was no exhilaration, no forgetfulness of misery; none of the pleasant gradations of excitement, hope, and confidence, through which men are accustomed to pass before arriving at the final stage, the complete oblivion, of intoxication. I felt myself getting gradually but hopelessly drunk. I struggled against the feeling, but in vain; the houses went round and round with me: my speech, when I tried to speak, became thick; the flags of the pavement flew up and struck me violently on the forehead, and I became unconscious of what happened afterwards.

*   *   *

In the morning I found myself lying on a stone bench in a small whitewashed room. My brows were throbbing and my throat was parched, and in my brain was ringing, I do not know why, the infernal 'Cluck-cluck!' of the negro with derisive iteration. I had not long to meditate; the door opened, and a constable appeared.

'Now then,' he said, roughly, 'if you can stand upright by this time, come along.'

It was clear enough to me now what had happened: I was in custody, in a police-cell, and I was going before the magistrate.

I dream of that ignominy still, though forty years have passed since I was placed in the dock and asked what I had to say for myself. 'Drunk and disorderly.'

I was charged by the constable—there were no police in 1823— with being drunk and disorderly. Twenty other poor wretches were waiting their trial for the same offence; one or two for graver charges. My case came first, and had the honour of being reported in the papers. Here is the extract cut out of the *Morning Chronicle*:

A young man, who gave his name as Henry Luke, and said he was an actor by profession, was charged with being drunk and disorderly in the streets. The constable found him at ten o'clock lying on the pavement of Bucklersbury, too drunk even to speak, and quite unable therefore to give any account of himself. A cheque, signed by the well-known firm of Crackett and Charges, for £30 was found on his person. The magistrate remarked that this was a suspicious circumstance, and decided to remand the case till these gentlemen could be communicated with. One of the partners appeared at twelve, and deposed that the prisoner's real name was Luke Lucraft, that he had been an actor, and that the cheque had been given him by the firm, acting for a client who wished to be anonymous, but whose motive was pure benevolence.

The magistrate, on hearing the facts of the case, addressed the prisoner with a suitable admonition. He bade him remember that such an abuse of a good man's charity, as he had been guilty of, was the worst form of ingratitude. It appeared that on the very day of receiving a gift, which was evidently intended to advance him in life, or to find him the means of procuring suitable employment, the prisoner deliberately made himself so hopelessly drunk that he could neither speak nor stand—where, it did not appear. The magistrate could not but feel that this conduct showed the gravest want of moral principle, and he strongly advised Mr Crackett to cancel the cheque till further orders.

As, however, it was a first offence, and in consideration of the prisoner's youth, the fine inflicted would be a small one of ten shillings, with costs.

That was the newspaper account of the affair. On his way out of the court, Mr Crackett stopped me.

'Young man,' he said, shaking his head, 'this is very dreadful. I warned my benevolent client against this act of generosity. You are the fifth young man whom he has assisted in this magnificent manner. The former, all four, took to drink, and died in a disgraceful manner. Take warning, and stop while it is yet time.'

I got away as fast as I could, and crept back to my lodging after the necessary miserable breakfast.

I am not ashamed to say that I sat down and cried. The tears *would* crowd into my eyes. It was too dreadful. Here I was, only twenty-four years of age, with my life before me, doomed, through my own folly, to a miserable ending and a disgraceful reputation. What good would come of having money under these dreadful conditions? Money, indeed! What had become of the fifty pounds given me only two days before? Gone. All gone but one single sovereign which served to pay my fine. Some one had robbed me. Perhaps the constables. Perhaps a street thief. It was gone. The sorry reward of my consent to the unholy bargain was clean swept away, and only the consequences of the contract remained.

In the afternoon, as I hastened home along the darkening streets, hoping to reach my lodging before the daily gorge began, a curious thing happened to me. On the other side of the street, in a dark corner, standing upright, and pointing to me with a finger of derision, I saw Boule-de-neige, the negro servant. I rushed at him, blind with rage. When I got to the spot I found nobody there. Was it a trick of a disordered brain? I had seen him, quite plainly, grinning at me with his wrinkled features. As I turned from the place I heard his familiar 'Cluck-cluck'.

Twice more on the way this strange phantom appeared to me; each time accompanied by the 'cluck' of his voice. It was a phantom with which I was to become familiar indeed, before I had finished with Boule-de-neige and his master.

It was clear that the demon to whom I had sold myself was incapable of the slightest consideration towards me. He would eat and drink as much as he felt disposed to do, careless of any consequences that might befall me. It was equally evident that he intended to make the most of his bargain, to eat enormously every day, and to drink himself drunk every night. And I was powerless. Meantime it was becoming evident that the consequences to me would be as serious as if I were myself guilty of these excesses. One drop of comfort alone remained: my appetite would fail, and my tormentor would be punished where he would feel it most. I lay down and waited till luncheon time; no sense of repletion came over me; it was certain, therefore, that he was already suffering a vicarious punishment, so to speak, for yesterday's debauch.

The next day, however, I really did meet my negro.

It was about five in the afternoon—the time when I was tolerably safe, because my owner, who took a plentiful luncheon at one, did not begin his nightly orgy much before seven. I was loitering about Bucklersbury, my favourite place of resort, in the hope of meeting the old man, when my arm was touched as I turned round. It *was* the negro. 'Massa Lucraft,' he said, 'you come along o' me. Massa him berry glad to see you.'

I declare that although the moment before I had been picturing such an encounter, although I had imagined myself with my fingers at his throat, dragging him off, and forcing him to tell me who and what he was, I felt myself unable to speak.

'Come along o' me, Massa Lucraft,' he said; 'this way—way you know berry well. Ho, ho!—Cluck.'

He stopped before the door I remembered, but had never been able to find, opened it with a little key, and led the way to the octagonal room.

There was no one in it, but the table was already laid for dinner.

'Massa come bymeby. You wait, young gegleman.'

Then he disappeared somehow.

As before, I could see no door. As before, the first sensation which came over me was of giddiness, from which I recovered immediately. I walked round and round the room looking at the heavy furniture, the pictures, which were all of fruit and game, and the silver plate. Everything showed the presence of great wealth, and, I supposed, though I knew nothing about it, great taste. I was kept waiting for nearly two hours. That I did not mind, because every moment brought me, I thought, nearer to the hour of my deliverance. I was certain that I had only to put the case to Mr Grumbelow—I remembered his name the moment I was back in that room—to appeal to his generosity, his honour, his pity, in order to obtain my release. Mr Grumbelow—Ebenezer Grumbelow—he was the charitable client of Messrs Crackett & Charges, was he? Why, I might show him up to popular derision and hatred. I might tell the world who and what this great benefactor of young men really was.

Suddenly, as the clock struck seven, he stood upon the carpet before me, while Boule-de-neige stood at the table with a soup tureen in his hand. I declare that I did not see at any time anyone enter the room or go out of it. They appeared to be suddenly in it.

I do hope that the appearance of small details like the above, at first incredible, will not be taken as proof of want of veracity on my own part. I wish that I could tell the tale without these particulars, but I cannot. I must relate the whole or none.

'You here?' said Mr Grumbelow, looking at me with an air of contempt. He seated himself at the table and unfolded his napkin. 'Soup, Boule-de-neige.'

'Massa hungry? Dat young debbel there he look berry pale already.'

'Pretty well, Boule-de-neige, considering. You, sir, come here, and let me look at you.' I obeyed. 'Hold out your hand. It shakes. Let me look at your eyes. They are yellow. Do you know that your appetite seems to me to be failing already—already—and it is only the fourth day.'

'It is not my fault,' I said.

'Nonsense. Don't talk to me, sir, because I will have none of your insolence. I say that you do not walk enough. I order you to walk twelve miles a day—do you hear?'

'It is not in the contract,' I replied, doggedly.

'It *is* in the contract. You are to use every means in your power to keep your faculties in vigour. What means have you used?'

He banged the spoon on the table and glanced at me so fiercely that I had nothing to say.

'Massa, soup get cold,' said Boule-de-neige.

He gobbled it up, every now and then looking up at me with an angry grunt.

'Now then, you and your contract. This is pretty ingratitude, this is. Here's a fellow, Boule-de-neige, I pick up out of the gutter, starving; whom I keep expensively; whom I endow with an income; whom I deprive of the temptation to gluttony.'

'Nebber see such a debbel in all my days,' said the negro; 'nebber hear such a ting told nowhere.'

'No nor ever will. Listen to me, sir. You will walk ten, twelve, or twenty miles a day, according to the dinner I have had. And, mark you, it will be the worse for you if you do not. Remember, if I cannot eat I can drink.'

There was a fiendish glare in his blood-stained eyes as he spoke, and I trembled. My spirit was so completely gone that I had not even the pluck to appeal to his pity. Perhaps a secret consciousness of the uselessness of such an appeal deterred me.

'You will now,' he said, 'watch me making as large a dinner as your miserably languid appetite will allow.'

'I have been drunk for four nights,' I pleaded.

'Then you have no business to get drunk so easily. Your head is contemptibly weak—what did I take yesterday, Boule-de-neige.'

'Big bottle champagne, big bottle port, eight goes whisky grog.'

'I did—and that was all. Why your predecessor stood double the quantity.'

'Beg pardon, massa. Last young gegleman poor trash—last but two—him mighty strong head—head like bull—nebber get drunk.'

'Ah, we wasted him, Boule-de-neige; we fooled him away in one imprudent evening. I told you at the time that noyeau punch is a very dangerous thing.'

'Ho, ho!' the diabolical negro laughed till his teeth showed like the grinning jaws of a death's head. 'Ho, ho! him so blind drunk he tumble out of window—break him neck. Ho, ho!'

This was a pleasant conversation for me to hear.

Then Mr Grumbelow resumed his dinner.

He ate a good deal in spite of his grumbling, and then he began to drink port. I observed that the wine had a peculiar effect upon him. It made him redder in the face, but not thicker in speech. He drank two bottles, talking to me all the time. I began to get drunk, he only got the more merrily fiendish.

'This is really delightful,' he said, as I reeled and caught at a chair for support. 'I wonder I never thought of this before. It is quite a new pleasure to watch the effects of my own drink on another man's brain, I shall write a book about you. I shall call it "The Young Christian deterred, or Leaves from Luke Lucraft's Wicked Life." Ho, ha! ha, ho! I saw the account in the *Morning Post*. Heigh, heigh!'—he nearly choked as he recalled the circumstance. 'The magistrate admonishing the wicked drunkard. Ho, ho! It is like a farce. Stand up, sir, stand up. He can't stand up. Can you sing? Can you dance? He could not even dance a hornpipe. Do you feel a little thickness in your speech? Would you be able to explain to the worthy magistrate the circumstances, quite beyond your own control, which brought you into that painful position in which you stood? It is the best situation that ever was put upon any stage. There's nothing like it in fiction. Nothing. Walter Scott never invented anything half so rich. Ho, ho, ho! he is really getting drunk already. What a poor creature it is!'

He paused for a moment and then went on.

'Boule-de-neige, coffee; brandy in it—plenty of brandy, and a glass of curaçoa afterwards. A large glass, sir! I'll have a night of it. Your health, Luke Lucraft, in this coffee; and you had better take care of it, or I'll pack you off with noyeau punch. Pleasant times you are having, eh? Might have been worse, you know. You might have been starving. What? Don't fall against the table in that way. Take care of the furniture. It cost a great deal more money than you are worth. So, sit down on the floor while I tell you about your predecessors, dead and gone, poor fellows.

'Let me see. The first was William Saunders, a poor devil of a clerk of mine. He disgraced himself in chapel one week-day prayer-meeting, the very evening of his signature; then he ran away, but Boule-de-neige found him out, and brought him back. He took to praying and crying. One day he died in St Bartholomew's Hospital of delirium tremens. He lasted about six months.

'The next was Hans Hansen, a Dane. He only lasted about three weeks, because he became melancholy directly he found he could no longer taste brandy. I was disappointed with Hansen, and when he jumped off London Bridge into the Thames one night, his appetite having quite gone, I was really very sorry on account of the temporary inconvenience it put me to; and I determined to be very careful in his successor. I remember I had a good deal of trouble to find one.

'However, at last I got a third man, a stout Cumberland chap, son of a statesman. You poor, puny little strolling actor, I suppose that you will hardly believe that I once took four and twenty tumblers of Scotch whisky and water without affecting that brave fellow's appetite one bit. He used to take it out in swearing; and really he was almost too often in trouble with the magistrates. He never clearly understood that his safety lay in being home early in the evening. Once he nearly killed Mr Crackett in his own office. Poor Crackett! that eminent Christian lawyer; I should never have forgiven myself had anything happened to the worthy Crackett. Well! he went too; at least, after a good tough twelvemonth. It was my own fault, and I ought not to grumble. That noyeau punch was strong enough to kill the devil.'

'Cluck,' said Boule-de-neige.

'Then we came to Tom Kirby. None of them looked so well or promised so much; none broke down so easily. A whining fellow too; a crying, sobbing, appealing rogue, who wanted to get off his bargain. However, *de mortuis*—Your health, Luke Lucraft. Hallo! hold up.

'I tell you what I mean to do after you are worked off, Luke Lucraft. I mean to have a brace of fellows. I shall go down to the London docks, or else to the railway stations, and find a couple of trusty young porters. They are the sort of men to have. Fine, strong, well-set-up rascals. Men with muscles like rigging ropes—don't clutch at the chair, Lucraft—if you can't sit up you may lie down—I shall make them come here—give them a blow out of steak—I wasted a splendid dinner on you—and then I shall make them sign.

'The great thing, then, will be to have the appetites of two men; twice as much to eat and twice as much to drink. I never thought of that before.

'And then to bring both the rogues up here of an evening and make them wait and see me eat; watch them gradually lolling and reeling about till they tumble over each other; go secretly and hear them curse me—me, their benefactor—Ho! ho! I think I shall not be long over you, Luke Lucraft. Hallo! keep your drunken legs away from the table. Boule-de-neige, roll this intoxicated log into the street.'

*　　*　　*

When I came to my senses it was of course the next morning, and I was lying in my own bedroom, whither I had been carried by two strange men, the landlady afterwards told me, who said they were paid for the job. I had a splitting headache. I was sick and giddy; my limbs trembled beneath me when I tried to stand; my hands shook. I looked at myself in the glass. Swollen features and bloodshot eyes greeted me.

Less than a week had wrought this ruin.

The ordinary drunkard refreshes himself in the morning with tea. Nothing refreshed me, because I could taste nothing, and because my sufferings sprang from a different source, though they were the same in kind. I had to bear them as best I might.

I remembered the command which Mr—Mr—strange, I had forgotten his name again—gave me, to walk twenty miles after a 'heavy night'. I started to obey him.

Outside London, beyond Islington, where there are now rows of houses, but were then fields, I saw a little modest cottage, standing alone in its garden. It was a cottage with four rooms only, covered over with creepers. On the board, standing at the gate, was an announcement that it was to let. A thought struck me: Here could be seclusion, at any rate. Here I could shut myself up every night, and await in comparative safety the dreadful punishment—fast becoming heavier than I could hear—which my tormenter inflicted upon me. Why should I not take the cottage, pay the rent in advance every month—for how many months should I have to pay it?—and so wait in patience and resignation the approach of my inevitable fate?

I made inquiries at once, and secured the place at a merely nominal rent. Then I moved in a little furniture, bought second hand in Islington High Street, and became the occupant, a lonely hermit, of the house. There were no houses within hearing, in case I should storm and rage in my drunken madness at night. The cottage stood removed from the road, and no callers were likely to trouble me. Within those walls I should be secure from some dangers at least. Here, night after night, I could await the attacks of surfeit and intoxication which regularly came; for my master knew no pity.

On the first evening I sat down at half-past six to prepare for what was coming. The day was drawing in, and a cold twilight— the month was March—covered the trees and shrubs in my little garden, as I opened the door and looked out.

Before me stood the negro.

My spirit was quite broken, and I could only groan.

'Do you want me to go with you again?' I asked, thinking of the last entertainment at which I provided amusement for his master.

'Massa say him berry glad you come hyar. You walk the twenty mile ebbery day, else massa know the reason why. How you feel, Massa Lucraft? Heigh! heigh! cluck. Dat most fortunate day for you when you sign dat little paper.'

He delivered his message and disappeared in the darkness. I heard his footsteps crunching the gravel in the road, and I longed, only now I had no courage or spirit left, to seize him and tear him limb from limb.

Then I shut myself in, lit one candle, and sat over the fire. I thought of the scenes by which my extravagant fancy had been excited; the garden full of lively girls—what were girls to me now? the country walks I was to have with Juliet—where was my passion for Juliet now? The ease and happiness, the lightness and innocence, of the life before me, drawn by an arch-deceiver, compared with my present, my actual misery, sitting alone, cut off from mankind, the slave and victim of a secret profligate and glutton, doomed to die slowly, unless it should please the murderer to kill me off quickly.

And then, because the first symptoms of the attack were coming on, I went to bed and stayed there.

So began my new life. A wretched life it was. There was no occupation possible for me—no amusement. I walked every day, in fair weather or foul, a measured twenty miles.

This in some degree restored vitality to my system. I never read; I took no interest in any politics. I sat by myself, and brooded.

As for my meals, I bought them ready prepared. They consisted almost wholly of bread and cold mutton. You may judge of the absolutely tasteless condition to which I was reduced, when I write calmly and truthfully that cold boiled mutton was as agreeable to me as any other form of food. I found, after repeated trials, that mutton forms the best fuel—it is better than either beef or pork—and keeps the human engine at work for the longest time. So I had mutton. As I discovered also that bulk was necessary, and that only a certain amount of animal food was wanted, I used to have cold potatoes always ready. I stoked twice a day, at eleven in the morning and about five in the afternoon. Thus fortified, I got through the miserable hours as best I could.

I look back on that period as one of unmitigated misery and despair. I was daily growing more bloated, fatter, and flabbier in the cheeks. My hands trembled in the morning. I seemed losing the power of connected thought. My very lips were thickening.

I hope I am making it clear what was the effect of my bargain on myself—I mean without reference to the sufferings inflicted on me by my tyrant. People, however, never can know, unless they happen to be like myself, which is unlikely, how great a part eating and drinking take in the conduct of life. Between the rest of the world and me there was a great gulf fixed. They could enjoy, I could not; they could celebrate every joyful event with something additional to eat; they could make a little festival of every day; they could give to happiness an outward and tangible form. Alas, not only was I debarred from this, but I was cut off even from joy itself; for, if you look at it steadily, you will find that most of human joy or suffering is connected with the senses. I had bartered away a good half of mine, and the rest seemed in mourning for the loss of their fellows. As for my pale and colourless life, it was as monotonous as the clock. If I neglected to stoke, the usual feebleness would follow. There was no gracious looking forward to a pleasant dinner; no trembling anticipations in hope and fear of what might be preparing; no cheerful contemplation of the joint while the carver sharpens his knife; no discussions of flavour and richness; no modestly hazarded conclusions as to more currants; no rolling of the wine-glass in the fingers to the light, and smacking of lips over the first sip—all these things were lost to me. Reader, if haply this memoir ever sees a posthumous light, think what would happen to yourself if eating and drinking, those perennial joys of humanity, which last from the infantine pap to the senile Revalenta Arabica, were taken away.

All things tasted alike, as I have said, and cold mutton formed my staple dish. As I could only distinguish between beer, wine, coffee, and tea by the look, I drank water. If I ventured, which was seldom, to take my dinner at a cookshop, I would choose my *piece de résistance* by the look, by some fancied grace in the shape, but not by taste or smell. The brown of roast beef might attract me one day and repel me the next. I was pleased with the comeliness of a game-pie, or tickled by some inexplicable external charm of a beefsteak-pudding. But three quarters of my life were gone, and with them all my happiness.

If you have no appetite for eating, you can enjoy nothing in the whole world. That is an axiom. I could not taste, therefore my eye ceased to feel delight in pleasant sights, and my ear in pleasant sounds. It was not with me as in the case of a blind man, that an abnormal development of some other sense ensued; quite the contrary. In selling one, I seem to have sold them all. For, as I discovered, man is one and inseparable; you cannot split him up; and when my arch-deceiver bought my appetite, he bought me out and out. A wine merchant might as well pretend to sell the bouquet of claret and preserve the body; or a painter the colour of his picture and preserve the drawing; or a sculptor the grace of his group and keep the marble.

As regards other losses, I found I had lost the perception of beauty in form or colour. Why this was so I cannot explain. I was no longer, I suppose, in harmony with other men on any single point. Pretty women passed me unheeded; pictures had no charm for me; music was only irritating to my nerves.

Then I found that I had lost the power of sympathy. I had formerly been a soft-hearted man. I remarked now that the sight of suffering found me entirely callous. There was a poor family living about half a mile from me, whose acquaintance I made through buying some of my supplies of them. They were in distress for rent; they applied to me . . . there, I cannot bear to think of it. I had the money and I refused them. They were sold up, and I sat at my door and watched them on their way to London—the mother, the two girls, the little boy, had in hand, homeless and penniless, without a pang and without a single prompting of the heart to help them. God knows what became of them. May He forgive me for the hard-hearted cruelty with which I regarded their fate.

Had I, then, sold everything to this man?

I had been pretty religious in a way—a young man's way. Now I had lost all religious feeling whatever. I had once ambition and hopes, these were gone; I had once the capacity of love, that was gone; I had once a generous heart, that was gone; I once loved things worth loving, I felt no emotion now for anything. I was a machine which could feel. I was a man with the humanity taken out of him.

This time lasted for about four months. On the first of each month I went to receive my pay—the wages of sin—from the clerk, who surveyed me critically, but said nothing till the morning of the fourth month. Then, while he handed me my money, he whispered confidentially across the table:

'Look here, old fellow, you know; you're going it worse than poor Tom Kirby. Why don't you stop it? What *is* the good of a feller's drinking himself to death? The old gentleman was here yesterday, asking me how you looked, and if you continued steady. Pull up, old man, and knock it off.'

I took the money in my trembling hands and slunk away abashed. When I got home again, I am not ashamed to say that I cried like a child.

Delirium tremens! That would begin soon, and then the end would not be far off. It was too awful. Think of my position. I was but four-and-twenty. Not only was I deprived of the pleasure—mind you, a very real pleasure—of eating and drinking; I was the most temperate man in the world, though that was no great credit to myself, considering; and yet I bore in my face and my apperance, and felt in my very brain, all the marks and signs of confirmed drunkenness and the hopelessness of it. That hardened old voluptuary, that demon of gluttony, that secret murderer, would have no pity. He must have felt, by the falling-off of the splendid appetite which he was doing his utmost to ruin, that things were getting worse, and he was resolved—I had suspected this for some time—to kill me off by drinking me to death.

I believe I should have been dead in another week, but for a blessed respite, due, I afterwards discovered, to my demon being laid up with so violent a sore throat that he could not even swallow. What was my joy at being able to go to bed sober, to wake without a headache, to feel my bad symptoms slowly disappearing, to recover my nerves! For a whole fortnight I was happy—so happy that I even believed the improvement would last and that the old man was penitent. One day, after fourteen days of a veritable earthly paradise, I was walking along the Strand—for I was no longer afraid of venturing out—and met my old manager, Juliet's father. He greeted me with a warmth that was quite touching under all the circumstances. 'My dear boy, I have been longing to know your whereabouts. Come and tell me all about it. Have you dined? Let us have some dinner together.'

I excused myself, and asked after Juliet.

'Juliet is but so-so. Ah, do you know, Lucraft, sometimes I think that I did wrong to part you. And yet, you know, you had no money. Make some, my boy, and come back to us.'

This was hearty. I forgot my troubles and my state of bondage and everything, except Juliet.

'I—I—I have money,' I said. 'I have come into a little money unexpectedly.'

'Have you?' he replied, clasping me by the hand. 'Then come down and see Juliet. Or—stay; no. The day after tomorrow is Juliet's ben. We are playing at Richmond. We have one of your own parts—you shall be Sir Harry Wildair. I will alter the bills. You are sure to come?'

'Sure to come,' I said, with animation. 'Capital! I know every line in the part. Tell Juliet an old friend will act with her.'

We made a few new arrangements and parted. I bought a copy of the play at Lacy's and studied the part over again.

Next day I got over to Richmond in good time. The day was fine, I remember; my spirits were rapidly rising because it was the fifteenth day since I had had one of my usual attacks. I was in great hopes that the old man was really going to change his life and behave with consideration towards me. With the birth of hope, there revived in my heart some of my old feelings. I had a real desire to see Juliet again, but yet the old warmth seemed gone. It was a desire to see one in whom I had once been interested; the desire to awake old memories, which, I think, principally actuated me.

I found the dear girl waiting for me with an impatience which ought to have touched my heart, but which, somehow, only seemed to remind me of old times. My heart was gone—sold to my master with eveything else. Mechanically I took her hands in mine, and kissed her on the lips as I used to do. She threw both arms round my neck, kissed me again and again, and burst into tears of joy.

'Oh, Luke, Luke!' she said, 'I have so longed to see you again. The time has been weary, weary, without you.'

We sat together for half an hour, she all the time talking to me, and I, remembering what I used to be with her, wondering where the old feelings were gone, and trying to act as I used to.

'Luke, you are not growing cold to me, are you?' she asked, as some little gesture or word of hers passed me unnoticed.

'Cold, Juliet?' I replied. 'What should make you think so?'

'I will not think so,' she said. 'It is too great happiness to meet again, is it not? And you are silent because you feel too happy to speak. Is not that so?'

Presently it became time to go and dress.

'Let me look at you, Sir Henry Wildair,' she said. 'Yes, we shall do it very well tonight. You are not looking, somehow, quite so well as you used, Luke dear. Is it that London does not agree with you? Are you working too hard? Your face is swollen and—fancy—Mrs Mould says you look as if you had been drinking.'

Mrs Mould was the dresser.

If Mrs Mould had seen me a fortnight before, she might well have said I had been drinking. A fortnight, however, of rest had done wonders for me.

I laughed, but felt a little uneasy.

We rang up at seven.

The house was quite full, because my Juliet was popular at Richmond.

I began with all my former fire and vigour, because I was acting again with her. The old life came back to me; I forgot my troubles; I was really happy, and I believe I acted well. At all events, the house applauded. Between the first and second acts a sudden terror seized me. I felt that the old man was eating again. That passed off, because he ate very little. But then he began to drink, and to drink fast.

It was no use fighting against it. I believe the villain must have been drinking raw brandy, because I was drunk in five minutes. I staggered and reeled about on the stage, I laughed wildly and sang foolishly, and then I tumbled down in a heap and could not get up again. The last thing I remember is the angry roar of poor old Kerrans, beside himself with passion, telling the carpenters to carry that drunken beast away and throw him into the road. I heard afterwards that they were obliged to drop the curtain, and that the *éclat* of poor Juliet's benefit was entirely spoiled. As for myself, the carpenters carried me out to the middle of Richmond-green, where they were going to leave me, only one of them had compassion, and wheeled me to his own house in a barrow.

In the morning I returned hastily to London, sought my cottage at Islington, and shut myself in with an agony of shame and humiliation.

I was quite crushed by this blow. For the first time I felt tempted to commit suicide and end it all. To be sure I ought to have foreseen this, and all the other dreadful things. Directly my master, my owner, got able to swallow, though he could not eat, he could drink, and ordered the most fiery liquor he could procure, with a view to kill me off and begin with another victim.

But Providence ruled otherwise.

Then began a week of cruel suffering. My master sent me word by Boule-de-neige that he intended to finish me off. My appetite, he said, had been long failing, and was now perfectly contemptible. He complained that I had neglected my part of the contract, that I must have been practising intemperance—the horrible hypocrite—to have reduced so fine an appetite to nothing in a short four months. Therefore he felt obliged to tell me that in a week or two I should probably find the agreement ended. That was his ferocious way of putting it. He meant that in a week I should be dead. His words were prophetic, but not in the sense in which he meant them.

He drank brandy now. He drank it morning, noon, and night. He drank it, not because he liked it, but in hopes of despatching me. I was no sooner partially recovered from one drunken bout than I plunged into another.

I lost all power of walking. I could not move about. I lay the whole day sick and feverish on my bed, or, if I got up at all, it was only to change it for an easy chair. I could eat nothing.

Then I began to have visions and to see spectres in my loneliness and misery.

First I saw all over again the scenes of my early life—my poor deserted mother; the tramp who took charge of me; the sleep in which I nearly perished; the strolling actors with whom I wandered; the girl with whom I fell in love. Only among them all there hovered perpetually the ugly face of Boule-de-neige, spoiling the pleasant memories, and corrupting the current of my thoughts with his 'Cluck-cluck', and his demoniac grin.

'How you do, Massa Lucraft? How you feel your stumjack this morning? Ole massa him berry fierce. Him gwine to make the noyeau punch tomorrow. Dat finish um off. Dat work um up. You wait till tomorrow, Massa Lucraft.'

I could only groan.

'You nice young gegleman,' he went on, with a grin. 'You berry grateful young gegleman. Massa him gib you thirty pounds a mouth, and you spend it all in 'temperate courses. Bad; berry bad, dam bad. What you say when you die—eh? Ho! ho!'

The creature seemed always with me during this time. If I opened my eyes I had the feeling that he was hovering about my bed. If it was dark I thought I saw his eyes glaring at me from some corner. If I was asleep he would waken me with his 'Cluck'. What he did in my cottage I never knew. The room was filled with the visions which passed through my brain, succeeding each other again and again like the acts of a play repeated incessantly. I saw the octagonal room with the old gentleman eating and drinking. I saw myself at Richmond. I saw myself before the magistrates; and I looked on as an outsider, as a spectator of a tragedy which would end in death and horror.

It was two days before the period allotted to me by my master, at eight o'clock in the evening, as I was sitting in my lonely cottage, expectant of the usual drunken bout, when I felt a curious agitation within me, an internal struggle, as if through all my veins a tempestuous wave was surging and rushing. I lay down.

'This is some new devilry of the old man,' I said to myself. 'Let him do his worst; at least, I must try to bear it with resignation.' I began to speculate on my inevitable and approaching end, and to wonder curiously, what proportion of the sin of all this drunkenness would be laid to my charge.

To my astonishment nothing more followed. The tumult of my system gradually subsided, and I fell asleep.

In the morning I awoke late, and missed the usual headache. I had, therefore, I was surprised to find, actually not been drunk the night before. I rose with my customary depression, and was astonished to discover that my nerves were steadier and spirits higher than I had known for a long time.

I mechanically went to the cupboard and pulled out my cold mutton and potatoes. Who can picture my joy when I found that I could taste the meat again, and that it was nasty? I hardly believed my senses; in fact, I had lost them for so long that it was difficult to understand that they had come back to me. I tried the potatoes. Heavens, what a horrible thing to a well-regulated palate is a cold boiled potato!

At first, as I said, I could not believe that I had recovered my taste; then, as the truth forced itself upon me, and I found that I could not only taste, but was actually hungry, I jumped and danced, and was beside myself with joy. Think of a convict suddenly released, and declared guiltless of the charges brought against him. Think of a prisoner on the very ladder of the gallows-tree, with the rope round his neck, reprieved and pardoned. Think of one doomed to death by his physician receiving the assurance that it was all a mistake, and that he would gather up long years of life as in a sheaf. And think that such joy as these would feel, I felt—and more!

I went to the nearest coffee-shop and ordered bacon, eggs, and tea, offering up a short grace with every plate as it came. And then, because I felt sure that my old tormentor must be dead, I repaired to my lawyers', and saw the clerk.

'Ah,' he said, 'the poor old man's gone at last! Went out like the snuff of a candle. His illness was only twenty-four hours. Well, he's gone to heaven, if ever man did.'

'What did he die of—too much eating and drinking?'

'Mr Lucraft,' said the clerk, severely, 'this is not the tone for *you* to adopt towards that distinguished man, your benefactor. He died, sir—being a man of moral, temperate, and even abstemious life, though of full habit—of apoplexy.'

'Oh!' I said, careless what the clerk said, but glad to be quite sure that the diabolical old villain was really dead. I suppose that never was such joy over the repentance of any sinner as mine over the death of that murdering glutton, for whom no words of hatred were too strong.

'I think you've got to see our senior partner,' said the clerk. 'Step this way.'

He led me to a room where I found a grave and elderly gentleman sitting at a table.

'Mr Lucraft?' he said. 'I was expecting you. I saw your late patron's negro this morning. He told me that you would call.'

I stared, but said nothing.

'I have a communication to make to you, on the part of our departed friend, Mr Ebenezer Grumbelow. It is dated a few weeks since, and is to the effect that a sum of money which I hold was to be placed in your hands in case of his death. This, it appears, he anticipated, for some reason or other.'

'Ebenezer Grumbelow'. That was the name which had so long escaped my memory—'Ebenezer Grumbelow'.

I said nothing, but stared with all my eyes.

'My poor friend,' the lawyer went on, 'after remarking that unless you change your unfortunate habits you will come to no good, gave me this money himself—here is the cheque—so that it will not appear in his last will and testament.'

I took it in silence.

'Well, sir'—he looked at me in some surprise—'have you no observation to make, or remark to offer, on this generosity?'

'None,' I said.

'I do not know,' he continued; 'I do not know—your signature here, if you please—what reason Mr Grumbelow had in taking you up, or what claim you possessed upon his consideration; but I think, sir, I do think, that some expression, some sense of regret, is due.'

I buttoned up the cheque in my pocket.

'Mr Grumbelow was a philanthropist, I believe, sir?'

'He was. As a philanthropist, as a supporter of charities, as a public donor of great amounts, Mr Grumbelow's name stands in the front. So much we all know.'

'A religious man, too?'

'Surely, surely; one of our most deeply religious men. A man who was not ashamed of his saintly profession.'

'Cluck-cluck!'

It was the familiar face of Boule-de-neige at the door.

'You know, I suppose,' said the lawyer, 'Mr Grumbelow's body-servant, a truly Christian negro?'

'Was there,' I asked, 'any clause in Mr Grumbelow's letter—any conditions attached to this gift?'

'None whatever. It is a free gift. Stay, there is a postscript which I ought to have read to you. You will perhaps understand it. In it Mr Grumbelow says that as to the services rendered by him to you, and by you to him, it will be best for your own sake to keep them secret.'

I bowed.

The date of the cheque corresponded with the first illness of the old man—his affection of the throat. Probably he was afraid that I should reveal his infamous story.

'I may now tell you, Mr Lucraft, without at all wishing to break any confidence that may have existed between you and the deceased, that a friend of Mr Grumbelow's—no other, indeed, than the Rev. Jabez Jumbles, a pulpit name doubtless known to you— intends to write the biography of this distinguished and religious man, as an example to the young. Any help you can afford to so desirable an end will be gratefully received. Particularly, Mr Lucraft, any communication on the subject of his continual help given to young men, who regularly disappointed him, and all, except yourself, died of drink.'

I bowed again and retired.

Did anyone ever hear of such a wicked old man?

Outside the office I was joined by the negro.

'What have you got to say to me, detestable wretch?' I cried, shaking my fist in his withered old face.

'Cluck-cluck! Massa not angry with poor old Boule-de-neige. How young massa? Young massa pretty well? How de lubly abbadide of de young gegleman? How him strong stumjack? Cluck-cluck!'

He kept at a safe distance from me. I think I should have killed him if I had ever clutched him by the throat.

'Ole massa him always ask, "How dat young debbel? Go and see, Boule-de-neige." I go to young massa's cottage daraway, and come back. "Him berry dam bad, sir," I say; "him going to be debbel berry fast, just like dem oders. De folk all say he drink too much for him berry fine constitution." Cluck-cluck! Ole massa he only say ebbery night, "Bring de brandy, Boule-de-neige; let's finish him." Cluck-cluck!'

Here was a Christian negro for you!

'Tell me, what did your master die of?'

'Apple perplexity, massa.'

'Ah! what else? Come, Boule-de-neige, I know a good deal; tell me more.'

'Massa's time up,' he whispered, coming close to me. 'Time quite up, and him berry much 'fraid. Massa Lucraft want servant? Boule-de-neige berry good servant. Cook lubly dinner; make massa rich, like Massa Grumbelow.'

'I'd rather hire the devil!' I exclaimed.

'Cluck-cluck-cluck!' grinned the creature; and really he looked at the moment as much like the devil as one could wish. 'Cluck! dat massa can do if massa like.'

I rushed away, too much excited by the recovery of my freedom to regard what he said.

I was free! What next?

First the restoration of my shattered nerves.

There was no permanent injury done to my constitution, because, after all, the drink had not actually gone down my throat, nor was it I who had consumed the gallons of turtle soup, the tons of fish, the shiploads of cattle with which he had punished me for that woeful signature of mine.

The contract, in some inexplicable manner, affected me with the punishment of my purchaser's excesses by a kind of sympathy. I remained a strictly temperate man for a month. I recovered gradually the tone of my system; my features lost their bloated look. I became myself again.

And then I sought the injured Kerrans.

It was no use trying to tell him a story which he never would have believed. I simply told him that I was taken suddenly and hopelessly ill on that fatal night. I asked him to remember, which is quite true, how I began the piece with a fire and animation quite impossible in a man who had been drinking; how I had certainly nothing between the scenes, during which intervals I was talking with him, and how the thing came upon me without any warning. If you try, you know, you can make yourself quite drunk with brandy in two minutes. This is just what Mr Grumbelow did to me.

Kerrans, good fellow, outraged in his best feelings, was difficult to smooth down.

He had asked me to act with Juliet in the hope of restoring to the girl her lost good spirits. I came; the misfortune happened, and she was worse than ever. But he forgave me at last, and allowed me another chance. This time it was not Juliet who threw her arms around me; it was I who implored her forgiveness, and the renewal of her love. I was cold no longer. I left off remembering, and lived

THE CASE OF MR LUCRAFT

again in the present. I was a lover, and my girl was trembling and blushing, with her hand in mine.

It all happened more than fifty years ago. The only record which remains of the events I have described are on the tablet to the memory of Ebenezer Grumbelow in St Rhadegunda's Church, City: and the little faded scrap from the *Morning Chronicle*, which I always carry in my pocket-book, and which tells the tale of my shame.

Juliet never believed my story, and I left off insisting on its truth.

She lies in Norwood Cemetery now, but we kept our golden wedding ere she died; and children and grandchildren live to bless her name.

THE MAN WHO COULDN'T TASTE PEPPER

G. B. Stern

Over the years, the huge diversity of national and regional foods has inspired hundreds of books of recipes, and led to the opening of innumerable restaurants specialising in the different cuisines. Gladys Bertha Stern (1890–1973), better known by her initials as G. B. Stern, was an enthusiast of international cooking and her work as a novelist and scriptwriter in Britain and Hollywood gave her the opportunity to patronise restaurants in many countries. Her story 'The Man Who Couldn't Taste Pepper' is set in Vienna in the year 1922 and features a small restaurant with the delightful name of 'The Little Hot Dog'. It is a story of a man with a very strange affliction and, of course, features death . . .

'So you like paprika, Niki?'

'I do. And for itself, not just because it's a national food. Though there's always a thrill about national food—like national anthems.'

'*Bouillabaisse* at Marseilles,' mused Franz, '*Fritto del mare* at Venice. Saddle of mutton in London. Ice-cream-soda in America—or is it pie?'

'There's something exciting in paprika,' went on Veronica. 'And it's such a glorious vermilion when it's in powder; a different red from cayenne. Though I don't think those people really appreciate it. Do you think they take our Little Hot Dog for a sort of Simpson's? I mean—one doesn't usually wallop into a nine-course dinner here, does one?'

'One can, but one doesn't. I'm glad you have a proper appreciation of paprika, Niki—though I knew a man once who couldn't taste pepper at all, black, white, cayenne or paprika.'

'Suppose one couldn't smell roses or hear Chopin! Tell me about your man, Franz. You haven't told me a story for ages. And I can't dance while those people are eating; it makes me feel like a tiger after a heavy kill, to watch them. What happened if you popped a whole lot of pepper into whatever your man was eating?'

'Well, what happened was that he killed a man and had to fly the country.'

'Ai-eee! Tell your darling-angel Niki. She likes red things—blood and paprika and soldiers' coats and lobsters.'

'It was twenty years ago—when wine was wine, and there were plenty of soldiers' coats, though not red ones. And the blood ran fast in your veins, and life was like one of Strauss's waltzes—all throb and sentiment, with a sob at the end of it. And I was a young lieutenant of dragoons, and I had an English friend—an acquaintance, rather, for I met him in a bar at midnight, and we knocked about together for a while. And La Belle Denise was dancing here at The Little Hot Dog, and he was madly infatuated with her—he and a Spaniard from Seville—I've even forgotten their names, though the Spaniard was called Juan de something, and the Englishman, I think, Charles.

'I don't believe she cared a flick of the eyelid for either of them, but they amused her, and she played off one against the other, till the two men hated each other to killing point. I've seen Juan finger his knife more than once when the Englishman was dancing with Denise. One of them would give her a bouquet that would cost a couple of million kronen nowadays, and the other would reply with a string of pearls, and next night the first would produce a ruby bracelet. And so it went on.

'She made a sort of game of keeping them exactly equal. A tour de force in equilibrium. We used to bet on it. A tilt in her favour on the Spanish or the English side, and the betting simply flickered like a compass needle.

'It got to be an absolute contest between them as to which could do the most extravagant and fantastic thing in her honour. Juan once had this place draped in black, and lit by luminous skeletons; Charles had the courtyard of the Imperial Hotel flooded and gave a Venetian fête in gondolas; Juan had a special tzigane band sent for from Hungary; Charles gave her seven brindled mastiffs, each with a spiked silver collar.

'Feeling ran very high at the "Dog". Everyone had money on it, and everyone was a fierce partisan of one or the other; and things got to such a pitch that one of Charles' men wouldn't drink with a Juanite, and vice versa.

'I tried to get Charles out of it. Things were going a bit too far. But he wouldn't listen to me. The silly fool said he wanted to marry Denise, and take her back to England. As if one married a dancer! especially a dancer like Denise. And as if she'd have had him—a younger son, who'd already squandered on her the little he had besides his pay. I found this out, you see, when I was trying to

show him how futile it was to contemplate marriage with a bird of
paradise like Denise. Why, she'd been the *chère amie* of at least two
Russian Grand Dukes, and her jewels were worth a small fortune.
And there were rumours about a reigning monarch. Anyway, they
say the Queen of Moldavia was markedly cold to her husband after
Denise left Blatzen.

'When I found that Charles couldn't be made to see reason, I
approached La Belle Denise herself. "What, mademoiselle," I said,
"do you hope to get by keeping these two silly moths fluttering
round the flame of your incomparable beauty? Mademoiselle is
charming, she is ravishing; one has but to see her to become her
slave. But an Englishman chooses for his wife someone a little less
exciting—more domestic. One who can cook and sew, and who
will be a good mother to his children. A Spaniard, too, admires the
homely virtues; and for him a marriage is arranged by the parents.
N'est ce pas?'

'Denise flashed her yellow eyes at me. "You think, then, that I
could not be a good wife? Bah! I have nothing to learn from your
Hausfrau, or your pudding-faced English miss! You shall see, *mon
ami*; me, I invite you to dinner, *chez moi* tomorrow night; you and
those two poor *drôles*. The arrangement, the cuisine, everything I
shall make myself."

'So the next evening found the three of us knocking at her flat.
Denise opened the door herself. To my intense amusement, she
was wearing an obvious fancy-dress of domesticity—blue cotton,
beautifully cut, of course, a white mob cap, and an apron. As a
matter of fact, she'd never looked prettier. She took us into the
sitting-room, which was also rather in fancy dress: no exotic
flowers, a work-box prominently displayed, a cosy fire burning
brightly in the grate, and all the photographs tucked away, except
two old-fashioned daguerrotypes of what might have been her
father and mother, or might have been bought at the curio shop
round the corner. The atmosphere was completed by a thoroughly
bourgeois cat—none of your blue-blooded Persians!—asleep on
the hearthrug, and a large doll propped in a baby's chair.

'"This," said Denise, taking it up and caressing it, "is my child,
my own little one. Her name is Joan, a little English miss." She
glanced wickedly at Juan. "You no like, *mon ami*? Then her name is
Juanita."

'And all that evening she worked that doll like the very devil, till
her rival adorers were simply at boiling point. It's a bad trick
among women, Niki—clever women—and I'm telling you this so
that you shouldn't do it, that when they know there's someone in
the room who wants to embrace them, they deliberately and

tantalisingly embrace something else—a dog, or a kitten, or even a sofa-cushion. It can drive a man to frenzy.'

'Yes,' mused Veronica, 'I suppose it could.' And absent-mindedly she began to kiss her own shoulder, very softly. Franz looked up. 'Fortunately,' he remarked, 'I am as leather. I've been pickled by the years . . .

'But Charles and Juan were very far from being leather that night. They were in a highly inflamed condition; and I, like a fool and a schoolboy, just to spite Denise, went and made it worse.'

'Oh, Franz, what did you do?'

'I tilted the entire contents of a pot of cayenne pepper into the omelette. The omelette, you see, was to be Denise's *chef d'oeuvre*. Her ultimate proof to me that she was thoroughly domesticated, thoroughly capable of running a home and making a man comfortable. She laid the table with her own hands. Tripping to and fro between the kitchen and sitting-room, giving a last polish to the glasses, calling us to come and admire the pile of snowy table napkins in the linen cupboard.

'Oh, it was well staged, the whole scene. I'll grant her that. And she could cook, the little devil; she knew her job. "But wait"! she cried. "Wait till you taste my omelette. There will not be a crumb left for *la p'tite* Juanita, I promise you that. But she—she prefers the rosbif." And she twinkled first at one and then at the other, and flung a glance of sheer triumph at me, and invited me to come into the kitchen and help beat the eggs.

'It was while she was carrying in the plates, that I tipped the pepper into the omelette. My object, you see, was to make her look a fool. I laughed when I pictured the grimaces of Charles and Juan. But what followed was more fantastic than funny.

'I refused omelette, on the grounds that I did not care for eggs. As for Denise, she insisted, still in the spirit of domestic masquerade, on remaining cook and waitress, and not eating, herself, till the others were done. So that the omelette was divided—with exact equality, as usual!—between Charles and Juan.

'Charles took a mouthful. "Delicious," he said, and fell to. But Juan began choking and spluttering and sneezing. He grew purple in the face. When he could speak, he glared fiercely first at Denise, then at Charles, who was halfway through his omelette. "So you try to poison me and me alone, because it is this English pig that you love? But he shall not live to love you long." And he smacked Charles twice across the face with his open hand.

'Charles sprang to his feet. A duel, of course, was inevitable. The very last thing that I had wanted.

'"I do not understand your talk of poison, Señor. I find the omelette of mademoiselle delicious. But you have called me a pig and struck me in the face. I am not a man to be insulted by a dago. When will you meet me and with what weapons?"

'I was simply amazed. Was Charles acting? If so, his nonchalance was superhuman, with all that pepper in his mouth and down his throat and up his nose. Denise, knowing nothing of the trick I had played, was merely insulted at the Spaniard's treatment of her cookery. With the sweetest of all smiles at Charles, and a cold flash of her eyes at Juan, she quitted the room. Then I burst out:

'"Charles—did you taste nothing wrong?"

'"Nothing," he replied.

'"That omelette—it was chockful of pepper—I tipped it in myself, for a joke!"

'Then I understood. Charles, by reason of some curious idiosyncrasy of palate, *could not taste pepper*. He had calmly eaten an omelette which was enough to make any ordinary man half-dead with choking and sneezing—exactly the effect it had had on Juan. Hence the quarrel—and from what I knew of Juan, one of them would have to die. He, obviously, did not believe a word of the pepper story, and Denise's parting glance of sweetness at Charles had not improved matters.

'Juan chose pistols. They were each to go and stand in opposite corners of a pitch dark room, with lighted cigarettes between their lips, and fire at the glowing end. I was sorry, for Charles was a fine swordsman but an indifferent revolver shot.

'We went in Denise's salon. I drew the blinds, placed them in position and extinguished the lights. Then the dancer and I had to wait with what patience we could while those two lunatics tried to kill each other.

'Six shots in quick succession. A seventh—a groan and a heavy fall. Like a madman I wrenched open the door, fumbled for the switch. Then I heard Charles' voice: "I believe I've killed him, Franz."

'Juan lay in a crumpled heap, the blood spreading through his shirt front in an ugly brown stain. In his hand was a still burning cigarette. Charles looked, and then turned away with a hunch of the shoulders. "So he cheated till the last!"

'"What d'you mean?"

'"Don't you see? He had his cigarette in his hand; I kept mine in my mouth all the time . . ."

'I managed to get him away. Duelling was more common then than now, but still it would have been an ugly thing for him if they'd been able to connect him with the sensational find of Juan's body in Denise's flat. As it was, we made it look like suicide. Everybody knew that he had been madly infatuated with her, and she, in her most exquisite clothes, reproached herself bitterly at the enquiry, and vowed that she would enter a convent and remain there for the rest of her life. I never heard from Charles again.'

'And did she go into a convent?' Niki asked.

Franz lit a cigarette with care, and shook his head, smiling a little to himself, as if amused at some ancient memory.

'And did you ever find out which of the two she had really loved?'

'No. She never told me. Not even during the perfectly charming six months we had together immediately after the regrettable affair.'

FINAL DINING

Roger Zelazny

The final tale of this section in a way brings history full circle by using the events of the Last Supper as the theme of a murder story set firmly in the present day. That fateful gathering of Jesus and his disciples might well be cited as the most famous instance of a meal which engendered a death—albeit that Christ's 'murder' was ordered by the Roman judiciary after Judas' treacherous act of betrayal. Fantasy writer Roger Zelazny (1937–   ) has used these facts as the basis for his account of a painter working on a picture of the 'Last Supper', who finds himself drawn inexorably into a last meal and a terrible act of murder. 'Final Dining' is a story in the best historical tradition as well as being chillingly contemporary.

I felt the cat's tongue lick of his brush, lining my cheeks, darkening my beard.

He touched my eyes and they were opened. First the left, then the right. Instantly.

There was no blur of sudden awakening. I stared back into his own dark eyes, intent upon my face. He held the brush delicately as a feather, his thumbnail a spectrum of pigment.

He stood there, admiring me.

'Yes!' he breathed at last. 'They *are* right! Lines of guilt, shame, terror—arrowing those target eyes!

'But they face into the light, nevertheless,' he continued, '—unflinching!—with all the insolence and pain of Lucifer. They will not drop as he dips the bread . . .

'Beard needs more red,' he added.

'Not much more,' I said.

He squinted.

'Not much more, though.'

He blew gently upon my face, then covered me.

Portrait sitting in fifteen minutes, he thought. *Have to stop*.

He was moving around. I felt him light a cigarette.

Mignon is coming at ten.

'Mignon is coming,' I said.

Yes. I will show you to her. She likes to look at paintings, and I've never done anything this good before. She doesn't think I can. I will show her. Of course, she doesn't know art . . .

'Yes.'

I heard a knock on the door.

He let her in. I felt his excitement.

'You're always on time,' he said.

She laughed, with the chime of an expensive clock.

'Always,' she said, 'until it's finished and I can see it. I'm eager.'

She is wearing her portrait smile already, he mused, hanging her coat on the rack. *She is sitting in the dark chair now. Dark as her hair. Green tweeds, and a silver pin. Why not diamonds? She's got them.*

'Why not diamonds?' I asked.

'Why not diamonds?'

'Huh?—Oh, my pin?' She touched it, glancing down at a youthful breast. 'You haven't painted that low yet, have you? I'm posing for a mantelpiece, not a cover story on family fortunes. So, I decided I'd rather have something simple.'

She's smiling again. Is she mocking me?

'What's that one you have covered?'

She walked to the canvas.

'Oh,' he said. Delighted. Anticipating. 'It's nothing, really.'

'Let me see it.'

'All right.'

The cloth rustled and I looked up at her.

'Goodness!' she said. 'Peter Halsey's "Last Supper"!—My, but it's fine.'

She moved farther back, intent.

'He looks as if he's about to step out of the frame and betray Him all over again.'

'I am,' I said, modestly.

'He probably is,' Peter observed. 'He's rather special.'

'Yes,' she decided. 'I've never seen those exact colours before. The depth, the texture—he's very unusual.'

'He ought to be,' he replied. 'He came from the stars.'

'The stars?' she puzzled. 'What do you mean?'

'His pigment was ground from a meteorite I found this summer. Its redness grabbed my attention right away, and it was small enough to throw in the trunk.'

She studied my brushwork.

'For something this good, you've painted it awfully fast.'

'No, it's been around for some time,' he said. 'I was waiting for the right notion of how to do him. That red stoned gave me the clue, the same week you began your sittings. Once I got started he practically painted himself.'

'He looks as if he enjoys it all,' she laughed.

'I don't mind a bit . . .'

'I doubt that he minds.'

'. . . for I am that organic changeling, left for a rock fancied as a footstool by the gods.'

'Who knows his origin?'

He covered me, with a matador's flourish.

'Shall we begin?'

'Yes.'

She returned to the chair.

After a while, he tried to read her posing eyes.

'Take her. She's willing.'

He put down the brush, stared at her, at his work, at her.

He picked up the brush again.

'Go ahead. What's to lose? And think of the gain. That silver could be diamonds on her breast. Think of her breast, think of the diamonds.'

He put the brush down.

'What's the matter?'

'I'm tired, all of a sudden. A cigarette and I'll be ready to go again.'

She rose, stretching her arms overhead.

'Want me to heat that coffee?'

He looked up, over at his cheap hot plate.

'No, that's all right. Cigarette?'

'Thanks.'

His hand shook.

She'll think it's fatigue.

'Your hand is shaking.'

'Tired, I guess.'

She sat on his studio bed. He seated himself beside her, slowly, half-reclining.

'Hot in here.'

'Yes.'

He took her hand.

'You're shaking, too.'

'Nerves. DTs. Who knows?'

He raised it to his lips.

'I love you.'

A frightened look widened her eyes, slackened her mouth.
'. . . and your teeth are lovely.'
He began to embrace her.
'Oh, please . . . !'
He kissed her, firmly.
'Don't. If you don't mean it . . .'
'I do,' he said. 'I do.'
'You're wonderful,' she sighed, 'and your art. I always felt . . .
But—'
He kissed her again, then drew her down beside him.
'Mignon.'
'—'

Peter Halsey looked out from his balcony, over the landscaped
garden with its Augustan walks, the picturesqueness, the
eighteenth-century prettiness, and down to the guard rails, the
cliffs, and the long, steep slant into the Gulf.
'It is good,' he said, and turned back toward his suite.
'Good,' I repeated.
I hung upon the side wall. He stopped before me.
'What are you smirking at, you old bastard?'
'Nothing.'
Blanche entered from the bedroom, right, patting her wide halo
of sunset-pink.
'Did you say something, honey?'
'Yes. But I wasn't talking to you.'
She looked up at me, pointing with her thumb.
'Him?'
'That's right. He's the only good thing I've ever done, and we get
along well.'
She shuddered.
'He looks something like you, at that—only meaner.'
He turned.
'Do you really think so?'
'Uh-huh. Especially the eyes.'
'Get out of here,' he said.
'What's wrong?'
'Nothing,' he controlled himself. 'But my wife will be back soon.'
'All right, daddy. When will I see you again?'
'I'll call you.'
'Okay.'
A swish of black skirts and she was gone.
Peter did not see her to the door. Not her sort. He studied me a
little longer, then crossed the room to the mirror and stared into it.

'Hm,' he announced. 'There *is* a little resemblance—subconscious pun or something.'

'Sure,' I said.

He strolled back toward the balcony, hands in the pockets of his silk dressing gown.

Once more, he looked at the ocean.

'Mater Oceana,' he invoked, 'I am happy and unhappy. Take . . . Take away my unhappiness.'

'What is that?'

He did not answer me, but I knew.

Outside, I heard Mignon coming. The door swung open. I knew. He stepped back into the room, looking at her.

'My, you're fresh. Why do you bother with beauty parlours?'

'To stay this way for you, dear, I'd hate to have you lose interest after two months.'

'Small chance of that.'

He embraced her.

I hate you, you rich bitch! You think you can run my life now, because you're footing the bills. You didn't make the loot either. It was your old man—Go ahead, ask me if I worked today.

She pulled away, reluctantly.

'Do any painting this afternoon, dear?'

No, I was in the bedroom with a blonde.

'No, I had a headache.'

'Oh, I'm sorry. Is it better now?'

'No, I still have it.' *You!*

'What about this evening?'

'What about it?'

'What was that French restaurant we passed yesterday?'

'Le Bois.'

'I thought you might like to try it. We've eaten in all the others.'

'No, not tonight.'

'Where, then?'

'How about right here?'

She looked troubled.

'I'll have to call downstairs now, then.'

I'll bet you can't even cook. I never have had a chance to find out!

'That'd be fine.'

'You're *sure* you don't want to go out?'

'Yes, I'm sure.'

Her face brightened.

'They'll set up a table in the garden, and send the food out on carts—for special guests.'

'Why go to all that bother?'

'Mother said she and Dad had it that way when they honey-mooned here. I've been meaning to suggest it.'

'Why not?' he shrugged.

Mignon looked at her watch. She raised her hand, hesitated, then tapped on the bedroom door.

'Aren't you dressed yet?'

'Just about.'

Why don't you die and leave me in peace? Maybe then I could paint again. You have no real appreciation of my art—of any art! Or anything else.—Phoney aesthete! What have you ever worked for? Die! So I can collect . . . and stop bothering me!

'Why not tonight?' I asked.

'I wonder . . . ?' he mused.

'You are a happy couple—honeymooners. There would be no suspicion. Keep her there until late. Pipe her champagne by the gallon. Dance with her. When the waiters have left, when the lights are dim, when there are just you two, music, the cham-pagne, and darkness—when she begins to laugh too much, when she stumbles as she dances,' I concluded, 'then there is the rail.'

There was another tap on the door.

'Ready?'

Peter Halsey adjusted his tie.

'Coming, dear.'

*   *   *

God! How much of that can she drink? I'll be under the table first!

'More champagne, darling?'

'Just a little.'

He filled it to the brim.

'Bottle is getting low. Might as well kill it.'

'You haven't been drinking much,' she accused.

'I wasn't raised on it.'

The candles were all. The trellises and islands of colour now wore impenetrable cloaks. It was deep, inky, outside the wavering halo. The Strauss waltzes whirled and circled from the hidden speaker—but dignified, dim, *sotto voce*, and excluded from the table. The aromas of invisible blossoms were dying, unmingling themselves, in the refrigerator of night.

He looked at her.

'Aren't you cold?'

'No! Let's stay here all night. This is wonderful!'

He squinted at his watch. It *was* getting late.

A drink, to brace the nerves.

He quaffed the sour fire. Like snowflakes falling upward into a yellow sky, its icy jewels jetted through his head.

'Now is the time.'

He leaned forward and blew out the candles.

'Why did you do that?'

'To be alone with you, in the dark.'

She giggled.

He found her and embraced her.

'Kiss her—that's it.'

He drew her to her feet, had a hard time unclasping her arms. But he led her, arm about the waist, to the white rail.

'How lovely the ocean, when there is no moon,' she said, thickly. 'Didn't Van Gogh once paint the Seine at ni—'

He struck her behind the knees with his left forearm. She toppled backwards, and he tried to catch her. Her head struck a flagstone. He cursed.

'No difference. She'll be bruised anyhow, when they find her.'

She moaned, softly, as he raised her warm stillness.

He leaned forward, shoving hard, and pushed her over the rail.

He heard her hit stone, once, but the *Blue Danube* covered all other sounds of descent.

'Good night, Mignon.'

'Good night, Mignon.'

'It was terrible,' he told the detective. 'I know I'm drunk and can't talk straight—that's why I couldn't save her. We were having such a good time, dancing and all. She wanted to look at the ocean, then I went back to the table for another drink. I heard her cry out, and, and—'

He covered his face with his hands, forcing a sobbing sound.

'—she was gone!'

He shook all over.

'—and we were having such a good time!'

'Take it easy, Mister Halsey.' The man put a hand on his shoulder. 'The desk clerk says he has some pills. Take them and go to bed. Honestly, that's the best thing you can do now. Your statement wouldn't be worth much, even though I can see what happened. I'll make my report in the morning.

'The Coast Guard has a cutter out there now,' he continued. 'You'll have to go to the morgue tomorrow. But just get some sleep now.'

'We were having such a good time,' Peter Halsey repeated, as he staggered to the elevator.

Inside, he lighted a cigarette.

*   *   *

He unlocked the door and switched on the light.

The suite was transformed.

It was divided into alcoves by the hastily-constructed partitions. Of the original furnishings, only a few chairs and a small table remained.

A placard stood on the table.

Beside the placard was a leather notebook. He opened it, dropping his cigarette to the floor. He read . . .

He read the names of the critics, the gallery scouts, the museum reviewers, the buyers, the makers of opinion.

It was the invitation list.

A wisp of smoke curled up from the carpet. Unconsciously, he moved his foot to crush it. He was reading the placard.

Peter Halsey Exhibition, it said, *Arranged by Mrs Peter Halsey, on the Anniversary of the Two Most Happy Months in Her Life. 1 AM to 2 PM. Friday, Saturday, Sunday.*

He walked from niche to niche, repainting with his eyes all the works his hands had ever executed.

His watercolours. His stab at cubism. His portraits.

She had hunted them all down, bought or borrowed all of them. *Portrait of Mignon.*

He looked at her smile, and her hair, dark as the chair; at her green tweeds; at the silver pin that could have been diamonds.

'—' she said.

Nothing.

She was dead.

And across the way, staring into her smile, with my beard of blood and bread in hand, amidst the dove-bright faces of the holy ones, with my halo also hammered from silver, I smiled back.

'Congratulations. The cheque will be in the mail promptly.'

Where's my palette knife?

'Come now! No Dorian Gray business, eh?'

Where's something that will cut?

'Why this? You painted me as I am. You could as easily have used the pigment for someone else.—Him, for example, or him.— But I was your inspiration. I! We drew life from one another, from your despair. Are we not a masterpiece?'

'No!' he cried, covering his face once more. 'No!'

'Take those pills and go to bed.'

'No!'

'Yes.'

'She wanted me to be great. She tried to buy it for me. But she *did* want me to be great . . .'

'Of course. She loved you.'

'I didn't know. I killed her . . .'

'Don't all men?—Wilde again, you know.'

'Shut up! Stop looking at me!'

'I can't. I am you.'

'I will destroy you.'

'That would take some doing.'

'*You* have destroyed me!'

'Ha! Who did the pushing?'

'Go away! Please!'

'And miss my exhibition?'

'Please.'

'Good night, Peter Halsey.'

And I watched him, shadow amidst shadows. He did not stagger. He moved like a machine, like a sleepwalker. Sure. Precise. Certain.

*   *   *

Ten hours have passed, and the sun is up. Soon now I will hear their footsteps in the hall. The cognoscenti, the great ones: the Berensons, the Duveens . . .

They will pause outside the door. They will knock, gently.

And after a while they will try the door.

It will open, and they will come in.

In fact, they are coming now.

They will behold the eyes, tearless windows of a sin-drenched soul . . .

They have paused outside.

They will see the lines of guilt, shame, terror, and remorse— arrowing those target eyes . . .

A knock.

—But they face into the light, nevertheless—unflinching! They will not drop!

The doorknob is turning.

'Come in, my lords, come in! Great art awaits you!—See yourselves a writhen soul—the halo hammered from insurance claims, from pride—see the betrayer betrayed!

'Come! See my masterpiece, my masters, where it hangs against the wall.'

And our teeth forever frozen in mid-gnash.

III

JUST DESSERTS

A Selection of Detective Cases

FOUR-AND-TWENTY BLACKBIRDS

Agatha Christie

The 1920s and 1930s are regarded as the 'Golden Age' of crime fiction, and reading the novels from this era it is intriguing to note how many victims are dispatched by the murderer at the dinner table. As one authority has noted, the dinner plate became the 'poisoner's playground', and because it was so easy to use has remained popular ever since—although the means of concealing the poison against the probing of forensic science has had to become increasingly more ingenious. A number of the most famous fictional sleuths have not only solved cases where murder was on the menu, but revealed themselves to be knowledgeable gourmets, too: their number ranging from Charles Dickens' pioneer Inspector Bucket by way of Hercule Poirot, Jules Maigret and Nero Wolfe to Nicolas Freeling's Van Der Valk. (Freeling, incidentally, was for a time a teacher at a cookery school.) Three of these detectives are featured in this section, starting with Poirot in the case of 'Four-and-Twenty Blackbirds' by Agatha Christie (1890–1976).

Hercule Poirot was dining with his friend, Henry Bonnington at the Gallant Endeavour in the King's Road, Chelsea.

Mr Bonnington was fond of the Gallant Endeavour. He liked the leisurely atmosphere, he liked the food which was 'plain' and 'English' and 'not a lot of made up messes'. He liked to tell people who dined with him there just exactly where Augustus John had been wont to sit and to draw their attention to the famous artists' names in the visitors' book. Mr Bonnington was himself the least artistic of men—but he took a certain pride in the artistic activities of others.

Molly, the sympathetic waitress, greeted Mr Bonnington as an old friend. She prided herself on remembering her customers' likes and dislikes in the way of food.

'Good evening, sir,' she said, as the two men took their seats at a corner table. 'You're in luck today—turkey stuffed with chestnuts—that's your favourite, isn't it? And ever such a nice

Stilton we've got! Will you have soup first or fish?'

Mr Bonnington deliberated the point. He said to Poirot warningly as the latter studied the menu:

'None of your French kickshaws now. Good well-cooked English food.'

'My friend,' Hercule Poirot waved his hand, 'I ask no better! I put myself in your hands unreservedly.'

'Ah—hruup—er—hm,' replied Mr Bonnington and gave careful attention to the matter.

These weighty matters, and the question of wine, settled, Mr Bonnington leaned back with a sigh and unfolded his napkin as Molly sped away.

'Good girl, that!' he said approvingly. 'Was quite a beauty once—artists used to paint her. She knows about food, too—and that's a great deal more important. Women are very unsound on food as a rule. There's many a woman if she goes out with a fellow she fancies—won't even notice what she eats. She'll just order the first thing she sees.'

Hercule Poirot, shook his head.

C'est terrible.'

'Men aren't like that, thank God!' said Mr Bonnington complacently.

'Never?' There was a twinkle in Hercule Poirot's eye.

'Well, perhaps when they're very young,' conceded Mr Bonnington. 'Young puppies! Young fellows nowadays are all the same—no guts—no stamina. I've no use for the young—and they,' he added with strict impartiality, 'have no use for me. Perhaps they're right! But to hear some of these young fellows talk you'd think no man had a right to be *alive* after sixty! From the way they go on, you'd wonder more of them didn't help their elderly relations out of the world.'

'It is possible,' said Hercule Poirot, 'that they do.'

'Nice mind you've got, Poirot, I must say. All this police work saps your ideals.'

Hercule Poirot smiled.

'*Tout de même,*' he said. 'It would be interesting to make a table of accidental deaths over the age of sixty. I assure you it would raise some curious speculations in your mind.'

'The trouble with you is that you've started going to look for crime—instead of waiting for crime to come to you.'

'I apologise,' said Poirot. 'I talk what you call "the shop". Tell me, my friend, of your own affairs. How does the world go with you?'

'Mess!' said Mr Bonnington. 'That's what's the matter with the world nowadays. Too much mess. And too much fine language.

The fine language helps to conceal the mess. Like a highly-flavoured sauce concealing the fact that the fish underneath it is none of the best! Give me an honest fillet of sole and no messy sauce over it.'

It was given him at that moment by Molly and he grunted approval.

'You know just what I like, my girl,' he said.

'Well, you come here pretty regular, don't you, sir? I ought to know what you like.'

Hercule Poirot said:

'Do people then always like the same things? Do not they like a change sometimes?'

'Not gentlemen, sir. Ladies like variety—gentlemen always like the same thing.'

'What did I tell you?' grunted Bonnington. 'Women are fundamentally unsound where food is concerned!'

He looked round the restaurant.

'The world's a funny place. See that odd-looking old fellow with a beard in the corner? Molly'll tell you he's always here Tuesdays and Thursday nights. He has come here for close on ten years now—he's a kind of landmark in the place. Yet nobody here knows his name or where he lives or what his business is. It's odd when you come to think of it.'

When the waitress brought the portions of turkey he said:

'I see you've still got Old Father Time over there?'

'That's right, sir. Tuesdays and Thursdays, his days are. Not but what he came in here on a *Monday* last week! It quite upset me! I felt I'd got my dates wrong and that it must be Tuesday without my knowing it! But he came in the next night as well—so the Monday was just a kind of extra, so to speak.'

'An interesting deviation from habit,' murmured Poirot. 'I wonder what the reason was?'

'Well, sir, if you ask me, I think he'd had some kind of upset or worry.'

'Why did you think that? His manner?'

'No, sir—not his manner exactly. He was very quiet as he always is. Never says much except good evening when he comes and goes. No, it was his *order.*'

'His order?'

'I dare say you gentlemen will laugh at me,' Molly flushed up, 'but when a gentleman has been here for ten years, you get to know his likes and dislikes. He never could bear suet pudding or blackberries and I've never known him take thick soup—but on that Monday night he ordered thick tomato soup, beefsteak and kidney pudding and blackberry tart! Seemed as though he just didn't notice *what* he ordered!'

'Do you know,' said Hercule Poirot, 'I find that extraordinarily interesting.'

Molly looked gratified and departed.

'Well, Poirot,' said Henry Bonnington with a chuckle. 'Let's have a few deductions from you. All in your best manner.'

'I would prefer to hear yours first.'

'Want me to be Watson, eh? Well, old fellow went to a doctor and the doctor changed his diet.'

'To thick tomato soup, steak and kidney pudding and blackberry tart? I cannot imagine any doctor doing that.'

'Don't believe it, old boy. Doctors will put you on to anything.'

'That is the only solution that occurs to you?'

Henry Bonnington:

'Well, seriously, I suppose there's only one explanation possible. Our unknown friend was in the grip of some powerful mental emotion. He was so perturbed by it that he literally did not notice what he was ordering or eating.'

He paused a minute and then said:

'You'll be telling me next that you know just *what* was on his mind. You'll say perhaps that he was making up his mind to commit a murder.'

He laughed at his own suggestion.

Hercule Poirot did not laugh.

He has admitted that at that moment he was seriously worried. He claims that he ought then to have had some inkling of what was likely to occur.

His friends assure him that such an idea is quite fantastic.

It was some three weeks later that Hercule Poirot and Bonnington met again—this time their meeting was in the Tube.

They nodded to each other, swaying about, hanging on to adjacent straps. Then at Piccadilly Circus there was a general exodus and they found seats right at the forward end of the car—a peaceful spot since nobody passed in or out that way.

'That's better,' said Mr Bonnington. 'Selfish lot, the human race, they won't pass up the car however much you ask 'em to!'

Hercule Poirot shrugged his shoulders.

'What will you?' he said. 'Life is too uncertain.'

'That's it. Here today, gone tomorrow,' said Mr Bonnington with a kind of gloomy relish. 'And talking of that, d'you remember that old boy we noticed at the Gallant Endeavour? I shouldn't wonder if *he'd* hopped it to a better world. He's not been there for a whole week. Molly's quite upset about it.'

Hercule Poirot sat up. His green eyes flashed.

'Indeed?' he said. 'Indeed?'

Bonnington said:

'D'you remember I suggested he'd been to a doctor and been put on a diet? Diet's nonsense of course—but I shouldn't wonder if he had consulted a doctor about his health and what the doctor said gave him a bit of a jolt. That would account for him ordering things off the menu without noticing what he was doing. Quite likely the jolt he got hurried him out of the world sooner than he would have gone otherwise. Doctors ought to be careful what they tell a chap.'

'They usually are,' said Hercule Poirot.

'This is my station,' said Mr Bonnington. 'Bye, bye. Don't suppose we shall ever know now who the old boy was—not even his name. Funny world!'

He hurried out of the carriage.

Hercule Poirot, sitting frowning, looked as though he did not think it was such a funny world.

He went home and gave certain instructions to his faithful valet, George.

Hercule Poirot ran his finger down a list of names. It was a record of deaths within a certain area.

Poirot's finger stopped.

'Henry Gascoigne. Sixty-nine. I might try him first.'

Later in the day, Hercule Poirot was sitting in Dr MacAndrew's surgery just off the King's Road. MacAndrew was a tall red-haired Scotsman with an intelligent face.

'Gascoigne?' he said. 'Yes, that's right. Eccentric old bird. Lived alone in one of those derelict old houses that are being cleared away in order to build a block of modern flats. I hadn't attended him before, but I'd seen him about and I knew who he was. It was the dairy people got the wind up first. The milk bottles began to pile up outside. In the end the people next door sent word to the police and they broke the door in and found him. He'd pitched down the stairs and broken his neck. Had on an old dressing-gown with a ragged cord—might easily have tripped himself up with it.'

'I see,' said Hercule Poirot. 'It was quite simple—an accident.'

'That's right.'

'Had he any relations?'

'There's a nephew. Used to come along and see his uncle about once a month. Lorrimer, his name is, George Lorrimer. He's a medico himself. Lives at Wimbledon.'

'Was he upset at the old man's death?'

'I don't know that I'd say he was upset. I mean, he had an affection for the old man, but he didn't really know him very well.'

'How long had Mr Gascoigne been dead when you saw him?'

'Ah!' said Dr MacAndrew. 'This is where we get official. Not less than forty-eight hours and not more than seventy-two hours. He was found on the morning of the sixth. Actually, we got closer than that. He'd got a letter in the pocket of his dressing-gown—written on the third—posted in Wimbledon that afternoon—would have been delivered somewhere around nine-twenty p.m. That puts the time of death at after nine-twenty of the evening of the third. That agrees with the contents of the stomach and the processes of digestion. He had had a meal about two hours before death. I examined him on the morning of the sixth and his condition was quite consistent with death having occurred about sixty hours previously—round about ten p.m. on the third.'

'It all seems very consistent. Tell me, when was he last seen alive?'

'He was seen in the King's Road about seven o'clock that same evening, Thursday the third, and he dined at the Gallant Endeavour restaurant at seven-thirty. It seems he always dined there on Thursdays. He was by way of being an artist, you know. An extremely bad one.'

'He had no other relations? Only this nephew?'

'There was a twin brother. The whole story is rather curious. They hadn't seen each other for years. It seems the other brother, Anthony Gascoigne, married a very rich woman and gave up art—and the brothers quarrelled over it. Hadn't seen each other since, I believe. But oddly enough, *they died on the same day*. The elder twin passed away at three o'clock on the afternoon of the third. Once before I've known a case of twins dying on the same day—in different parts of the world! Probably just a coincidence—but there it is.'

'Is the other brother's wife alive?'

'No, she died some years ago.'

'Where did Anthony Gascoigne live?'

'He had a house on Kingston Hill. He was, I believe, from what Dr Lorrimer tells me, very much of a recluse.'

Hercule Poirot nodded thoughtfully.

The Scotsman looked at him keenly.

'What exactly have you got in your mind, M. Poirot?' he asked bluntly. 'I've answered your questions—as was my duty seeing the credentials you brought. But I'm in the dark as to what it's all about.'

Poirot said slowly:

'A simple case of accidental death, that's what you said. What I have in mind is equally simple—a simple push.'

Dr MacAndrew looked startled.

'In other words, murder! Have you any grounds for that belief?'

'No,' said Poirot. 'It is a mere supposition.'

'There must be something—' persisted the other.

Poirot did not speak. MacAndrew said:

'If it's the nephew, Lorrimer, you suspect, I don't mind telling you here and now that you are barking up the wrong tree. Lorrimer was playing bridge in Wimbledon from eight-thirty till midnight. That came out at the inquest.'

Poirot murmured:

'And presumably it was verified. The police are careful.'

The doctor said:

'Perhaps you know something against him?'

'I didn't know that there was such a person until you mentioned him.'

'Then you suspect somebody else?'

'No, no. It is not that at all. It's a case of the routine habits of the human animal. That is very important. And the dead M. Gascoigne does not fit in. It is all wrong, you see.'

'I really don't understand.'

Hercule Poirot murmured:

'The trouble is, there is too much sauce over the bad fish.'

'My dear sir?'

Hercule Poirot smiled.

'You will be having me locked up as a lunatic soon, *Monsieur le Docteur*. But I am not really a mental case—just a man who has a liking for order and method and who is worried when he comes across a fact *that does not fit in*. I must ask you to forgive me for having given you so much trouble.'

He rose and the doctor rose also.

'You know,' said MacAndrew, 'honestly I can't see anything the least bit suspicious about the death of Henry Gascoigne. I say he fell—you say somebody pushed him. It's all—well—in the air.'

Hercule Poirot sighed.

'Yes,' he said. 'It is workmanlike. Somebody has made the good job of it!'

'You still think—?'

The little man spread out his hands.

'I'm an obstinate man—a man with a little idea—and nothing to support it! By the way, did Henry Gascoigne have false teeth?'

'No, his own teeth were in excellent preservation. Very creditable indeed at his age.'

'He looked after them well—they were white and well brushed?'

'Yes, I noticed them particularly. Teeth tend to grow a little yellow as one grows older, but they were in good condition.'

'Not discoloured in any way?'

'No. I don't think he was a smoker if that is what you mean?'

'I did not mean that precisely—it was just a long shot—which probably will not come off! Good-bye, Dr MacAndrew, and thank you for your kindness.'

He shook the doctor's hand and departed.

'And now,' he said, 'for the long shot.'

At the Gallant Endeavour, he sat down at the same table which he had shared with Bonnington. The girl who served him was not Molly. Molly, the girl told him, was away on a holiday.

It was only just seven and Hercule Poirot found no difficulty in entering into conversation with the girl on the subject of old Mr Gascoigne.

'Yes,' she said. 'He'd been here for years and years. But none of us girls ever knew his name. We saw about the inquest in the paper, and there was a picture of him. "There," I said to Molly. "If that isn't our 'Old Father Time'" as we used to call him.'

'He dined here on the evening of his death, did he not?'

'That's right. Thursday, the third. He was always here on a Thursday. Tuesdays and Thursdays—punctual as a clock.'

'You don't remember, I suppose, what he had for dinner?'

'Now let me see, it was mulligatawny soup, that's right, and beefsteak pudding or was it the mutton?—no pudding, that's right, and blackberry and apple pie and cheese. And then to think of him going home and falling down those stairs that very same evening. A frayed dressing-gown cord they said it was as caused it. Of course, his clothes were always something awful—old-fashioned and put on anyhow, and all tattered, and yet he *had* a kind of air, all the same, as though he was *somebody*! Oh, we get all sorts of interesting customers here.'

She moved off.

Hercule Poirot ate his filleted sole. His eyes showed a green light.

'It is odd,' he said to himself, 'how the cleverest people slip over details. Bonnington will be interested.'

But the time had not yet come for leisurely discussion with Bonnington.

Armed with introductions from a certain influential quarter, Hercule Poirot found no difficulty at all in dealing with the coroner for the district.

'A curious figure, the deceased man Gascoigne,' he observed. 'A lonely, eccentric old fellow. But his decease seems to arouse an unusual amount of attention?'

He looked with some curiosity at his visitor as he spoke.

Hercule Poirot chose his words carefully.

'There are circumstances connected with it, Monsieur, which make investigation desirable.'

'Well, how can I help you?'

'It is, I believe, within your province to order documents produced in your court to be destroyed, or to be impounded—as you think fit. A certain letter was found in the pocket of Henry Gascoigne's dressing-gown, was it not?'

'That is so.'

'A letter from his nephew, Dr George Lorrimer?'

'Quite correct. The letter was produced at the inquest as helping to fix the time of death.'

'Which was corroborated by the medical evidence?'

'Exactly.'

'Is that letter still available?'

Hercule Poirot waited rather anxiously for the reply.

When he heard that the letter was still available for examination he drew a sigh of relief.

When it was finally produced he studied it with some care. It was written in a slightly cramped handwriting with a stylographic pen. It ran as follows:

Dear Uncle Henry,

I am sorry to tell you that I have had no success as regards Uncle Anthony. He showed no enthusiasm for a visit from you and would give me no reply to your request that he would let bygones be bygones. He is, of course, extremely ill, and his mind is inclined to wander. I should fancy that the end is very near. He seemed hardly to remember who you were.

I am sorry to have failed you, but I can assure you that I did my best.

Your affectionate nephew,

George Lorrimer

The letter itself was dated 3rd November. Poirot glanced at the envelope's postmark—4.30 p.m. 3 Nov.

He murmured:

'It is beautifully in order, is it not?'

Kingston Hill was his next objective. After a little trouble, with the exercise of good-humoured pertinacity, he obtained an interview with Amelia Hill, cook-housekeeper to the late Anthony Gascoigne.

Mrs Hill was inclined to be stiff and suspicious at first, but the charming geniality of this strange-looking foreigner would have had its effect on a stone. Mrs Amelia Hill began to unbend.

She found herself, as had so many other women before her, pouring out her troubles to a really sympathetic listener.

For fourteen years she had had charge of Mr Gascoigne's household—*not* an easy job! No, indeed! Many a woman would have quailed under the burdens *she* had had to bear! Eccentric the poor gentleman was and no denying it. Remarkably close with his money—a kind of mania with him it was—and he as rich a gentleman as might be! But Mrs Hill had served him faithfully, and put up with his ways, and naturally she'd expected at any rate a *remembrance*. But no—nothing at all! Just an old will that left all his money to his wife and if she predeceased him then everything to his brother, Henry. A will made years ago. It didn't seem fair!

Gradually Hercule Poirot detached her from her main theme of unsatisfied cupidity. It was indeed a heartless injustice! Mrs Hill could not be blamed for feeling hurt and surprised. It was well known that Mr Gascoigne was tight-fisted about money. It had even been said that the dead man had refused his only brother assistance. Mrs Hill probably knew all about that.

'Was it that that Dr Lorrimer came to see him about?' asked Mrs Hill. 'I knew it was something about his brother, but I thought it was just that his brother wanted to be reconciled. They'd quarrelled years ago.'

'I understand,' said Poirot, 'that Mr Gascoigne refused absolutely?'

'That's right enough,' said Mrs Hill with a nod. '"*Henry?*" he says, rather weak like. "*What's this about Henry? Haven't seen him for years and don't want to. Quarrelsome fellow, Henry.*" Just that.'

The conversation then reverted to Mrs Hill's own special grievances, and the unfeeling attitude of the late Mr Gascoigne's solicitor.

With some difficulty Hercule Poirot took his leave without breaking off the conversation too abruptly.

And so, just after the dinner hour, he came to Elmcrest, Dorset Road, Wimbledon, the residence of Dr George Lorrimer.

The doctor was in. Hercule Poirot was shown into the surgery and there presently Dr George Lorrimer came to him, obviously just risen from the dinner table.

'I'm not a patient, Doctor,' said Hercule Poirot. 'And my coming here is, perhaps, somewhat of an impertinence—but I'm an old man and I believe in plain and direct dealing. I do not care for lawyers and their long-winded roundabout methods.'

He had certainly aroused Lorrimer's interest. The doctor was a clean-shaven man of middle height. His hair was brown but his eyelashes were almost white which gave his eyes a pale, boiled appearance. His manner was brisk and not without humour.

'Lawyers?' he said, raising his eyebrows. 'Hate the fellows! You rouse my curiosity, my dear sir. Pray sit down.'

Poirot did so and then produced one of his professional cards which he handed to the doctor.

George Lorrimer's white eyelashes blinked.

Poirot leaned forward confidentially. 'A good many of my clients are women,' he said.

'Naturally,' said Dr George Lorrimer, with a slight twinkle.

'As you say, naturally,' agreed Poirot. 'Women distrust the official police. They prefer private investigations. They do not want to have their troubles made public. An elderly woman came to consult me a few days ago. She was unhappy about a husband she'd quarrelled with many years before. This husband of hers was your uncle, the later Mr Gascoigne.' George Lorrimer's face went purple.

'My uncle? Nonsense! His wife died many years ago.'

'Not your uncle, Mr *Anthony* Gascoigne. Your uncle, Mr *Henry* Gascoigne.'

'Uncle Henry? But *he* wasn't married?'

'Oh yes, he was,' said Hercule Poirot, lying unblushingly. 'Not a doubt of it. The lady even brought along her marriage certificate.'

'It's a lie!' cried George Lorrimer. His face was now as purple as a plum. 'I don't believe it. You're an impudent liar.'

'It is too bad, is it not?' said Poirot. 'You have committed murder for nothing.'

'Murder?' Lorrimer's voice quavered. His pale eyes bulged with terror.

'By the way,' said Poirot, 'I see you have been eating blackberry tart again. An unwise habit. Blackberries are said to be full of vitamins, but they may be deadly in other ways. On this occasion I rather fancy they have helped to put a rope round a man's neck—your neck, Dr Lorrimer.'

'You see, *mon ami*, where you went wrong was over your fundamental assumption.' Hercule Poirot, beaming placidly across the table at his friend, waved an expository hand. 'A man under severe mental stress doesn't choose that time to do something that he's never done before. His reflexes just follow the track of least resistance. A man who is upset about something *might* conceivably come down to dinner dressed in his pyjamas—but they will be his *own* pyjamas—not somebody else's.

'A man who dislikes thick soup, suet pudding and blackberries suddenly orders all three one evening. *You* say, because he is thinking of something else. But *I* say *that a man who has got something on his mind will order automatically the dish he has ordered most often before.*

'*Eh bien*, then, what other explanation could there be? I simply could not think of a reasonable explanation. And I was worried! The incident was all wrong. It did not fit! I have an orderly mind and I like things to fit. Mr Gascoigne's dinner order worried me.

'Then you told me that the man had disappeared. He had missed a Tuesday and a Thursday the first time for years. I liked that even less. A queer hypothesis sprang up in my mind. If I were right about it *the man was dead*. I made inquiries. The man *was* dead. And he was very neatly and tidily dead. In other words the bad fish was covered up with the sauce!

'He had been seen in the King's Road at seven o'clock. He had had dinner here at seven-thirty—two hours before he died. It all fitted in—the evidence of the stomach contents, the evidence of the letter. Much too much sauce! You couldn't see the fish at all!

'Devoted nephew wrote the letter, devoted nephew had beautiful alibi for time of death. Death very simple—a fall down the stairs. Simple accident? Simple murder? Everyone says the former.

'Devoted nephew only surviving relative. Devoted nephew will inherit—but is there anything *to* inherit? Uncle notoriously poor.

'But there is a brother. And brother in his time had married a rich wife. And brother lives in a big rich house on Kingston Hill, so it would seem that rich wife must have left him all her money. You see the sequence—rich wife leaves money to Anthony, Anthony leaves money to Henry, Henry's money goes to George—a complete chain.'

'All very pretty in theory,' said Bonnington. 'But what did you do?'

'Once you *know*—you can usually get hold of what you want. Henry had died two hours after a *meal*—that is all the inquest really bothered about. But supposing that meal was not dinner, but *lunch*. Put yourself in George's place. George wants money—badly. Anthony Gascoigne is dying—but his death is no good to George. His money goes to Henry, and Henry Gascoigne may live for years. So Henry must die too—and the sooner the better—but his death must take place *after* Anthony's, and at the same time

George must have an alibi. Henry's habit of dining regularly at a restaurant on two evenings of the week suggests an alibi to George. Being a cautious fellow, he tries his plan out first. *He impersonates his uncle on Monday evening at the restaurant in question.* It goes without a hitch. Everyone there accepts him as his uncle. He is satisfied. He has only to wait till Uncle Anthony shows definite signs of pegging out. The time comes. He writes a letter to his uncle on the afternoon of the second November but dates it the third. He comes up to town on the afternoon of the third, calls on his uncle, and carries his scheme into action. A sharp shove and down the stairs goes Uncle Henry. George hunts about for the letter he has written, and shoves it in the pocket of his uncle's dressing-gown. At seven-thirty he is at the Gallant Endeavour, beard, bushy eyebrows all complete. Undoubtedly Mr Henry Gascoigne is alive at seven-thirty. Then a rapid metamorphosis in a lavatory and back full speed in his car to Wimbledon and an evening of bridge. The perfect alibi.'

Mr Bonnington looked at him.

'But the postmark on the letter?'

'Oh, that was very simple. The postmark was smudgy. Why? It had been altered with lamp black from second November to third November. You would not notice it *unless you were looking for it.* And finally there were the blackbirds.'

'Blackbirds?'

'Four-and-twenty blackbirds baked in a pie! Or blackberries if you prefer to be literal! George, you comprehend, was after all not quite a good enough actor. Do you remember the fellow who blacked himself all over to play Othello? That is the kind of actor you have got to be in crime. George *looked* like his uncle and *walked* like his uncle and *spoke* like his uncle and had his uncle's beard and eyebrows, but he forgot to *eat* like his uncle. He ordered the dishes that he himself liked. Blackberries discolour the teeth—the corpse's teeth were not discoloured, and yet Henry Gascoigne ate blackberries at the Gallant endeavour that night. But there were no blackberries in the stomach. I asked this morning. And George had been fool enough to keep the beard and the rest of the make-up. Oh! plenty of evidence once you look for it. I called on George and rattled him. That finished it! He had been eating blackberries again, by the way. A greedy fellow—cared a lot about his food. *Eh bien*, greed will hang him all right unless I am very much mistaken.'

A waitress brought them two portions of blackberry and apple tart.

'Take it away,' said Mr Bonnington. 'One can't be too careful. Bring me a small helping of sago pudding.'

THE LONG DINNER

H. C. Bailey

The aristocratic sleuth Reggie Fortune, a practising physician and surgeon who acts as special adviser to Scotland Yard, has been described as 'probably the msot popular detective in England between World Wars I and II'. Rather plump and younger-looking than his years, Reggie is a gourmet who enjoys virtually all fine food and drink. He is also said to be a man who loves life and feasts on its pleasures—as the reader will discover in the case of 'The Long Dinner'. Fortune was created by H. C. Bailey (1877–1961), a classical scholar and newspaper drama critic who delighted in making little jibes at English class-consciousness. In this story, however, it is snobbery over food which leads to a murder . . .

'I dislike you,' said Mr Fortune. 'Some of the dirtiest linen I've seen.' He gazed morosely at the Chief of the Criminal Investigation Department.

'Quite,' Lomas agreed. 'Dirty fellow. What about those stains?'

'Oh, my dear chap!' Mr Fortune mourned. 'Paint. All sorts of paint. Also food and drink and assorted filth. Why worry me? What did you expect? Human gore?'

'I had no expectations,' said Lomas sweetly.

A certain intensity came into Mr Fortune's blue eyes. 'Yes. I hate you,' he murmured. 'Anything else you wanted to know?'

'A lot of things,' Lomas said. 'You're not useful, Reginald. I want to know what sort of fellow he was, and what's become of him.'

'He was an artist of dark complexion. He painted both in oils and water-colours. He lived a coarse and dissolute life, and had expensive tastes. What's become of him, I haven't the slightest idea. I should say he was on the way to the devil. What's it all about? Why this interest in the debauched artist?'

'Because the fellow's vanished,' said Lomas. 'He is a painter of sorts, as you say. Name—Derry Farquhar. He had a talent and a bit of success years ago, and he's gone downhill ever since. Not altogether unknown to the police—money under false pretences and that sort of thing—but never any clear case. Ten days ago a woman turned up to give information that Mr Derry Farquhar was missing. He had some money out of her—a matter of fifty pounds—three months ago. She don't complain of that. She was used to handing him donations—that kind of woman and that kind of man. What worries her is that, since this particular fifty pounds, he's faded out. And it is a queer case. He's lived these ten years in a rat-hole of a flat in Bloomsbury. He's not been seen there for months. That's unlike him. He's never been long away before. A regular London loafer. And his own money—he's got a little income from a trust—has piled up in the bank. August and September dividends untouched. That's absolutely unlike him. Besides that: one night about a fortnight ago—we can't fix the date—somebody was heard in the flat making a good deal of noise. When Bell went to have a look at things, he found the place in a devil of a mess, and a heap of foul linen. So we sent that to you.'

'Hoping for proof of bloodshed,' Reggie murmured. 'Hopeful fellow. Shirts extremely foul, but affordin' no evidence of foul play. Blood is absent. Almost the only substance that is.'

'So you don't believe there's anything in the case?'

'My dear chap! Oh, my dear chap,' Reggie opened large, plaintive eyes. 'Belief is a serious operation. I believe you haven't found anything. That's all. I should say you didn't look.'

'Thank you,' said Lomas acidly. 'Bell raked it all over' He spoke into the telephone, and Superintendent Bell arrived with a fat folder.

'Mr Fortune thinks you've missed something, Bell,' Lomas smiled.

'If there was anything any use, I have,' Bell said heavily. 'I'll be glad to hear what it is. Here's some photographs of the place, sir. And an inventory.'

'You might pick up a bargain, Reginald,' said Lomas, while Reggie, with a decent solemnity, perused the inventory and contemplated the photographs.

'Four oil paintings, fifteen water-colours. Unframed,' he read, and lifted a gaze of innocent enquiry to Bell.

'I'd call 'em clever, myself,' said Bell. 'Not nice, you know, but very bright and showy. Nudes of ladies, and that sort of thing. I should have thought he could have made a tidy living out of them. But a picture dealer that's seen 'em priced 'em at half a dollar each. Slick rubbish, he called 'em. I'm no hand at art. Anyway—it don't tell us anything.'

'I wouldn't say that. No,' Reggie murmured. 'Builds up the

character of Mr Farquhar for us. Person of no honour, even in his pot-boilin' art. However. Nothing else in the flat?'

'Some letters—mostly bills and duns. Nothing to show what he was up to. Nothing to work on.'

Reggie turned over the correspondence quickly. 'Yes. As you say.' He stopped at a crumpled, stained card. 'Where was this?'

'In a pocket of a dirty old sports coat,' Bell said. 'It's only a menu. I don't know why he kept it. Some faces drawn on the back. Perhaps he fancied 'em. No accounting for taste. Looks like drawing devils to me.'

'Rather diabolical, yes,' Reggie murmurd. 'Conventional devil. Mephistopheles in a flick.' The faces were sketched, in pencil, with a few accomplished strokes, but had no distinction: the same face in variations of grin and scowl and leer: a face of black brows, moustache, and pointed beard. 'Clever craftsman. Only clever.' He turned the card to the menu written on the front. 'My only aunt!' he moaned, and, in a hushed voice of awe read out:

DÎNER

Artichauts à l'Huile

Pommes de Terre à l'Huile

Porc frais froid aux Cornichons

Langouste Mayonnaise

Canard aux Navets

Omelette Rognons

Filet garni

Fromage à la Crème

Fruits, Biscuits

'Good Gad! Some dinner,' Lomas chuckled.

'I don't say I get it all,' Bell frowned. 'But what's it come to? He did himself well some time.'

'Well!' Reggie groaned. 'Oh, my dear chap! Artichokes in oil, cold pork, lobster, duck and turnips—and a kidney omelette and roast beef and trimmings.'

'I've got to own it wants a stomach,' said Bell gloomily. 'What then?'

'Died of indigestion,' said Lomas. 'Or committed suicide in the pangs. Very natural. Very just. There you are, Bell. Mr Fortune has solved the case.'

'I was taking it seriously myself,' Bell glowered at them.

'Oh, my Bell!' Reggie sighed. 'So was I.' He turned on Lomas. 'Incurably flippant mind, your mind. This is the essential fact. Look for Mr Farquhar in Brittany.'

Bell breathed hard. 'How do you get to that, sir?'

'No place but a Brittany inn ever served such a dinner.'

Bell rubbed his chin. 'I see. I don't know Brittany myelf, I'm glad to say. I got to own I never met a dinner like it.' He looked at Lomas. 'That means putting it back on the French.'

'Quite,' Lomas smiled. 'Brilliant thought, Reginald. Would you be surprised to hear that Paris is asking us to look for Mr Derry Farquhar in England?'

'Well, well,' Reggie surveyed him with patient contempt. 'Another relevant fact which you didn't mention. Also indicatin' an association of your Mr Farquhar with France.'

'If you like,' Lomas shrugged. 'But the point is they are sure he's here. Dubois is coming over today. I'm taking him to dine at the club. You'd better join us.'

'Oh, no. No,' Reggie said quickly. 'Dubois will dine with me. You bring him along. Your club dinner would destroy his faith in the English intelligence. If any. And I like Dubois. Pleasant to discuss the case with a serious mind. Good-bye. Half past eight.' . . .

With a superior English smile, Lomas sat back and watched Reggie and Dubois consume that fantasia on pancakes, Crêpes Joan, which Reggie invented as an expression of the way of his wife with her husband. . . .

Dubois wiped his flowing moustaches. 'My homage,' he said reverently.

By way of a devilled biscuit, they came to another claret. Dubois looked and smelt and tasted, and his eyes returned thanks. 'Try it with a medlar,' Reggie purred.

'You are right. There is no fruit better with wine.'

They engaged upon a ritual of ecstasy while Lomas gave himself a glass of port and lit a cigarette. At that, Reggie gave a reproachful stare. 'My only aunt! Forgive him, Dubois. He's mere modern English.'

'I pity profoundly,' Dubois sighed. 'A bleak life. This is a great wine, my friend. Of Pauillac, I think, eh? Of the last century?'

'Quite good, yes,' Reggie purred. 'Mouton Rothschild 1900.'

Dubois's large face beamed. 'Aha. Not so bad for poor old Dubois.'

They proceeded to a duet on claret. . . .

Lomas became restive. 'This unanimity is touching. Now you've embraced each other all over, we might come to business and see if you can keep it up.'

Dubois turned to him with a gesture of deprecation. 'Pardon, my friend. Have no fear. We agree always. But I will not delay you. The affair is, after all, very simple—'

'Quite,' Lomas smiled. 'Tell Fortune. He has his own ideas about it.'

'Aha,' Dubois's eyebrows went up. 'I shall be grateful. Well, I begin, then, with Max Weber. He is what you call a profiteer, but, after all, a good fellow. It is a year ago he married a pretty lady. She was by courtesy an actress, the beautiful Clotilde. One has nothing else against her. They live together very happily in an apartment of luxury. Two weeks ago, they find that some of her jewels, which she had in her bedroom, are gone. Not all that Weber had given her, the most valuable are at the bank, but diamonds worth five hundred thousand francs. Weber comes to the Sûreté and makes a complaint. What do we find? The servants, they have been with Weber many years, they are spoilt, they are careless; but dishonest—I think not. There is no sign of a burglary. But the day before the jewels were missed a man came to the Weber apartment who asked for Madame Weber and was told she was not at home. That was true in fact, but, also, Weber's man did not like his look. A *gouape* of the finest water—that is the description. What you call a blackguard, is it not? The man was shabby but showy; he resembled exactly a loafer in the Quartier Latin, an artist *décavé*—how do you say that.'

'On his uppers. Yes. Still more interesting. But not an identification, Dubois.'

'Be patient still. You see—here is a type which might well have known *la belle* Clotilde before she was Madame Weber. Very well. This gentleman, when he was refused at the Weber door, he did not go far away. We have a *concierge* who saw him loitering till the afternoon at least. In the afternoon the Weber servants take their ease. The man went to a café—he admits it—one woman calls on a friend here, another there. What more easy than for the blackguard artist to enter, to take the jewel case, to hop it, as you say.'

'We do. Yes.'

'Well, then, I begin from a description of Monsieur the Blackguard. It is not so bad. A man who is plump and dark, with little dark whiskers, who has front teeth which stand out, who walks like a bird running, with short steps that go pit pat. He speaks French well enough, but not like a Frenchman. He wears clothes of orange colour, cut very loose, and a soft black hat of wide brim. Then I find that a man like this got into the night train from the Gare St Lazare for Dieppe—that is, you see, to come back to England by the cheap way. Very well. We have worked in the Quartier Latin, we find that a man like this was seen a day or two in some of the cafés. They remember him well, because they knew him ten years ago when he was a student. They are like that, these old folks of the Quartier—it pays. Then his name was Farquhar, Derek Farquhar, an Englishman.' Dubois twirled his moustaches. 'So you see, my friend, I dare to trouble Mr Lomas to find me in England this Farquhar.'

'Yes. Method quite sound,' Reggie mumbled. 'As a method.'

'My poor Reginald,' Lomas laughed. 'What a mournful, reluctant confession! You've hurt him, Dubois. He was quite sure Mr Farquhar was traversing the wilds of Brittany.'

'Aha,' Dubois put up his eyebrows, and made a gesture of respect to Reggie. 'My dear friend, never I consult you but I find you see farther than I. Tell me then.'

'Oh, no. No. Don't see it all,' Reggie mumbled, and told him of the menu of the long dinner.

'Without doubt that dinner was served in Brittany,' Dubois nodded. 'I agree, it is probable he had been there not so long ago. But what of that? He was a painter, he had studied in France, and Brittany is always full of painters.'

'Yes. You're neglectin' part of the evidence. Faces on the back of the menu.' He took out his pocketbook, and sketched the black-browed, black-bearded countenance. 'Like that.'

'The devil,' said Dubois.

'As you say. Devil of opera and fancy ball. The ordinary Mephistopheles. Associated by your Mr Farquhar with Brittany.'

'My dear Fortune!' Dubois's big face twisted into a quizzical smile. 'You are very subtle. Me, I find this is to make too much of little things. After all, drawing devils, it is common sport—you find devils all over our comic papers—a devil and a pretty lady—and he drew pretty ladies often, you say, this Farquhar—and this is a very common devil.'

'Yes, rational criticism,' Reggie murmured, looking at him with dreamy eyes. 'You're very rational, Dubois. However. Any association of the Webers with Brittany?'

'Oh, my friend!' Dubois smiled indulgently. 'None at all. And when they go out of Paris, it is to Monte Carlo, to Aix, not to rough it in Brittany, you may be sure. No. You shall forgive me, but I find nothing in your menu to change my mind. I must look for my Farquhar here.' He shook his head sadly at Reggie. 'I am desolated that you do not agree.' He turned to Lomas. 'But this is the only way, *hein*?'

'Absolutely. There's no other line at all,' said Lomas, with satisfaction. 'Don't let Fortune worry you. He lives to see what isn't there. Wonderful imagination.'

'My only aunt!' Reggie moaned. 'Not me, no. No imagination at all. Only simple faith in facts. You people ignore 'em when they're not rational. Unscientific and superstitious. However. Let's pretend and see what we get. Go your own way.'

'One does as one can,' Dubois shrugged.

'Quite. Fortune is never content with the possible. We must work it out here. I've put things in train for you. We have a copy of Farquhar's photograph. That's been circulated with description, and there's a general warning out for him and the jewels. We're combing out all his friends and his usual haunts.'

'"So runs my dream, but what am I?"' Reggie murmured. '"An infant cryin' in the night. An infant cryin' for the light—" Well, well. Are we downhearted? Yes. A little Armagnac would be grateful and comfortin'.' He turned the conversation imperatively to the qualities of that liqueur, and Dubois was quick with respectful responses. Lomas relapsed upon Olympian disdain and whisky and soda.

When he took Dubois away, 'Fantastic fellow, Fortune, isn't he?' Lomas smiled. 'Mind of the first order, but never content to use it.'

'An artist, my friend,' said Dubois. 'A great artist. He feels life. We think about it.'

'Damme, you don't believe he's right about this Brittany guess?'

'What do I know?' Dubois shrugged. 'It means nothing. Therefore it is nothing for us. However, one must confess, he is disconcerting, your Mr Fortune. He makes one always doubt.'

This, when he heard of it, Reggie considered the greatest compliment which he ever had, except from his wife. He also thinks it deserved. . . .

Some days later he was engaged upon the production in his marionette theatre of the tragedy of *Don Juan*, lyrics by Lord Byron, prose and music by Mr Fortune, when the telephone called him from a poignant passage on the rejection of his hero by hell.

'Yes, Fortune speaking. "Between two worlds life hovers like a star." Perhaps you didn't know that, Lomas. "How little do we know that which we are." Discovery of the late Lord Byron. I'm settin' it to music. Departmental ditty for the Criminal Investigation Department. I—'

'Could you listen for a moment?' said Lomas sweetly. 'You might be interested.'

'Not likely, no. However. What's worryin' you?'

'Nothing, except sympathy for you, Reginald. I'm afraid you'll suffer. To break it gently, we've traced Farquhar. But not in Brittany, Reginald.'

Reggie remained calm. 'No. Of course not,' he moaned. 'You weren't trying. I don't want to hear what you've missed. Takes too long.'

A sound of mockery came over the wire. 'Are you ever wrong, Reginald? No. It's always the other fellow. But the awkward fact is, Farquhar hadn't gone to Brittany, he'd gone to Westshire. So that was the only place we could find him. We have our limitations.'

'You have. Yes. *C'est brutal, mais ça marche.* You're clumsy, but you move—sometimes—like the early cars. What has he got to say for himself?'

'I don't know. We haven't put our hands on him yet. We— what?'

'Pardon me. It was only emotion. A sob of reverence. Oh, my Lomas. You found the only place you could find him, so you haven't found him. The perfect official. No results, but always the superior person.'

'Results quite satisfactory,' Lomas snapped. 'We had a clear identification. He's been staying at Lyncombe. He's bolted again. No doubt found we were on his track. But we shall get him. They're combing out the district. Bell's gone down with Dubois.'

'Splendid. Always shut the stable door when the horse has been removed. I'll go too. I like watching that operation. Raises my confidence in the police force.' . . .

As the moon rose over the sea, Reggie's car drove into Lyncombe. It is a holiday town of some luxury. The affronts to nature of its blocks of hotel and twisting roads of villas for the opulent retired have not yet been able to spoil all the beauty of cliff and cove.

When Reggie saw it, the banal buildings and the headlands were mingled in moonlight to make a dreamland, and the sea was a black mystery with a glittering path on it.

He went to the newest hotel, he bathed well and dined badly, and, as he sat smoking his consolatory pipe on a balcony where the soft air smelt of chrysanthemums and the sea, Dubois came to him with Bell.

'Aha.' Dubois spoke. 'You have not gone to Brittany then, my friend?'

'No. No. Followin' the higher intelligence. I have a humble mind. And where have you got to?'

'We have got to the tracks of Farquhar, there is no doubt of that. What is remarkable, he had registered in his own name at the hotel, and the people there they recognise his photograph—they are sure of it. In fact, it is a face to be sure of, a rabbit face.'

'The identification's all right,' Bell grunted. 'The devil of it is, he's gone again, Mr Fortune. He went in a hurry too. Left all his traps behind, such as they were. The hotel people think he was just bilking them. He'd been a matter of ten days and not paid anything, and his baggage is worth about nothing—a battered old suitcase and some duds fit for the dust-bin.'

'Oh, Peter!' Reggie moaned. 'No, Bell, no. I haven't got to look at his shirts again?'

'I'm not asking you, sir. There's no sort of reason to think there was anything done to him. He just went out and didn't come back. Three days ago. I don't see any light at all. What he was doing here, beats me. You can say he was hiding with the swag he got in Paris. But then, why did he register in his own name? Say he was just a silly ass—you do get that kind of amateur thief. But what has he bolted for? He couldn't have had any suspicions we were on to him. We weren't, at the time he faded out.'

'But, my friend, you go too fast,' said Dubois. 'From you, no, he could not have had any alarm. But there is the other end—Paris. It is very possible that a friend in Paris warned him the police were searching for him.'

'All right,' Bell grunted. 'I give you that. Why would he make the hotel people notice him by bolting without paying his bill? Silly again. Sheer silly. He'd got a pot of money, if he did have the jewels, like you say. Going off without paying 'em just sent them to inform the police quick.'

'That is well argued. You have an insight, a power of mind, my friend.' Dubois's voice was silky. 'But what have we then? It is quite natural that Farquhar should disappear again, it is not natural that he should disappear like this. For me, I confess I do not find myself able to form an idea of Farquhar. That he is the type to rob such a woman as Clotilde, there is evidence enough—he had the knowledge, he had the opportunity. So far, there are a thousand cases like it. But that he should then retire to such a paradise of the bourgeois, that is not like his type at all.'

'That's right,' said Bell. 'No sense in it anyway.'

'No. As you say,' Reggie murmured. 'That struck me. Happy to agree with everybody. We don't know anything about anything.'

'*Bigre!* You go a little strong,' Dubois rumbled. 'Come, there is at least a connection with Clotilde, and her jewels are gone. Be sure of that. Weber is an honest man—except in business. And what, now, is your hypothesis? You said look for him in Brittany. This at least is certain—he had not gone there. What the devil should he have to do with this so correct Lyncombe? As much as with our rough Brittany.'

'Yes. Quite obscure. I haven't the slightest idea what he's been doing. However. Are we downhearted? No. We're in touch with the fundamental problem now. Why does Mr Farquhar deal with Brittany and Clotilde and Lyncombe? First method of solution clearly indicated. Find out what he did do in Lyncombe. That ought to be an easy one, Bell. He must have been noticed. He'd be conspicuous in this correct place. Good night.'

The next day he sat upon the same balcony, spreading the first scone of his tea with clotted cream and blackberry jelly, when the two returned.

'What! Have you not moved since last night?' Dubois made a grimace at him.

'My dear chap! Just walked all along one of the bays. And back. Great big bay. Exercise demanded by impatient and fretful brain. Rest is better. Have a splitter. They're too heavy. But the cream is sound.'

Dubois shuddered. 'Brr! You are a wonderful animal. Me, I am only human. But Bell has news for you. Tell him, old fellow.'

'It's like this,' Bell explained. 'About a week ago—that's three or four days before he disappeared, we can't fix the date nearer— Farquhar went to call at one of the big houses here. There's no doubt about that. It's rather like the Paris case. He was seen loafing round before and after—as you said, he's the sort of chap to get noticed. The house he went to belongs to an old gentleman—Mr Lane Hudson. Lived here for years. Very rich, they say. Made his money in South Wales, and came here when he retired. Well, he's eighty or more; he's half paralysed—only gets about his house and grounds in a wheeled chair. I've seen him; I've had a talk with him. His mind's all right. He looks like a mummy, only a bit plumped out. Sort of yellow, leathery face that don't change or move. Sits in his chair looking at nothing, and talks soft and thick. He tells me he never heard of Farquhar: didn't so much as know Farquhar had been to his house: that's quite in order, it's his rule that the servants tell anybody not known he's not well enough to see people, and I don't blame him. I wouldn't want strangers to come and look at me if I was like he is. I gave him an idea of the sort of fellow Farquhar was, and watched him pretty close, but he didn't turn a hair. He just said again he had no knowledge of any such person, and I believe him. He wasn't interested. He told me the fellow had no doubt come begging for money; he was much exposed to that sort of thing—we ought to stop it—and good day Mr Superintendent. Anyhow, it's certain Farquhar didn't see him. The old butler and the nurse bear that out, and they never heard of Farquhar before. The butler saw him and turned him away—had a spot of bother over it, but didn't worry. Like the old man, he says they do have impudent beggars now and then. So here's another nice old dead end.'

'Yes. As you say. Rather weird isn't it? The flamboyant

debauched Farquhar knockin' at the door—to get to a paralysed old rich man who never heard of him. I wonder. Curious selection of people to call on by our Mr Farquhar. A pretty lady of Paris who's married money and settled down on it; a rich old Welshman who's helpless on the edge of the grave. And neither of 'em sees Mr Farquhar—accordin' to the evidence—neither will admit to knowin' anything about him. Very odd. Yes.' Reggie turned large, melancholy eyes on Dubois. 'Takes your fancy, what? The black-guard artist knockin', knockin', and, upstairs, a mummy of a man helpless in his chair.'

'Name of a name!' Dubois rumbled. 'It is fantasy pure. One sees such things in dreams. This has no more meaning.'

'No. Not to us. But it happened. Therefore it had a cause. Mr Lane Hudson lives all alone, what—except for servants?'

'That's right, sir,' Bell nodded. 'He's been a widower this long time. Only one child—daughter—and there's a grandson, quite a kid. Daughter's been married twice—first to a chap called Tracy, now to a Mr Bernal—son by the first marriage, no other children.'

'You have taken pains, Bell,' Reggie smiled.

'Well, I got everything I could think of,' said Bell, with gloomy satisfaction. 'Not knowing what I wanted. And there's nothing I do want in what I've got. The Bernals come here fairly regular—Mr and Mrs Bernal, not the child—they've been staying with the old man just now. Usual autumn visit. They were there when Far-quhar called, and after—didn't go away till last Wednesday; that's before Farquhar disappeared, you see, the day before. Farquhar didn't ask for the Bernals, and they didn't see him at all, the servants say. So there you are. The Bernals don't link up any way. That peters out, like everything else.'

'Yes. Taken a lot of pains,' Reggie murmured.

'What would you have?' Dubois shrugged. 'To amass useless knowledge—it is our only method; one is condemned to it. Ours is a slow trade, my friend. We gather facts and facts and facts, and so, if we are lucky, eliminate ninety-nine of the hundred and use, at last, one.'

'Yes. As you say,' Reggie mumbled. 'Where do the Bernals live, Bell?'

'In France, sir,' said Bell, and Reggie opened his eyes.

'Aha!' Dubois made a grimace, and pointed a broad finger at him. 'There, my friend. The one grand fact, is it not? In France! And Brittany is in France! But alas, my dear Fortune, they do not live in Brittany! Far from it. They live in the south, near Cannes; they have lived there—what do I know?—since they were married, *hein*?' he turned to Bell.

'That's right,' Bell grunted. 'Lady set up house there with her first husband. He had to live in the south of France—gassed in the war.'

'You see?' Dubois smiled. 'It is still the useless knowledge. And your vision of Brittany, my friend, it has no substance still.'

'I wonder,' Reggie mumbled, and sank deep in his chair. . . .

He is, even without hope, conscientious. That night he examined another set of Farquhar's dirty linen, but neither in that nor the rest of the worthless luggage found any information. Prodded by him, Bell enquired of the Hudson household where the Bernals were to be found, but could obtain only the address of their Cannes villa, for they were reported to be going back by car. Dubois was persuaded to telegraph Cannes and received the reply that the Bernal villa was shut up; monsieur and madame were away motoring, and their boy at school—what school nobody knew.

'Then what?' Dubois summed up. 'Nothing to do.'

'Not tonight, no,' Reggie yawned. 'I'm going to bed.'

'To dream of Brittany, *hein*?'

'I never dream,' said Reggie, with indignation. . . .

But he was waked in the night. He rubbed his eyes and looked up to see Dubois's large face above him. 'Oh, my hat,' he moaned. 'What is it? Why won't it wait?'

'Courage, my friend. They have found him. At least, they think so. Some fishermen, going out yesterday evening, they found a body on the rocks at what they call Granny's Cove. Come. The brave Bell wants you to see.'

'Bless him,' Reggie groaned, and rolled out of bed. 'What is life that one should seek it? I ask you.' And, slipping clothes on him, swiftly he crooned, '"Three fishers went sailin' out into the west, out into the west, as the sun went down"—and incredibly caught the incredible Farquhar.'

'You are right,' Dubois nodded. 'Nothing clear, nothing sure. The more it changes, the more it is the same, this accursed case. It has no shape; there is no reason in it.'

'Structure not yet determined. No,' Reggie mumbled, parting his hair, for he will always be neat. 'We're not bein' very clever. Ought to be able to describe the whole thing from available evidence of its existence. Same like inferrin' the age of reptiles from a fossil or two—"dragons of the prime, tearin' each other in the slime, were mellow music unto him." Yes. The struggle for life of the reptiles might be mellow music compared to the diversions of Mr Farquhar and friends. Progressive world, Dubois.'

'Name of a dog!' Dubois exclaimed. 'When you are philosophic, my stomach turns over. What is in your mind?'

'Feelin' of impotence. Very uncomfortable,' Reggie moaned, and muffled himself to the chin and made haste out.

In the mortuary Bell introduced them to a body covered by a sheet. 'Here you are, sir.' He stepped aside. 'The clothes seem to be Farquhar's clothes all right. Sort of orange tweed and green flannel trousers. But I don't know about the man.'

Reggie drew back the sheet from what was left of a face.

'*Saprelotte!*' Dubois rumbled. 'The fish have bitten.'

'Well, I leave it to you,' said Bell thickly. . . .

Under a sunlit breeze the sea was dancing bright, the mists flying inland from the valleys to the dim bank of the moor, when Reggie came out again.

He drove back to his hotel, and shaved and bathed and rang up the police station. Bell and Dubois arrived to find him in his room, eating with appetite grilled ham and buttered eggs.

'My envy; all my envy,' Dubois pulled a face. 'This is greatness. The English genius at the highest.'

'Oh, no. No,' Reggie protested. 'Natural man. Well. The corpse is that of Mr Farquhar as per invoice. Prominent teeth not impaired by activities of the lobsters. Some other contours still visible. The marmalade—thanks. Yes. Hair, colourin', size and so forth agree. Mr Farquhar's been in the sea three or four days. Correspondin' with date of disappearance. Cause of death, drowning. Severe contusions on head and body, inflicted before death. Possibly by blows, possibly by fall. Might have fallen from cliff; might have been dashed on rocks by sea. No certainty to be obtained. That's the medical evidence.'

'You are talking!' Dubois exclaimed. '*Flute!* There we are again. Whatever arrives, it will mean nothing for us. Here is murder, suicide, accident—what you please.'

'I wonder.' Reggie began to peel an apple. 'Anything in his pockets, Bell?'

'A lot of money, sir. Nothing else. The notes are all sodden, but it's a good wad, and some are fifties. Might be five or six hundred pounds. So he wasn't robbed.'

'And then?' said Dubois. 'It is not enough for all the jewels of Clotilde, but it is something in hand. Will you tell me what the devil he was doing at the door of this paralysed millionaire? It means nothing, none of it.'

'No. Still amassin' useless knowledge, as you were sayin'.' Reggie gazed at Dubois with dreamy eyes. 'I should say that's what we came here for. Don't seem the right place, does it? However. As we are here, let's try and get a little more before departure. Usin' the local talent. Bell—your fishermen—have they got any ideas where a fellow would tumble into the sea to be washed up into Granny's Cove?'

'Ah.' Bell was pleased. 'I have been asking about that, sir. Supposing he got in from the land, they think it would be somewhere round by Shag Nose. That's a bit o' cliff west o' the town. I'm having men search round and enquire. But the scent's pretty cold by now.'

'Yes. As you say,' Reggie sighed. His eyes grew large and melancholy. 'Is it far?' he said, in a voice of fear.

'Matter of a mile or two.'

'Oh, my Bell.' Reggie groaned. He pushed back his chair. He rose stiffly. 'Come on.'

Shag Nose is a headland from which dark cliffs fall sheer. Below them stretches seaward a ridge of rocks, which stand bare some way out at low tide, and in the flood make a turmoil of eddies and broken water.

The top of the headland is a flat of springy turf, in which are many tufts of thrift and cushions of stunted gorse.

'Brr. It is bleak,' Dubois complained. 'Will you tell me why Farquhar should come here? He was not—how do you say?—a man for the great open spaces.'

'Know the answer, don't you?' Reggie mumbled.

'Perfectly. He came to meet somebody in secret who desired to make an end of him. Very well. But who then? Not the paralysed one. Not the son-in-law either. It is in evidence that the son-in-law was gone before Farquhar disappeared.'

'That's right. I verified that,' Bell grunted. 'Bernal and his wife left the night before.'

'There we are again,' Dubois shrugged. 'Nothing means anything. For certain, it is not a perfect alibi. They went by car; they could come back and not be seen. But it is an alibi that will stand unless you have luck, which you have not yet, my dear Bell, God knows.'

'Not an easy case. No,' Reggie murmured. 'However. Possibilities not yet examined. Lyncombe's on the coast. Had you noticed that? I wonder if any little boat from France came in while Farquhar was still alive.'

Dubois laughed. Dubois clapped him on the shoulder. 'Magnificent! How you are resolute, my friend. Always the great idea! A boat from Brittany, *hein*? That would solve everything. The good Farquhar was so kind as to come here and meet it and be killed by the brave Bretons. And the paralysed millionaire, he was merely a diversion to pass the time.'

'Yes. We are not amused,' Reggie moaned. 'You're in such a

hurry. Bell—what's the local talent say about the tide? When was high water on the night Farquhar disappeared?'

'Not till the early morning, sir. Tide was going out from about three in the afternoon onwards.'

'I see. At dusk and after, that reef o' rocks would be comin' out of the water. Assumin' he went over the cliff in the dark or twilight, he'd fall on the rocks.'

'That's right. Of course he might bounce into the sea. But I've got a man or two down there searching the shore and the cliff-side.'

'Good man.' Reggie smiled, and wandered away to the cliff edge.

'Yes. It is most correct,' Dubois shrugged. 'I should do it, I avow. But also I should expect nothing, nothing. After all, we are late. We arrive late at everything.'

Reggie turned and stared at him. 'I know. That's what I'm afraid of,' he mumbled.

He wandered to and fro about the ground near the cliff edge, and found nothing which satisfied him, and at last lay down on his stomach where a jutting of the headland gave him a view of the cliffs on either side.

Two men scrambled about over the rocks below, scanning the cliff face, prying into every crevice they could reach . . . one of them vanished under an overhanging ledge, appeared again, working round it, was lost in a cleft . . . when he came out he had something in his hand.

'Name of a pipe!' Dubois rumbled. 'Is it possible we have luck at last?'

'No.' Reggie stood up. 'Won't be luck, whatever it is. Reward of virtue. Bell's infinite capacity for takin' pains.' . . .

A breathless policeman reached the top of the cliff, and held out a sodden book. 'That's the only perishing thing there is down there, sir,' he panted. 'Not a trace of nothing else.'

Bell gave it to Reggie. It was a sketch-book of the size to slide into a man's pocket. The first leaf bore, in a flamboyant scrawl, the name Derek Farquhar.

'Ah. That fixes it, then,' said Bell. 'He did go over this cliff, and his sketch-book came out of his pocket as he bounced on the ledges.'

'Very well,' Dubois shrugged. 'We know now as much as we guessed. Which means nothing.'

Reggie sat down and began to separate the book's wet pages.

Farquhar had drawn, in pencil, notes rather than sketches at first, scraps of face and figure and scene which took his unholy fancy, a drunken girl, a nasty stage dance, variations of impropriety. Then came some parades of men and women bathing, not less unpleasant, but more studied. 'Aha! Here is something seen at least,' said Dubois.

'Yes, I think so,' Reggie murmured, and turned the page.

The next sketch showed children dancing—small boys and girls. Some touch of cruelty was in the drawing—they were made to look ungainly—but it had power; it gave them an intensity of frail life which was at once pathetic and grotesque. They danced round a giant statue—a block in which the shape of a woman was burlesqued, hideously fat and thin, with a flat, foolish face. There were no clothes on it, but rough lines which might be girdle and necklace.

'What the devil!' Dubois exclaimed. 'This is an oddity. He discovers he had a talent, the animal.'

Reggie did not answer. For a moment more he gazed at the children and the statue, and he shivered, then he turned the other pages of the book. There were some notes of faces, then several satires on the respectability of Lyncombe—the sea front, with nymphs in Bath chairs propelled by satyrs and satyrs propelled by nymphs. He turned back to the dancing children and the giant female statue, and stared at it, and his round face was pale. 'Yes. Farquhar had talent,' he said. 'Played the devil with it all his life. And yet it works on the other side. What's the quickest way to Brittany? London and then Paris by air. Come on.'

Dubois swore by a paper bag and caught him up. 'What, then? How do you find your Brittany again in this?'

'The statue,' Reggie snapped. 'Sort of statue you see in Brittany. Nowhere else. He didn't invent that out of his dirty mind. He'd seen it. It meant something to him. I should say he'd seen the children too.'

'You go beyond me,' said Dubois. 'Well, it is not the first time. A statue of Brittany, eh? You mean the old things they have among the standing stones and the menhirs and dolmens. A primitive goddess. The devil! I do not see our Farquhar interested in antiquities. But it is the more striking that he studied her. I give you that. And the children? I will swear he was not a lover of children.'

'No. He wasn't. That came out in the drawing. Not a nice man. It pleased him to think of children dancin' round the barbarous female.'

'I believe you,' said Dubois. 'The devil was in that drawing.'

'Yes. Devilish feelin'. Yes. And yet it's going to help. Because the degenerate fellow had talent. Not wholly a bad world.'

'Optimist. Be it so. But what can you make the drawing mean, then?'

'I haven't the slightest idea,' Reggie mumbled. 'Place of child life in the career of the late Farquhar very obscure. Only trace yet discovered, the Bernals have a child. No inference justified. I'm going to Brittany. I'm goin' to look for traces round that statue. And meanwhile—Bell has to find out if a French boat has been in to Lyncombe—you'd better set your people findin' the Bernals—with child. Have the Webers got a child?'

'Ah, no.' Dubois laughed. 'The beautiful Clotilde, she is not that type.'

'Pity. However. You might let me have a look at the Webers as I go through Paris.'

'With all my heart,' said Dubois. 'You understand, my friend, you command me. I see nothing, nothing at all, but I put myself in your hand.' He made a grimace. 'In fact there is nothing else to do. It is an affair for inspiration. I never had any.'

'Nor me, no,' Reggie was indignant. 'My only aunt! Inspired! I am not! I believe in evidence. That's all. You experts are so superior.' . . .

Next morning they sat in the *salon* of the Webers. It was overwhelming with the worst magnificence of the Second Empire—mirrors and gilding, marble and malachite and lapis lazuli. But the Webers, entering affectionately arm in arm, were only magnificent in their opulent proportions. Clotilde, a dark full-blown creature, had nothing more than powder on her face, no jewels but a string of pearls, and the exuberance of her shape was modified by a simple black dress. Weber's clumsy bulk was all in black too.

They welcomed Dubois with open arms; they talked together. What had he to tell them? They had heard that the cursed Farquhar had been discovered dead in England—it was staggering; had anything been found of the jewels?

Nothing, in effect, Dubois told them. Only, Farquhar had more money than such an animal ought to have. It was a pity.

Clotilde threw up her hands. Weber scolded.

Dubois regretted—but what to do? They must admit one had been quick, very quick, to trace Farquhar. They would certainly compliment his *confrère* from England—that produced perfunctory bows. What the English police asked—and they were right—it was could one learn anything of who had worked with Farquhar, why had he come to the apartment Weber?

The Webers were contemptuous. What use to ask such a question? One had not an acquaintance with thieves. As to why he came, why he picked out them to rob—a thief must go where there was something to steal—and they—well, one was known a little. Weber smirked at his wife, and she smiled at him.

'For sure. Everyone knows monsieur—and madame.' Dubois bowed. 'But I seek something more.'

They stormed. It was not to be supposed they should know anything of such a down-at-heel.

'Oh, no. No,' said Reggie quickly. 'But in the world of business'—he looked at Weber—'in the world of the theatre'—he looked at Clotilde—'the fellow might have crossed your path, what?'

That was soothing. They agreed the thing was possible. How could one tell? They chattered of the detrimentals they remembered—to no purpose.

Under plaintive looks from Reggie, Dubois broke that off with a brusque departure. When they were outside—'Well, you have met them!' Dubois shrugged. 'And if they are anything which is not ordinary I did not see it.'

Reggie gazed at him with round reproachful eyes. 'They were in mourning,' he moaned. 'You never told me that. Were they in mourning when you saw 'em before?'

'But yes,' Dubois frowned. 'Yes, certainly. What is the matter? Did you think they had put on mourning for the animal Farquhar?'

'My dear chap! Oh, my dear chap,' Reggie sighed. 'Find out why they are in mourning. Quietly, quite quietly. Good-bye. Meet you at the station.' . . .

The night express to Nantes and Quimper drew out of Paris. They ate a grim and taciturn dinner. They went back to the sleeping car and shut themselves in Reggie's compartment. 'Well, I have done my work,' said Dubois. 'The Webers are in mourning for their nephew. A child of ten, whom Weber would have made his heir—his sister's son.'

'A child,' Reggie murmured. 'How did he die?'

'It was not in Brittany, my friend,' Dubois grinned. 'Besides it is not mysterious. He died at Fontainebleau, in August, of diphtheria. They had the best doctors of Paris. There you are again. It means nothing.'

'I wonder,' Reggie mumbled. 'Any news of the Bernals?'

'It appears they have passed through Touraine. If it is they, there was no child with them. Have no fear, they are watched for. One does not disappear in France.'

'You think not? Well, well. Remains the Bernal child. Not yet known to be dead. Of diphtheria or otherwise! I did a job o' work too. Talked to old Huet at the Institut. You know—the prehistoric man. He says Farquhar's goddess is the Woman of Sarn. Recognised her at once. She stands on about the last western hill in France. Weird sort o' place, Huet says. And he can't imagine why

Farquhar thought of children dancin' round her. The people are taught she's of the devil.'

'But you go on to see her?' Dubois made a grimace. 'The fixed idea.'

'No. Rational inference. Farquhar thought of her with children. And there's a child dead—and another child we can't find—belongin' to the people linked with Farquhar. I go on.'

'To the land's end—to the end of the world—and beyond. For your faith in yourself. My dear Fortune, you are sublime. Well, I follow you. Poor old Dubois. Sancho Panza to your Don Quixote, *hein*?' . . .

They came out of the train to a morning of soft sunshine and mellow ocean air. The twin spires of Quimper rose bright among their minarets, its sister rivers gleamed, and the wooded hill beyond glowed bronze. Dubois bustled away from breakfast to see officials. 'Don Quixote is a law to himself, but Sancho had better be correct, my friend.'

'Yes, rather,' Reggie mumbled, from a mouth full of honey. 'Conciliate the authorities. Liable to want 'em.'

'Always the optimist, my Quixote.'

'No. No. Only careful. Don't tell 'em anything.'

'Name of a name!' Dubois exploded. 'That is necessary, that warning. I have so much to tell!'

In an hour, they were driving away from Quimper, up over high moorland of heather and gorse and down again to a golden bay and a fishing village of many boats, then on westward, with glimpses of sea on either hand. There was never a tree, only, about the stone walls which divided the waves of bare land into a draught-board of little fields, thick growth of bramble and gorse. Beyond the next village, with its deep inlet of a harbour, the fields merged into moor again, and here and there rose giant stones, in line, in circle, and solitary.

'Brrr,' Dubois rumbled. 'Tombs or temples, what you please, it was a gaunt religion which put them up here on this windy end of the earth.'

The car stopped, the driver turned in his seat and pointed, and said he could drive no nearer, but that was the Woman of Sarn. 'She is lonely,' Dubois shrugged. 'There is no village near, my lad?'

'There is Sarn.' The driver pointed towards the southern sea. 'But it is nothing.'

Reggie plodded away through the heather. 'Well, this is hopeful, is it not?' Dubois caught him up. 'When we find her, what have we found? An idol in the desert. But you will go on to the end, my Quixote. Forward, then.'

They came to the statue, and stood, for its crude head rose high above theirs, looking up at it. 'And we have found it, one must avow,' Dubois shrugged. 'This is the lady Farquhar drew, devil a doubt. But, *saperlipopette*, she is worse here than on paper. She is real; she is a brute—all that there is of the beast in woman, emerging from the shapeless earth.'

'Inhuman and horrid human, yes,' Reggie murmured. 'Cruelty of life. Yes. He knew about that, the fellow who made her, poor beggar. So did Farquhar.'

'I believe it! But do you ask me to believe little children come and dance round this horror. Ah, no!'

'Oh, no. No. That never happened. Not in our time. Point of interest is, Farquhar thought it fittin' they should. Very interestin' point.' Reggie gave another look at the statue, and walked on towards the highest point of the moor.

From that he could see the tiny village of Sarn, huddled in a cove, the line of dark cliff, a long rampart against the Atlantic. Below the cliff top he made out a white house, of some size, which seemed to stand alone.

His face had a dreamy placidity as he came back to Dubois. 'Well, well. Not altogether desert,' he murmured. 'Something quite residential over there. Let's wander.'

They struck southward towards the sea. As they approached the white house, they saw that it was of modern pattern—concrete, in simple proportions, with more window than wall. Its site was well chosen, in a little hollow beneath the highest of the cliff, sheltered, yet high enough for a far prospect, taking all the southern sun.

'Of the new ugliness, eh?' said Dubois, whose taste is for elaboration in all things. 'All the last fads. It should be a sanatorium, not a house.'

'One of the possibilities, yes.' Reggie went on fast.

They came close above the house. It stood in a large walled enclosure, within which was a trim garden, but most of the space was taken by a paved yard with a roofed platform like a bandstand in the middle. Reggie stood still and surveyed it. Not a creature was to be seen. The acreage of window blazed blank and curtainless.

'The band is not playing.' Dubois made a grimace. 'It is not the season.'

Reggie did not answer. His eyes puckered to stare at a window within which the sun glinted on something of brass. He made a little inarticulate sound, and walked on, keeping above the house. But they saw no one, no sign of life, till they were close to the cliff edge.

Then a cove opened below them in a gleaming stretch of white shell sand, and on the sand children were playing: some of them at a happy-go-lucky game of rounders, some building castles, some tumbling over each other like puppies. On a rock sat, in placid guard over them, a man who had the black pointed beard, the heavy black brows, which Farquhar had sketched on his menu. But these Mephistophelean decorations did not display the leer and sneer of Farquhar's drawing. The owner watched the children with a grave and kindly attention which seemed to be interested in everyone. He called to them cheerily, and had gay answers. He laughed jovial satisfaction at their laughter.

Reggie took Dubois's arm and walked him away. 'Ah, my poor friend!' Dubois rumbled chuckles. 'There we are at last. We arrive. We have the brute goddess, we have the children, we have even the devil of our Farquhar. And behold! he is a genial paternal soul, and all the children love him. Oh, my poor friend!'

'Yes. Funny isn't it?' Reggie snapped. 'Dam' funny. Did you say the end? Then God forgive us. Which He wouldn't. He would not!'

Dubois gave him a queer look—something of derision, something of awe, and a good deal of doubt. 'When you talk like that'— a shrug, a wave of the hands—'it is outside reason, is it not? An inspiration of faith.'

'Faith that the world is reasonable. That's all,' Reggie snarled. 'Come on.'

'And where?'

'Down to this village.'

The huddled cottages of Sarn were already in sight. Then odours, a complex of stale fish and the filth of beast and man, could be smelt. Women clattered in sabots and laboured. Men lounged against the wall above the mess of the beach. A few small and ancient boats lay at anchor in the cove, and one of a larger size, and better condition, which had a motor engine.

They found a dirty *estaminet* and obtained from the landlord a bottle of nameless red wine. He said it was old, it was marvellous, but, being urged to share it, preferred a glass of the apple spirit, Calvados. 'Marvellous, it is the world,' Dubois grinned. 'You are altogether right. Calvados for us also, my friend. It is more humane.'

The landlord was slow of speech, and a pessimist. Even with several little glasses of Calvados inside him he would talk only of the hardness of life and the poverty of Sarn and the curse upon the modern sardine. Reggie agreed that life was dear and life was difficult, but, after all, they had still their good boats at Sarn— motor-boats indeed. The landlord denied it with gloomy vehemence: motors—not one—only in the *Badebec*, and that was no fishing-boat, that one. It was M. David's.

'Is it so?" Reggie yawned, and lit his pipe. He gazed dreamily down the village street to the hideous little church. From that— under a patched umbrella, to keep off the wind, which was high, or the sun, which was grown faint—came a fat and shabby *curé*. 'Well, better luck my friend,' Reggie murmured, left Dubois to pay the bill, and wandered away.

He met the *curé* by the church gate. Was it permitted to visit that interesting church? Certainly, it was permitted, but monsieur would find nothing of interest—it was new; it was, alas! a poor place.

The *curé* was right—it was new; it was garish, it was mean. He showed it to Reggie with an affecting simplicity of diffident pride, and Reggie was attentive. Reggie praised the care with which it was kept. 'You are kind, sir,' the *curé* beamed. 'You are just. In fact they are admirably pious, my poor people, but poor—poor.'

'You will permit the stranger—' Reggie slipped a note into his hand.

'Ah, monsieur! You are generous. It will be rewarded, please God.'

'It is nothing,' said Reggie quickly. 'Do not think of it.' They passed out of the church. 'I suppose this is almost the last place in France?'

'Sometimes I think we are forgotten,' the *curé* agreed. 'Yes, almost the last. Certainly we are all poor folk. There is only M. David, who is sometimes good to us.'

'A visitor?' Reggie said.

'Ah, no. He lives here. The Maison des Iles, you know. No? It is a school for young children—a school of luxury. He is a good man, M. David. Sometimes he will take, for almost a nothing, children who are weakly, and in a little while he has them as strong as the best. I have seen miracles. To be sure it is the best air in the world, here at Sarn. But he is a very good man. He calls his school 'of the islands' because of the islands out there'—the *curé* pointed to what looked like a reef of rocks. 'My poor people call them the islands of the blessed. It is not good religion, but they used to think the souls of the innocent went there. Yes, the Maison des Iles, his school is. But you should see it, sir. The children are charming.'

'If I had time—' said Reggie, and said good-bye.

Dubois was at the gate. Dubois took his arm and marched him off. 'My friend, almost thou persuadest me—' He spoke into Reggie's ear. 'Guess what I have found, will you? That motor-yacht, the yacht of M. David, she was away a week ten days ago.

And M. David on board. You see? It is possible she went over to England. A guess, yes, a chance, but one must avow it fits devilish well, if one can make it fit. A connection with all your fantasy—M. David over in England when Farquhar was drowned. Is it possible we arrive at last?'

'Yes, it could be. Guess what I've heard. M. David keeps school. That wasn't a bandstand. Open-air class-room. M. David is a very good man, and he uses his beautiful school to cure the children of the poor. He does miracles. The old *curé* has seen 'em.'

'The devil!' said Dubois. 'That does not fit at all. But a priest would see miracles. It is his trade.'

'Oh, no. No. Not unless they happen,' Reggie murmured.

'My friend, you believe more than any man I ever knew,' Dubois rumbled. 'Come, I must know more of this David. The sooner we were back at Quimper the better.'

'Yes. That is indicated. Quimper and telephone.' He checked a moment, and gazed anguish at Dubois. 'Oh, my hat, how I hate telephones.'

Dubois has not that old-fashioned weakness. Dubois, it is beyond doubt, enjoyed the last hours of that afternoon, shut into privacy at the post office with its best telephone, stirring up London and Paris and half France till sweat dripped from his big face and the veins of his brow dilated into knotted cords.

When he came into Reggie's room at the hotel it was already past dinner-time. Reggie lay on his bed, languid from a bath. 'My dear old thing,' he moaned sympathy. 'What a battle! You must have lost pounds.'

'So much the better,' Dubois chuckled. 'And also I have results. Listen. First. I praise the good Bell. He has it that a French boat—cutter rig with motor—was seen by fishermen in the bay off Lyncombe last week. They watched her, because they had suspicions she was poaching their lobsters and crabs, which they unaccountably believe is the habit of our honest French fishermen. She was lying in the bay the night of Tuesday—you see, the night that Farquhar disappeared. In the morning she was gone. They are not sure of the name, but they thought it was *Badboy*. That is near enough to Badebec, *hein*? In fact, myself, I do not understand the name Badebec.'

'Lady in Rabelais,' Reggie murmured. 'Rather interestin'. Shows the breadth of M. David's taste.'

'Aha. Very well. Here is a good deal for M. David to explain. Second, M. David himself. He is known: there is nothing against him. In fact he is like you, a man of science, a biologist, a doctor. He

was brilliant as a student, which was about the same time that
Farquhar studied art—and other things—in the Quartier Latin.
David had no money. He served in hospitals for children; he set up
his school here—a school for delicate children—four years ago. Its
record is very good. He has medical inspection by a doctor from
Quimper each month. But, third, Weber's nephew was at this
school till July. He went home to Paris, they went out to Fontainebleau, and—piff!' Dubois snapped his fingers. 'He is dead
like that. There is no doubt it was diphtheria. Do you say fulminat-
ing diphtheria? Yes, that is it.'

'I'd like a medical report,' Reggie murmured.

'I have asked for it. However—the doctors are above suspicion,
my friend. And now, fourth—the Bernals are found. They are at
Dijon. They have been asked what has become of their dear little
boy, and, they reply, he is at school in Brittany. At the school of M.
David, Maison des Iles, Quimper.'

'Yes. He would be. I see.'

'Name of a name! I think you have always seen everything.'

'Oh, no. No. Don't see it now,' Reggie mumbled. 'However.
We're workin' it out. You've done wonderfully.'

'Not so bad.' Dubois smiled. 'My genius is for action.'

'Yes. Splendid. Yes. Mine isn't. I just went and had a look at the
museum.'

'My dear friend,' Dubois condescended. 'Why not? After all, the
affair is now for me.'

'Thanks, yes. Interestin' museum. Found a good man on the
local legends there. Told me the Woman of Sarn used to have
children sacrificed to her. That'll be what Farquhar had in his nice
head. Though M. David is so good to children.'

'Aha. It explains, and it does not explain,' Dubois said. 'In spite
of you, M. David remains an enigma. Let poor old Dubois try. I
have all these people under observation—the Webers, the
Bernals—they cannot escape me now. And there are good men
gone out to watch over M. David in his Maison des Iles. Tomorrow
we will go and talk to him, hein?'

'Pleasure,' Reggie murmured. 'You'd better go and have a bath
now. You want it. And I want my dinner.' . . .

When they drove out to Sarn in the morning a second car
followed them. In a blaze of hot sunshine they started, but they
had not gone far before a mist of rain spread in from the sea, and by
the time they reached the Maison des Iles they seemed to be in the
clouds.

'An omen, hein?' Dubois made a grimace. 'At least it may be
inconvenient—if he is alarmed; if he wishes to play tricks. We have

no luck in this affair. But courage, my friend. Poor old Dubois, he is not without resource.'

Their car entered the walled enclosure of the Maison des Iles, the second stopped outside. When Dubois sent in his card to M. David, they were shown to a pleasant waiting-room, and had not long to wait.

David was dressed with a careless neatness. He was well groomed and perfectly at ease. His full red lips smiled; his dark eyes quizzed them. 'What a misery of a morning you have found, gentlemen. I apologise for my ocean. M. Dubois?' he made a bow.

'Of the Sûreté.' Dubois bowed. 'And M. Fortune, my distinguished *confrère* from England.'

David was enchanted. And what could he do for them?

'We make some little enquiries. First, you have here a boy— Tracy, the son of Mme Bernal. He is in good health?'

'Of the best.' David lifted his black brows. 'You will permit me to know why you ask.'

'Because another boy who was here is dead. The little nephew of M. Weber. You remember him?'

'Very well. He was a charming child. I regret infinitely. But you are without doubt aware that he fell ill on the holidays. It was a tragedy for his family. But the cause is not here. We have had no illness, no infection at all. I recommend you to Dr Lannion, at Quimper. He is our medical inspector.'

'Yes. So I've heard,' Reggie murmured. 'Have you had other cases of children who went home for the holidays and died?'

'It is an atrocious question!' David cried.

'But you are not quite sure of the answer?' said Dubois.

'If that is an insinuation, I protest,' David frowned. 'I have nothing to conceal, sir. It is impossible, that must be clear, I should know what has become of every child who has left my school. But, I tell you frankly, I do not recall any death but that of the little nephew of Weber, poor child.'

'Very well. Then you can have no objection that my assistant should examine your records,' said Dubois. He opened the window, and whistled and lifted a hand.

'Not the least in the world. I am at your orders.' David bowed. 'Permit me, I will go and get out the books,' and he went briskly.

'Now if we had luck he would try to run away,' Dubois rumbled. 'But do not expect it.'

'I didn't,' Reggie moaned.

And David did not run away. He came back and took them to his office, and there Dubois's man was set down to work at registers. 'You wish to assist?' David asked.

'No, thanks. No,' Reggie murmured. 'I'd like to loook at your school.'

'An inspection!' Dubois smiled. 'I shall be delighted. I dare to hope for the approval of a man of science so eminent.'

They inspected dormitories and dining-room and kitchen, class-rooms and workshop and laboratory. M. David was expansive and enthusiastic, yet modest. Either he was an accomplished actor, or he had a deep interest in school hygiene, and his arrangements were beyond suspicion. In the laboratory Reggie lingered. 'It is elementary,' David apologised. 'But what would you have? Some general science, that is all they can do, my little ones: botany for the most part; as you see, a trifle of chemistry to amuse them.'

'Yes. Quite sound. Yes. I'd like to see the other laboratory.'

'What?' David stared. 'There is only this.'

'Oh, no. Another one with a big microscope,' Reggie murmured. 'North side of the house.'

'Oh, la, la,' David laughed. 'you have paid some attention to my poor house. I am flattered. You mean my own den, where I play with marine biology still. Certainly you shall see it. But a little moment. I must get the key. You will understand. One must keep one's good microscope locked up. These imps, they play every-where.' He hurried out.

'Bigre! How the devil did you know there was another laboratory?' said Dubois.

'Name of a dog! Is there anything you do not see?' Dubois complained. 'Well, if we have any luck he has run away this time.'

They waited some long while, and Dubois's face was flattened against the window to peer through the rain at the man on watch. But David had not run away, he came back at last, and apologised for some delay with a fool of a master, heaven given him patience! He took them briskly to the other laboratory, his den.

It was not pretentious. There were some shelves of bottles, and a bench with a sink, and a glass cupboard which stood open and empty. On the broad table in the window was a microscope of high power, and some odds and ends.

Reggie glanced at the bottles of chemicals and came to the microscope. 'I play at what I worked at. That is middle age,' David smiled. 'Here is something a little interesting.' He slipped a slide into the microscope and invited Reggie to look.

'Oh, yes. One of the diatoms. Pretty one,' Reggie murmured, and was shown some more. 'Thanks very much.' A glance set Dubois in a hurry to go. David was affably disappointed. He had hoped they would lunch with him. The gentleman with the registers could hardly have finished his investigations. He desired an investigation the most complete.

'I will leave him here,' Dubois snapped, and they got away. 'Nothing, my friend?' Dubois muttered.

'No. That was the point,' Reggie said. ' "When they got there the cupboard was bare." '

As their car passed the gate, a man signalled to them out of the rain. They stopped just beyond sight of the house, and he joined them. 'Bouvier has held someone,' he panted. 'A man with a sack.' They got out of the car and Dubois waved him on.

Through the blinding rain-clouds they came to the back of the house, and, on the way up to the cliffs, found Bouvier with his hand on the collar of a sullen, stupefied Breton. A sack lay on the ground at their feet.

'He says it is only rubbish,' Bouvier said, 'and he was taking it to throw into the sea, where they throw their waste. But I kept him.'

'Good. Let us see.' Dubois pulled the sack open. 'The devil, it is nothing but broken glass!'

Reggie grasped the hand that was going to turn it over. 'No, you mustn't do that,' he said sharply. 'Risky.'

'Why? What then? It is broken glass and bits of jelly.'

'Yes. As you say. Broken glass and bits of jelly. However.' Over Reggie's wet face came a slow benign smile. 'Just what we wanted. Contents of cupboard which was bare. I'll have to do some work on this. I'm going to the hospital. You'd better collect David—in the other car. Good-bye.' . . .

Twenty-four hours, later, he came into a grim room of the *gendarmerie* at Quimper. There Dubois and David sat with a table between them, and neither man was a pleasant sight. David's florid colour was gone, he had become untidy, he sagged in his chair, unable to hide fatigue and pain. Dubois also was dishevelled, and his eyes had sunk and grown small, but the big face wore a look of hungry cruelty. He turned to Reggie. 'Aha. Here you are at last. And what do you tell M. David?'

'Well, we'll have a little demonstration.' Reggie set down a box on the table and took from it a microscope. 'Not such a fine instrument as yours, M. David, but it will do.' He adjusted a slide. 'You showed me some beautiful marine diatoms in your laboratory. Let me show you this. Also from your laboratory. From the sackful of stuff you tried to throw into the sea.'

David dragged himself up and looked, and stared at him, and dropped back in his chair.

'Oh, that's not all, no.' Reggie changed the slide. 'Try this one.'

Again, and more wearily, David looked. He sat down again. His

full lips curled back to show his teeth in a grin. 'And then?' he said.
'What have you?' Dubois came to the microscope. 'Little chains of dots, eh?' Reggie put back the first slide. 'And rods with dots at the end.'

'Not bad for a layman, is it, M. David?' Reggie murmured. 'Streptococcus pyogenes, and the diphtheria bacillus. I've got some more—'

'Indeed?' David sneered.

'Oh, yes. But these will do. Pyogenes was found in poor little Weber: accountin' for the virulence of the diphtheria. Very efficient and scientific murder.'

'And the others?' Dubois thundered. 'The other children who went home for their holidays and died. Two, three, four, is it, David?'

David laughed. 'What does it matter? Yes, there are others who have gone to the isles of the blessed. But, also, there are many who have been made well and strong. I mock at you.'

'You have cause, Herod,' Dubois cried. 'You have grown rich on the murder of children. But it is we who laugh last. We deliver you to justice now.'

'Justice! Ah, yes, you believe that.' David laughed again. 'You are primitive, you are barbarous. Me, I am rational, I am a man of science. I sacrifice one life that a dozen may live well and happy. These who stand in the way of the rich, their deaths are paid for, and with the money I heal many. What, if life is valuable, is not this wisdom and justice? Let one die to save many—it is in all the religions, that. But no one believes his religions now. I—I believe in man. Well, I am before my time. But some day the world will be all Davids. With me it is finished.'

'Not yet, name of God!' Dubois growled.

'Oh yes, my friend. I am sick to death already. I have made sure of that.' He waved his hand at Reggie. 'You will not save me—no, not even you, my clever confrère. Good night! Go chase the Weber and the Bernal and the rest. David, he is gone into the infinite.' He fell back, a hand to his head.

Reggie went to him, and looked close and felt at him. 'Better take him away,' he pronounced. 'Hospital, under observation.'

Dubois gave the orders. . . . 'Play-acting, my friend,' he shrugged.

'Oh, no. No. That kind of man. Logical and drastic. He's ill all right. There was the diplococcus of meningitis in his collection. Might be that.' And it was. . . .

Ten days afterwards Dubois came to London with Reggie and gave Lomas a lecture on the case. 'I am desolated that I cannot offer you anyone to hang, my friend. But what can one do? The wretched Farquhar—I have no doubt he was murdered between David and Bernal. But there is no evidence. And, after all, David, he is dead, and we have Bernal for conspiracy to murder his stepson. That will do. It was, in fact, a case profoundly simple, like all the great crimes. To make a trade of arranging the deaths of unwanted children, that is very old. The distinction of David was to organise it scientifically, that is all. The child who was an heir to fortune, with a greedy one waiting to succeed, that was the child for him. Weber's nephew stood in the way of the beautiful Clotilde to Weber's fortune. Mrs Bernal's little boy was in the way of her second husband to the fortune of her father, the old millionaire. And the others! Well here is a beautiful modern school for delicate children, nine out of ten of them thrive marvellously. But, for the tenth, there is David's bacteriological laboratory, and a killing disease to take home with him when he goes for his holidays. Always at home, they die; always a disease of infection they could pick up anywhere. *Bigre!* It was a work of genius. And it would have gone on for ever but that this worthless Farquhar blunders into Brittany upon it, and begins to blackmail the beautiful Clotilde, the Bernal. Clotilde pays with her jewels, and has to pretend a robbery. Bernal will not pay—cannot, perhaps. Farquhar approaches the old grandfather, and Bernal calls in David, and the blackmailer is killed. The oldest story in the world. Rascals fall out, justice comes in. There is your angel of justice.' He bowed to Reggie. 'Dear master. You have shown me the way. Well, I am content to serve. Does he serve badly, poor old Dubois?'

'Oh, no. No. Brilliant,' Reggie murmured. 'Queer case, though. I believe David myself. He wanted to be a god. Make lives to his desire. And he did. Cured more than he killed. Far more. Then this fellow, who never wanted to be anything but a beast, blows in and beats him. Queer world. And David might have been a kindly, human fellow, if he hadn't had power. Dangerous stuff, science. Lots of us not fit for it.'

THE ASSASSINS' CLUB

Nicholas Blake

Nigel Strangeways, who finds himself eyewitness to a murder during a dinner of 'The Assassins' Club', is another of the highly regarded detectives to have emerged during the 'Golden Age' of crime fiction. An erudite man and an astute judge of character, he has something in common with his creator, Nicholas Blake (1904–1972) otherwise known as Cecil Day Lewis, the novelist and critic who became Poet Laureate in 1968. Lewis began writing his pseudonymous stories about Strangeways in 1935 to supplement his income, and the detective has been described as 'more believable than most fictional sleuths'. Lewis was a great admirer of the detective story which he once described as 'the folk myth of the twentieth century', and is at his best in the following example.

'No,' thought Nigel Strangeways, looking round the table, 'no one would ever guess.'

Ever since, a quarter of an hour ago, they had assembled in the ante-room for sherry, Nigel had been feeling more and more nervous—a nervousness greater than the prospect of having to make an after-dinner speech seemed to warrant. It was true that, as the guest of honour, something more than the usual postprandial convivialities would be expected of him. And of course the company present would, from its nature, be especially critical. But still, he had done this sort of thing often enough before; he knew he was pretty good at it. Why the acute state of jitters, then? After it was all over, Nigel was tempted to substitute 'foreboding' for 'jitters'; to wonder whether he oughtn't to have proclaimed these very curious feelings, like Cassandra, from the house-top—even at the risk of spoiling what looked like being a real peach of a dinner party. After all, the dinner party did get spoiled, anyway, and soon enough, too. But, taking all things into consideration, it probably wouldn't have made any difference.

It was in an attempt to dispel this cloud of uneasiness that Nigel began to play the old game of identity-guessing with himself. There was a curious uniformity among the faces of the majority of the twenty-odd diners. The women—there were only three of them—looked homely, humorous, dowdy-and-be-damned-to-it. The men, Nigel finally decided, resembled in the mass sanitary inspectors or very minor Civil Servants. They were most of them rather undersized, and ran to drooping moustaches, gold-rimmed spectacles and a general air of mild ineffectualness. There were exceptions, of course. That elderly man in the middle of the table, with the face of a dyspeptic and superannuated bloodhound—it was not difficult to place him; even without the top-hat or the wig with which the public normally associated him, Lord Justice Pottinger could easily be recognised—the most celebrated criminal judge of his generation. Then that leonine, mobile face on his left; it had been as much photographed as any society beauty's; and well it might, for Sir Eldred Travers' golden tongue had—it was whispered—saved as many murderers as Justice Pottinger had hanged. There were one or two other exceptions, such as the dark-haired, poetic-looking young man sitting on Nigel's right and rolling bread-pellets.

'No,' said Nigel, aloud this time, 'no one would possibly guess.'

'Guess what?' inquired the young man.

'The bloodthirsty character of this assembly.' He took up the menu-card, at the top of which was printed in red letters:

THE ASSASSINS

Dinner, December 20th

'No,' laughed the young man, 'we don't look like murderers, I must admit—not even murderers by proxy.'

'Good lord! are you in the trade, too?'

'Yes. Ought to have introduced myself. Name of Herbert Dale.'

Nigel looked at the young man with increased interest. Dale had published only two cime-novels, but he was already accepted as one of the *élite* of detective writers; he could not otherwise have been a member of that most exclusive of clubs, the Assassins; for, apart from a representative of the Bench, the Bar, and Scotland Yard, this club was composed solely of the princes of detective fiction.

It was at this point that Nigel observed two things—that the hand which incessantly rolled bread-pellets was shaking, and that, on the glossy surface of the menu-card Dale had just laid down, there was a moist finger-mark.

'Are you making a speech, too?' Nigel said.

'Me? Good lord, no. Why?'

'I thought you looked nervous,' said Nigel, in his direct way.

The young man laughed, a little too loudly. And, as though that was some kind of signal, one of those unrehearsed total silences fell upon the company. Even in the street outside, the noises seemed to be damped, as though an enormous soft pedal had been pressed down on everything. Nigel realised that it must have been snowing since he came in. A disagreeable sensation of eeriness crept over him. Annoyed with this sensation—a detective has no right to feel psychic, he reflected angrily, not even a private detective so celebrated as Nigel Strangeways—he forced himself to look round the brilliantly lighted room, the animated yet oddly neutral-looking faces of the diners, the *maître d'hôtel* in his white gloves—bland and uncreased as his own face, the impassive waiters. Everything was perfectly normal; and yet . . . Some motive he was never after able satisfactorily to explain forced him to let drop into the yawning silence:

'What a marvellous setting this would be for a murder.'

If Nigel had been looking in the right direction at the moment, things might have happened very differently. As it was, he didn't even notice the way Dale's wine-glass suddenly tilted and split a few drops of sherry.

At once the whole table buzzed again with conversation. A man three places away on Nigel's right raised his head, which had been almost buried in his soup plate, and said:

'Tchah! This is the one place where a murder would never happen. My respected colleagues are men of peace. I doubt if any of them has the guts to say boo to a goose. Oh, yes, they'd *like* to be men of action, tough guys. But, I ask you, just look at them! That's why they became detective-story writers. Wish-fulfilment, the psychoanalysts call it—though I don't give much for that gang, either. But it's quite safe, spilling blood, as long as you only do it on paper.'

The man turned his thick lips and small, arrogant eyes towards Nigel. 'The trouble with you amateur investigators is that you're so romantic. That's why the police beat you to it every time.'

A thick-set, swarthy man opposite him exclaimed: 'You're wrong there, Mr Carruthers. We don't seem to have beaten Mr Strangeways to it in the past every time.'

'So our aggressive friend is *the* David Carruthers. Well, well,' whispered Nigel to Dale.

'Yes,' said Dale, not modifying his tone at all. 'A squalid fellow, isn't he? But he gets the public all right. We have sold our thousands, but David has sold his tens of thousands. Got a yellow streak though, I'll bet, in spite of his bluster. Pity somebody doesn't bump him off at this dinner, just to show him he's not the Mr Infallible he sets up to be.'

Carruthers shot a vicious glance at Dale. 'Why not try it yourself? Get you a bit of notoriety, anyway; might even sell your books. Though,' he continued, clapping on the shoulder a nondescript little man who was sitting between him and Dale, 'I think little Crippen here would be my first bet. You'd like to have my blood, Crippen, wouldn't you?'

The little man said stiffly: 'Don't make yourself ridiculous, Carruthers. You must be drunk already. And I'd thank you to remember that my name is Cripps.'

At this point the president interposed with a convulsive change of subject, and the dinner resumed its even tenor. While they were disposing of some very tolerable trout, a waiter informed Dale that he was wanted on the telephone. The young man went out. Nigel was trying at the same time to listen to a highly involved story of the president's and decipher the very curious expression on Cripps' face, when all the lights went out too. . . .

There were a few seconds of astonished silence. Then a torrent of talk broke out—the kind of forced jocularity with which man still comforts himself in the face of sudden darkness. Nigel could hear movement all around him, the pushing back of chairs, quick, muffled treads on the carpet—waiters, no doubt. Someone at the end of the table, rather ridiculously, struck a match; it did nothing but emphasize the pitch-blackness.

'Stevens, can't someone light the candles?' exclaimed the president irritably.

'Excuse me, sir,' came the voice of the *maître d'hôtel*, 'there are no candles. Harry, run along to the fuse-box and find out what's gone wrong.'

The door banged behind the waiter. Less than a minute later the lights all blazed on again. Blinking, like swimmers come up from a deep dive, the diners looked at each other. Nigel observed that Carruther's face was even nearer his food than usual. Curious, to go on eating all the time—But no, his head was right on top of the food—lying in the plate like John the Baptist's. And from between his shoulder-blades there stood out a big white handle; the handle—good God! it couldn't be; this was too macabre altogether—but it *was* the handle of a fish-slice.

A kind of gobbling noise came out of Justice Pottinger's mouth. All eyes turned to where his shaking hand pointed, grew wide with horror, and then turned ludicrously back to him, as though he was about to direct the jury.

'God bless my soul!' was all the Judge could say.

But someone had sized up the whole situation. The thick-set man who had been sitting opposite Carruthers was already standing with his back to the door. His voice snapped:

'Stay where you are, everyone. I'm afraid there's no doubt about this. I must take charge of this case at once. Mr Strangeways, will you go and ring up Scotland Yard—police surgeon, fingerprint men, photographers—the whole bag of tricks; you know what we want.'

Nigel sprang up. His gaze, roving around the room, had registered something different, some detail missing; but his mind couldn't identify it. Well, perhaps it would come to him later. He moved towards the door. And just then the door opened brusquely, pushing the thick-set man away from it. There was a general gasp, as though everyone expected to see something walk in with blood on its hands. It was only young Dale, a little white in the face, but grinning amiably.

'What on earth—?' he began. Then he, too, saw . . .

An hour later, Nigel and the thickset man, Superintendent Bateman, were alone in the anteroom. The princes of detective fiction were huddled together in another room, talking in shocked whispers.

'Don't like the real thing, do they, sir?' the Superintendent had commented sardonically; 'do 'em good to be up against a flesh-and-blood problem for once. I wish 'em luck with it.'

'Well,' he was saying now. 'Doesn't seem like much of a loss to the world, this Carruthers. None of 'em got a good word for him. Too much food, to much drink, too many women. But that doesn't give us a motive. Now this Cripps. Carruthers said Cripps would like to have his blood. Why was that, d'you suppose?'

'You can search me. Cripps wasn't giving anything away when we interviewed him.'

'He had enough opportunity. All he had to do when the lights went out was to step over to the buffet, take up the first knife he laid hands on—probably thought the fish slice was a carving-knife—stab him, and sit down and twiddle his fingers.'

'Yes, he could have wrapped his handkerchief round the handle. That would account for there being no fingerprints. And there's no one to swear he moved from his seat; Dale was out of the room—and it's a bit late now to ask Carruthers, who was on his other side. But, if he *did* do it, everything happened very luckily for him.'

'Then there's young Dale himself,' said Bateman, biting the side of his thumb. 'Talked a lot of hot air about bumping Carruthers off before it happened. Might be a double bluff. You see, Mr Strangeways, there's no doubt about that waiter's evidence. The main switch was thrown over. Now, what about this? Dale arranged to be called up during dinner; answers call; then goes and turns off the main switch—in gloves, I suppose, because there's only the waiter's fingerprints on it—comes back under cover of darkness, stabs his man, and goes out again.'

'Mm,' ruminated Nigel, 'but the motive? And where are the gloves? And why, if it was premeditated, such an outlandish weapon?'

'If he's hidden the gloves, we'll find 'em soon enough. And—' the Superintendent was interrupted by the tinkle of the telephone at his elbow. A brief dialogue ensued. Then he turned to Nigel.

'Man I sent round to interview Morton—bloke who rang Dale up at dinner. Swears he was talking to Dale for three to five minutes. That seems to let Dale out, unless it was collusion.'

That moment a plainclothes man entered, a grin of ill-concealed triumph on his face. He handed a rolled-up pair of black kid gloves to Bateman. 'Tucked away behind the pipes in the lavatories, sir.'

Bateman unrolled them. There were stains on the fingers. He glanced inside the wrists, then passed the gloves to Nigel, pointing at some initials stamped there.

'Well, well,' said Nigel. 'H. D. Let's have him in again. Looks as if that telephone call *was* collusion.'

'Yes, we've got him now.'

But when the young man entered and saw the gloves lying on the table his reactions were very different from what the Superintendent had expected. An expression of relief, instead of the spasm of guilt, passed over his face.

'Stupid of me,' he said, 'I lost my head for a few minutes, after— But I'd better start at the beginning. Carruthers was always bragging about his nerve and the tight corners he's been in and so on. A poisonous specimen. So Morton and I decided to play a practical joke on him. He was to phone me up. I was to go out and throw the main switch, then come back and pretend to strangle Carruthers from behind—just give him a thorough shaking-up—and leave a bloodcurdling message on his plate to the effect that this was just a warning, and next time the Unknown would do the thing properly. We reckoned he'd be gibbering with fright when I turned up the lights again! Well, everything went all right till I came up behind him; but then—then I happened to touch that knife, and I knew somebody had been there before me, in earnest. Afraid, I lost my nerve then, especially when I found I'd got some of his blood on my gloves. So I hid them, and burnt the spoof message. Damn silly of me. The whole idea was damn silly, I can see that now.'

'Why gloves at all?' asked Nigel.

'Well, they say it's your hands and your shirt-front that are likely to show in the dark; so I put on black gloves and pinned my coat over my shirt-front. And, I say,' he added in a deprecating way, 'I don't want to teach you fellows your business, but if I had really meant to kill him, would I have worn gloves with my initials on them?'

'That is as may be,' said Bateman coldly, 'but I must warn you that you are in—'

'Just a minute,' Nigel interrupted. 'Why should Cripps have wanted Carruthers's blood?'

'Oh, you'd better ask Cripps. If he won't tell you, I don't think I ought to—'

'Don't be a fool. You're in a damned tight place, and you can't afford to be chivalrous.'

'Very well. Little Cripps may be dim, but he's a good sort. He told me once, in confidence, that Carruthers had pirated an idea of his for a plot and made a best-seller out of it. But—dash it—no one would commit murder just because—'

'You must leave that for us to decide, Mr Dale,' said the Superintendent.

When the young man had gone out, under the close surveillance of a constable, Bateman turned wearily to Nigel.

'Well,' he said, 'it may be him; and it may be Cripps. But with all these crime authors about, it might be any of 'em.'

Nigel leapt up from his seat. 'Yes,' he exclaimed, 'and that's why we've not thought of anyone else. And'—his eyes lit up—'by Jove! now I've remembered it—the missing detail. Quick! Are all those waiters and chaps still there?'

'Yes; we've kept 'em in the dining-room. But what the—?'

Nigel ran into the dining-room, Bateman at his heels. He looked out of one of the windows, open at the top.

'What's down below there?' he asked the *maître d'hôtel.*

'A yard, sir; the kitchen windows look out on it.'

'And now, where was Sir Eldred Travers sitting?'

The man pointed to the place without hesitation, his imperturbable face betraying not the least surprise.

'Right; will you go and ask him to step this way for a minute. Oh, by the way,' he added, as the *maître d'hôtel* reached the door, *'where are your gloves?'*

The man's eyes flickered. 'My gloves, sir?'

'Yes; before the lights went out you were wearing white gloves; after they went up again, I remembered it just now, you were not wearing them. Are they in the yard by any chance?'

The man shot a desperate glance around him; then the bland composure of his face broke up. He collapsed, sobbing, into a chair.

'My daughter—he ruined her—she killed herself. When the lights went out, it was too much for me—the opportunity. He deserved it. I'm not sorry.'

'Yes,' said Nigel, ten minutes later, 'it was too much for him. He picked up the first weapon at hand. Afterwards, knowing everyone would be searched, he had to throw the gloves out of the window. There would be blood on them. With luck we mightn't have looked in the yard before he could get out to remove them. And unless one was looking, one wouldn't see them against the snow. They were white.'

'What was that about Sir Eldred Travers?' asked the Superintendent.

'Oh, I wanted to put him off his guard, and to get him away from the window. He might have tried to follow his gloves.'

'Well, that fish-slice might have been a slice of bad luck for young Dale if you hadn't been here,' said the Superintendent, venturing on a witticism. 'What are you grinning away to yourself about?'

'I was just thinking, this must be the first time a Judge has been present at a murder.'

DINNER FOR TWO

Roy Vickers

The Department of Dead Ends at Scotland Yard does what its name suggests—takes on the cases where all the clues and bits of evidence about a case have ended up in 'dead ends'. Detective Inspector Rason is the man from this obscure branch of the police who has to go methodically through what all his colleagues have already investigated in the hope of finding something that everyone has overlooked. The series of cases about this department were written by Roy Vickers (1889–1965), a former court reporter who, with tales like 'Dinner For Two', pioneered the 'inverted' detective story in which the reader follows the police methods from the discovery of a crime to its eventual solution.

Today, if you were to mention the Ennings mystery, you would be assured that 'everyone knows' that Dennis Yawle murdered Charles Ennings. In this case, 'everyone' happens to be right, though for the wrong reasons. The public of the day decided that he was guilty because he denounced an attractive young woman of pleasing manners and assumed respectability. And 'everyone knows' that nice young women don't commit murder, whatever their walk in life, and that self-centred, solitary, aggressive little men sometimes do.

Charles Ennings was a patent agent. He lived in a flat on the third floor at Barslade Mansions, Westminster, the kind of flats that are occupied by moderately successful professional men and junior directors. A bachelor, with a promiscuous impulse freely indulged, he nevertheless managed to avoid scandalising his neighbours.

His dead body was found in his sitting-room by the daily help at eight-thirty. Death, which had occurred upwards of ten hours previously, had been caused by a knife—thrust in the throat—an ordinary pocket knife such as could then be bought in any cutler's for a few shillings. The news, of course, did not appear before the lunchtime editions.

Dennis Yawle, the murderer, was a prematurely embittered man of thirty-two. He had taken a science degree in chemistry and had been employed by a well-known firm of soap manufacturers for the last nine years at a modest salary. His personality, rather than his science, had precluded him from promotion. The firm had given him a chance as manager of their depot in the Balkans; but he disappointed them in everything except his routine work. Incidentally, it was in the Balkans that he had learned how to use a knife for purposes other than the cutting of string.

In chemistry alone he was enterprising. He had worked out some useful little compounds, unconnected with soap, and had patented them through Ennings. His income had been substantially increased, but not to the point where he could prudently resign his job.

He believed that Ennings had tricked him over his patents, which was true. He believed that he had lost Aileen Daines because he had insufficient money—which may have been true. Hysteria was added to grievance by the further belief that Ennings himself had enjoyed the lady's favours for a brief period before discarding her for another, which was probably an exaggeration. By that particular exaggeration many a man has been flicked from hatred to murderous intent.

Daily at lunchtime he would emerge from the laboratory in North London with his colleague, Holldon. Holldon had his daily bet on the races, and always bought a paper from a stand outside the restaurant. He would prop it up during lunch, while Yawle generally read a book. But on January 18th, 1933, he brought no book, because he had to stage a little pantomime with Holldon's paper.

First, he must eat his lunch, which was not too easy. When the coffee arrived he delivered his line, which began with a yawn:

'Any news in that thing?'

'No. They've had to plug a murder to fill space.'

Holldon was doing everything right, even to pushing the paper across the table. Yawle's stage business with the paper was easy enough.

'Good—lord!' He shot it out, and Holldon was sufficiently startled to attend. 'I know this chap who's been murdered. I say, Holldon, this is pretty ghastly for me! I was with him last evening—I must ring the police.'

'I'd keep out of it, if I were you. You have to turn up at court day after day in case they want you to give evidence.'

'But they've called in Scotland Yard, which means that the local police can't produce a suspect.' Yawle kept it up until the other professed himself convinced.

Five minutes later he was speaking on the telephone to Chief

Inspector Karslake, giving particulars of himself.

'I was at that flat last night between seven and half-past. I don't suppose I can tell you anything you don't know but I thought I'd better give you a ring.'

Karslake thanked him with some warmth, and said he would send a man to Mr Yawle's office.

'Well-l, I have rather a crowded afternoon in front of me. I could make Scotland Yard in about twenty minutes. If you could see me then, we could get my little bit tidied up right away.'

In his pocket was a crystal of cyanide to complete the tidying-up process if necessary.

To walk up to the tiger and stoke it was a desperate improvisation, necessitated by the blunders of an ill-designed murder. Indeed, it is doubtful whether his plans had ever emerged from the fantasy stage, until he struck the blow—if we except the solitary precaution of observing the porter's movements.

For three nights previously he had strolled past the flats on the opposite side of the road, noting that between seven and eight the porter was extremely busy—with three entrances and forty-five flats, most of whose tenants were arriving or departing by taxi or car. It would be child's play to slip in—and out again—without being seen.

In the fantasy, he eluded the porter, passed through an empty hall, ascended an empty staircase.

In actuality, he did elude the porter. But the hall was not empty. In the miniature lounge, consisting of one palm, a radiator, and three chairs, stood a girl who, as he fancied, bore some resemblance to Aileen Daines. That is, she was neither tall nor short; she was slim and dark, with regular features and liberal eyebrows. She glanced at the electric clock, sat down and began to sort her shopping parcels. Yawle looked straight into her eyes, but she took no notice of him, which, irrationally, inflamed his sense of the loss of Aileen.

The staircase, too, contributed its quota of trouble. Most people used the automatic elevator—that was why he had chosen the staircase. On the first turn, between floors, he all but crashed into an elderly lady from behind: it was such a near thing that she dropped a parcel.

He was himself startled and at a loss. The woman, small but imposing, fiftyish, glared at him with an indignation that had a quality of voraciousness—to his nerve-racked fancy, she looked as if she wanted to pounce upon him, spiderwise, and eat him.

'I'm most awfully sorry, madam! Very careless of me! I hope I didn't frighten you.'

The voracious, spiderlike quality vanished from a face which was ordinary enough and even pleasing. She accepted the parcel with a graceful, old-fashioned bow and the kind of smile that used to go with the bow.

He hurried on to the first floor—up the next flight, to the second.

'I say! Do you know you really *lose* time when you do two stairs at once?'

The thin, piping treble had come from a boy of about ten.

'Do I? Pr'aps you're right. I'll take your advice.'

This was a nightmare journey. The murder, still in part a fantasy, receded. Funny how that girl had reminded him of Aileen! Must have been like her, in a way. But that girl was sure of herself and happy. If only he could tell what had happened to Aileen!

The device of writing to her parents to inquire had not occurred to him. By the time he reached the third floor Aileen's present condition was deplorable and even unmentionable—as a result of the general behaviour of Charles Ennings.

When Ennings opened the door he was wearing a dinner jacket, which somehow made everything worse. He seemed younger than his fifty years, the heavy lips had become masterful, he had pulled himself in, probably with corsets. He looked successful, confident, insolent.

'I want to talk to you, Ennings.'

'By all means!' Ennings was unenthusiastic, if not positively damp. 'Between ourselves, I don't do business at home, but—come in, won't you?'

The hall was but a bulge in the corridor of the flat. Opposite were two doors some ten feet apart. Ennings opened one and Yawle entered the kind of near-luscious sitting-room he had expected, littered with cabinet photographs of the current inamorata—not even attractive, in Yawle's eyes.

The telephone rang, as if to emphasise that Yawle's presence was an intrusion.

'No, it was a washout,' said Ennings into the receiver. 'I got home at the usual time after all, and I'm taking an evening off. Can't talk now. I have a client who's in a hurry.'

Ennings cut off. He pointed to an armchair, but Yawle remained standing. Ennings sat in the other armchair.

'Gronston's,' said Yawle, 'have put my Cleanser in every grocer's, and every oil shop and every hardware store in the country. And it's selling.'

'Of course it's selling! It's a damn fine fluid, old man. Who's saying it isn't!'

'Why do I get such measly royalties? Why is the contract signed by Lanberry's instead of by Gronston's?'

'So that's what's biting you!' Ennings had had this conversation, in one form or another, with a good many inventors. 'Between ourselves, Lanberry's is a holding company, if you know what that means—'

'I know that Lanberry's *holds* one desk in one room in a back street off Holborn. And I know that the Chairman is a clerk employed by you. I've been there.'

'You've been there!' snorted Ennings. 'So it only remains for the bloodsucking financier to burst into tears and disgorge the loot! My good young man, you're poking your nose into things you don't understand—and you're making an infernal fool of yourself.'

The main purpose, of course, was to talk about Aileen. Yawle had given no detailed thought to the matter of the royalties. Ennings and his dinner jacket—successful, confident, insolent— was riding him.

'I shall take it up with Gronston's! There's another thing—'

'Good! I hope you'll be fool enough to do just that. In the meantime you can take yourself and your business to the devil. Your business! Your *invention!* Between ourselves, there are a good few others who've rediscovered that old formula, or copied it out of a back number—'

So, in the end, Aileen's name hadn't even been mentioned.

The skill of the Balkan bandits with their short knives—very like our pocket knives—is based on a knowledge of how to hold the knife. If you hold it properly, as Yawle did, in the palm of the hand, you leave no fingerprints on the haft. Your index finger lies along the back of the blade, slides down it as the blade impacts with an upward sweep: so there's no detectable fingerprint there, either. If your aim is accurate, as Yawle's was, there is neither bother nor noise in the killing.

Ennings remained sitting in his armchair as he had sat in life.

If all the movements were performed correctly, there should be no stains. Yawle studied himself in the mirror. There were no stains. The brainstorm, the moment of hysteria, had passed, leaving him cool, tingling with a sense of achievement and well-being. He felt successful, confident, insolent.

He noted that Ennings's electric clock registered seven twenty-three. He had been in the flat for less than six minutes, all told.

He shut the door of the sitting-room. He was halfway to the front door when he heard footsteps on the landing. He backed away from the front door, found himself opposite the room next to that of the sitting-room. The dining-room. He opened the door.

The footsteps died away. The light from the corridor of the flat had fallen on a white tablecloth. Using his sleeve, he switched on the room light.

The table was laid for two, and the food was on the table. Cold food. Smoked salmon; chicken; trifle in fairy glasses, with a peach on top—canned peach! So Ennings had been expecting a girl! Who might turn up at any minute!

Yawle was in the act of opening the front door, was reaching forward for the latch, when he again heard footsteps approaching. This time he did not panic. He merely stood back, so that his shadow should not fall on the glass panel.

This time the footsteps stopped outside the door. The knocker was lifted and discreetly applied. Yawle kept still. In due course, people go away when there is no response to a knock.

But this caller did not go away. There came the unmistakable sound of a latchkey being inserted.

There was no time to rush back to the dining-room. He slipped into the sitting-room, locked himself in with the dead man, turning the key with his handkerchief.

He did not hear the outer door of the flat being shut. For a moment he was ready to believe that his over-taut nerves had tricked him—that there had been no footsteps and no latchkey.

Some ten seconds later there came a light knock on the door of the sitting-room. Then the handle was turned. Yawle held his breath.

'*Char*-lie! It's *me-e*!'

A full throated, middle-contralto Aileen had a middle contralto voice, too. But that voice was not—could not be—Aileen's voice. If it were Aileen, would she hand him over to the police?

As, by hypothesis, it was not Aileen, there was a danger amounting to certainty that the owner of the voice *would* hand him over to the police.

Seconds passed without any sound to give him a clue as to what was happening.

Then the sound of the front door being shut.

Within a minute or so he had evolved a feasible theory of his predicament. The girl has been given a latchkey, so she's one of Ennings's harem. She thinks he's cut a date with her, so she's gone off in a huff. If she's waiting for him on the landing—but she won't be! She's on latchkey terms and would curl herself up in the flat. Give her a couple of minutes to get clear.

When the two minutes had passed he slipped out of the flat, pausing only to shut the outer door as silently as possible. The main thing was to avoid being seen or heard leaving the flat.

No footsteps. No one on the staircase. By the time he reached the second floor, his confidence returned.

That table spread with a meal for two was nothing less than a first-class alibi, provided the body were not discovered in the next ten minutes or so. No man, he could point out, would be such a fool as to murder another in a flat when he knew that a guest was momentarily expected.

He had merely to pretend that he had seen the table when he entered the flat, and he could add that Ennings had explained that he was expecting a girl friend. He need not even bother to dodge the porter.

When Yawle reached the ground floor, the porter was not there to be dodged or not dodged, being occupied with a tenant who had arrived with luggage at another entrance. Yawle strode on.

In the miniature lounge the girl who resembled Aileen Daines was adjusting her make-up. Unaware of his presence, she snapped her bag, gathered up her shopping parcels and went out of the building.

Might be Ennings's girl friend, he reflected—but without deep interest, for his ego was fully inflated. He had done what he had done—he had turned deadly peril to positive advantage. He would top it off by making use of the porter.

Luckily, he had a pen on him. He began to write a noncommital message for Ennings, but found to his surprise that his hand was shaking. Never mind! His resourcefulness was equal to any emergency.

He found the porter at the third entrance.

'I've just left Mr Ennings and I find that I've absent-mindedly pocketed his fountain pen.' It was a standard model, unidentifiable. He gave it to the porter, with a florin. 'If I were you, I wouldn't return it until the morning. The fact is, porter, he is entertaining—well, let's say a *friend!*'

By bedtime, Yawle's confidence had ebbed. Again and again he reviewed his movements, with increasing alarm. He had got clean away, but could he be dragged back? He ticked off the items.

The first person to see him enter the block had been the girl, but she obviously had not noticed him and could be ignored. Then the old lady who had looked at him like a spider. She might or might not remember him enough to give a description.

Then there was that wretched boy—almost certainly a Boy Scout obsessed with stairs and footsteps, who would love telling the police everything.

With that sterling alibi of the dinner table it would be safe to come forward, unsafe to hang back.

'There's the boy, the middle-aged woman, and the girl—all three saw you entering the building at about seven-ten, Mr Yawle?' Chief Inspector Karslake was making notes as he spoke. 'Can you remember what they looked like?'

'The boy I didn't notice—an ordinary boy of about ten or so. The woman, smallish, about fifty, old-fashioned, but not exactly old, round sort of face. The girl—middle twenties, about my height, dark, good looking, well-marked eyebrows, slim, quietly dressed. But I'm sure she didn't know I was there—if you're thinking of asking these people whether they saw me.'

'It's only for checking up with others,' Karslake assured him. 'Please go on, Mr Yawle.'

'I went to the flat. Ennings opened the door. He was in a dinner jacket and told me he was expecting a friend to dinner. The way he said it, I guessed it was a girl. He showed me the dining-room—I suppose so that I shouldn't think he was stalling me—cold supper set for two. I said I would only keep him a few minutes. As soon as we got into his sitting-room the phone rang. He answered briefly and cut off.'

Yawle waited while Karslake wrote. He had not anticipated that everything he said would be noted.

'And then you both sat down and discussed your business?'

'If we are to be literal, I didn't sit down—wanted to make it clear that I wasn't going to stick around.'

The next bit was tricky. In the night he had worked out that the porter might have noticed when Ennings' guest went upstairs—that must have been while he was in the flat.

'We were about halfway through our business when his girl turned up.

'And he got up to let her in?'

Confound the man with his passion for footling little details! Be careful to tell no unnecessary lies.

'She let herself in with a latchkey. I said I'd just write out a note and then—'

'Half a minute. Don't think I'm niggling, Mr Yawle. The fact is, we use everything an honest witness tells us to check on the people who are not public spirited and may be hiding something. How did you know some one had come in with a latchkey if you were shut up in a room talking business?'

'Ennings had one ear listening for that latchkey.' Yawle managed a realistic snigger. 'He got up, spoke to her, said he would be with her in a few minutes.'

Karslake passed him a chart of Ennings's sitting-room.

'Will you show me on that chart where you were standing when he went to speak to the girl?'

There was only one spot where one could stand to talk to a man sitting as Ennings had sat.

'Oh the hearth rug— here.'

'Could you identify the girl, Mr Yawle?'

'Oh, no—no! Certainly not!'

'But you must have seen her if you were standing there!' It was a statement rather than a question, and Yawle shrank from contradicting.

'Well—yes—but—in these circumstances, Inspector, I simply can't make a statement involving someone else unless I'm sure of what I say.'

'You couldn't put it better, Mr Yawle. All I want you to tell me now is what you saw. To begin with, you saw it was a girl and not a man. Tall or short? Fair or dark?'

'I don't think we need winkle it out that way. I can go as far as this—she was of the same physical type as the girl I noticed in the hall when I was coming in. But I cannot state that she was the same girl.'

It would be better, he had decided, not to add that he had also seen the girl when he was leaving the building.

'From your description of the girl in the hall the thing a man would notice first would be those eyebrows,' persisted Karslake.

'Y-yes. But—'

'Was she in evening dress?'

'No.'

'Same sort of clothes as the girl in the hall, eh?' As Yawle did not deny it, 'Very natural that you won't state it's the same girl, because you aren't quite positive. Very proper attitude, if I may say so. Where did Ennings park the girl in the flat?'

'I don't know. He came back to me. I wanted to make that note. I'd forgotten my pen and he lent me his. I went on talking a minute or so and absent-mindedly pocketed his pen. When I got downstairs—which I suppose was about half-past seven—I looked for the porter and asked him to return the fountain pen—' Yawle repeated the snigger '—in the morning.'

Karslake had the air of an inspector who is not only satisfied but even grateful.

'I think that's about all, Mr Yawle. We shall round up the boy and the woman on the stairs so that you can identify each other. The local police will probably want you for the inquest. Otherwise, I don't suppose we shall trouble you—' he pressed a bell push '—if you'll be good enough to give us your fingerprints before you go.'

A junior entered with a frame and Yawle obliged.

'As far as I know,' he said when the process had been completed, 'I didn't leave any fingerprints in the flat. Don't think I touched anything except that fountain pen.'

'But look at it from our point of view, Mr Yawle.' Karslake was urbane and even confidential. 'Until we've taken your prints we can't prove that it wasn't you who had dinner with Ennings.'

'Dinner with Ennings?' echoed Yawle, genuinely puzzled.

'Well, supper if you like, as it was cold stuff. There were prints other than those of the deceased on the cutlery, the plates, the glasses, some of the dishes—someone who doesn't take salt or pepper but fairly shovels the sugar on a sweet.'

'D'you mean that meal was eaten?' gasped Yawle.

'You bet it was! Look here, I'm not supposed to show this, but you'll see it at the inquest tomorrow.'

Karslake displayed photographs of the dining-room and of the table, of the débris of a meal consumed by two persons. Yawle observed particularly the fairy glasses that had held the trifle. The glasses in the photograph were opaque, with nothing showing above the rims. Before consumption the trifle had topped the rim and the canned peach had topped the trifle.

Yawle left Scotland Yard, dazed to the point of being but barely aware of his surroundings. That dinner had been untouched when he left the flat. As Ennings was dead, he could not possibly have had dinner with the girl. Therefore, somebody else had dinner with the girl—which was absurd.

Alternatively, the flat had been burgled after the girl had gone. The burglars, notwithstanding the presence of a corpse in the flat, had sat down to a meal—which was even more absurd.

Which all proved that the dinner had not been eaten when, in point of fact, it had been eaten.

That it removed all danger from himself was scarcely heeded. That photograph gave him a creeping doubt of his own sanity. He had read of eye-witnesses making wholly false statements in wholly good faith. In some amazing way he must have seen an untouched meal when he was really looking at the débris of a meal.

That meal cropped up again at the inquest. One of the jurymen, unsupported by the others, challenged Yawle's evidence in a question to the Coroner.

'How do we know that this meal was eaten after Mr Yawle had left the flat? It might have been eaten before—I mean, it might have been lunch or anything. I'm not suggesting it was but as it's important evidence I think we ought to have that point cleared up.'

'I think I can help there, sir,' said Yawle. 'When the deceased took me into his dining-room I happened to notice particularly two fairy glasses containing trifle, with a canned peach on the top. If the police can confirm that statement I think it must prove that I saw the meal laid out before it was consumed.'

The police could confirm that statement. The jury returned a verdict of murder against a person unknown, with a rider indicating the young woman who had entered the flat with a latchkey at approximately seven-twenty.

The boy was found some six weeks later. He had spent a couple of nights with an uncle, one of the tenants, who suddenly remember that fact and reported it with profuse apologies. The boy had gone back to board in school at Brighton: the incident had utterly passed from his mind, and he failed to identify Yawle.

The elderly lady with the parcel was another unexpected stumbling block. When appeals through press and radio failed to solicit response, the Yard was ready to believe that she was an invention of Yawle's, prompted by a desire to tie the time of his presence at the flat at both ends. Innocent people often did that kind of thing.

The porter was interviewed again and again. His story remained sufficiently consistent. It was his busy time, dodging from one of the three entrances to another. There had never been any trouble with the police—they weren't that kind of tenant, and he was not given to observing their actions. He had not seen Mr Yawle until he made his request concerning the fountain pen—which was close to seven-thirty.

He had certainly noticed a young woman sitting in the hall-lounge round about ten past seven. That was nothing unusual. He had only noticed her because, as he passed, she was fiddling with her bag and dropped something, but picked it up before he could do it for her. He mentioned her eyebrows and her dress, which was not the expensive kind.

The dragnet went out through the West End, though from the description of the porter and of Yawle, she was not likely to be found in any of the bars or night clubs. The search became intensive, was carried to the theatres, including the dress circles and stalls, with the result that, some six weeks after the inquest, Yawle was asked to accompany a plainclothes man and wait outside a City office about lunch time.

Out of the office came Aileen Daines.

'Hullo, Dennis!' She shook hands with frank friendliness. 'I'm so glad to see you—I was going to write. You see, Leonard and I—yes, at Easter.'

When she had gone, Yawle rejoined the plainclothes man.

'You saw her speak to me. She is not the one we want. I know her very well indeed.'

The porter, at the same time on the next day, was not so positive. By a majority vote, as it were, of his muddled recollections, he decided that he did not think this young lady was that young lady.

'All the same, there's the bare possibility that this young lady *is* that young lady,' said Karslake when he was discussing the report with his staff. 'Used to be Yawle's girl, eh? There might be some tangled sex stuff there. We haven't enough to sail in with a request for her dabs. Now, if one of you boys could manage to watch her eating—when she isn't with her young man—we might get a line.'

None of them did see her eating, but one of them obtained her fingerprints without her knowledge. And that dropped her out of the case—and dropped the case itself into the Department of Dead Ends.

As weeks lengthened into months, Yawle ceased to worry about his sanity in the matter of the dinner which could not possibly have been—but had been—eaten. He still carried the crystal of cyanide in a dummy petrol lighter, but it had become a talisman rather than a menace.

Learning that Ennings's estate had been proved at £60,000 he went to see Gronston's, who gladly gave him details of the royalties paid to Lanberry's. Yawle brought an action against the estate for balance of royalties withheld by a fraudulent device.

The action was heard in the following Spring. Detective Inspector Rason was present, not because he expected to find in the public gallery the girl who had murdered Ennings, but because it was a routine duty to keep contact with the principals in an unsolved crime.

The hearing was very brief, for there was in effect no defence. Yawle obtained judgement for some four thousand pounds and his costs. The judge remarked that the deceased had behaved as an unscrupulous scoundrel and that Hendricks, his shabby little clerk who survived him, would do well to examine his own conscience.

Rason decided to do a little examining of the clerk's conscience himself, for he had the glimmer of an idea. Over a pint of beer and a sandwich Hendricks was willing to talk.

'I knew there was going to be a rumpus when Mr Yawle turned up at my room,' said Hendricks. 'I gave the guv'nor the wire, but he only laughed at me.'

'When did Mr Yawle turn up at your room?' asked Rason.

'I dunno—not the date anyhow. Must've been about a week before the guv'nor copped out.'

That was the sort of thing Rason was hoping for. What business had Yawle transacted with Ennings when he knew that Ennings had been cheating him? No business. He had gone to demand restitution. And had he borrowed Ennings's fountain pen to make a note of it? Rats!

Barking up the wrong tree, muttered Rason. Proving that Yawle quarrelled with Ennings and killed him, when the job is to find the girl and prove she did.

Back in the office he was reluctant to admit that he had wasted his morning. He tried hard to squeeze a bit into the discovery that Yawle had known that Ennings was swindling him. No link-up.

Start with the girl, now! She comes in with a latchkey, has her dinner and then knifes him. Why? She must've expected him to get free. Can't pull the dewy innocent with that latchkey in her bag. Suppose she was an inventor, too? In the sitting-room she finds something, proving that Ennings has been buying her the stockings out of her own money?

The next morning he paddled back to Hendricks.

'Have you got on your books a girl middle twenties, height about five six, thickish eyebrows—'

'I've never seen any of 'em except Mr Yawle. And we got no girls. Only a couple o' widows, legatees of course.'

'Let's have the widows!'

Mrs Siegman lived in Hampstead, was middle-aged and had virtually no eyebrows. Mrs Deaker lived in Surbiton, which was an hour's drive out of London, allowing for traffic. With some difficulty Rason found a small house with a brick wall surrounding the garden on the outskirts of the suburb.

The door was opened by a good-looking girl in the middle twenties, height about five-six, dark, with well-defined eyebrows.

'Are you Mrs Deaker?'

'No. Mrs Deaker is in town. I'm her companion and at the moment her domestic staff too. Do you want to leave a message?'

Rason presented his official card.

'Oh!' said the girl, and Rason decided to spring it on her.

'What were you doing in Barslade Manions, Westminster, the night Charles Ennings was killed?'

'Oh!' said the girl again. 'I'm not going to tell you anything until I have a lawyer.'

'In that case I'm afraid you'll have to come with me to Scotland Yard,' said Rason.

He was with her while she packed a suitcase and left a note for her employer, kept her within arm's reach while he telephoned the Yard. On the journey the only admission she made was that her name was Margaret Halling. On arrival at the Yard she made no objection to having her fingerprints taken.

Some three hours later Dennis Yawle turned up at Scotland Yard in response to a request by telephone. Some five minutes previously Margaret Halling's employer had arrived with a lawyer. All three, with some half a dozen others, were enduring time in a waiting-room.

Detective Inspector Rason thanked Yawle profusely, took him along a corridor behind the waiting-room.

'I want you to look through this little panel, Mr Yawle—they can't see you—and tell me if there's anybody in the room you recognise.'

Yawle looked through the panel. A smile broadened.

'Yes,' he said. 'I shall never forget that face! That is the elderly lady whose parcel I picked up on the stairs.'

'Well, I'm—' Rason was more astonished than he had been for a long time. 'Excuse me, Mr Yawle.' In his agitation he pushed Yawle back to the panel, put his hand on the crown of Yawle's head, and gently twisted until Yawle could be presumed to have a view of the seat in the window.

This time there was no broad smile. Rason had the impression that he saved Yawle from subsiding to the floor.

'That's the girl with the eyebrows—the girl I saw in the hall.'

'And she's the girl you saw when she let herself in with the latchkey?'

'I don't know. I said at the time I couldn't be sure the girls were the same.'

'That's all right, Mr Yawle—we never lead a witness,' said Rason unblushingly. He was now in extremely high spirits, for he had had another glimmer. 'Your statement in my file says they were of similar type. That passes the buck to us.'

They went to Chief Inspector Karslake's room. The chair at the roll-top desk was placed at Rason's disposal, with Karslake on his left, for this was Rason's case, and his own room was too much of a museum for interviews.

'Well, I suppose the first thing to do,' hinted Karslake, when he had heard the news, 'is to have the girl in for a formal identification.'

'No, it isn't, sir,' said Rason, picking up Karslake's house telephone.

'Mrs Deaker, in the waiting-room—ask her if she would like to see me. If so, bring her in.'

'Mr Yawle,' said Rason. 'This old girl has given Mr Karslake a

good deal of trouble, one way and another.' Karslake's surprise
change to profound disapproval, as Rason went on: 'If she hands
us anything you know to be phoney, I'd be grateful if you'd chip in
and flatten her out.'

Yawle assented politely. The 'old woman' presented no
problem. She could do nothing but confirm his statement.

Mrs Deaker chose to brave the detective without the support of
the lawyer, who was earmarked for Margaret Halling.

'I think you have seen this gentleman before, Mrs Deaker?'
Rason indicated Yawle.

'Not to my recollection,' answered Mrs Deaker. 'Perhaps if you
were to tell me his name—?'

'At Barslade Mansions, Westminster, on the evening of January
17th 1933, this gentleman retrieved a parcel you had dropped on
the staircase.

'Did he! Then it was very kind of him, and it is ungracious of me
to forget.'

'We advertised in the press and on the radio, asking you to come
forward, Mrs Deaker,' said Rason severely.

'I remember those advertisements, I didn't realise you meant
me!' She glared at Yawle. 'Did you describe me as an *elderly*
woman? That's what the advertisement said!' Before Yawle could
excuse himself, she went on: 'I suppose I do seem elderly to a man
of your age. However, if we may consider the incident of the parcel
is closed I would like to tell the police about Margaret Halling, my
companion. She was there solely because my taxi brought her
there. I was dining with a friend. Her train home from Waterloo
was not until eight-ten. It was a cold night and I told her to sit in the
lounge by the radiator until it was time to leave.'

'Who was the friend with whom you were dining, Mrs Deaker?'

'The man who was murdered. Mr Ennings. But of course, you
must know all about him, as you're still looking for the murderer.
Now that we have mentioned the subject, you may wish me
to account for my own movements, though they are of no
significance, or I would have reported them.

'Mr Ennings was a friend—a very intimate friend—before I
married, somewhat injudiciously, the man who invented the
Deaker commutator. He handled my husband's affairs. In recent
years, after his death, Mr Ennings and I—Mr Ennings and I
resumed our friendship, which was cemented by the fact that my
husband had made him trustee.

'Mr Ennings telephoned me in the morning that he might be
detained at some special meeting or other. As I was doing a day's
shopping, I was to come—he would have a cold meal prepared—

and I was not to wait dinner for him after seven-thirty.

'As to the parcel incident, I never enter an elevator unless there is a responsible-looking man in charge. I selected the staircase— which took a long time—no doubt because I am *elderly*! I duly waited until seven-thirty, and then I sat down to dinner by myself. I waited in the flat until a little after nine-thirty and then caught the ten-five home.'

Rason had taken from the dossier the photographs of the débris of the meal.

'When did you see Mr Ennings?'

'Obviously, I didn't see him at all.'

'How did you obtain entry to the flat?'

'I lifted the knocker, as there was a light in the hall.' Her words were laboured as she went on: 'I thought I had sufficiently emphasised the fact of our friendship. I have a latchkey. Here it is.' She took it from her bag and gave it to Rason. 'I went to the sitting-room, but the door was locked. I knocked, then called his name. Then I looked about the flat, shut the front door and went into the dining-room to wait for him. Once, I thought I heard the front door being closed, but it was a false alarm, so I sat down and had my dinner.'

Yawle had reached forward and snatched from Rason's desk the photograph of the débris of the meal.

'I don't think so, Mrs Deaker!' cried Yawle. 'Look at this photograph. Two persons ate that dinner!'

They were glaring at each other.

'Half a minute, Mr Yawle!' interposed Rason. 'I thought Mr Karslake had told you everything! Did he forget to tell you that there was *only one set of fingerprints on those dishes*?'

'Then they must be mine!' sighed Mrs Deaker. 'I had hoped to escape this public humiliation. The degrading truth is that I can eat—and I often do—as much as two men! By nine, I concluded that Mr Ennings must have had his dinner. So I—I—I really *did*—'

Rason left Mrs Deaker floundering in a whirlpool of social shame.

'Well, Yawle, let's get back to that young girl you saw in the flat, whom you can't *quite* identify with the young girl you saw in the hall. Eyebrows an' all, too! Or would you rather ask Mrs Deaker some questions about that sitting-room door *that was locked on the inside*? At about twenty past seven, as near as makes no matter to you, Yawle!'

But Yawle possessed a talisman in a dummy petrol lighter that warded off all further assaults on his dignity.

A CASE FOR GOURMETS

Michael Gilbert

The author of the next story has been hailed as 'one of the finest of the post-World War II generation of detective story writers', to quote that doyen, Ellery Queen. Michael Gilbert (1912–   ) is a lawyer by profession and a crime writer by inclination, having discovered the genre while a prisoner of war in Italy and later, more intimately, as legal adviser to Raymond Chandler. Gilbert's most memorable series character is Detective Inspector Patrick Petrella who made his debut in Blood and Judgement *(1959)—acclaimed as one of the best mystery novels of the year—and a number of short stories including 'A Case for Gourmets' which introduces the inspector to the puzzling affair of the Herring Jam . . .*

The curious and involved transaction which is recorded in the annals of Gabriel Street under the title of 'Herring Jam' may be traced to its beginning in the Court of Mr Whitcomb, the South Borough Stipendiary Magistrate.

Detective-Inspector Patrick Petrella, who was there on duty, was reminded of a remark once made to him by Sergeant Drage of the British Railways Police—to the effect that the travelling public were divisible into three classes. One, people who travelled without tickets; two, people who stole goods in transit; and three, people who defaced posters.

In the dock when he arrived, Petrella found an apple-checked old lady accused of travelling from Wimbledon to Charing Cross with a threepenny ticket. Her defence, which she was conducting herself, was that she had asked for a ticket to the Kennington Oval, but the booking clerk had misheard her.

'But surely, madam,' said Mr Whitcomb with the courtesy for which he was renowned, 'it costs more than threepence to travel from Wimbledon to the Oval.'

Certainly, agreed the old lady, but since the booking clerk was clearly stone-deaf, what was more likely was that when *she* had said the Kennington Oval, *he* had thought she said Colliers Wood.

'But did it not occur to you that the fare to the Oval must be more than threepence?'

The old lady rode this one off. She said that she always paid exactly what booking clerks asked for. In her experience, sometimes they asked for more, sometimes less. She never argued with them.

'And why,' said Mr Whitcomb, who believed in leaving no avenue unexplored, 'if you had been given a ticket to Colliers Wood, in mistake for a ticket to the Oval, did you ultimately alight at Charing Cross?'

The old lady said she had mistaken it for Trafalgar Square.

It took some time to get this one sorted out (absolute discharge—coupled with a severe warning) and then Ronald Duckworth was called forward. Mr Duckworth was charged with an act of wilful damage, committed on the premises of the London Passenger Transport Board, in that he, on the previous Tuesday, had attempted to tear down a poster at Borough High Street Underground Station, the property of Barleymow Breakfast Bricks Ltd., the said poster advertising their wares.

Mr Duckworth pleaded guilty, and an LPTB Inspector stated that at about five minutes past eleven on the evening before last, one of the porters at Borough High Street Station, a Mr Sampson, returning to the platform, had observed the accused, who had apparently thought he was alone, seize a loose corner of the advertisement in question and tear it sharply in an upward direction.

'Are you perhaps not fond of Barleymow's Breakfast Bricks?' inquired Mr Whitcomb with every evidence of sympathy.

Mr Duckworth said no. It wasn't that—it was just an impulse.

Mr Whitcomb said that such impulses, though understandable (he much preferred porridge himself) ought to be resisted. He ordered Mr Duckworth to pay the costs of the prosecution and bound him over conditionally on his undertaking to leave all posters, however offensive the products they advertised, alone for the next twelve months.

Mr Duckworth departed thankfully. The next case was Petrella's, and it was not one which he viewed with any enthusiasm at all.

The charge, against Albert Mundy, was one of receiving goods well knowing them to be stolen goods. The facts were simple enough. Mr Mundy, an electrician working in the Wandsborough Power Station, had purchased a television set from a man he had met in the Saloon Bar of a public house.

They had had a few drinks and the man had told Mundy a long story of a mix-up which had resulted in the man being in possession of two television sets. 'It's a brand-new set,' he said. 'I've got it outside in the car now. I'd be glad to get rid of it for half what I paid for it.'

Mr Mundy was not only an electrician. He knew quite a lot about television sets. It was, as he saw when he went out to inspect it, a brand-new one. The maker's and wholesaler's labels were still on it. Even if (as Mr Mundy half suspected) it contained some hidden defect, he was confident that he could put it right, and it was still a staggering bargain. He hurried home, produced the money from a reserve which he kept under a loose floorboard, and clinched the deal. The set proved to be in perfect condition. It also, unfortunately, turned out to have been one of a consignment of twelve stolen in transit between Manchester and Tooley Street Goods Depot—probably at the depot itself.

There was a good deal to be said on both sides: on the side of Mr Mundy, that he was an honest citizen with a hitherto unblemished record, and that he had no positive proof that the set was a stolen one; on the side of the authorities, that Mr Mundy had himself admitted that he thought the deal a fishy one, and that people who buy television sets for half the list price from strangers in public houses must take the consequences of their actions.

There was also a third powerful, but unexpressed, argument— that several million pounds worth of goods was being lost every year by pilfering in transport, a loss which fell on the Transport services, their insurers, and, ultimately, on the public.

It was a very close thing, and the sweat stood in beads on Mr Mundy's forehead before the Magistrate finally decided to give weight to his previously blameless record and dismiss the case.

Petrella thought that substantial justice had been done. Mr Mundy had been given a bad fright. To imprison him would have been bad luck on Mr Mundy's family and would not have hurt the real criminals—those who stole and organised the stealing. For the losses were now so large and so regular that they had a look of organisation about them.

'We do what we can,' said Sergeant Drage. 'We can't watch the men at work. To do that properly you'd need one railway policeman for each worker. Anyway, most of them are honest enough. The few who aren't do a disproportionate amount of damage. It's worst towards Christmas—more stuff about and a lot of casual labour taken on for the holiday season.'

'If you can't watch them, how do you hope to stop them?'

'Keep your eyes and ears open. Make the places as difficult as we can to get in and out, and organise snap searches when they come off duty.'

'I see,' said Petrella. 'The old ring-fence system. You can't stop them taking it, but you can make it difficult for them to get away with it.'

Superintendent Benjamin held monthly conferences at Causeway, which the Detective-Inspectors in charge of stations attended. Petrella, from Gabriel Street, Groves from the Common, and Merriam from Tooley Street. In October, and again in November, the first item on his agenda, displacing even such established favourites as shoplifting and juvenile delinquency, was thefts from the railways.

'The Insurance Companies are starting to kick,' said Benjamin. 'They're bullying the Commissioner, the Commissioner's given a rocket to District, and the tail-end of the stick's landed on me.'

'Isn't it really a job for the Railway Police?' said Merriam.

'Surely,' said Benjamin. 'But once stuff's been stolen, it's our job too. If they can't stop them lifting it, we must stop them disposing of it. At least, that's the idea. We've got three big goods yards plumb in our area—Tooley Street, Red Cross, and Bricklayers Arms. What I suggest is—'

He went on to lay down certain principles for patrolling outside these depots. They were sound enough, in their way, but his subordinates knew as well as Benjamin did that it was like trying to watch an acre of rabbit warren with one man and one dog.

It was in the second week in November that Mr Duckworth reappeared in Mr Whitcomb's Court. The charge this time had rather more serious elements in it.

It appeared that the staff of Southwark Underground Station had been on the point of closing down for the night. The last passenger train had gone through, and the last passenger, as they imagined, had been shepherded out into the street. Happening to come down to the platform for a final look-round, the porter had heard a suspicious noise from inside the closet where cleaning materials and other odds and ends were stored.

Being a man of discretion, he had fetched the stationmaster and the ticket collector before investigating, and the three of them had then returned to the platform. The closet door was open, and the accused, who must have been hiding in the cubicle, was engaged in tearing down a number of posters affixed only that morning to the wall of the station.

Mr Duckworth, who looked even more embarrassed than on the previous occasion, again pleaded guilty and said that he had again acted on impulse.

'As I said on the previous occasion,' observed Mr Whitcomb, 'it is understandable that a man might have a sudden, and perhaps overmastering, impulse to tear down a poster. But to secrete yourself in a cupboard, after the station had been closed for the night, and then come out and start systematically to pull down posters hardly seems to me to be conduct which could be properly described as impulsive.'

Mr Duckworth looked unhappy, and said that he was very sorry. Mr Whitcomb, a copy of the record of the earlier case in front of him, pondered for a few minutes, and then announced that he was far from happy about the matter. He wished further inquiries to be made (the Court Missioner sighed audibly) and he would put back Mr Duckworth's case for one week. He understood that the accused was a respectable family man. He could have bail on his own recognisances, for seven days.

Petrella, who was in Court in connection with another matter, caught the Missioner at the door and said, 'When you've finished with him, let me have a go at him.'

'Have him first if you like,' said the Missioner. 'He's daft as a coot. His mother was probably frightened by a railway poster when she was a girl.'

'I'm not sure,' said Petrella. He had, by now, a fairly extensive knowledge of the cranks, crackpots, and fanatics who took up so much police time and afforded such entertaining copy for the court reporters of the leading evening newspapers; but he was far from convinced that Mr Duckworth was a crank or crackpot.

So he took Duckworth out and bought him a cup of tea, and listened with infinite patience to the story of his life. Mr Duckworth was an interior decorator, and an amateur soldier of the late War, during which he had served with credit in an Artillery Regiment, rising to the rank of Sergeant. He had a wife and three children (whose photographs Petrella inspected). He was a supporter of Charlton Athletic, and a keen darts player. And, he added, there was nothing at all wrong with his eyes.

Petrella felt that they might now be approaching the heart of the mystery. He ordered second cups of tea for both of them.

'Nothing wrong with my eyes at all,' repeated Mr Duckworth.

'Who suggested there was?' said Petrella.

'No one actually suggested it,' said Mr Duckworth crossly. 'It was just that—look here, if I tell you this story from the beginning, will you promise not to laugh at me?'

'I never laugh on duty,' said Petrella.

'No, I mean that. It's—it's quite mad. It's—it's sort of fourth dimensional. You know what I mean?'

'Science fiction?' suggested Petrella helpfully.

'That's right—that's just what I mean! You walk out of one life into another. That's why I'd rather people thought I was a crook than they thought I was cracked, if you follow me.'

'Lots of people think like that,' said Petrella. 'Just you tell me about it.'

It was, in its elements, quite a simple story. Mr Duckworth had been attending a reunion at the Regimental Headquarters in North London, a function he attended annually and which was, as he put it, 'the one time in the year he really let his hair down.'

Being an old soldier, before plunging into the fray, he had carefully secured his line of retreat. The nearest station to the headquarters in question was Highgate Archway, on the Northern Line. His home station was Colliers Wood, on the same line. The last train left Highgate at ten minutes before midnight.

With these essential facts firmly engraved in his memory, Mr Duckworth had settled down to enjoy himself in congenial company, had drunk quite a few pints of beer and a couple (but, he thought, not more than a couple) of whiskies, and had caught his train at Highgate with two minutes to spare. As soon as the train started, he had gone to sleep.

An indeterminate number of minutes later he had wakened with a start and with the strong conviction that he had reached his own station and was about to be carried past it. The train, sure enough, was stationary, and the doors were open. There was not a moment to lose. Fortunately, he was sitting in a seat near to, and facing, the doors, and just as they closed he hurled himself between them.

The doors shut behind him, the train jerked into motion, and disappeared. A solitary porter, in the far distance, also disappeared, leaving Mr Duckworth still dazed from the combined effects of sleep and drink, alone on the platform.

His overmastering desire was to sit down somewhere for a few minutes and recuperate. Behind him, at the far end of the platform, was a recess which had possibly once contained a seat. It seemed to Mr Duckworth to be exactly what he wanted. He got his back comfortably against one end, his feet against the other, and settled down to a period of reflection.

When he opened his eyes he was in darkness—a sort of dim-blue darkness, broken by one very bright light.

His head, he said, was comparatively clear. He had discovered earlier that no matter how much beer he drank, give him half an hour's sleep, and he'd be more or less all right.

Petrella interupted to say, 'How long do you think you had been asleep?'

Difficult to say, said Mr Duckworth, but not, he thought, more than half an hour. He had then staggered to his feet and had seen that the bright light was a small floodlight at platform level. It was so placed that it lit up the platform side of the station which (he was clear-headed enough to note) was not one of the modern type, all gleaming tiles and cement, but quite an old-fashioned one with upright wooden billboards.

The light, as he observed when he reached it, was shining directly onto one of these billboards—almost as if it had been placed there purposely to illuminate it. The effect was emphasised by the fact that the billboards on both sides were blank.

'I take it,' said Petrella, 'you'd realised by this time you weren't at Colliers Wood?'

'Oh, yes. I realised I'd jumped off the train too soon and should have a long walk home. I wasn't worried about being locked up in the station. If there were lights on, there must be people still working. The next bit is something I can't remember very clearly at all. I thought I heard a noise behind me, a sort of scraping noise—and then the ceiling fell on me. Or that's what it felt like. Something hard and heavy landed on top of my head, and before I had time to feel anything else, I was falling forward and—well, the next thing I knew, I was opening my eyes. It was five o'clock of a perishing grey morning, and I was on a seat, just off the road, in the middle of South Borough Common.'

He waited, defiantly, for comment.

Petrella said, 'You might have dreamed it all, of course. Someone might have given you a lift back from the reunion and tried to find out where you lived. You were too pickled to give him your address, so he propped you up on the seat to cool off. Not very friendly, but it could have happened.'

'All right,' said Mr Duckworth. 'Then how do you account for the fact that I'd still got my ticket with me? I found it in my waistcoat pocket.'

'Then,' agreed Petrella, 'it might have happened just as you said. You butted in on something you weren't meant to see, got slugged and dumped.'

'I thought that out for myself,' said Mr Duckworth. 'Only not quite as quickly, because I had a nasty lump on the back of my head —that wasn't imaginary. It was sore as hell—and the father and mother of a hangover—and I had my wife to deal with. She'd got into a real state and gone to the police, and then when I turned up—'

'I can imagine that bit,' said Petrella.

'Yes, well, I thought about it, and I had the same idea as you. I thought I'd start by finding what station it really was.'

'That shouldn't have been too difficult,' said Petrella. 'Most of the stations on that bit of line have been modernised, and besides, you saw at least one of the advertisements—the one the light was shining on.'

'That's just it,' said Mr Duckworth.

'*Didn't* you see it?'

'Yes, I did. And I wish I hadn't. It's been getting me down. Here's where you've promised not to laugh. What I saw—and I saw it quite clearly—and if I shut my eyes I can see it now—what I saw was three lines of writing, with one word on each line. It said GET HERRING JAM.'

Petrella stared at him.

'Now be honest,' said Mr Duckworth. 'Isn't that where you start thinking I've got a screw loose? If you do, you're not the only one. I began to think it myself.'

Petrella said, 'You say you can visualise it? What sort of print was it, and how were the three lines arranged?'

'Ordinary capital letters. On the large side, but not enormous. The GET was on the top and a bit to the left. The middle was HERRING—that ran right across. The JAM was the bottom line and a bit to the right.'

'I see,' said Petrella. 'I suppose there isn't some other advertisement rather like—'

'I've been up and down every perishing station between Waterloo and Balham twenty times and there's nothing like it at all—nothing remotely like it! Most of 'em are pictures of girls. There's some in writing, like notices telling you to buy Premium Bonds and drink somebody or other's stout.'

'But no herrings?'

'Not a fish among 'em. That's how I got the idea that it might have been an advertisement that had been covered up with another one. They change 'em about once a week. So—'

Light dawned on Petrella.

'So you started pulling off the new ones to see what the old ones said underneath.'

'It'd sort of got me by that time,' said Mr Duckworth. 'I can't explain it. But what I felt was, if I can find that advert, then perhaps I can find out what happened to me that night. If I can't—well, maybe I'm mad. I expect you think I'm mad anyway.'

'No,' said Petrella slowly. 'I don't think you're mad at all.'

He said the same thing to Mr Wetherall that evening. Mr Wetherall was headmaster of the South Borough Secondary School, and when Petrella had fallen out with two landladies in succession (in both cases over the peculiar house kept and his excessive use of the telephone) Wetherall had suggested to Petrella that he set up house in the two empty rooms below his own in the big house in Brinkman Road. It was a bit far from Gabriel Street, but otherwise it suited Petrella perfectly. It had been great fun furnishing the rooms, and he enjoyed an occasional after-dinner gossip with Mr Wetherall.

'I don't think I'd have started trespassing and pulling down advertisements,' said Mr Wetherall. 'I'd have gone to one of the big agents who does advertising on the Underground, and asked him to find out what advertisements were showing that week.'

'You might have,' said Petrella, 'and so might I, and the agent might have told us. But not someone like Mr Duckworth.'

'Have you located the station?'

'I've had a shot at it. The trouble is that going from Highgate to Colliers Wood, Mr Duckworth could have gone one of two ways— via Charing Cross—that's the West End route—or via Bank. All the stations on the West End route are modern tile and chromium jobs. But one or two of the stations on the Bank route would fit. London Bridge, Southwark, and Borough High Street are all possibles.'

'Since you've done some work on it, I take it you don't think he made the whole thing up?'

'No, I don't,' said Petrella. 'But I couldn't explain why.'

Mr Wetherall puffed his horrible pipe for a few seconds and then said, 'No, you can't, can you? I mean, you can't tell how you know when people are telling the truth, but it's a fact that you can. I've found that often with boys.' He reflected again and said, 'I think you'd better have a word with my friend, Raynor-Hasset. He'll tell you all you want to know about the London railway system. He used to be a schoolmaster, but he's retired now. He lives in one of those little houses up on the Heath. I'll give him a ring and let him know you're coming.'

Petrella knew that Mr Wetherall seldom made recommendations idly. So the following evening he called on Mr Raynor-Hasset. Mr Wetherall's friend had a corvine face and a slight stoop, as if much of his life had been spent in exploring places with low roofs.

'I don't imagine,' he said, when they had settled down in front of the fire, 'that you have ever heard of the Spurs?'

'The Spurs?'

'Not the football team,' said Mr Raynor-Hasset with a thin smile. 'The Society for the Preservation of Unused Railway lines. I have the honour to be their Secretary.'

'I'm afraid not,' said Petrella. 'What do you do?'

'Just as speleologists explore the recesses and convolutions of our caves, we delight in tracking down the railway lines which run under this great city. It is a curious fact but once a railway line has been constructed, it may be covered over—*but it is hardly ever filled in again.'*

'I suppose not.'

'Most people imagine, when they think about it, that our main railway lines stop well short of the centre of London. The Northern ones at Euston, Kings Cross, and St Pancras. The Southern ones at Waterloo and Victoria. It is far from true, of course. I could name you half a dozen ways of crossing London from North to South by steam train. I conducted a special trip along the Blackfriars, Holborn, Kentish Town line myself last year. And did you know that there was an old but still usable railway line, part of the original Charing Cross Bayswater switch, which runs within a hundred yards of the Eros statue in Piccadilly? The entrance to it is through a shop—'

Petrella listened, entranced, as Mr Raynor-Hasset described and expounded to him that curious system of disused passages and tunnels, of unsuspected tracks, of forgotten stairways and phantom stations (akin to the traces in the human system of some dread but dead disease) which the private enterprise of our railway pioneers had left under the unsuspecting surface of London.

During an interval, while his host brewed cocoa for them, Petrella explained the idea which had come into his head.

Mr Raynor-Hasset cleared the table and spread on it a map of large scale. 'It's a very feasible idea,' he said. 'I think that the Tooley Street Goods Yard would be the one to start with. You have had losses from there—serious losses. Quite so. You'll note that although it is now linked to London Bridge by part of the ordinary Southern system, its previous history is far from simple. It began life as a private depot for goods coming up the river to St Saviour's Dock—a horse-drawn tramway connected it to Dockhead; or you could get at it under the River by the old subway—it's disused now—that came out at Stanton's Wharf. Plenty of possibilities there. As for the underground stations—' Mr Raynor-Hasset shook his head. 'If people had any idea what lay behind those shiny, well-lit platforms, they'd be pretty surprised.'

He consulted his chart again. 'If I had to make a guess I'd say that the connection lies between Tooley Street and Southwark. And I'll tell you why. Southwark Underground must be within a very short distance of the connecting line which the old Brighton and South Coast—who shared London Bridge with the South Easter and Chatham—ran across to Waterloo. It was never a great success, as passengers found it just as easy to go straight through from London Bridge, and it was closed to traffic in the eighties. You can see it marked here.'

Petrella followed the spidery lines on the map and found his excitement kindling.

'I really believe,' he said, 'that you must be right.'

'There's no need to rely on guesswork. Why don't we go and see?'

Petrella looked at him.

'With your authority,' said Mr Raynor-Hasset, 'and my experience, I should anticipate no difficulty. I take it you can square it with the authorities.'

'Yes, certainly.'

'Then I suggest tomorrow night. We will meet at—shall we say, eleven o'clock at Bermondsey South? The old Station, on the North side of the Rotherhithe Road. Dress in your oldest clothes.'

At a few minutes after eleven the following night Petrella was following Mr Raynor-Hasset down a flight of wooden steps. At the bottom of the steps a man was waiting for them.

'I've opened her up,' he said. 'Had to use a pint of oil. Must be five years since anyone went through there.'

'Almost exactly five years,' said Mr Raynor-Hasset. 'I took a party along there myself. Thank you very much, Sam.' Some coins changed hands. 'You lock up behind. We'll probably be coming out at Waterloo.'

'I'll give 'em a ring,' said Sam. The door opened into what looked at first sight, like a brick wall, but which was in fact the bricked-up entrance to a railway tunnel. It shut behind them with a solid thud, cutting off light, air, and sound.

'I should have asked you before we started,' said Mr Raynor-Hasset, 'whether you suffered at all from claustrophobia.'

'I don't think so,' said Petrella. 'I've never really found out.'

'One man I took with me was so severely overcome that he fell flat on his face and when I endeavoured to assist him he bit me—in the left leg. Straight ahead now.'

It was quite easy going. The rails were gone, and the old permanent way had become covered, in the course of time, by a thin deposit of dried earth mixed with soot from the tunnel roof. The only discomfort was the dust they kicked up as they walked.

'Ventilation is sometimes a problem,' said Mr Raynor-Hasset. 'It was originally quite adequate, but one or two of the shafts have become blocked with the passage of time. In a really old tunnel I have used a safety lamp, but we should be all right here.' He paused to consult the map, and a pedometer which was pinned to the front of his coat. 'There's an air shaft somewhere here. Yes—you can catch a glimpse of the sky.'

Petrella looked up a narrow opening and was pleased to see the stars winking back at him. The light of the torch shone on something white. It was a tiny heap of bones.

'A dog, I should imagine,' said Mr Raynor-Hasset. 'On we go. We've much ground to cover.'

They went on in silence. Petrella soon lost count of time and distance. His guide used his torch sparingly, and as they paced forward into the blackness, Petrella began to feel the oppression of the entombed, a consciousness of the weight of earth above him. The air grew thicker, and was there—or was it his imagination—greater difficulty in breathing?

'We must,' he said, his voice coming out in a startling croak, 'we must be nearly the other side of London by now.'

Mr Raynor-Hasset halted, clicked on his torch, and said, 'One mile and nearly one furlong. By my calculations we are just passing under Bricklayers Arms Depot. We go past the North East corner, and then we should swing through nearly a quarter turn to the right . . . Yes, here we are. Better keep an eye for possible entrances on our left.'

He kept his torch alight for two hundred yards, but the brick walls remained unbroken. Ahead of them pink beads winked and flushed in the light, retreating before them.

'Rats,' said Mr Raynor-Hasset. 'But a timid bunch. I carry a few Guy Fawkes squibs to throw at them, but I've never had to use them.'

They walked on in silence.

Petrella, who was gradually becoming acclimatised, calculated that they had gone forward another mile when Mr Raynor-Hasset spoke again.

'Can you feel,' he said, 'a slight dampness?'

'It's less dusty, certainly.'

'There's a water seepage here. Nothing serious—some defect in drainage. We must be almost under the old Leathermarket.'

Petrella tried to visualise the geography of the part of London.

'In that case,' he said, 'we shouldn't be far from Tooley Street.'

'About two hundred yards.'

The torch came on again. Ahead of them the surface shone, black and slimy. The smell was unspeakable. Even Mr Raynor-Hasset noticed it.

'Quite fresh, isn't it?' he said. 'We'll keep the torch on now for a bit.'

When they came to it, the side entrance was easy to see. It sloped upward, gently, to the right. Mr Raynor-Hasset took a compass bearing and marked his map.

'I should think there's no doubt at all,' he said. 'That's an old loading track and it goes straight to Tooley Street Depot. You'll probably find it comes out in a loading pit. Do you wish to follow it?'

But Petrella's eyes were on the ground. 'Could you point your torch here a moment,' he said. 'Look. That's not five years old.'

It was a cigarette carton.

'No, indeed,' said Mr Raynor-Hasset. 'And those, I think, are footprints. How very interesting!'

Clearly to be seen in the mud was a beaten track of men's boot prints that led from the mouth of the shaft and onward up the tunnel.

'Keep your torch on them,' said Petrella. 'This is going to save me a lot of trouble.'

'It looks as if an army has passed this way.'

An army of soldier-ants, thought Petrella. An army bearing burdens.

Four hundred yards, and the line of footprints turned into a track branching down to the left. Mr Raynor-Hasset again checked his position, and said, 'Southwark Underground Station, or I'm a Dutchman.'

They went sharply down for a short distance, then the track levelled out, ran along, and climbed again, finally emerging into a circular antechamber. Above their heads an iron staircase spiralled upward into the gloom.

'Southwark,' said Mr Raynor-Hasset, 'was one of those stations which was developed forward. I mean that when they redesigned it, they put in a moving staircase at the far end, with the lifts, and closed the old emergency stair shaft altogether. That is what we have come out into.'

But Petrella was not listening to him. The light of the torch had revealed, strewn around the foot of the staircase, an astonishing jumble of cartons, crates, boxes, sacks, and containers of every shape and size.

'This is where they unpack the stuff,' he said. 'I wonder where they store it. Can we get out onto the platform?'

'Certainly. I think this must be the way.'

There was a door in the boarding ahead of them, secured by three stout bolts.

'What time is it?'

'Just after two o'clock.'

'Should be all right,' said Petrella.

He slid the bolts and swung the door open. They stepped through and found themselves on the platform of Southwark Underground Station, lit only by the ghostly blue lamps which shine all night to guide the maintenance trolleys.

'What are we looking for?' said Mr Raynor-Hasset.

'There must, I think, be more storage space. Have you a knife? It would be about here, I'd guess. Hold the torch steady a moment.'

Petrella slid the blade between the boards, choosing the place with precision. He felt a latch lifting and levered strongly with the knife blade. A section of boarding hinged out towards them.

'Good gracious,' said Mr Raynor-Hasset mildly.

The deep recess contained, stacked on shelves and floor, an astonishing assortment of goods. There were piled cartons of cigarettes, wooden boxes with the stamp of a well-known whisky firm, portable typewriters, wireless and television sets, bales of textiles, a pair of sporting rifles, boxes of shoes, cases of tinned food.

'A producer-to-consumer service,' said Petrella grimly.

His mind was already busy constructing exactly the sort of police trap that would be necessary: two cars in the street above, to catch the people when they came to collect; men in the tunnel itself, beyond the opening, to seal the far end; and a very cautious reconnaissance to find out how the Tooley Street end worked.

He was standing on the platform, thinking about all this, when suddenly he started to laugh. Mr Raynor-Hasset edged perceptibly away.

'It's quite all right,' said Petrella. 'I'm not going to start biting you in the leg. Hold the torch on that wall. Now watch, while I open and shut those two doors.'

Mr Raynor-Hasset did so, and then himself gave a dry cackle. 'Very ingenious,' he said.

Two advertisements stood next to each other on the billboard. They were very close, with only a thin margin between them.

When the doors were shut, the two advertisements read:

THIS YEAR'S TARGET
BUY YOURSELF ANOTHER   RING PARK 0906
PREMIUM BOND   JAMES BOND & SONS
                        Everything for your car

When both doors were opened, most of the left-hand advertisement and most of the right-hand advertisement were neatly cut away; and when the cut-away parts vanished into the darkness of the opened doors, all that remained of the adjoining advertisements was:

GET
HER RING
JAM

'I couldn't help thinking,' said Petrella, 'that we have, at least, set Mr Duckworth's mind at rest.'

RUM FOR DINNER

Lawrence G. Blochman

The next tale, 'Rum for Dinner', features the unlikely trio of tenacious sleuths, Dr Dan Coffee, Dr Motilal Mookerji and Lieutenant Max Ritter, who have combined their talents in a number of crime novels and short stories in which food and beverages have frequently played a major part. Dr Coffee is a physician, Dr Mookerji a rotund Hindu pathologist, while Lieutenant Ritter works for the Northbank Police Force. The stories were written by Lawrence G. Blochman (1900–1975), who received a certificate in forensic pathology and then worked in several branches of the US government before turning to writing crime fiction and scripts for radio and television. The story demonstrates the power of team-work in criminal investigation—in a case where a man has died most mysteriously after dinner . . .

The interne on emergency duty looked at the man in the back seat of the car and shook his head.

'Sorry, madam,' he said. 'There's nothing I can do.'

'But you must!' The woman at the wheel made an imperious gesture that glittered expensively. 'He's quite ill.'

'He's dead,' said the interne.

'That's impossible,' the woman said. 'He was dining with me tonight and he took ill about an hour ago. You must admit him.'

The interne hooked his stethoscope into his ears and leaned over the man in the dinner jacket. He unfastened the pearl studs and slipped the microphone inside the man's pleated silk shirt.

'Dead, all right,' the interne said. 'Sorry, but we can't accept dead-on-arrival cases.'

The woman got out of the car. Her evening cape of midnight-blue velvet had slipped down, revealing one alabaster shoulder and an important constellation of first-magnitude jewels which twinkled astronomically at the low horizon of her dinner gown. There was a cold, classic beauty—an abstract, inhuman beauty—

in the pale symmetry of her finely-chiselled features. There was a majesty in her bearing of which she was aware but not self-conscious.

'You must take care of Mr Otto,' she said. 'Perhaps you do not know who I am. I am Madeline Starkey—Mrs Herbert Starkey.'

The interne glanced at the impressive display of precious stones flashing blue-white fire for his benefit, but he was not impressed. At least he was not impressed in the manner intended by Mrs Starkey. The interne, who had worked his way through medical school, had just been wondering if the girl he loved would wait another three years until he could support a wife. So he merely stepped to the telephone at the entrance and called the Northbank police.

'This is Pasteur Hospital,' said the interne. 'A lady just drove up with a dead man in her car. Yes, DOA. I can't make her understand this is a hospital not a morgue. Better send the wagon.'

Mrs Starkey felt suddenly faint—although she seemed considerably stronger than the two red-faced gentlemen in dinner clothes who got out of the car behind hers to support her.

'I'll drive you home, darling,' said the red-faced man with the paunch and the greying hair.

'You and Sydney stay here with poor Mr Otto,' said Mrs Starkey. 'I'll drive your car home.'

As Mrs Starkey backed noisily out of the hospital driveway, the man called Sydney climbed unsteadily into the car with the late Mr Otto and promptly fell asleep.

The red-faced gentleman with the paunch approached the interne and said in thick, alcoholic syllables: 'I'm Herbert Starkey. So don't spare any expense in—'

'The police will be here shortly,' said the interne.

Dr Daniel Webster Coffee walked thoughtfully next morning as he returned to his laboratory from Operating Room B. He had just listened to a long and voluble complaint by a surgeon about his new resident pathologist. There had been other complaints about the new man, Dr Motilal Mookerji, on scholarship from Calcutta Medical College—most of them based on the fact that Dr Mookerji was a Hindu. Dr Coffee was confident that the new resident would work out all right, although he had to admit that the shakedown period was a little difficult. The Hindu was not only learning laboratory medicine and American hospital routine, but also the American language.

Dr Mookerji spoke an English of sorts—a high-flown, ornate,

peculiar idiom he himself called 'Babu English', pronounced with what he apologised for as a chi-chi accent, and blended with the Americanisms he was rapidly acquiring. Dr Mookerji was well on his way to becoming the linguistic wonder of the century. He was already the popular wonder of Pasteur Hospital, and, to a lesser extent, of all Northbank. Any Hindu would be a novelty in the brick-paved streets of the mid-western city of Northbank, and a Hindu who was almost perfectly spherical in shape was a positive sensation. Dr Mookerji was not only spheroidal; he was a diminutive spheroid; the summit of the huge pink turban which he wore with his occidental clothes came only to the shoulders of tall, sandy-haired Dr Coffee.

Dr Mookerji was probably in his late twenties, although he could have been forty. The baby-like rotundity of his ageless, olive-tinted face was given romantic maturity by the dark circles under his clear brown eyes. His long, straight nose was incongruously thin. His long, dark eyelashes were the envy of every nurse at Pasteur Hospital. The nurses, in fact, had been popping into the pathology laboratory with unusual frequency and at the slightest excuse since the Hindu's arrival, no doubt on the chance that they would find him performing the Indian Rope Trick, casting oriental spells, or telling fortunes from the smoke of sandalwood incense.

Despite his queer personal topography, his castigation of the President's English, and his general exoticism, however, the Hindu was going to make a first-rate pathologist. Dr Coffee was convinced that he knew his bacteriology and histology, that he had a quick, diagnostic eye, the same fine scientific curiosity and the same dogged patience that characterised such Hindu minds as C. V. Raman, Jagadis Chandra Bose, and P. C. Roy.

'Welcome, Doctor Sahib, five times welcome,' said Dr Mookerji, as Dr Coffee entered the laboratory. 'Was hoping for early arrival because am somewhat nonplussed by parcel just now delivered to laboratory by small-size messenger boy.'

'What parcel, Doctor?' Dan Coffee asked.

'Having taken slight liberty of unpackaging said package,' said Dr Mookerji, 'am able to report contents as consisting of semi-private anatomical specimens as follows, to wit. Item: One stomach. Item: One liberal portion of gentleman's liver. Item: One complete cerebrum with cerebellum attached: One glass jar enclosing assorted personal organs, all somewhat fragmentary. However, regret to state, Doctor, that could discover no card enclosed. Was unable to unearth further clues to identity of owner of said detached anatomy.'

'That must be the police case that Lieutenant Ritter phoned me about last night,' said Dr Coffee. 'They want us to make an analysis for suspected poisoning.'

'Police?' exclaimed Dr Mookerji. 'Do not American police officials analyse own poisons?'

'Not in Northbank. The Northbank police have a beautiful and expensive new jail and a fleet of fast automobiles equipped with two-way radio. But not a single microscope or test tube.'

'Quite similar to natal village in Bengal,' said the Hindu, 'where scientific criminology is practised exclusively with lengthy stick applied to wrong-doers. What poisons are under suspicion?'

'I'm not sure,' said Dr Coffee. 'The man died after dinner, and the symptoms seemed to be gastric, so you'd better set up a Reinsch test. If you get presumptive reactions for either arsenic or mercury, we can go ahead with more specific tests.' Dr Coffee glanced at his watch. 'I may have more details for you after lunch. I'm meeting Lieutenant Ritter in half an hour. Meanwhile, label those jars "Clifford Otto" and start work on them.'

'Will initiate analytical procedures instantly,' said Dr Mookerji.

Dr Coffee was meeting Lieutenant of Detectives Max Ritter at Raoul's. Dr Coffee liked to eat at Raoul's. He liked to eat anywhere, although the meagre upholstery of his big, bony, gangling frame gave no indication of his epicurean tendencies. He could, in fact, go for days without thought of food once he was shut up in his laboratory with his microscope and a problem in pathology, consuming the sandwiches and coffee his technician brought him without him even being aware that he was eating. But when he got his knees under a well-stocked table, he knew very well that he was eating—and what.

Raoul's was a pint-sized restaurant on the wrong side of the tracks in Northbank's grimy industrial section. It was one flight up and there was sawdust on the floor. The chequered red tablecloths had only a nodding acquaintance with the laundry. The little place stank beautifully of garlic and browning onions and spicy things stewing in wine. The cooks from the Barzac Cannery in the next block came there regularly to eat plebeian dishes off thick, chipped crockery—veal kidneys in red wine, corned pork with lentils, rabbit stew, tripe. Raoul, the red-faced Norman who ran the place, was particularly proud of his tripe, which simmered all day in earthenware pots filled with white wine and carrots and big onions studied with cloves. He sealed the lid on the pot with pastry dough to keep in the savoury steam, and he had small gas plates on the three tables in the back room, behind the kitchen, especially reserved for tripe eaters; Raoul did not consider tripe fit for a civilised palate unless it was kept piping hot while it was eaten.

Dr Coffee liked to eat tripe at Raoul's because it was a relief from the wholesome, dietician-planned meals of the Pasteur Hospital dining hall, with its sanitary whiteness and shop-talking internes, its counted calories and its pitchers of milk on the spotless tables. He had not lunched at Raoul's since the first difficult days of breaking in his new Hindu resident, but Max Ritter had been insistent; so Dan Coffee had stolen an hour from the hospital to drive across town.

Lieutenant Ritter had already demolished eight inches of the long French bread on the table when Dr Coffee arrived. He wasted no time on preliminaries.

'It's about that DOA case last night,' Ritter said. 'The guy that drives up dead with Mrs Madeline Starkey in her Plushmobile Twelve. Clifford Otto, she says his name was. What are you going to eat, Doc? Tripe? Or maybe some of that beef in Burgundy?'

'Tripe,' said Dr Coffee. 'When you phoned last night, you said you thought you knew the bird. Who was he?'

'Tripe, Raoul,' said Max Ritter. 'Doc, I never saw the guy before last night, but when I came up to the hospital after the emergency ward phoned, I knew there was something about his mug that looked familiar. So I had him printed and then went back to my shop to look at pictures until two in the morning. I looked at old circulars—post-office wanteds, FBI, out-of-town police, private agencies. But before I could find out where I'd seen that mug, the old eyelids started dropping on me. So I wired Otto's fingerprint classification to Washington and went to bed. This morning I got this answer.'

The detective handed Dr Coffee a telegram which read:

YOUR QUERY RE FOLLOWING HENRY CLASSIFICATION RECEIVED

32 L 1 U 101 7
     L 1 U 101 13

ABOVE CLASSIFICATION FILED FOR OTTO CLIFTON, ALIAS CLIFTON FORD, ALIAS CLIFF OTFORD, ARRESTED NEW YORK 1937, CHARGE JEWEL ROBBERY, DISMISSED AT REQUEST COMPLAINING WITNESS MRS ANDREW VAN CARSEN, WIDOW DUTCH OIL MAGNATE, ARRESTED MIAMI 1938 SIMILAR CHARGE, ALSO DISMISSED. SERVED ONE YEAR JAMAICA, B.W.I., POSSESSING STOLEN GOODS. CURRENTLY WANTED HAVANA POLICE SUSPICION STEALING DIAMOND NECKLACE FROM COUNTESS ZLATA OF YUGOSLAVIA

'So it was a Havana circular where I saw this Otto's pretty puss,' Lieutenant Ritter said. 'I dug the Havana circular out of the files. It says the rocks which this Countess Zlata smuggled out of

Yugoslavia, before Tito declared her an enemy of the people's republic, were worth $200,000. It also says that Otto has been coaxing little baubles out of lonely middle-aged ladies in the West Indies for quite a while now.'

'How does a guy like that get to Northbank?' Dr Coffee interrupted.

'I'm coming to that,' Max Ritter said. 'Seems he used to know Mrs Starkey down in Jamaica. She was living in Jamaica when she met Starkey—you know, when he took one of those Caribbean cruises just before the war. She told me last night, before I knew this guy Otto's story, that he was an old Chicago boy who was tired of living abroad. So, on his way home, he stopped off here to say hello to an old friend and he fell in love with our green little, clean little city and he decided to settle here if he could find a suitable business opportunity. He's been living at River House the last two weeks at twenty bucks a day—a suite, naturally—and last night Mrs Starkey gave a little dinner party so Otto could meet some of Northbank's best people and maybe make a few business connections. Only Otto got sick from the dinner and died on the way to the hospital. Do you know a Dr Perry, Doc?'

'George Perry? Sure. A first-rate man.'

'He honest?'

'And a yard wide. They don't come any finer than George Perry.'

'The reason I asked,' Ritter said, 'is that this Otto went to see Doc Perry about a week ago. Bum stomach. So the Coroner says Otto died of acute gastritis. Maybe the old man's right. After all, why shouldn't a gigolo and a gem snatcher die from bellyache just like anybody else? Only I ain't quite sure. There's something funny about this dinner last night.'

'How funny?' Dr Coffee asked.

'Well, the people that were there,' the detective replied. 'Some of the biggest collectors of emerald bracelets in Northbank. So when a crooked diamond fancier sits down to dinner with about a million dollars' worth of shiny gewgaws and then drops dead . . . Well, I got a right to be kind of suspicious, don't I, Doc?'

'Who was there, Max?'

The detective reached into his pocket for a dog-eared envelope and consulted the back. 'First the host and hostess, Mr and Mrs Herbert Starkey,' he read. 'Then, Mr and Mrs Peter Brooks, Mr and Mrs Wally Drew, and Mr and Mrs Sydney Kelling. See what I mean, Doc? Small and cosy, but very high class.'

The chef-proprietor interrupted the conversation by placing a steaming earthenware pot on the gas plate.

'Don't touch the marmite,' Raoul said. 'Very hot.' He carefully wiped his ruddy face with his apron, leaving a drop of perspiration gleaming at each end of his black moustache. 'Some wine, maybe? A bottle of white, like last time?'

Dr Coffee looked at his watch. 'Sure, Raoul,' he said. 'Some of that Lake Erie Islands white.'

There was no talk for the next few minutes, and no sound but the pleasant bubbling of the marmite, the crusty whisper of breaking French bread, the squeak and gasp of a cork withdrawn, the clink of forks on plates. But Dr Coffee was thinking. He was reviewing mentally the Starkey guest list: Brooks, Drew, Kelling, all men with wives who could be models for an advertisement by DeBeers Consolidated.

Dr Coffee himself never thought in terms of carats or cabochons, but several times each year—after the opening of the symphony, the two-night stand of the Metropolitan Opera Company's annual visit to Northbank, or the Northbank Community Chest Ball—he was forced to lie awake for several hours while his wife catalogued, described, appraised, and speculated on the probable origin of the most spectacular jewellery paraded on these occasions. And Mesdames Starkey, Brooks, Drew and Kelling always led the parade.

Madeline Starkey's rings were above reproach, Julia Coffee had always said, but her tiara and necklace were a little too gaudy to be in good taste. However, they were all honestly come by, if you accepted the source of Herbert Starkey's money as legitimate. Starkey was president of Lakeside Development Co, the realty firm that launched Northbank's swank Lakeside Park. Lakeside Park overlooked an artificial lake created by the City of Northbank as a spare reservoir for the municipal water system. It was pure coincidence, of course, that when the time came to subdivide the hillslopes around the lake into desirable residence sites, forty per cent of the land turned out to belong to two members of the City Council, and the remaining sixty per cent to Starkey's Lakeside Development Co. However, Lakeside Park had become a thing of beauty and civic pride, and Starkey had become a slightly pot-bellied, highly-respected member of the community, a trustee of orphanages, director of the local Red Cross, and a leader in the Community Chest. His whirlwind courtship and marriage of Madeline during a three-weeks West Indies cruise had caused some talk, but she had made him a most ornamental wife and her brilliant little dinners always made the society pages.

Mrs Peter Brooks wore the largest diamonds in Northbank, and, according to Julia Coffee, the yellowest. They represented profits

JUST DESSERTS

on Peter Brooks' municipal paving contracts.

Mrs Wally Drew had started collecting emerald bracelets when she was Mrs Somebody Else, the wife of an investment banker who had bought his freedom with a settlement that allowed her to continue her collection and acquire a husband ten years her junior. Wally Drew had been golf pro at the Northbank Country Club at the time of his marriage, but he now played golf for pleasure. His present career consisted in admiring his wife's profile and bracelets.

Mrs Sydney Kelling was very unobtrusive in her adornment—just a few strands of matched pearls, a ruby brooch, and an oriental sapphire ring—but then everyone knew that they were flawless and expensive because her husband was Northbank's leading jeweller.

It was indeed a coincidence, Dr Coffee mused, that a notorious jewel thief should be having dinner with such a bejewelled coterie—unless, of course, his sudden death should prove not to be a coincidence . . .

'More tripe, Doc?' said Lieutenant Ritter.

'Thanks,' said Dr Coffee. 'Tell me more about the dinner, Max.'

'Well, it was a West Indies dinner,' the detective said. 'Yesterday was the anniversary of the Starkey's engagement, and the Brookses and the Drews and the Kellings were all along on the Caribbean cruise where Starkey met his Madeline. Besides, the guest of honour also happened to be temporarily from Jamaica. So it was strictly Caribbean chow. Here's the menu. Seems that when there's more than two to dinner at the Starkey house, they always have printed menus.'

Ritter handed the pathologist a printed card. Dr Coffee read:

Rougail de Crevettes
Ackees with Cod
Poulet aux bananes en cocotte
Eggplant, Sauce au Chien
Hearts of Palm Salad
Spiced Avocados with Kirsch
Puerto Rican Coffee
Various West Indies Rums

'The only things on there I understand,' continued Max Ritter, 'are the coffee and rum. And boy, did they have rum! I put seals on the kitchen last night, just in case you wanted to run some of the leftovers through your lab, Doc. I got samples of all the bottles. Six kinds of rum, they drank. Cuban rum for daiquiri cocktails. Then Barbados rum with the—whatever they kick off with. Jamaica rum with the ackees, whatever they are. What are they, Doc?'

'I don't know. We'll ask Raoul.'

'Anyhow, there was Martinician rum with the chicken. Seems that Poulet and stuff means chicken.'

'With bananas,' said Dr Coffee. 'I wonder how she cooks that.'

'And Haitian rum with the palm hearts. Then Demerara rum—that's 150 proof—with the dessert. Maybe this Otto really did die of bellyache after all. Anything else fatal on the menu, Doc?'

Dr Coffee shook his head. Then he called Raoul. What, he wanted to know, was 'Rougail'?

Raoul studied the menu and fingered his moustache. Rougail, he believed, was a West Indies hors d'oeuvre, made by pounding shrimps in a mortar with oil and salt and little bird peppers, until they become a smooth paste. Ackees? Raoul had never heard of them. Certainly not a French West Indies dish. No, Raoul didn't know how one cooked chicken with bananas. He knew it was a Martinician dish, and he understood the bananas were the small variety and not quite ripe when cooked. He did not know the recipe.

'Thanks, Raoul,' said Dr Coffee. 'Max, where do we go from here?'

'That's what I don't know, Doc,' the detective said. 'If this guy Otto was poisoned, you'll catch it in the lab. Right? The Coroner promised to send you the guy's innards. He don't mind so much my working with you since that time you told the newspapers that he was the one who did the autopsy in the Harriet Baron case. Did he send everything?'

Dr Coffee nodded. 'Dr Mookerji is making the preliminary tests now,' he said.

'That Swami? Is he up to it, Doc?'

'Dr Mookerji is an excellent chemist,' said Dr Coffee.

'Because it's got to be good. I'm scared shiftless that the Coroner is going to have the laugh on me, Doc.'

'Why, Max?'

'Because everybody at the Starkey dinner ate the same food. I talked to the servants this morning. They were all sore at having to dress up like Jamaicans, with bandannas around their hair—you know, local colour stuff—and they talked their heads off. The cook said Mrs Starkey came out in the kitchen to boss the job because she knew how everything ought to taste and how to make it taste that way. Seems she brought in a lot of the stuff by air from Jamaica. The maids say everybody was served from the same dishes. The maids passed the dishes at the table, so there was no chance of Otto getting a special helping of cyanide. The rum bottles got passed around, too, so I can't figure how there was a special mickey for Otto. But I'll be damned, Doc, if I can get rid of the hunch that I got a homicide case on my hands.'

'Anything beside the hunch and Otto's record?' Dr Coffee asked.

'Well, maybe three things,' the detective said. 'First, what happened to the Countess Zlata's sparklers? Maybe Otto lost them somewhere between Havana and Northbank and maybe he didn't. Anyhow I went through Otto's suite at River House with a fine comb, and the answer is zero. Second, why did Madeline Starkey leave the hospital alone, when the emergency interne called police, instead of letting her husband drive her home, like he offered to? I don't say that he got to River House ahead of me, but I do know that Otto's hotel key is missing. Third, a couple of Otto's pockets were turned inside out when I first saw him. I can't tell you why, but I can tell you that when Mrs Starkey drove off alone, this guy Sydney Kelling who came over with Starkey behind Mrs Starkey's car, climbed in the car with Otto and passed out next to him. He's got a perfect right to pass out after inhaling all that rum, and I don't accuse a high-class jeweller of being a dip. But where's Countess Zlata's shiny horse-collar, and where's the key to Otto's River House suite?'

'I see what you mean,' said Dr Coffee. He looked at his watch. 'I've got to get back to the hospital, Max. I'll tell you what turns up in the lab.'

Exactly nothing had turned up in the lab when Dr Coffee returned. The thin copper strips had come through the Reinsch test bright and shining. Therefore there was no arsenic and no mercury in the dead man's digestive system.

'Have also completed tests for phosphorous, antimony, and fluorine,' Dr Motilal Mookerji announced. 'Reactions likewise negative. You are not desiring tests for alkaloids, Doctor Sahib?'

'I guess you ought to try Mayer's reagent,' Dr Coffee said. 'But if we start running the whole two dozen colour reactions for alkaloids, the hospital administration is going to be on my neck for tying up the lab for extracurricular purposes. Let's narrow the field. Dr Mookerji, you're from the tropics. Did you ever hear of a tropical fruit, vegetable, fish, or animal called an ackee?'

'Ackees? Quite!' said the plump Hindu. 'Although same is not common in India, am familiar with ackee fruits via descriptions by Cousin Lal Gupta Mookerji, former inhabitant of Trinidad and Jamaica in minor medical capacity. Ackee fruits resemble small red apple with large blackish seeds in yellow interior. Cousin Lal Gupta reports same quite tasty when stewed with certain fishes.

Latin appellation called *Blighia sapida* because Captain Bligh introduced same to Jamaica from New Guinea somewhat anterior to mutinous unpleasantness with Clark Gable on board HMS *Bounty*. Have you been eating ackess this luncheon-time, Doctor Sahib?'

'No,' said Dr Coffee, 'but the late Mr Otto ate ackees for dinner last night, shortly before his death.'

The pink turban bobbed from side to side. 'Most indicative,' said the Hindu interne. 'Am of distant impression that ackees cause poisonous actions when unripe or overripe. Perhaps should dispense with alkaloid tests and proceed to glucosides, since ackee poisoning somewhat akin to saponin.'

Dr Coffee lit a cigarette and allowed two thoughtful wisps of smoke to curl from his nostrils before he replied. 'Test for saponin,' he said, 'although I don't know what good it will do. Eight people ate ackees for dinner last night, and only one died.'

'Quite unusual mortality rate,' said Dr Mookerji.

At eight-thirty that night Dr Coffee was just finishing dinner when he was called to the phone.

'Hello, Doctor Sahib,' said the Hindu's cheery voice. 'Have completed preliminary testings on deceased stomach of late Mr Otto. Gentleman's digestive tissues gave positive reaction for saponin. Therefore can state gentleman's decease no doubt caused by poisoning from eating ackee-fruits of improper ripeness. However can discover no reasons for immunity of other dinner guests. Mortality rate from ackees frequently attains ninety per cent.'

'Maybe he got the only bad ackee in the lot,' Dr Coffee said. 'Have you done an analysis of the brain tissue yet?'

'Am beginning at once,' said Dr Mookerji. 'Have not forgotten instructions for molybdic-acid test for alcohol in brains.'

'I'm sure you'll get a beautiful blue reaction,' said Dr Coffee. 'Call me if anything develops.'

He had scarcely hung up when Max Ritter called. 'I'll be by for you in five minutes,' the detective said. 'Put your coat on because we got a fifty-mile drive. If you have to leave a phone number for emergencies, you can be reached at Valley 1776. Goodbye.'

As he got into Max Ritter's car, Dr Coffee said: 'I don't know where we're going, Max, but I'm afraid Otto's death was an accident. He died of ackee poisoning. He must have eaten the only bad fruit in the dish.'

'We're going to the Starkeys' weekend rumpus cabin, which they call their hunting lodge,' said Ritter. 'It's twenty-five miles out of town. And I ain't so sure it was an accident, Doc. I just got a cable from the police in Kingston, Jamaica. Seems they used to know Mrs Starkey before she got married. She used to give expensive little parties for expensive winter visitors in all the Jamaica swank spots, and this guy Otto was always around. They never had enough on Madeline to make a pinch, but they're pretty sure she was the come-on and finger gal for Otto whenever he worked the Carribbean diamond fields. Now suppose Otto decided he had a meal ticket in Northbank for the rest of his life as long as Madeline wanted to hang on to her new plush-bottomed respectability with platinum zippers; and suppose Madeline decided to eliminate the danger of getting unzipped by a black-mailer . . .'

'Is that why we're going to the hunting lodge, Max?'

'Well, no. The servants told me that Mrs Starkey didn't get home last night till more than an hour after she left the hospital. That would give her time to drive to the lodge and back. Then this afternoon I been working on this Sydney Kelling. He's scared. He says he didn't know Otto was a crook and he's scared his reputation as an honest jeweller ain't going to be improved by his having dinner with a diamond thief. So when Madeline Starkey called him this afternoon and asked him to come to the lodge at ten tonight, Kelling tipped me right away. He'll do anything to get off the hook.'

'I can't see that you have anything very definite on Mrs Starkey, Max,' Dr Coffee said.

'That's why I want you along, Doc,' said the detective. 'If you give her enough scientific double-talk about what your lab is digging up, maybe she'll come clean.'

Dr Coffee shook his head dubiously as the police car sped through the night.

The Starkey hunting lodge stood on a hilltop in a clump of evergreens. Max Ritter pounded the heavy knocker on the front door. After a moment Madeline Starkey opened it. If she was surprised she did not show it. She stood regally in the doorway, her head poised so that the cold, impersonal beauty of her classic profile would show to advantage against the fire burning in the grate behind her. Her dark braids, coiled tightly about her imperious head, shone like jet through the diaphanous crown of her hat. There was a twenty-thousand-dollar glitter to the clasp which held the ends of the sables carelessly draped over one shoulder.

The room behind her was in shadow except for the light from the fireplace. The skins and heads of animals adorned the walls and two huge brass dog's-heads gleamed on the andirons.

'We just dropped in to see if Kelling agreed to reset the Countess Zlata's necklace,' Max Ritter said.

'I don't understand you,' said Mrs Starkey.

Ritter stepped past her and Dr Coffee followed. From somewhere in the shadows, Sydney Kelling said aplogetically: 'I just got here, Lieutenant. We were discussing the unfortunate death of Mr Otto.'

'That's good,' said Ritter, 'because Dr Coffee here has been doing a little laboratory work on Mr Otto. The doctor thinks maybe you killed him, Mrs Starkey.'

The door banged shut. 'That's ridiculous,' said Mrs Starkey. 'Why would I kill Cliff Otto?'

'To keep your husband from finding out how thick you used to be with a jewel thief. I got a cable here from the Jamaica police about you two.'

Mrs Starkey's laugh was as light and tinkling as ice in a highball. 'How ridiculous!' she said. 'I've hidden nothing from my husband. Why should a man who has been as successful as Herbert Starkey in filching many thousands of dollars from Northbank taxpayers be at all squeamish about my knowing Cliff Otto, who never did anything more reprehensible than accept gifts of jewellery from foolish elderly ladies?'

'Otto served time,' Ritter said. 'Maybe it wouldn't help the Starkey's social standing if you kept having a jailbird to dinner.'

'So that's it,' Mrs Starkey said. 'How am I supposed to have killed poor Cliff?'

'Ackee poisoning,' Dr Coffee said. 'You know of course that ackees are sometimes poisonous.'

'I recall that children in Jamaica sometimes got very sick from eating ackees they picked up from the ground,' said Mrs Starkey. 'As a matter of fact—'

Mrs Starkey stopped talking. Her head turned toward the door that was opening slowly at one side of the fireplace. A paunchy, balding man stood in the doorway. There were red velvet lapels on his smoking jacket. When he moved his hand, gunmetal gleamed in the firelight.

'Sorry, folks.' Herbert Starkey grinned and pocketed his revolver. 'I was asleep in the other room and I heard voices. I didn't know who was in here.'

Mrs Starkey was rigid as she glared at her husband. 'What are you doing here, Herbert?' she demanded.

'I overheard you phoning Syd Kelling to meet you here, so I came up early. I always check on you when you make a rendezvous with another man these days, Madeline.'

'These gentlemen say Cliff Otto was poisoned with ackees, Herbert,' Mrs Starkey said.

'We all ate ackees,' Starkey said. 'Personally, I feel very much alive.'

A telephone rang somewhere in the room. Max Ritter stumbled through the shadows to grab the ringing instrument. He grunted a few times, then said, 'For you, Doc. I think it's your Swami.'

Dr Mookerji's voice was shrill in Dan Coffee's ear. 'Have just completed qualitative analysis of deceased gentleman's brains.' The Hindu was excited. 'Tissues demonstrated complete lack of alcohol. Therefore can report that abstemiousness of deceased regarding alcoholic beverages was great and fatal misfortune. Because consultation of standard works on tropical medicine this evening-time revealed discovery by Dr Sir Harold Scott that alcohol is first-rate antidote for ackee poison. Alcohol precipitates venomous substances before morbid activities begin. Perhaps surviving ackee eaters were less abstemious, Doctor Sahib?'

'About six kinds of rum away from being abstemious, Dr Mookerji,' Dan Coffee said. 'Thanks. And congratulations on a damned fine job of post-mortem analysis.'

Dr Coffee sat for a moment looking at the fire. Than he telephoned Dr George Perry and spoke briefly in low tones. At last he walked slowly back to the group by the fireplace.

'Mrs Starkey,' he asked, 'was Otto the only one of your dinner guests who drank no rum last night?'

'Now that you mention it, I guess he was.'

'Why didn't you tell Lieutenant Ritter about this?'

'He didn't ask me. Is it important?' Madeline Starkey asked.

'Alcohol is an antidote for ackee poisoning,' said Dr Coffee. 'Your other guests were not poisoned because they were saturated with rum.'

'What a tragic accident!' said Madeline Starkey.

'It was no accident,' said Dr Coffee. 'Max, you'd better take that gun Mr Starkey has in his pocket. Because Mr Starkey murdered Clifford Otto.'

'Why, that's nonsense.' Starkey obediently handed his revolver to the detective. 'I knew nothing about alcohol and ackee poisoning.'

Madeline Starkey was staring at her husband with cold, accusing eyes. 'That's not true, Herbert,' she said. 'I remember telling you how I nearly died once, after eating ackees as a little girl . . . and how the doctor in Kingston saved my life by giving me rum until I was quite drunk.'

'I'd forgotten.' Starkey smiled with his lips as he returned his wife's stare, but his eyes did not smile.

'And you arranged for the tropical foods to be flown here from

Jamaica, Herbert,' Mrs Starkey continued. 'You ordered the ackees, Herbert.'

'That's not murder, Madeline. That's not—'

'It was murder, Mr Starkey,' Dr Coffee interrupted, 'when you referred Otto to Dr Perry a week ago, and you told Dr Perry to scare Otto into going on the wagon for a few weeks because he was an alcoholic.'

'I may have told Perry that Otto was drinking too much,' said Starkey with a suave gesture. 'But Otto's death was completely accidental. You can't prove otherwise. You can't prove that I knew anything about ackee poisoning. You can't . . .'

Starkey's voice died. He stared at his wife. Madeline Starkey still stood rigidly facing him, but her impersonal, classic mask was gone. Horror contorted her face and there was hate in her eyes.

Starkey smiled again. 'If you gentlemen of the police really want a case that will stand up in court,' he said, 'I advise you to examine the gun rack in the far corner of this room. I happened to be poking about there a few hours ago, and I noticed a rather handsome diamond necklace hidden behind the guns. I don't know if the necklace is stolen property, or who brought it here, but . . .'

Once more Starkey's voice failed. He did not take his eyes from his wife's face, even when Max Ritter stepped up to handcuff his hands in front of him.

'Madeline,' he said after a moment, 'you lied to me. You still loved him.'

Madeline Starkey did not reply. But her silence was eloquent. The utter scorn, the primitive hate that curled her thin lips was a complete confession of her love for the dead man, an accusation of his murderer.

Herbert Starkey lunged forward. His manacled hands swung swiftly against the side of his wife's face.

Madeline's head turned slightly. There was blood on her cheek, but her expression did not change. She collapsed slowly, quietly. Her head struck the gleaming brass nose of the dog on the nearest andiron. She lay motionless on the hearth.

Dr Coffee lifted her and carried her to a couch. Two minutes later he said: 'She must have struck the base of her skull. She was killed instantly.'

As Herbert Starkey sank to his knees beside the couch, Max Ritter said: 'This one won't be hard to prove in court, Starkey.'

Driving back to town, Max Ritter remarked: 'You know, Doc, we can only hang a manslaughter rap on Starkey for his wife's death, but it's better than nothing. He's probably right about our not

JUST DESSERTS

being able to prove in court that he killed Otto. That ackee business was clever.'

'If it hadn't been for Dr Mookerji,' Dr Coffee said, 'it would have been too clever.'

'Doc, there's a reward for this Countess Zlata's sparklers. Maybe we could cut the Swami in on the reward.'

'Dr Mookerji didn't have much to do with the necklace,' Don Coffee said 'but he really cracked the case for us.'

'We'll cut him in,' said Ritter. 'You, too, Doc.'

'You can give my share to the hospital. Then maybe the adminstration will stop squawking about my lab being cluttered up with police cases.' Dr Coffee pulled the lighter from the dashboard and pressed a cigarette against the glowing disk. 'I don't suppose we'll ever know how Mrs Starkey cooked that Poulet aux bananes en cocotte,' he said.

UNDER THE HAMMER

Georges Simenon

Inspector Maigret ranks high both as a detective—he has been called the 'French Sherlock Holmes'—and as a gourmet, although he does tend to prefer his wife's excellent cuisine and only dines out when duty calls, according to the many novels and short stories in which he has appeared. Indeed, he shares the distinction with Holmes and the American sleuth, Nero Wolfe, of having had a collection of his favourite dishes issued as a separate work, Madame Maigret's Own Cookbook. *Created by the prolific Belgian-born writer, Georges Simenon (1903–1989), who was something of a gourmet himself, Maigret always has to exercise restraint to keep his weight down, a trait which will be found in the following case of murder which he investigates at Frederic Michaux's little inn . . .*

Maigret pushed away his plate, got up from the table, grunted, shook himself, went over to the stove, and raised the lid mechanically.

'Well, now, let's get to work. We're going to be in bed early.'

And the others, sitting around the big table in the inn, looked at him with resignation. Frédéric Michaux, the proprietor, three days' stubble on his chin, was the first to get up and move to the bar. 'What'll you—?'

'No,' cried Maigret. 'No more. We've had enough. White wine, calvados, more wine and—'

They had all reached that stage of weariness where one's eyes smart and one's whole body aches. Julia, who passed for Frédéric's wife, went into the kitchen with a platter that bore the congealed remains of a dish of baked beans. Thérèse, the servant girl, wiped her eyes, but not because she was crying: she had a cold in the head.

'Where do we go back to?' she asked. 'Where I've cleared away?'

'It's eight o'clock now, so we pick it up from eight o'clock in the evening.'

'Then I'll bring the tablecloth and the cards.'

It was hot in the inn, too hot in fact, but outside the wind was driving gusts of icy rain through the darkness.

'Nicholas, you sit where you were last night. Monsieur Groux, you hadn't yet arrived.'

'It was when I heard Groux's footsteps outside,' the innkeeper interrupted, 'that I said to Thérèse, "Put the cards out."'

'Have I got to pretend to come in all over again?' groaned Groux, a six-foot farmer, solid as a kitchen dresser.

You would have thought they were actors rehearsing a play for the twentieth time—their minds blank, their gestures limp, their eyes vacant. Maigret himself, in his role of stage manager, had some difficulty in believing it was all real. Even the place itself— imagine spending three days in an inn miles from the nearest village, in the middle of the fens of the Vendée!

The place was called Pont-du-Grau, and there was in fact a bridge, a long wooden bridge over a sort of muddy canal, filled twice a day by the tide. But the sea could not be seen: all there was to see was fenland, crisscrossed by ditches, and far away on the horizon flat roofs, farms—called 'cabins' in these parts.

Why this inn here by the roadside? For sportsmen after duck and plover? There was a red-painted petrol pump in the yard, and on the gable end there was a big blue advertisment for a brand of chocolate.

On the other side of the bridge, a hovel—nothing more than a rabbit hutch—the home of old Nicholas, who was an eel-fisher. Three hundred yards away, quite a big farm, with long single-storey buildings: Groux's place.

January 15th . . . 1 p.m. sharp at the place known as La Mulatière, sale by auction . . . farm, 30 hectares, equipment and stock . . . farm machinery, furniture, china . . . the transaction will be by cash.

That is how it had all started. For years life at the inn had been the same every evening. Old Nicholas would arrive, always half drunk, and before he settled down with his pint, he would go over for a drink at the bar. Then Groux would arrive from his farm. Thérèse would spread a red cloth on the table, and bring the cards and the counters. They still had to wait for the excise man to make the fourth; if he didn't turn up, Julia took his place.

Now, on the 14th, the eve of the sale, there were two other customers, farmers who had come from farther way—one of them a man called Borchain, from near Angoulême, the other a certain Canut, from Saint Jean-d'Angély.

'Just a minute,' said Maigret, as the innkeeper was about to shuffle the cards. 'Borchain went to bed before eight o'clock—

that's to say, straight after his supper. Who was it who took him to his room?'

'I did,' Frédèric answered.

'He'd been drinking?'

'Not too much. A little, of course. He asked me who the chap was who looked so glum, and I told him it was Groux, the man whose property was going to be sold . . . Then he asked me how Groux had come to fail with such good land, and I—'

'That's enough of that,' Groux groaned. The big fellow was in a gloomy mood. He refused to admit that he had never looked after his land and his beasts, and be blamed fate for his failure.

'All right! By that time who had seen his wallet?'

'All of us. He had taken it out of his pocket during the meal to show us a photograph of his wife . . . so we saw it was full of notes. Even if we hadn't seen them we would have known, as he had come with the intention of buying, and the sale had been advertised as a cash one.'

'Same thing for you, Canut? You, too, had over a hundred thousand francs on you?'

'A hundred and fifty. I did not mean to go any higher . . .'

Ever since his arrival there Maigret, who was at that time in charge of the flying squad at Nantes, had been studying Frédèric Michaux thoughtfully. Michaux, who was about forty-five, hardly looked like a country innkeeper, with his boxer's jersey and his broken nose.

'Tell me, don't you have the feeling we've seen one another before somewhere?'

'It's not worth beating about the bush—you're quite right, Inspector. But I'm going straight now.'

Loitering with intent in the Ternes district of Paris, assault and battery, illegal bets, slot machines . . . In short, Frédèric Michaux, innkeeper at Pont-du-Grau in the depths of the Vendée, was better known to the police under the name of Fred the Boxer.

'You'll recognise Julia, too, no doubt . . . You put the two of us away ten years ago. But you can see she's a respectable woman now . . .'

It was true. Bloated and flabby, blowsy, her hair greasy, shuffling back and forth between kitchen and dining-room, Julia in no way resembled the girl of the Place des Ternes, and, what was more unexpected, she was a first-class cook.

'We brought Thérèse with us. She's an orphanage kid.'

Eighteen years old, slim and tall, with a sharp nose and a funny little mouth, and a bold stare.

'Have we got to play in earnest?' asked the excise man, whose name was Gentil.

'Play as you did then. You, Canut, why haven't you gone to bed?'

'I was watching the game,' the farmer muttered.

'Or, rather, he kept running after me,' snapped Thérèse, 'making me promise to go to his room afterwards.'

Maigret noted that Fred threw a black look at the man, and that Julia was watching Fred.

Good, they were all in their places. And the other night it had been raining, too. Borchain's room was on the ground floor, at the far end of the passage. In that corridor there were three doors: one that led into the kitchen, another that opened on to the cellar stairs, and a third numbered 100.

Maigret sighed and ran his hand wearily over his brow. In the three days he had been there, the smell of the place had been soaking into him, the atmosphere clung to his skin until it sickened him. And yet what else could he do?

A little before midnight on the 14th, while the card game was going on quietly, Fred had sniffed once or twice, and shouted to Julia in the kitchen, 'Is there something burning on the stove?'

He had got up and opened the door into the passage.

'Heavens, it reeks of burning out here!'

Groux had followed him, and Thérèse, too. It was coming from Borchain's room. He had banged on the door, then he had opened it, for it had no lock.

It was the mattress that was smouldering, a wool mattress, which gave off an acrid fatty smell. On the bed, in shirt and drawers, Borchain lay stretched out, his skull smashed in.

Then the telephone. At one in the morning Maigret had been roused. By four he was arriving, in the middle of a downpour, his nose red with cold, his hands frozen.

Borchain's wallet had disappeared. The window of the room was closed. No one could have come in from outside, for Michaux had a disagreeable Alsatian dog.

Impossible to arrest them all. They were all under suspicion, except Canut, the only one who had not left the inn parlour the whole evening.

'Come, now, my friends! I'm listening to you, and I'm watching . . . Do exactly what you did at this time on the 14th.'

The sale had been postponed to a later date. All day on the 15th people had been passing up and down in front of the house, whose doors the inspector had had closed.

Now it was the 16th. Maigret had hardly left the room, except to get a few hours' sleep. The same for the rest of them. They were sick to death of seeing each other from morning to night, of hearing the same questions over and over again, of going through the same actions time after time.

Julia was cooking. The rest of the world was forgotten. It was hard to realise that there were people in other places, in the towns, who were not saying the same things over and over, endlessly. 'Let's see . . . I had just cut hearts . . . Groux threw down his hand, saying: "It's not worth playing . . . I haven't a single card . . . Just my luck!" He got up—'

'Get up, Groux,' ordered Maigret, 'just as you did that night.'

The big man shrugged. 'How many more times are you going to send me along that corridor?' he grumbled. 'Ask Frédéric—ask Nicholas—don't I go along there at least twice most evenings? Eh? What do you think I do with the four or five bottles of white wine I drink during the day?'

He spat, and went towards the door, slouched along the passage, and banged open the door marked 100 with his fist. 'There! Have I got to stay here, at this time of night?'

'As long as necessary, yes . . . Now, what did the rest of you do while he was out?'

The excise man laughed nervously at Groux's show of temper, and his laughter sounded forced. He was the least tough of them all. It was as if his nerves were too near the surface.

'I said to Gentil and Nicholas that no good would come of it,' said Fred.

'No good would come of what?'

'Groux and his farm . . . He never really believed the sale would take place. He was sure he would find some way to borrow the money . . . When they came to put up the notice he threatened the bailiff with his gun. At his age, when you've always been your own master, it's not easy to go back to being somebody else's farmhand . . .'

Groux had come back without a word and was looking at them balefully.

'Now what?' he shouted. 'Have you got it all fixed? Was it me who killed him and set fire to the mattress? Say so now, and chuck me into prison! Having got this far . . .'

'Where were you, Julia?' Maigret asked. 'It seems to me you're not where you should be . . .'

'I was cleaning the vegetables in the kitchen. We were expecting a lot of people to lunch because of the sale. I had ordered two gigots, and we've only just finished one of them now . . .'

'And you, Thérèse?'

'I went up to my room . . .'

'When, exactly?'

'A little after Monsieur Groux came back . . .'

'All right, we'll go up together. The rest of you carry on—you started playing again?'

'Not right away: Groux didn't want to. We talked . . . I went to get a packet of cigarettes from the bar.'

'Come along, Thérèse . . .'

The room where Borchain had died we certainly strategically placed. The staircase was barely six feet away, so Thérèse could have . . .

A narrow room, an iron bed, clothes and underwear on a chair.

'What did you come up for?'

'To write.'

'To write what?'

'That we certainly wouldn't have a moment alone together the next day . . .' She was looking him straight in the eye, defiantly. 'You know very well what I'm talking about—I could tell from the looks you gave me and from your questions . . . The old woman suspects something. She's always on top of us. I begged Fred to take me away, and we had made up our minds to clear off in the spring . . .'

'Why the spring?'

'I don't know—Fred fixed the date. We were to go to Panama, where he once lived, and open a bistro . . .'

'How long did you stay in your room?'

'Not long. I heard the old woman coming upstairs. She asked me what I was doing. I answered, 'Nothing.' She hates me and I hate her—I'd swear she suspected what we were planning . . .'

And Thérèse returned Maigret's gaze. She was a girl who knew what she wanted, and she wanted it badly.

'You don't think Julia would rather see Fred in prison than have him go off with you?'

'She's capable of it!'

'What was she going to her room for?'

'To take off her corset. She has to wear a rubber one to keep what's left of her figure . . .'

Thérèse's pointed teeth reminded him of some small animal; she had the same unfeeling cruelty. Her lips curled as she spoke of the woman who had preceded her in Fred's affections.

'In the evenings, especially when she has eaten too much—it's revolting how she stuffs herself!—her corset kills her, and she goes upstairs to take it off . . .'

'How long did she stay?'

'Maybe ten minutes. When she came down again I helped her with the vegetables. The others were still playing cards . . .'

'The door was open between the kitchen and the parlour?'

'It's always open.'

Maigret gave her a last look, then tramped heavily down the creaking stairs. From the courtyard came the sound of the dog pulling at its chain.

Just behind the cellar door was a heap of coal, and it was there that the murder weapon had been found—a heavy coal hammer.

No fingerprints. The killer must have picked up the tool with a cloth. Through the rest of the house, including the doorknob of Borchain's room, innumerable blurred prints belonging to all those who were there on the night of the 17th.

As for the wallet, ten of them had looked for it, even in the unlikeliest places—all men accustomed to searches of this kind— and the day before the sanitary department had been called in to drain the cesspool.

The unfortunate Borchain had come from his place to buy Groux's farm. Until then he had been only a farmer; he wanted to become a landowner. He was married and had three daughters. He had had dinner at one of the tables. He had chatted with Canut, who was another prospective buyer. He had shown around his wife's photograph.

Weighed down with too heavy a meal and liberal helpings of drink, he had made for bed, thet way country people do when they feel sleep coming on. No doubt he had slipped the wallet under his pillow.

In the inn parlour, four men playing *belote*, as on any other evening, and drinking white wine: Fred, Groux, old Nicholas, whose face turned purplish when he had drunk his fill, and the excise man Gentil, who would have been better off doing his rounds.

Behind them, straddling a chair, Canut, dividing his attention between the cards and Thérèse, in the hope that this night of his away from home would be marked by some adventure.

In the kitchen, two women: Julia and the young girl from the orphanage, at work on a pail of vegetables.

One of these people, at a given moment, went into the passage, on some pretext or other, opened first the cellar door, to take out the coal hammer, and then Borchain's door.

No one had heard anything. It could not have taken long as nobody had noticed any lengthy absence—even though the murderer had also to put the wallet in a safe place, for, as the mattress was set on fire, it would not be long before the alarm was given. They would telephone the police, and each of them would be searched.

'When I think,' Maigret said plaintively on returning to the parlour, 'that you haven't even any decent beer . . .' A glass of cool, frothy beer straight from the barrel . . . instead of these contemptible bottles of so-called family brew.

'How about the game?'

Fred looked at the time on the clock with its sky-blue pottery frame and its advertising slogan. He was used to the police: he was tired, like the others, but rather less strung up.

'Twenty to ten . . . Not started yet. We were still talking. It was you, Nicholas, who wanted more wine?'

'That's possible.'

'I called through to Thérèse, "Go and draw some wine." Then I got up and went down to the cellar myself.'

'Why?'

He paused, then shrugged his shoulders. 'Oh well, can't be helped. What does it matter if she does hear it, after all? When all this is over, life won't carry on as it was before, anyway . . . I had heard Thérèse got up to her room. I thought she had probably left me a note. It would be put in the keyhole of the cellar door. Do you hear, Julia? I can't help it, old girl. The few happy moments we've spent together have been more than paid for by your endless scenes.'

Canut reddened. Only Nicholas sniggered into his ginger whiskers. Monsieur Gentil averted his eyes, for he, too, had often made a pass at Thérèse.

'Was there a note?' Maigret asked.

'Yes. I read it down there while the bottle was filling. All Thérèse said was we probably wouldn't have a moment by ourselves the next day.'

Strange, but one sensed real feeling in Fred, and even a totally unexpected depth of emotion . . . In the kitchen Thérèse got up suddenly and came towards the card table.

'Haven't you had enough?' she said, with trembling lips. 'I'd rather they arrested us all and put us in prison. It would soon . . . But to go round and round like this, as if—as if . . .' She burst out sobbing, and ran over to bury her head in her arms against the wall.

'So you stayed in the cellar for several minutes?' Maigret went on imperturbably.

'Three or four minutes yes,' Fred replied.

'What did you do with the note?'

'I burnt it in the candle.'

'Are you afraid of Julia?'

Fred strongly resented Maigret's question. 'Surely you understand? You who arrested us ten years ago—don't *you* understand that when one's been through a lot together . . . Anyway, have it your own way. Don't you upset yourself, Julia dear.'

And a calm voice came from the kitchen: 'I'm not upset.'

As for motive—the classic motive that all the lectures on criminology stress—each one of these people had a motive. Groux even more than the others, as he was at the end of his tether, about to be sold up the day after, thrown out of house and home without even furniture or belongings, and with no alternative but to hire himself out as labourer. He knew the house well—the way to the cellar, the coal, the hammer . . .

And Nicholas—an old drunk, certainly, but he was penniless. Although he had a daughter in service at Niort, all her earnings went to the upkeep of her child. So couldn't he have . . . ? Besides, as Fred had just said, it was Nicholas who came in each week to chop the wood and break the coal.

Now, at about ten, Nicholas has gone along the passage, zigzagging drunkenly. Gentil had said, 'Hope he doesn't mistake the door.' It was an extraordinary coincidence: why had Gentil, sitting there, shuffling the cards mechanically, suddenly said that?

And why shouldn't Gentil have had the idea of committing the crime himself when a few moments later he followed in Nicholas' footsteps? Granted he was an excise officer, but everyone knew he didn't take that very seriously; he did his rounds at the café table, and was always ready to come to an arrangement . . .

'Listen, Inspector—' Fred started.

'One moment. It's five past ten. Where had we reached the other night?'

At that Thérèse, who was still sniffling, came and sat down behind Fred, her shoulder touching his back.

'You were sitting there?' Maigret asked.

'Yes. I had finished the vegetables. I took up the sweater I was knitting, but I didn't do any of it . . .'

Julia was still in the kitchen, but she couldn't be seen.

'What was it you wanted to say, Fred?' Maigret asked.

'Just an idea—it seems to me there's one point that proves it wasn't one of us who killed him, because—suppose—No, that's what I mean . . . If I killed someone in my house, do you think I'd start a fire? What for? To draw attention . . . ?'

Maigret had just filled his pipe, and was taking his time over lighting it. 'I think I'll have a calvados, after all, Thérèse,' he said.

'Now, Fred, why wouldn't you start a fire?'

'Well, because . . .' Fred was struck dumb. 'If that fire hadn't started, we wouldn't have worried about the fellow. The others would have gone home . . . and . . .'

Maigret smiled; the stem of his pipe stretched his mouth into an odd grin. 'A pity you're proving exactly the opposite of what you wanted to prove, Fred. The start of that fire was the only real clue— it struck me immediately. Suppose you do kill the old man, as you say. Everyone knows he's at your place, so you wouldn't dream of disposing of the body . . . The next morning you will just be compelled to open the door of his room and raise the alarm. When did he in fact ask to be called?'

'Six o'clock. He wanted to go over the farm and the fields before the sale . . .'

'So if the body had been found at six o'clock, there would be no one in the house but you, Julia, and Thérèse—I don't include Monsieur Canut, whom no one would have suspected. Nor would anyone have thought the crime could have been committed during the card game.'

Fred was following the Inspector's reasoning carefully, and it seemed to Maigret that he had grown paler. He even tore a playing-card absently into bits and dropped the pieces on the floor.

'Look what you're doing! Next time you try to play, you'll have a hard time finding the ace of spades. What was I saying? Ah, yes. How could one make sure the crime was discovered before the departure of Groux, Nicholas, and Monsieur Gentil, so that suspicion might fall on them? No reason for going into Borchain's room . . . Except one—the fire . . .'

This time Fred shot to his feet, fists clenched, grimfaced. 'In heaven's name!' he shouted.

There was dead silence: they were shocked to the core. They had become so exhausted that they had gradually ceased to believe in the murderer. They no longer grasped that he was there, in the house, talking to them, eating at the same table with them, perhaps playing cards with them, and raising his glass to them.

Fred strode up and down the inn parlour. Maigret seemed to have sunk into himself, his eyes almost closed; he wondered if he was going to succeed at last. For three days he had kept them on the go, hour after hour, making them repeat ten times over the same actions, the same words, partly in the hope that a forgotten detail would suddenly emerge, but above all to wear them down, to push the murderer to breaking-point.

'The whole thing—' His voice was quiet, the words punctuated by little puffs on his pipe—'hangs on knowing who had a safe enough hiding-place for the wallet never to be found . . .'

Everyone had been searched. One after the other, that first night, they had been stripped stark naked. The coal behind the cellar door had been searched through. The walls had been tapped, and the casks sounded. In spite of that, a fat wallet holding more than a hundred thousand-franc notes . . .

'You're making me dizzy, Fred, going round and round like that . . .'

'But, for heaven's sake, don't you understand—'

'Understand what?'

'That I didn't kill him! I'm not fool enough for that—me with a police record long enough to—'

'It was in the spring, then, you meant to take Thérèse to South America and buy a bistro?'

Fred glanced towards the kitchen door. 'So what?' he asked through clenched teeth.

'Where was the money coming from?'

Fred's eyes bored into Maigret's. 'So that's what you're getting at! You're on the wrong tack, Inspector. I'll have money on the 15th of May. It was a comfortable little idea that came to me when I was doing nicely as a boxing promoter. I took out an insurance policy for a hundred thousand francs to come at the age of fifty. I shall be fifty on the 15th of May—ah, yes, Thérèse, I'm a bit longer in the tooth than I usually let on.'

'Julia knew about this insurance?'

'That's nothing to do with a woman.'

'So, Julia, you didn't know Fred was coming into a hundred thousand francs?'

'I knew.'

'What?' Fred started.

'I also knew he wanted to go off with that trashy little—'

'And you would have let them go?'

Julia stayed quite still, her gaze fixed on Fred; there was a strange calm about her.

'You haven't answered me,' Maigret persisted.

She turned her gaze on him. Her lips moved, perhaps she was going to say something important—but instead she shrugged her shoulders. 'Can you ever tell what a man will do?'

Fred was not listening. He looked as if he was suddenly pre-occupied with something else. Brows furrowed, he was deep in thought, and Maigret had the impression that they were thinking along the same lines.

'Well, now, Fred?'

'What?' It was as if he had been jolted out of a dream.

'About this insurance policy—this policy that Julia saw without your knowing—I'd also like to take a look at it.'

How oddly the truth can come to light! Maigret was sure he had thought of everything. Thérèse told him in her room about the departure, therefore there had to be money . . . Fred confessed to the existence of an insurance policy. And now—it was so simple, so obvious, that he almost burst out laughing—the house had been combed ten times over but no insurance policy had been found, no identity papers, no military service record.

'As you like, Inspector,' Fred answered calmly with a sigh. 'At least you'll be able to see how much I've saved up . . .' He went towards the kitchen.

'You can come in. When one lives at the back of beyond like this . . . Not to mention some papers I have that my pals from the old days wouldn't mind pinching . . .'

Thérèse followed them, astonished. Groux's heavy footsteps could be heard, and Canut getting up in turn.

'Don't think this is anything special,' Fred went on. 'I just happen to have been a coppersmith in my young days . . .'

To the right of the kitchen range there was an enormous dustbin of galvanised iron. Fred emptied the contents out right in the middle of the floor, and released the concealed double bottom in its base. He was the first to look inside. Slowly a frown spread over his face. Slowly he raised his head; his mouth hung open . . .

Lying there, among other papers, was a bulging wallet, grubby with use and held together with a band of red rubber cut from an innertube.

'Well, Julia?' Maigret asked softly.

Then, it seemed to him, through the woman's flabby features he saw a flash of the old Julia. She looked round at them all, and her upper lip curled disdainfully. She looked as if the tears were not far away, but they did not come. Her voice was flat when she spoke.

'Well, that's that. I'm done for . . .'

The extraordinary thing was that it was Thérèse who suddenly burst into tears, like a dog howling in the presence of death. Meanwhile the woman who had done the killing asked, 'I suppose you're taking me off straight away? As you have the car? Can I bring my things?'

Maigret let her pack her bits and pieces. He felt sad: reaction, after prolonged nervous tension.

How long, he wondered, had Julia known about Fred's hiding-place? On seeing the insurance policy, which he had never told her about, she must have realised that the day that money came he would be off with Thérèse.

Then came her chance: more money even than Fred would be getting. And she would be the one who would bring it to him, a few days or a few weeks after the affair was all over—*Look, Fred, I know everything . . . You wanted to go away with her, didn't you? You thought I was no good any more . . . Take a look in your hiding-place—It's your 'old girl' who . . .*

Maigret kept close watch over her as she moved about the bedroom where there was only a big mahogany bed and, above it, a photograph of Fred in boxing rigout. 'Have to put my corset on,' she said. 'You won't look, will you? It's not very pretty . . .'

It was not until she was in the car that she broke down. Maigret kept his eyes fixed on the raindrops sliding down the windows. He wondered what the others were doing now, back at the inn. And who would get Groux's farm when the auctioneer's voice rang out—going, going, gone!—and the hammer fell.

POISON À LA CARTE

Rex Stout

The amazing Nero Wolfe—amazing in terms of his genius at solving crimes, and similarly in his physical appearance: 5 feet 11 inches tall and weighing one seventh of a ton!—is certainly the gourmand among detectives. Not only does he employ a chef, Fritz Brenner, to prepare the epicurean dishes he loves, but a full-time assistant, Archie Goodwin, to do his leg-work and prevent him having to leave his New York apartment except when absolutely necessary, claming that, 'I carry this fat to insulate my feelings.' The Nero Wolfe Cookbook has long been a favourite with the detective's admirers, and a group of them, known as the Wolfe Pack, meet once a year for a banquet derived from its pages. Rex Stout (1886– 1975) was unlike either his creation or his own name, being a thin, wiry man, though he did share Nero Wolfe's love of food and orchids. Gourmet meals feature in most of the Nero Wolfe stories, but among these epicurean delights there are few more elaborate than the one in the story that follows.

I slanted my eyes down to meet her big brown ones, which were slanted up. 'No,' I said, 'I'm neither a producer nor an agent. My name's Archie Goodwin, and I'm here because I'm a friend of the cook. My reason for wanting it is purely personal.'

'I know,' she said, 'it's my dimples. Men often swoon.'

I shook my head. 'It's your earrings. They remind me of a girl I once loved in vain. Perhaps if I get to know you well enough—who can tell?'

'Not me,' she declared. 'Let me alone. I'm nervous, and I don't want to spill the soup. The name is Nora Jaret, without an H, and the number is Stanhope five, six-six-two-one. The earrings were a present from Sir Laurence Olivier. I was sitting on his knee.'

I wrote the number down in my notebook, thanked her, and looked around. Most of the collection of attractive young females were gathered in an alcove between two cupboards, but one was over by a table watching Felix stir something in a bowl. Her profile

was fine and her hair was the colour of corn silk just before it starts
to turn. I crossed to her, and when she turned her head I spoke.
'Good evening, Miss—Miss?'
    'Annis,' she said. 'Carol Annis.'
    I wrote it down, and told her my name. 'I am not blunt by
nature,' I said, 'but you're busy, or soon will be, and there isn't
time to talk up to it. I was standing watching you and all of a
sudden I had an impulse to ask you for your phone number, and
I'm no good at fighting impulses. Now that you're closed up it's
even stronger, and I guess we'll have to humour it.'
    But I may be giving a wrong impression. Actually I had no
special hankering that Tuesday evening for new telephone
numbers; I was doing it for Fritz. But that could give a wrong
impression too, so I'll have to explain.
    One day in February, Lewis Hewitt, the millionaire orchid
fancier for whom Nero Wolfe had once handled a tough problem,
had told Wolfe that the Ten for Aristology wanted Fritz Brenner to
cook their annual dinner, to be given as usual on April first, Brillat-
Savarin's birthday. When Wolfe said he had never heard of the Ten
for Aristology, Hewitt explained that it was a group of ten men
pursuing the ideal of perfection in food and drink, and he was one
of them. Wolfe had swivelled to the dictionary on its stand at a
corner of his desk, and after consulting it had declared that
'aristology' meant the science of dining, and therefore the Ten
were witlings, since dining was not a science but an art. After a
long argument Hewitt had admitted he was licked and had agreed
that the name should be changed, and Wolfe had given him
permission to ask Fritz to cook the dinner.
    In fact, Wolfe was pleased, though of course he wouldn't say so.
It took a big slice of his income as a private detective to pay Fritz
Brenner, chef and housekeeper in the old brownstone on West
35th Street—about the same as the slice that came to me as his
assistant detective and man Friday, Saturday, Sunday, Monday,
Tuesday, Wednesday, and Thursday—not to mention what it took
to supply the kitchen with the raw materials of Fritz's productions.
Since I am also the bookkeeper, I can certify that for the year 1957
the kitchen and Fritz cost only slightly less than the plant rooms on
the roof bulging with orchids.
    So when Hewitt made it clear that the Ten, though they might be
dubs at picking names, were true and trustworthy gourmets, that
the dinner would be at the home of Benjamin Schriver, the ship-
ping magnate, who wrote a letter to *The Times* every year on
September first denouncing the use of horseradish on oysters, and
that the cook would have a free hand on the menu and the Ten

would furnish whatever he desired, Wolfe pushed a button to summon Fritz. There was a little hitch when Fritz refused to commit himself until he had seen the Schriver kitchen, but Hewitt settled that by escorting him out front to his Heron town car and driving him down to Eleventh Street to inspect the kitchen.

That's where I was that Tuesday evening, April first, collecting phone numbers—in the kitchen of the four-storey Schriver house on Eleventh Street west of Fifth Avenue. Wolfe and I had been invited by Schriver, and though Wolfe dislikes eating with strangers and thinks that more than six at table spoils a meal, he knew Fritz's feeling would be hurt if he didn't go; and besides, if he stayed home who would cook his dinner? Even so, he would probably have balked if he had learned of one detail which Fritz and I knew about but had carefully kept from him: that the table was to be served by twelve young women, one for each guest.

When Hewitt had told me that, I had protested that I wouldn't be responsible for Wolfe's conduct when the orgy got under way, that he would certainly stamp out of the house when the girls started to squeal. Good lord, Hewitt said, nothing like that; that wasn't the idea at all. It was merely that the Ten had gone to ancient Greece not only for their name but also for other precedents. Hebe, the goddess of youth, had been cupbearer to the gods, so it was the custom of the Ten for Aristology to be waited on by maidens in appropriate dress. When I asked where they got the maidens he said through a theatrical agency, and added that at that time of year there were always hundreds of young actresses out of a job glad to grab at a chance to make fifty bucks, with a good meal thrown in, by spending an evening carrying food, one plate at a time. Originally they had hired experienced waitresses from an agency, but they had tripped on their stolas.

Wolfe and I had arrived at seven on the dot, and after we had met our host and the rest of the Ten, and had sampled oysters and our choice of five white wines, I had made my way to the kitchen to see how Fritz was making out. He was tasting from a pot on the range, with no more sign of fluster than if he had been at home getting dinner for Wolfe and me. Felix and Zoltan, from Rusterman's, were there to help, so I didn't ask if I was needed.

And there were the Hebes, cupbearers to the gods, twelve of them, in their stolas, deep rich purple, flowing garments to their ankles. Very nice. It gave me an idea. Fritz likes to pretend that he has reason to believe that no damsel is safe within a mile of me, which doesn't make sense since you can't tell much about them a mile off, and I thought it would do him good to see me operate at close quarters. Also, it was a challenge and an interesting sociological experiment. The first two had been a cinch: one named Fern Faber, so she said, a tall blonde with a wide lazy mouth, and Nora Jaret with the big brown eyes and dimples. Now I was after this Carol Annis with hair like corn silk.

'I have no sense of humour,' she said and turned back to watch Felix.

I stuck. 'That's a different kind of humour and an impulse like mine isn't funny. It hurts. Maybe I can guess it. Is it Hebe one, oh-oh-oh-oh?'

No reply.

'Apparently not. Plato two, three-four-five-six?'

She said, without turning her head, 'It's listed. Gorham eight, three-two-one-seven.' Her head jerked to me. 'Please?' It jerked back again.

It rather sounded as if she meant please go away, not please ring her as soon as possible, but I wrote it down anyway, for the record, and moved off. The rest of them were still grouped in the alcove, and I crossed over. The deep purple of the stolas was a good contrast for their pretty young faces topped by nine different colours and styles of hairdos. As I came up the chatter stopped and the faces turned to me.

'At ease,' I told them. 'I have no official standing. I am merely one of the guests, invited because I'm a friend of the cook, and I have a personal problem. I would prefer to discuss it with each of you separately and privately, but since there isn't time for that—'

'I know who you are,' one declared. 'You're a detective and you work for Nero Wolfe. You're Archie Goodwin.'

She was a redhead with milky skin. 'I don't deny it,' I told her, 'but I'm not here professionally. I don't ask if I've met you because if I had I wouldn't have forgot—'

'You haven't met me. I've seen you and I've seen your picture. You like yourself. Don't you?'

'Certainly. I string along with the majority. We'll take a vote. How many of you like yourselves? Raise your hands.'

A hand went up with a bare arm shooting out of the purple folds, then two more, then the rest of them, including the redhead.

'Okay,' I said, 'that's settled. Unanimous. My problem is that I decided to look you over and ask the most absolutely irresistibly beautiful and fascinating one of the bunch for her phone number, and I'm stalled. You are all it. In beauty and fascination you are all far beyond the wildest dreams of any poet, and I'm not a poet. So obviously I'm in a fix. How can I possibly pick on one of you, any one, when—'

'Nuts.' It was the redhead. 'Me, of course. Peggy Choate. Argyle two, three-three-four-eight. Don't call before noon.'

'That's not fair,' a throaty voice objected. It came from one who looked a little too old for Hebe, and just a shade too plump. It went on, 'Do I call you Archie?'

'Sure, that's my name.'

'All right, Archie, have your eyes examined.' She lifted an arm, baring it, to touch the shoulder of one beside her. 'We admit we're all beautiful, but we're not in the same class as Helen Iacono. Look at her!'

I was doing so, and I must say that the throaty voice had a point. Helen Iacono, with deep dark eyes, dark velvet skin, and wavy silky hair darker than either skin or eyes, was unquestionably rare and special. Her lips were parted enough to show the gleam of white teeth, but she wasn't laughing. She wasn't reacting at all, which was remarkable for an actress.

'It may be,' I conceded, 'that I am so dazzled by the collective radiance that I am blind to the glory of any single star. Perhaps I'm a poet after all, I sound like one. My feeling that I must have the phone numbers of *all* of you is certainly no reflection on Helen Iacono. I admit that that will not completely solve the problem, for tomorrow I must face the question which one to call first. If I feel as I do right now I would have to dial all the numbers simultaneously, and that's impossible. I hope to heaven it doesn't end in a stale-mate. What if I can never decide which one to call first? What if it drives me mad? Or what if I gradually sink—'

I turned to see who was tugging at my sleeve. It was Benjamin Schriver, the host, with a grin on his ruddy round face. He said, 'I hate to interrupt your speech, but perhaps you can finish it later. We're ready to sit. Will you join us?'

The dining room, on the same floor as the kitchen, three feet or so below street level, would have been too gloomy for my taste if most of the dark wood panelling hadn't been covered with pictures of geese, pheasants, fish, fruit, vegetables, and other assorted edible objects; and also it helped that the tablecloth was white as snow, the wineglasses seven of them at each place, glistened in the soft light from above, and the polished silver shone. In the centre was a low gilt bowl, or maybe gold, two feet long, filled with clusters of Phalaenopsis Aphrodite, donated by Wolfe, cut by him that afternoon from some of his most treasured plants.

As he sat he was scowling at them, but the scowl was not for the orchids; it was for the chair, which, though a little fancy, was perfectly okay for you or me but not for his seventh of a ton. His fundament lapped over at both sides. He erased the scowl when

Schriver, at the end of the table, complimented him on the flowers, and Hewitt, across from him, said he had never seen Phalaenopsis better grown, and the others joined in the chorus, all but the aristologist who sat between Wolfe and me. He was a Wall Street character and a well-known theatrical angel named Vincent Pyle, and was living up to his reputation as an original by wearing a dinner jacket, with tie to match, which looked black until you had the light at a certain slant and then you saw that it was green. He eyed the orchids with his head cocked and his mouth puckered, and said, 'I don't care for flowers with spots and streaks. They're messy.'

I thought, but didn't say, Okay, drop dead. If I had known that that was what he was going to do in about three hours I might not even have thought it. He got a rise, not from Wolfe and me, or Schriver or Hewitt, but from three others who thought flowers with spots and streaks were wonderful: Adrian Dart, the actor who had turned down an offer of a million a week, more or less, from Hollywood; Emil Kreis, Chairman of the Board of Codex Press, book publishers; and Harvey M. Leacraft, corporation lawyer.

Actually, cupbearers was what the Hebes were not. The wines, beginning with the Montrachet with the first course, were poured by Felix; but the girls delivered the food, with different routines for different items. The first course, put on individual plates in the kitchen, with each girl bringing in a plate for her aristologist, was small blinis sprinkled with chopped chives, piled with caviar, and topped with sour cream—the point, as far as Fritz was concerned, being that he had made the blinis, starting on them at eleven that morning, and also the sour cream, starting on that Sunday evening. Fritz's sour cream is very special, but Vincent Pyle had to get in a crack. After he had downed all his blinis he remarked loud enough to carry around the table, 'A new idea, putting sand in. Clever. Good for chickens, since they need grit.'

The man on my left, Emil Kreis, the publisher, muttered at my ear, 'Ignore him. He backed three flops this season.'

The girls, who had been coached by Fritz and Felix that afternoon, handled the green turtle soup without a splash. When they had brought in the soup plates Felix brought the bowl, and each girl ladled from it as Felix held it by the plate. I asked Pyle cordially, 'Any sand?' but he said no, it was delicious, and cleaned it up.

I was relieved when I saw that the girls wouldn't dish the fish—flounders poached in dry white wine, with a mussel-and-mushroom sauce that was one of Fritz's specialties. Felix did the dishing at a side table, and the girls merely carried. With the first taste of the sauce there were murmurs of appreciation, and Adrian Dart, the actor, across from Wolfe, sang out, 'Superb!' They were making various noises of satisfaction, and Leacraft, the lawyer, was asking Wolfe if Fritz would be willing to give him the recipe, when Pyle, on my right, made a face and dropped his fork on his plate with a clatter.

I thought he was putting on an act, and still thought so when his head drooped and I heard him gnash his teeth, but then his shoulders sagged and he clapped a hand to his mouth, and that seemed to be overdoing it. Two or three of them said something, and he pushed his chair back, got to his feet, said, 'You must excuse me, I'm sorry,' and headed for the door to the hall. Schriver arose and followed him out. The others exchanged words and glances.

Hewitt said, 'A damn shame, but I'm going to finish this,' and used his fork. Someone asked if Pyle had a bad heart, and someone else said no. They all resumed with the flounder and the conversation, but the spirit wasn't the same.

When, at a signal from Felix, the maidens started removing the plates, Lewis Hewitt got up and left the room, came back in a couple of minutes, sat, and raised his voice. 'Vincent is in considerable pain. There is nothing we can do, and Ben wishes us to proceed. He will rejoin us when—when he can.'

'What is it?' someone asked.

Hewitt said the doctor didn't know. Zoltan entered bearing an enormous covered platter, and the Hebes gathered at the side table, and Felix lifted the cover and began serving the roast pheasant, which had been larded with strips of pork soaked for twenty hours in Tokay, and then—but no. What's the use? The annual dinner of the Ten for Aristology was a flop. Since for years I have been eating three meals a day cooked by Fritz Brenner I would like to show my appreciation by getting in print some idea of what he can do in the way of victuals, but it won't do here. Sure, the pheasant was good enough for gods if there had been any around, and so was the suckling pig, and the salad, with a dressing which Fritz calls Devil's Rain, and the chestnut croquettes, and the cheese—only the one kind, made in New Jersey by a man named Bill Thompson under Fritz's supervision; and they were all eaten, more or less. But Hewitt left the room three more times and the last time was gone a good ten minutes, and Schriver didn't rejoin the party at all, and while the salad was being served Emil Kreis went out and didn't come back.

When, as coffee and brandy were being poured and cigars and cigarettes passed, Hewitt left his chair for the fifth time, Nero Wolfe got up and followed him out. I lit a cigar just to be doing something, and tried to be sociable by giving an ear to a story Adrian Dart was telling, but by the time I finished my coffee I was getting fidgety. By the glower that had been deepening on Wolfe's face for the past hour I knew he was boiling, and when he's like that, especially away from home, there's no telling about him. He might even have had the idea of aiming the glower at Vincent Pyle for ruining Fritz's meal. So I put what was left of the cigar in a tray, arose, and headed for the door, and was halfway to it when here he came, still glowering.

'Come with me,' he snapped, and kept going.

The way to the kitchen from the dining room was through a pantry, twenty feet long, with counters and shelves and cupboards on both sides. Wolfe marched through with me behind. In the kitchen the twelve maidens were scattered around on chairs and stools at tables and counters, eating. A woman was busy at a sink. Zoltan was busy at a refrigerator. Fritz, who was pouring a glass of wine, presumably for himself, turned as Wolfe entered and put the bottle down.

Wolfe went to him, stood, and spoke. 'Fritz. I offer my apologies. I permitted Mr Hewitt to cajole you. I should have known better. I beg your pardon.'

Fritz gestured with his free hand, the wineglass steady in the other. 'But it is not to pardon, only to regret. The man got sick, that's a pity, only not from my cooking. I assure you.'

'You don't need to. Not from your cooking as it left you, but as it reached him. I repeat that I am culpable, but I won't dwell on that now; it can wait. There is an aspect that is exigent.' Wolfe turned. 'Archie. Are those women all here?'

I had to cover more than half a circle to count them, scattered as they were. 'Yes, sir, all present. Twelve.'

'Collect them. They can stand'—he pointed to the alcove—'over there. And bring Felix.'

It was hard to believe. They were eating; and for him to interrupt a man, or even a woman, at a meal, was unheard of. Not even me. Only in an extreme emergency had he ever asked me to quit food before I was through. Boiling was no name for it. Without even bothering to raise a brow, I turned and called out, 'I'm sorry, ladies, but if Mr Wolfe says it's urgent that settles it. Over there, please? All of you.'

Then I went through the pantry corridor, pushed the two-way door, caught Felix's eye, and wiggled a beckoning finger at him, and he came. By the time we got to the kitchen the girls had left the chairs and stools and were gathering at the alcove, but not with enthusiasm. There were mutterings, and some dirty looks for me as I approached with Felix. Wolfe came, with Zoltan and stood, tight-lipped, surveying them.

'I remind you,' he said, 'that the first course you brought to the table was caviar on blinis topped with sour cream. The portion served to Mr Vincent Pyle, and eaten by him, contained arsenic. Mr Pyle is in bed upstairs, attended by three doctors, and will probably die within an hour. I am speaking—'

He stopped to glare at them. They were reacting, or acting, no matter which. There were gasps and exclamations, and one of them clutched her throat, and another, baring her arms, clapped her palms to her ears. When the glare had restored order Wolfe went on, 'You will please keep quiet and listen. I am speaking of conclusions formed by me. My conclusion that Mr Pyle ate arsenic is based on the symptoms—burning throat, faintness, intense burning pain in the stomach, dry mouth, cool skin, vomiting. My conclusion that the arsenic was in the first course is based, first, on the amount of time it takes arsenic to act; second, on the fact that it is highly unlikely it could have been put in the soup or the fish; and third, that Mr Pyle complained of sand in the cream or caviar. I admit the possibility that one or both of my conclusions will be proven wrong, but I regard it as remote and I am acting on them.' His head turned. 'Fritz. Tell me about the caviar from the moment it was put on the individual plates. Who did that?'

I had once told Fritz that I could imagine no circumstances in which he would look really unhappy, but now I wouldn't have to try. He was biting his lips, first the lower and then the upper. He began, 'I must assure you—'

'I need no assurance from you, Fritz. Who put it on the plates?'

'Zoltan and I did.' He pointed. 'At that table.'

'And left them there? They were taken from that table by the women?'

'Yes, sir.'

'Each woman took one plate?'

'Yes, sir. I mean, they were told to. I was at the range.'

Zoltan spoke up. 'I watched them, Mr Wolfe. They each took one plate. And believe me, nobody put any arsenic—'

'Please, Zoltan. I add another conclusion: that no one put arsenic in one of the portions and then left to chance which one of the guests would get it. Surely the poisoner intended it to reach a certain one—either Mr Pyle, or, as an alternative, some other one and it went to Mr Pyle by mishap. In any case, it was the portion Pyle ate that was poisoned, and whether he got it by design or by mischance is for the moment irrelevant.' His eyes were at the girls. 'Which one of you took that plate to Mr Pyle?'

No reply. No sound, no movement.

Wolfe grunted. 'Pfui. If you didn't know his name, you do now.

The man who left during the fish course and who is now dying. Who served him?'

No reply; and I had to hand it to them that no pair of eyes left Wolfe to fasten on Peggy Choate, the redhead. Mine did. 'What the heck,' I said. 'Speak up, Miss Choate.'

'I didn't!' she cried.

'That's silly. Of course you did. Twenty people can swear to it. I looked right at you while you were dishing his soup. And when you brought the fish—'

'But I didn't take him that first thing! He already had some!'

Wolfe took over. 'Your name is Choate?'

'Yes.' Her chin was up. 'Peggy Choate.'

'You deny that you served the plate of caviar, the first course, to Mr Pyle?'

'I certainly do.'

'But you were supposed to? You were assigned to him?'

'Yes. I took the plate from the table there and went in with it, and started to him, and then I saw that he had some, and I thought I had made a mistake. We hadn't seen the guests. That man'—she pointed to Felix—'had shown us which chair our guest would sit in, and mine was the second from the right on this side as I went in, but that one had already been served, and I thought someone else had made a mistake or I was mixed up. Anyway, I saw that the man next to him, on his right, hadn't been served, and I gave it to him. That was you. I gave it to you.'

'Indeed.' Wolfe was frowning at her. 'Who was assigned to me?'

That wasn't put on. He actually didn't know. He had never looked at her. He had been irritated that females were serving, and besides, he hates to twist his neck. Of course I could have told him, but Helen Iacono said, 'I was.'

'Your name, please?'

'Helen Iacono.' She had a rich contralto that went fine with the deep dark eyes and dark velvet skin and wavy silk hair.

'Did you bring me the first course?'

'No. When I went in I saw Peggy serving you, and a man on the left next to the end didn't have any, so I gave it to him.'

'Do you know his name?'

'I do,' Nora Jaret said. 'From the card. He was mine.' Her big brown eyes were straight at Wolfe. 'His name is Kreis. He had his when I got there. I was going to take it back to the kitchen, but then I thought, someone had stage fright but I haven't, and I gave it to the man at the end.'

'Which end?'

'The left end. Mr Schriver. He came and spoke to us this afternoon.'

She was corroborated by Carol Annis, the one with hair like corn silk who had no sense of humour. 'That's right,' she said. 'I saw her. I was going to stop her, but she had already put the plate down, so I went around to the other side of the table with it when I saw that Adrian Dart didn't have any. I didn't mind because it was him.'

'You were assigned to Mr Schriver?'

'Yes. I served him the other courses, until he left.'

It was turning into a ring-around-a-rosy, but the squat was bound to come. All Wolfe had to do was get to one who couldn't claim a delivery, and that would tag her. I was rather hoping it wouldn't be the next one, for the girl with the throaty voice had been Adrian Dart's, and she had called me Archie and had given Helen Iacono a nice tribute. Would she claim she had served Dart herself?

No. She answered without being asked. 'My name is Lucy Morgan,' she said, 'and I had Adrian Dart, and Carol got to him before I did. There was only one place that didn't have one, on Dart's left, the next but one, and I took it there. I don't know his name.'

I supplied it. 'Hewitt. Mr Lewis Hewitt.' A better name for it than ring-around-a-rosy would have been passing-the-buck. I looked at Fern Faber, the tall blonde with a wide lazy mouth who had been my first stop on my phone-number tour. 'It's your turn, Miss Faber,' I told her. 'You had Mr Hewitt. Yes?'

'I sure did.' Her voice was pitched so high it threatened to squeak.

'But you didn't take him his caviar?'

'I sure didn't.'

'Then who did you take it to?'

'Nobody.'

I looked at Wolfe. His eyes were narrowed at her. 'What did you do with it, Miss Faber?'

'I didn't do anything with it. There wasn't any.'

'Nonsense. There are twelve of you, and there were twelve at the table, and each got a portion. How can you say there wasn't any?'

'Because there wasn't. I was in the john fixing my hair, and when I came back in she was taking the last one from the table, and when I asked where mine was he said he didn't know, and I went to the dining room and they all had some.'

'Who was taking the last one from the table?'

She pointed to Lucy Morgan.

'Whom did you ask where yours was?'

She pointed to Zoltan. 'Him.'

Wolfe turned. 'Zoltan?'

'Yes, sir. I mean, yes, sir, she asked where hers was. I had turned away when the last one was taken. I don't mean I know where she had been, just that she asked me that. I asked Fritz if I should go in and see if they were one short and he said no, Felix was there and would see to it.'

Wolfe went back to Fern Faber. 'Where is that room where you were fixing your hair?'

She pointed toward the pantry. 'In there.'

'The door's around the corner,' Felix said.

'How long were you in there?'

'My God, I don't know, do you think I timed it? When Archie Goodwin was talking to us, and Mr Schriver came and said they were going to start, I went pretty soon after that.'

Wolfe's head jerked to me. 'So that's where you were. I might have known there were young women around. Supposing that Miss Faber went to fix her hair shortly after you left—say three minutes—how long was she at it, if the last plate had been taken from the table when she returned to the kitchen?'

I gave it a thought. 'Fifteen to twenty minutes.'

He growled at her, 'What was wrong with your hair?'

'I didn't say anything was wrong with it.' She was getting riled. 'Look, Mister, do you want all the details?'

'No.' Wolfe surveyed them for a moment, not amiably, took in enough air to fill all his middle—say two bushels—let it out again, turned his back on them, saw the glass of wine Fritz had left on a table, went and picked it up, smelled it, and stood to make noises, and, hearing them, he put the glass down and came back.

'You're in a pickle,' he said. 'So am I. You heard me apologise to Mr Brenner and avow my responsibility for his undertaking to cook that meal. When, upstairs, I saw that Mr Pyle would die, and reached the conclusions I told you of, I felt myself under compulsion to expose the culprit. I am committed. When I came down here I thought it would be a simple matter to learn who had served poisoned food to Mr Pyle, but I was wrong.

'It's obvious now that I have to deal with one who is not only resourceful and ingenious, but also quick-witted and audacious. While I was closing in on her just now, as I thought, inexorably approaching the point where she would either have to contradict one of you or deny that she had served the first course to anyone, she was fleering at me inwardly, and with reason, for her coup had worked. She had slipped through my fingers, and—'

'But she didn't!' It came from one of them whose name I didn't have. 'She said she didn't serve anybody!'

Wolfe shook his head. 'No. Not Miss Faber. She is the only one who is eliminated. She says she was absent from this room during the entire period when the plates were being taken from the table, and she wouldn't dare to say that if she had in fact been here and taken a plate and carried it in to Mr Pyle. She would certainly have been seen by some of you.'

He shook his head again. 'Not her. But it could have been any other one of you. You—I speak now to that one, still to be identified—you must have extraordinary faith in your attendant godling, even allowing for your craft. For you took great risks. You took a plate from the table—not the first probably, but one of the first—and on your way to the dining room you put arsenic in the cream. That wasn't difficult; you might even have done it without stopping if you had the arsenic in a paper spill. You could get rid of the spill later, perhaps in the room which Miss Faber calls a john. You took the plate to Mr Pyle, came back here immediately, got another plate, took it to the dining room, and gave it to one who had not been served. I am not guessing; it had to be like that. It was a remarkably adroit stratagem, but you can't possibly be impregnable.'

He turned to Zoltan. 'You say you watched as the plates were taken, and each of them took only one. Did one of them come back and take another?'

Zoltan looked fully as unhappy as Fritz. 'I'm thinking, Mr Wolfe. I can try to think, but I'm afraid it won't help. I didn't look at their faces, and they're all dressed alike. I guess I didn't watch very close.'

'Fritz?'

'No, sir. I was at the range.'

'Then try this, Zoltan. Who were the first ones to take plates—the first three or four?'

Zoltan slowly shook his head. 'I'm afraid it's no good, Mr Wolfe. I could try to think, but I couldn't be sure.' He moved his eyes right to left and back again, at the girls. 'I tell you, I wasn't looking at their faces.' He extended his hands, palms up. 'You will consider, Mr Wolfe, I was not thinking of poison. I was only seeing that the plates were carried properly. Was I thinking which one has got arsenic? No.'

'I took the first plate,' a girl blurted—another whose name I didn't know. 'I took it in and gave it to the man in my chair, the one at the left corner at the other side of the table, and I stayed there. I never left the dining room.'

'Your name, please?'

'Marjorie Quinn.'

'Thank you. Now the second plate. Who took it?'

Apparently nobody. Wolfe gave them ten seconds, his eyes moving to take them all in, his lips tight. 'I advise you,' he said, 'to jog your memories, in case it becomes necessary to establish the order in which you took the plates by dragging it out of you. I hope it won't come to that.' His head turned. 'Felix, I have neglected you purposely, to give you time to reflect. You were in the dining room. My expectation was that after I had learned who had served the first course to Mr Pyle you would corroborate it, but now that there is nothing for you to corroborate I must look to you for the fact itself. I must ask you to point her out.'

In a way Wolfe was Felix's boss. When Wolfe's oldest and dearest friend, Marko Vukcic, who had owned Rusterman's restaurant, had died, his will had left the restaurant to members of the staff in trust, with Wolfe as the trustee, and Felix was the *maître d'hôtel*. With that job at the best restaurant in New York, naturally Felix was both bland and commanding, but now he was neither. If he felt the way he looked, he was miserable.

'I can't,' he said.

'Pfui! You, trained as you are to see everything?'

'That is true, Mr Wolfe. I knew you would ask me this, but I can't. I can only explain. The young woman who just spoke, Marjorie Quinn, was the first one in with a plate, as she said. She did not say that as she served it one of the blinis slid off onto the table, but it did. As I sprang toward her she was actually about to pick it up with her fingers, and I jerked her away and put it back on the plate with a fork, and I gave her a look. Anyway, I was not myself. Having women as waiters was bad enough, and not only that, they were without experience. When I recovered command of myself I saw the red-headed one, Choate, standing back of Mr Pyle, to whom she had been assigned, with a plate in her hand, and I saw that he had already been served. As I moved forward she stepped to the right and served the plate to you. The operation was completely upset, and I was helpless. The dark-skinned one, Iacono, who was assigned to you, served Mr Kreis, and the—'

'If you please.' Wolfe was curt. 'I have heard them, and so have you. I have always found you worthy of trust, but it's possible that in your exalted position, *maître d'hôtel* at Rusterman's, you would rather dodge than get involved in a poisoning. Are you dodging, Felix?'

'Good God, Mr Wolfe, I *am* involved!'

'Very well. I saw that woman spill the blini and start her fingers for it, and I saw you retrieve it. Yes, you're involved, but not as I am.' He turned to me. 'Archie. You are commonly my first resort, but now you are my last. You sat next to Mr Pyle. Who put that plate before him?'

Of course I knew that was coming, but I hadn't been beating my brain because there was no use. I said merely but positively, 'No.' He glared at me and I added, 'That's all, just no, but like Felix I can explain. First, I would have had to turn around to see her face, and that's bad table manners. Second, I was watching Felix rescue the blini. Third, there was an argument going on about flowers with spots and streaks, and I was listening to it and so were you. I didn't even see her arm.'

Wolfe stood and breathed. He shut his eyes and opened them again, and breathed some more. 'Incredible,' he muttered. 'The wretch had incredible luck.'

'I'm going home,' Fern Faber said. 'I'm tired.'

'So am I,' another one said, and was moving, but Wolfe's eyes pinned her. 'I advise you not to,' he said. 'It is true that Miss Faber is eliminated as the culprit, and also Miss Quinn, since she was under surveillance by Felix while Mr Pyle was being served, but I advise even them to stay. When Mr Pyle dies the doctors will certainly summon the police, and it would be well for all of you to be here when they arrive. I had hoped to be able to present them with an exposed murderer. Confound it! There is still a chance. Archie, come with me. Fritz, Felix, Zoltan, remain with these women. If one or more of them insist on leaving do not detain them by force, but have the names and the times of departure. If they want to eat, feed them. I'll be—'

'I'm going home,' Fern Faber said stubbornly.

'Very well, go. You'll be got out of bed by a policeman before the night's out. I'll be in the dining room, Fritz. Come, Archie.'

He went and I followed, along the pantry corridor and through the two-way door. On the way I glanced at my wrist watch: ten past eleven. I rather expected to find the dining room empty, but it wasn't. Eight of them were still there, the only ones missing being Schriver and Hewitt, who were probably upstairs. The air was heavy with cigar smoke. All of them but Adrian Dart were at the table with their chairs pushed back at various angles, with brandy glasses and cigars. Dart was standing with his back to a picture of honkers on the wing, holding forth. As we entered he stopped and heads turned.

Emil Kreis spoke. 'Oh, there you are. I was coming to the kitchen but didn't want to butt in. Schriver asked me to apologise to Fritz Brenner. Our custom is to ask the chef to join us with champagne,

which is barbarous but gay, but of course in the circumstances . . .'
He let it hang, and added, 'Shall I explain to him? Or will you?'

'I will.' Wolfe went to the end of the table and sat. He had been on his feet for nearly two hours—all very well for his twice-a-day sessions in the plant rooms, but not elsewhere. He looked around. 'Mr Pyle is still alive?'

'We hope so,' one said. 'We sincerely hope so.'

'I ought to be home in bed,' another one said. 'I have a hard day tomorrow. But it doesn't seem . . .' He took a puff on his cigar.

Emil Kreis reached for the brandy bottle. 'There's been no word since I came down.' He looked at his wrist. 'Nearly an hour ago. I suppose I should go up. It's so damned unpleasant.' He poured brandy.

'Terrible,' one said. 'Absolutely terrible. I understand you were asking which one of the girls brought him the caviar. Kreis says you asked him.'

Wolfe nodded. 'I also asked Mr Schriver and Mr Hewitt. And Mr Goodwin and Mr Brenner, and the two men who came to help at my request. And the women themselves. After more than an hour with them I am still at fault. I have discovered the artifice the culprit used, but not her identity.'

'Aren't you a bit premature?' Leacraft, the lawyer, asked. 'There may be no culprit. An acute and severe gastric disturbance may be caused—'

'Nonsense. I am too provoked for civilty, Mr Leacraft. The symptoms are typical of arsenic, and you heard Mr Pyle complain of sand, but that's not all. I said I have discovered the artifice. None of them will admit serving him the first course. The one assigned to him found he had already been served and served me instead. There is indeed a culprit. She put arsenic in the cream *en passant*, served it to Mr Pyle, returned to the kitchen for another portion, and came and served it to someone else. That is established.'

'But then,' the lawyer objected, 'one of them served no one. How could that be?'

'I am not a tyro at inquiry, Mr Leacraft. I'll ravel it for you later if you want, but now I want to get on. It is no conjecture that poison was given to Mr Pyle by the woman who brought him the caviar; it is a fact. By a remarkable combination of cunning and luck she has so far eluded identification, and I am appealing to you. All of you. I ask you to close your eyes and recall the scene. We are here at table, discussing the orchids—the spots and streaks. The woman serving that place'—he pointed—'lets a blini slip from the plate and Felix retrieves it. It helps to close your eyes. Just about then a woman enters with a plate, goes to Mr Pyle, and puts it before him. I appeal to you: which one?'

Emil Kreis shook his head. 'I told you upstairs, I don't know. I didn't see her. Or if I did, it didn't register.'

Adrian Dart, the actor, stood with his eyes closed, his chin up, and his arms folded, a fine pose for concentration. The others, even Leacraft, had their eyes closed too, but of course they couldn't hold a candle to Dart. After a long moment the eyes began to open and heads to shake.

'It's gone,' Dart said in his rich musical baritone. 'I must have seen it, since I sat across from him, but it's gone. Utterly.'

'I didn't see it,' another said. 'I simply didn't see it.'

'I have a vague feeling,' another said, 'but it's too damn vague. No.'

They made it unanimous.

Wolfe put his palms on the table. 'Then I'm in for it,' he said grimly. 'I am your guest, gentlemen, and would not be offensive, but I am to blame that Fritz Brenner was enticed to this deplorable fiasco. If Mr Pyle dies, as he surely will—'

The door opened and Benjamin Schriver entered. Then Lewis Hewitt, and then the familiar burly frame of Sergeant Purley Stebbins of Manhattan Homicide West.

Schriver crossed to the table and spoke. 'Vincent is dead. Half an hour ago. Doctor Jameson called the police. He thinks that it is practically certain—'

'Hold it,' Purley growled at his elbow. 'I'll handle it if you don't mind.'

'My God,' Adrian Dart groaned, and shuddered magnificently.

That was the last I heard of the affair from an aristologist.

'I did not!' Inspector Cramer roared. 'Quit twisting my words around! I didn't charge you with complicity! I merely said you're concealing something, and what the hell is that to scrape your neck? You always do!'

It was a quarter to two Wednesday afternoon. We were in the office on the first floor of the old brownstone on West 35th Street— Wolfe in his oversized chair. The daily schedule was messed beyond repair. When we had finally got home, at five o'clock in the morning, Wolfe had told Fritz to forget about breakfast until further notice, and had sent me up to the plant rooms to leave a note for Theodore saying that he would not appear at nine in the morning and perhaps not at all. It had been not at all. At half-past eleven he had buzzed on the house phone to tell Fritz to bring up the breakfast tray with four eggs and ten slices of bacon instead of two and five, and it was past one o'clock when the sounds came of his elevator and then his footsteps in the hall, heading for the office.

If you think a problem child is rough, try handling a problem elephant. He is plenty knotty even when he is himself, and that day he was really special. After looking through the mail, glancing at his desk calendar, and signing three cheques I had put on his desk, he snapped at me, 'A fine prospect. Dealing with them singly would be interminable. Will you have them all here at six o'clock?'

I kept calm. I merely asked, 'All of whom?'

'You know quite well. Those women.'

I still kept calm. 'I should think ten of them would be enough. You said yourself that two of them can be crossed off.'

'I need them all. Those two can help establish the order in which the plates were taken.'

I held on. I too was short on sleep, shorter even than he, and I didn't feel up to a fracas. 'I have a suggestion,' I said. 'I suggest that you postpone operations until your wires are connected again. Counting up to five hundred might help. You know damn well that all twelve of them will spend the afternoon either at the District Attorney's office or receiving official callers at their homes—probably most of them at the DA's office. And probably they'll spend the evening there too. Do you want some aspirin?'

'I want *them*,' he growled.

I could have left him to grope back to normal on his own and gone up to my room for a nap, but after all he pays my salary. So I picked up a sheet of paper I had typed and got up and handed it to him. It read:

	Assigned to	Served
Peggy Choate	Pyle	Wolfe
Helen Iacono	Wolfe	Kreis
Nora Jaret	Kreis	Schriver
Carol Annis	Schriver	Dart
Lucy Morgan	Dart	Hewitt
Fern Faber	Hewitt	No one

'Fern Faber's out,' I said, 'and I realise it doesn't have to be one of those five, even though Lucy Morgan took the last plate. Possibly one or two others took plates after Peggy Choate did, and served the men they were assigned to. But it seems—'

I stopped because he had crumpled it and dropped it in the wastebasket. 'I heard them,' he growled. 'My faculties, including my memory, are not impaired. I am merely ruffled beyond the bounds of tolerance.'

For him that was an abject apology, and a sign that he was beginning to regain control. But a few minutes later, when the bell rang, and after a look through the one-way glass panel of the front door I told him it was Cramer, and he said to admit him, and Cramer marched in and planted his fanny on the red leather chair and opened up with an impolite remark about concealing facts connected with a murder, Wolfe had cut loose; and Cramer asked him what the hell was that to scrape his neck, which was a new one to me but sounded somewhat vulgar for an Inspector. He had probably picked it up from some hoodlum.

Ruffling Cramer beyond the bounds of tolerance did Wolfe good. He leaned back in his chair. 'Everyone conceals something,' he said placidly. 'Or at least omits something, if only because to include everything is impossible. During those wearisome hours, nearly six of them, I answered all questions, and so did Mr Goodwin. Indeed, I thought we were helpful. I thought we had cleared away some rubble.'

'Yeah.' Cramer wasn't grateful. His big pink face was always a little pinker than normal, not with pleasure, when he was tackling Wolfe. 'You had witnessed the commission of a murder, and you didn't notify—'

'It wasn't a murder until he died.'

'All right, a felony. You not only failed to report it, you—'

'That a felony had been committed was my conclusion. Others present disagreed with me. Only a few minutes before Mr Stebbins entered the room, Mr Leacraft, a member of the bar and therefore himself an officer of the law, challenged my conclusion.'

'You should have reported it. You're a licensed detective. Also you started an investigation, questioning the suspects—'

'Only to test my conclusion. I would have been a ninny to report it before learning—'

'Damn it,' Cramer barked, 'will you let me finish a sentence? Just one?'

Wolfe's shoulders went up an eight of an inch and down again. 'Certainly if it has import. I am not baiting you, Mr Cramer. But I have already replied to these imputations, to you and Mr Stebbins and an Assistant District Attorney. I did not wrongly delay reporting a crime, and I did not usurp the function of the police. Very well, finish a sentence.'

'You knew Pyle was dying. You said so.'

'Also my own conclusion. The doctors were trying to save him.'

Cramer took a breath. He looked at me, saw nothing inspiring, and returned to Wolfe. 'I'll tell you why I'm here. Those three men—the cook, the man that helped him, and the man in the dining room—Fritz Brenner, Felix Courbet, and Zoltan Mahany—were all supplied by you. All close to you. I want to know about them, or at least two of them. I might as well leave Fritz out of it. In the first place, it's hard to believe that Zoltan doesn't know who took the first two or three plates or whether one of them came back for a second one, and it's also hard to believe that Felix doesn't know who served Pyle.'

'It is indeed,' Wolfe agreed. 'They are highly trained men. But they have been questioned.'

'They sure have. It's also hard to believe that Goodwin didn't see who served Pyle. He sees everything.'

'Mr Goodwin is present. Discuss it with him.'

'I have. Now I want to ask your opinion of a theory. I know yours, and I don't reject it, but there are alternatives. First, a fact. In a metal trash container in the kitchen—not a garbage pail—we found a small roll of paper, ordinary white paper that had been rolled into a tube, held with tape, smaller at one end. The laboratory has found particles of arsenic inside. The only two fingerprints on it that are any good are Zoltan's. He says he saw it on the kitchen floor under a table some time after the meal had started, he can't say exactly when, and he picked it up and dropped it in the container, and his prints are on it because he pinched it to see if there was anything in it.'

Wolfe nodded. 'As I surmised. A paper spill.'

'Yeah. I don't say it kills your theory. She could have shaken it into the cream without leaving prints, and she certainly wouldn't have dropped it on the floor if there was any chance it had her prints. But it *has* got Zoltan's. What's wrong with the theory that Zoltan poisoned one of the portions and saw that it was taken by a certain one? I'll answer that myself. There are two things wrong with it. First, Zoltan claims he didn't know which guest any of the girls were assigned to. But Felix knew, and they could have been in collusion. Second, the girls all deny that Zoltan indicated which plate they were to take, but you know how that is. He could have done it without her knowing it. What else is wrong with it?'

'It's not only untenable, it's egregious,' Wolfe declared. 'Why, in that case, did one of them come back for another plate?'

'She was confused. Nervous. Dumb.'

'Bosh. Why doesn't she admit it?'

'Scared.'

'I don't believe it. I questioned them before you did.' Wolfe waved it away. 'Tommyrot, and you know it. My theory is not a theory; it is a reasoned conviction. I hope it is being acted on. I suggested to Mr Stebbins that he examine their garments to see if some kind of pocket had been made in one of them. She had to have it readily available.'

'He did. They all had pockets. The laboratory has found no trace of arsenic.' Cramer uncrossed his legs. 'But I wanted to ask you about those men. You know them.'

'I do, yes. But I do not answer for them. They may have a dozen murders on their souls, but they had nothing to do with the death of Mr Pyle. If you are following up my theory—my conviction, rather—I suppose you have learned the order in which the women took the plates.'

Cramer shook his head. 'We have not, and I doubt if we will. All we have is a bunch of contradictions. You had them good and scared before we got to them. We do have the last five, starting with Peggy Choate, who found that Pyle had been served and gave it to you, and then—but you got that yourself.'

'No. I got those five, but not that they were the last. There might have been others in between.'

'There weren't. It's pretty well settled that these five were the last. After Peggy Choate the last four plates were taken by Helen Iacono, Nora Jaret, Carol Annis, and Lucy Morgan. Then that Fern Faber, who had been in the can, but there was no plate for her. It's the order in which they took them before that, the first seven, that we can't pry out of them—except the first one, that Marjorie Quinn. You couldn't either.'

Wolfe turned a palm up. 'I was interrupted.'

'You were not. You left them there in a huddle, scared stiff, and went to the dining room to start in on the men. Your own private murder investigation, and to hell with the law. I was surprised to see Goodwin here when I rang the bell just now. I supposed you'd have him out running errands like calling at the agency they got the girls from. Or getting a line on Pyle to find a connection between him and one of them. Unless you're no longer interested?'

'I'm interested willy-nilly,' Wolfe declared. 'As I told the Assistant District Attorney, it is on my score that a man was poisoned in food prepared by Fritz Brenner. But I do not send Mr Goodwin on fruitless errands. He is one and you have dozens, and if anything is to be learned at the agency or by inquiry into Mr Pyle's associations your army will dig it up. They're already at it, of course, but if they had started a trail you wouldn't be here. If I send Mr Goodwin—'

The doorbell rang and I got up and went to the hall. At the rear the door to the kitchen swung open part way and Fritz poked his head through, saw me, and withdrew. Turning to the front for a look through the panel, I saw that I had exaggerated when I told Wolfe that all twelve of them would be otherwise engaged. At least one wasn't. There on the stoop was Helen Iacono.

It had sounded to me as if Cramer had about said his say and would soon be moving along, and if he bumped into Helen Iacono in the hall she might be too embarrassed to give me her phone number, if that was what she had come for; so as I opened the door I pressed a finger to my lips and *sshh*ed at her, and then crooked the finger to motion her in. Her deep dark eyes looked a little startled, but she stepped across the sill, and I shut the door, turned, opened the first door on the left, to the front room, motioned to her to enter, followed, and closed the door.

'What's the matter?' she whispered.

'Nothing now,' I told her. 'This is soundproofed. There's a police inspector in the office with Mr Wolfe and I thought you might have had enough of cops for now. But if you want to meet him—'

'I don't. I want to see Nero Wolfe.'

'Okay, I'll tell him as soon as the cop goes. Have a seat. It shouldn't be long.'

There is a connecting door between the front room and the office, but I went around through the hall, and here came Cramer. He was marching by without even the courtesy of a grunt, but I stepped to the front to let him out, and then went to the office and told Wolfe, 'I've got one of them in the front room. Helen Iacono, the tawny-skinned Hebe who had you but gave her caviar to Kreis. Shall I keep her while I get the rest of them?'

He made a face. 'What does she want?'

'To see you.'

He took a breath. 'Confound it. Bring her in.'

I went and opened the connecting door, told her to come, and escorted her across to the red leather chair. She was more ornamental in it than Cramer, but not nearly as impressive as she had been at first sight. She was puffy around the eyes and her skin had lost some glow. She told Wolfe she hadn't had any sleep. She said she had just left the District Attorney's office, and if she went home her mother would be at her again, and her brothers and sister would come home from school and make noise, and anyway she had decided she had to see Wolfe. Her mother was old-fashioned and didn't want her to be an actress. It was beginning to sound as if what she was after was a place to take a nap, but then Wolfe got a word in.

He said drily, 'I didn't suppose, Miss Iacono, you came to consult me about your career.'

'Oh, no. I came because you're a detective and you're very clever and I'm afraid. I'm afraid they'll find out something I did, and if they do I won't have any career. My parents won't let me even if I'm still alive. I nearly gave it away already when they were asking

me questions. So I decided to tell you about it and then if you'd
help me I'll help you. If you promise to keep my secret.'

'I can't promise to keep a secret if it is a guilty one—if it is a
confession of a crime or knowledge of one.'

'It isn't.'

'Then you have my promise, and Mr Goodwin's. We have kept
many secrets.'

'All right. I stabbed Vincent Pyle with a knife and got blood on
me.'

I stared. For half a second I thought she meant that he hadn't
died of poison at all, that she had sneaked upstairs and stuck a
knife in him, which seemed unlikely since the doctors would
probably have found the hole.

Apparently she wasn't going on, and Wolfe spoke. 'Ordinarily,
Miss Iacono, stabbing a man is considered a crime. When and
where did this happen?'

'It wasn't a crime because it was in self-defence.' Her rich
contralto was as composed as if she had been telling us the
multiplication table. Evidently she saved the inflections for her
career. She was continuing. 'It happened in January, about three
months ago. Of course I knew about him—everybody in show
business does. I don't know if it's true that he backs shows just so
he can get girls, but it might as well be. There's a lot of talk about
the girls he gets, but nobody really knows because he was always
very careful about it. Some of the girls have talked but he never did.
I don't mean just taking them out, I mean the last ditch. We say that
on Broadway. You know what I mean?'

'I can surmise.'

'Sometimes we say the last stitch, but it means the same thing.
Early last winter he began on me. Of course I knew about his
reputation, but he was backing *Jack in the Pulpit* and they were
about to start casting, and I didn't know it was going to be a flop,
and if a girl expects to have a career she has to be sociable. I went
out with him a few times, dinner and dancing and so forth, and
then he asked me to his apartment, and I went. He cooked the
dinner himself—I said he was very careful. Didn't I?'

'Yes.'

'Well, he was. It's a penthouse on Madison Avenue, but no one
else was there. I let him kiss me. I figured it like this, an actress gets
kissed all the time on the stage and the screen and TV, and what's
the difference? I went to his apartment three times and there was
no real trouble, but the fourth time—that was in January—he
turned into a beast right before my eyes, and I had to do something, and I grabbed a knife from the table and stabbed him with it.

I got blood on my dress, and when I got home I tried to get it out but it left a stain. it cost forty-six dollars.'

'But Mr Pyle recovered.'

'Oh, yes. I saw him a few times after that, I mean just by accident, but he barely spoke and so did I. I don't think he ever told anyone about it, but what if he did? What if the police find out about?'

Wolfe grunted. 'That would be regrettable, certainly. You would be pestered even more than you were now. But if you have been candid with me you are not in mortal jeopardy. The police are not simpletons. You wouldn't be arrested for murdering Mr Pyle last night, let alone convicted, merely because you stabbed him in self-defence last January.'

'Of course I wouldn't,' she agreed. 'That's not it. It's my mother and father. They'd find out about it because they would ask them questions, and if I'm going to have a career I would have to leave home and my family, and I don't want to. Don't you see?' She came forward in the chair. 'But if they find out right away who did it, who poisoned him, that would end it and I'd be all right. Only I'm afraid they won't find out right away, but I think you could if I help you, and you said last night that you're committed. I can't offer to help the police because they'd wonder why.'

'I see.' Wolfe's eyes were narrowed at her. 'How do you propose to help me?'

'Well, I figure it like this.' She was on the edge of the chair. 'The way you explained it last night, one of the girls poisoned him. She was one of the first ones to take a plate in, and then she came back and got another one. I don't quite understand why she did that, but you do, so all right. But if she came back for another plate that took a little time, and she must have been one of the last ones, and the police have got it worked out who were the last five. I know that because of the questions they asked this last time. So it was Peggy Choate or Nora Jaret or Carol Annis or Lucy Morgan.'

'Or you.'

'No, it wasn't me.' Just matter-of-fact. 'So it was one of them. And she didn't poison him just for nothing, did she? You'd have to have a very good reason to poison a man, I know I would. So all we have to do is find out which one had a good reason, and that's where I can help. I don't know Lucy Morgan, but I know Carol a little, and I know Nora and Peggy even better. And now we're in this together, and I can pretend to them I want to talk about it. I can talk about him because I had to tell the police I went out with him a few times, because I was seen with him and they'd find out, so I thought I'd better tell them. Dozens of girls went out with him, but he was so careful that nobody knows which ones went to the last ditch except the ones that talked. And I can find out which one of those four girls had a reason, and tell you, and that will end it.'

I was congratulating myself that I hadn't got her phone number; and if I had got it, I would have crossed it off without a pang. I don't say that a girl must have true nobility of character before I'll buy her a lunch, but you have to draw the line somewhere. Thinking that Wolfe might be disgusted enough to put into words the way I felt, I horned in. 'I have a suggestion, Miss Iacono. You could bring them here, all four of them, and let Mr Wolfe talk it over with them. As you say, he's very clever.'

She looked doubtful. 'I don't believe that's a good idea. I think they'd be more apt to say things to me, just one at a time. Don't you think so, Mr Wolfe?'

'You know them better than I do,' he muttered. He was controlling himself.

'And then,' she said, 'when we find out which one had a reason, and we tell the police, I can say that I saw her going back to the kitchen for another plate. Of course just where I saw her, where she was and where I was, that will depend on who she is. I saw you, Mr Wolfe, when I said you could if I helped you, I saw the look on your face. You didn't think a twenty-year-old girl could help, did you?'

He had my sympathy. Of course what he would have liked to say was that it might well be that a twenty-year-old hellcat could help, but that wouldn't have been tactful.

'I may have been a little sceptical,' he conceded. 'And it's possible that you're oversimplifying the problem. We have to consider all the factors. Take one: her plan must have been not only premeditated but also thoroughly rigged, since she had the poison ready. So she must have known that Mr Pyle would be one of the guests. Did she?'

'Oh, yes. We all did. Mr Buchman at the agency showed us a list of them and told us who they were, only of course he didn't have to tell us who Vincent Pyle was. That was about a month ago, so she had plenty of time to get the poison. Is arsenic very hard to get?'

'Not at all. It is in common use for many purposes. That is of course one of the police lines of inquiry, but she knew it would be and she is no bungler. Another point: when Mr Pyle saw her there, serving food, wouldn't he have been on his guard?'

'But he didn't see her. They didn't see any of us before. She came up behind him and gave him that plate. Of course he saw her afterwards, but he had already eaten it.'

Wolfe persisted. 'But then? He was in agony, but he was

conscious and could speak. Why didn't he denounce her?'

She gestured impatiently. 'I guess you're not as clever as you're supposed to be. He didn't know she had done it. When he saw her she was serving another man, and—'

'What other man?'

'How do I know? Only it wasn't you, because I served you. And anyway, maybe he didn't know she wanted to kill him. Of course she had a good reason, I know that, but maybe he didn't know she felt like that. A man doesn't know how a girl feels—anyhow, some girls. Look at me. He didn't know I would never dream of going to the last ditch. He thought I would give up my honour and my virtue just to get a part in that play he was backing, and anyhow it was a flop.' She gestured again. 'I thought you wanted to get her. All you do is make objections.'

Wolfe rubbed the side of his nose. 'I do want to get her, Miss Iacono. I intend to. But like Mr Pyle, though from a different motive, I am very careful. I can't afford to botch it. I fully appreciate your offer to help. You didn't like Mr Goodwin's suggestion that you get them here in a body for discussion with me, and you may be right. But I don't like your plan, for you to approach them singly and try to pump them. Our quarry is a malign and crafty harpy, and I will not be a party to your peril. I propose an alternative. Arrange for Mr Goodwin to see them, together with you. Being a trained investigator, he knows how to beguile, and the peril, if any, will be his. If they are not available at the moment, arrange it for this evening—but not here. Perhaps one of them has a suitable apartment, or if not, a private room at some restaurant would do. At my expense, of course. Will you?'

It was her turn to make objections, and she had several. But when Wolfe met them, and made it plain that he would accept her as a colleague only if she accepted his alternative, she finally gave in. She would phone to let me know how she was making out with the arrangements. From her manner, when she got up to go, you might have thought she had been shopping for some little item, say a handbag, and had graciously deferred to the opinion of the clerk. After I graciously escorted her out and saw her descend the seven steps to the sidewalk, I returned to the office and found Wolfe sitting with his eyes closed and his fists planted on the chair arms.

'Even money,' I said.

'On what?' he growled.

'On her against the field. She knows damn well who had a good reason and exactly what it was. It was getting too hot for comfort and she decided that the best way to duck was to wish it on some dear friend.'

His eyes opened. 'She would, certainly. A woman whose conscience has no sting will stop at nothing. But why come to me? Why didn't she cook her own stew and serve it to the police?'

'I don't know, but for a guess she was afraid the cops would get too curious and find out how she had saved her honour and her virtue and tell her mother and father, and father would spank her. Shall I also guess why you proposed your alternative instead of having her bring them here for you?'

'She wouldn't. She said so.'

'Of course she would, if you had insisted. That's your guess. Mine is that you're not desperate enough yet to take on five females in a bunch. When you told me to bring the whole dozen you knew darned well it couldn't be done, not even by me. Okay, I want instructions.'

'Later,' he muttered, and closed his eyes.

It was on the fourth floor of an old walk-up in the West Nineties near Amsterdam Avenue. I don't know what it had in the way of a kitchen or bedroom—or bedrooms—because the only room I saw was the one we were sitting in. It was medium-sized, and the couch and chairs and rugs had a homey look, the kind of homeyness that furniture gets by being used by a lot of different people for fifty or sixty years. The chair I was on had a wobbly leg, but that's no problem if you keep it in mind and make no sudden shifts. I was more concerned about the spidery little stand at my elbow on which my glass of milk was perched. I can always drink milk and had preferred it to Bubble-Pagne, registered trademark, a dime a bottle, which they were having. It was ten o'clock Wednesday evening.

The hostesses were the redhead with milky skin, Peggy Choate, and the one with big brown eyes and dimples, Nora Jaret, who shared the apartment. Carol Annis, with the fine profile and the corn-silk hair, had been there when Helen Iacono and I arrived, bringing Lucy Morgan and her throaty voice after detouring our taxi to pick her up at a street corner. They were a very attractive collection, though of course not as decorative as they had been in their ankle-length purple stolas. Girls always look better in uniforms or costumes. Take nurses or elevator girls or Miss Honeydew at a melon festival.

I was now calling her Helen, not that I felt like it, but in the detective business you have to be sociable, of course preserving your honour and virtue. In the taxi, before picking up Lucy Morgan, she told me she had been thinking it over and she doubted if it would be possible to find out which one of them had a good reason to kill Pyle, or thought she had, because Pyle had been so very careful when he had a girl come to his penthouse. The only way would be to get one of them to open up, and Helen doubted if she could get her to, since she would be practically confessing murder. So the best way would be for Helen and me, after spending an evening with them, to talk it over and decide which one was the most likely, and then she would tell Wolfe she had seen her going back to the kitchen and bringing another plate, and Wolfe would tell the police, and that would do it.

No, I didn't feel like calling her Helen. I would just as soon have been too far away from her to call her at all.

Helen's declared object in arranging the party—declared to them—was to find out from me what Nero Wolfe and the cops had done and were doing, so they would know where they stood. Helen was sure I would loosen up, she had told them, because she had been to see me and found me very nice and sympathetic. So the hostesses were making it sort of restive and intimate by serving Bubble-Pagne, though I preferred milk. I had a suspicion that at least one of them, Lucy Morgan, would have preferred whiskey or gin or rum or vodka, and maybe they all would, but that might have made me suspect that they were not just a bunch of wholesome, hard-working artists.

They didn't look festive. I wouldn't say they were haggard, but much of the bloom was off. And they hadn't bought Helen's plug for me that I was nice and sympathetic. They were absolutely sceptical, sizing me up with sidewise looks, especially Carol Annis, who sat cross-legged on the couch with her head cocked. It was she who asked me, after a few remarks had been made about how awful it had been and still was, how well I knew the chef and the other man in the kitchen. I told her she could forget Fritz. He was completely above suspicion, and anyway he had been at the range while the plates were taken. As for Zoltan, I said that though I had known him a long while we were not intimate, but that was irrelevant because, granting that he had known which guest each girl would serve, if he poisoned one of the portions and saw that a certain girl got it, why did she or some other girl come back for another plate?

'There's no proof that she did,' Carol declared. 'Nobody saw her.'

'Nobody *noticed* her.' I wasn't aggressive; I was supposed to be nice and sympathetic. 'She wouldn't have been noticed leaving the dining room because the attention of the girls who were in there was on Felix and Marjorie Quinn, who had spilled a blini, and the men wouldn't notice her. The only place she would have been noticed was in the corridor through the pantry, and if she met another girl there she could have stopped and been patting her hair or something. Anyhow, one of you must have gone back for a second plate, because when Fern Faber went for hers there wasn't any.'

'Why do you say one of us?' Nora demanded. 'If you mean one of us here. There were twelve.'

'I do mean one of you here, but I'm not saying it, I'm just quoting the police. They think it was one of you here because you were the last five.'

'How do you know what they think?'

'I'm not at liberty to say. But I do.'

'I know what I think,' Carol asserted. She had uncrossed her legs and slid forward on the couch to get her toes on the floor. 'I think it was Zoltan. I read in the *Gazette* that he's a chef at Rusterman's, and Nero Wolfe is the trustee and so he's the boss there, and I think Zoltan hated him for some reason and tried to poison him, but he gave the poisoned plate to the wrong girl. Nero Wolfe sat right next to Pyle.'

There was no point in telling her that she was simply ignoring the fact that one of them had gone back for a second helping, so I just said, 'Nobody can stop you thinking. But I doubt very much if the police would buy that.'

'What would they buy?' Peggy asked.

My personal feelings about Peggy were mixed. For: she had recognized me and named me. Against: she had accused me of liking myself. 'Anything that would fit,' I told her. 'As I said, they think it was one of you five that went back for more, and therefore they have to think that one of you gave the poison to Pyle, because what other possible reason could you have had for serving another portion? They wouldn't buy anything that didn't fit into that. That's what rules out everybody else, including Zoltan.' I looked at Carol. 'I'm sorry, Miss Annis, but that's how it is.'

'They're a bunch of dopes,' Lucy Morgan stated. 'They get an idea and then they haven't got room for another one.' She was on the floor with her legs stretched out, her back against the couch. 'I agree with Carol, there's no proof that any of us went back for another plate. That Zoltan said he didn't see anyone come back. Didn't he?'

'He did. He still does.'

'Then he's a dope too. And he said no one took two plates. Didn't he?'

'Right. He still does.'

'Then how do they know which one he's wrong about? We were

all nervous, you know that. Maybe one of us took two plates instead of one, and when she got to the dining room there she was with an extra, and she got rid of it by giving it to some guest that didn't have any.'

'Then why didn't she say so?' I asked.

'Because she was scared. The way Nero Wolfe came at us was enough to scare anybody. And now she won't say so because she has signed a statement and she's even more scared.'

I shook my head. 'I'm sorry, but if you analyse that you'll see that it won't do. It's very tricky. You can do it the way I did this afternoon. Take twenty-four little pieces of paper, on twelve of them write the names of the guests, and arrange them as they sat at the table. On the other twelve pieces write the names of the twelve girls. Then try to manipulate the twelve girl pieces so that one of them either took in two plates at once, and did not give either of them to Pyle, or went back for a second plate, and did not give either the first one or the second one to Pyle. It can't be done. For if either of those things happened there wouldn't have been one mix-up, there would have been two. Since there was only one mix-up, Pyle couldn't possibly have been served by a girl who neither brought in two plates at once nor went back for a second one. So the idea that a girl *innocently* brought in two plates is out.'

'I don't believe it,' Nora said flatly.

'It's not a question of believing.' I was still sympathetic. 'You might as well say you don't believe two plus two is four. I'll show you. May I have some paper? Any old kind.'

She went to a table and brought some, and I took my pen and wrote the twenty-four names, spacing them, and tore the paper into twenty-four pieces. Then I knelt on a rug and arranged the twelve guest pieces in a rectangle as they had sat at table—not that that mattered, since they could have been in a straight line or a circle, but it was plainer that way. The girls gathered around.

'Okay,' I said, 'show me.' I took *Quinn* and put it back of *Leacraft*. 'There's no argument about that, Marjorie Quinn brought the first plate and gave it to Leacraft. Remember there was just one mix-up, started by Peggy when she saw Pyle had been served and gave hers to Nero Wolfe. Try having any girl bring in a second plate—or bring in two at once if you still think that might have happened—without either serving Pyle or starting a second mix-up.'

My memory has had a long stiff training under the strains and pressure Wolfe has put on it, but I wouldn't undertake to report all the combinations they tried, huddled around me on the floor. They stuck to it for half an hour or more. The most persistent was Peggy Choate, the redhead. After the others had given up she stayed

390   JUST DESSERTS

with it, frowning and biting her lip, propped first on one hand and then the other. Finally she said, 'Nuts,' stretched an arm to make a jumble of all the pieces of paper, guests and girls, got up, and returned to her chair.

'It's just a trick,' said Carol Annis, perched on the couch again.

'I still don't believe it,' Nora Jaret declared. 'I do not believe that one of us deliberately poisoned a man—one of us sitting here.' Her big brown eyes were at me. 'Good lord, look at us! Point at her! Point her out! I dare you to!'

That, of course, was what I was there for—not exactly to point her out, but at least to get a hint. I had had a vague idea that one might come from watching them manoeuvre the pieces of paper, but it hadn't. Nor from anything any of them had said. I had been expecting Helen Iacono to introduce the subject of Vincent Pyle's *modus operandi* with girls, but apparently she had decided it was up to me. She hadn't spoken more than twenty words since we arrived.

'If I could point her out,' I said, 'I wouldn't be bothering the rest of you. Neither would the cops if *they* could point her out. Sooner or later, of course, they will, but it begins to look as if they'll have to get at it from the other end. Motive. They'll have to find out which one of you had a motive, and they will—sooner or later—and on that maybe I can help. I don't mean help them, I mean help you—not the one who killed him, the rest of you. That thought occurred to me after I learned that Helen Iacono had admitted that she had gone out with Pyle a few times last winter. What if she had said she hadn't? When the police found out she had lied, and they would have, she would have been in for it. It wouldn't have proved she had killed him, but the going would have been mighty rough. I understand that the rest of you have all denied that you ever had anything to do with Pyle. Is that right? Miss Annis?'

'Certainly.' Her chin was up. 'Of course I had met him. Everybody in show business has. Once when he came backstage at the Coronet, and once at a party somewhere, and one other time but I don't remember where.'

'Miss Morgan?'

She was smiling at me, a crooked smile. 'Do you call this helping us?' she demanded.

'It might lead to that after I know how you stand. After all, the cops have your statement.'

She shrugged. 'I've been around longer than Carol, so I had seen him to speak to more than she had. Once I danced with him at the Flamingo, two years ago. That was the closest I had ever been to him.'

'Miss Choate?'

'I never had the honour. I only came to New York last fall. From Montana. He had been pointed out to me from a distance, but he never chased me.'

'Miss Jaret?'

'He was Broadway,' she said. 'I'm TV.'

'Don't the twain ever meet?'

'Oh, sure. All the time at Sardi's. That's the only place I ever saw the great Pyle, and I wasn't with him.'

'So there you are,' I said, 'you're all committed. If one of you poisoned him, and though I hate to say it I don't see any way out of that, that one is lying. But if any of the others are lying, if you saw more of him than you admit, you had better get from under quick. If you don't want to tell the cops tell me, tell me now, and I'll pass it on and say I wormed it out of you. Believe me, you'll regret it if you don't.'

'Archie Goodwin, a girl's best friend,' Lucy said. 'My bosom pal.'

No one else said anything.

'Actually,' I asserted, 'I *am* your friend, all of you but one. I have a friendly feeling for all pretty girls, especially those who work, and I admire and respect you for being willing to make an honest fifty bucks by coming there yesterday to carry plates of grub to a bunch of finickers. I *am* your friend, Lucy, if you're not the murderer.'

I leaned forward, forgetting the wobbly chair leg, but it didn't object. It was about time to put a crimp in Helen's personal project. 'Another thing. It's quite possible that one of you *did* see her returning to the kitchen for another plate, and you haven't said so because you don't want to squeal on her. If so, spill it now. The longer this hangs on, the hotter it will get. When it gets so the pressure is too much for you and you decide you have got to tell it, it will be too late. Tomorrow may be too late. If you go to the cops with it tomorrow they probably won't believe you; they'll figure that you did it yourself and you're trying to squirm out. If you don't want to tell me here and now, in front of her, come with me down to Nero Wolfe's office and we'll talk it over.'

They were exchanging glances, and they were not friendly glances. When I had arrived probably not one of them, excluding the murderer, had believed that a poisoner was present, but now they all did, or at least they thought she might be; and when that feeling takes hold it's goodbye to friendliness. It would have been convenient if I could have detected fear in one of the glances, but fear and suspicion and uneasiness are too much alike on faces to tell them apart.

'You *are* a help,' Carol Annis said bitterly. 'Now you've got us hating each other. Now everybody suspects everybody.'

I had quit being nice and sympathetic. 'It's about time,' I told her. I glanced at my wrist. 'It's not midnight yet. If I've made you all realise that this is no Broadway production, or TV either, and the longer the payoff is postponed the tougher it will be for everybody, I *have* helped.' I stood up. 'Let's go. I don't say Mr Wolfe can do it by just snapping his fingers, but he might surprise you. He has often surprised me.'

'All right,' Nora said. She arose. 'Come on. This is getting too damn painful. Come on.'

I don't pretend that that was what I had been heading for. I admit that I had just been carried along by my tongue. If I arrived with the gang at midnight and Wolfe had gone to bed, he would almost certainly refuse to play. Even if he were still up, he might refuse to work, just to teach me a lesson, since I had not stuck to my instructions. Those thoughts were at me as Peggy Choate bounced up and Carol Annis started to leave the couch.

But they were wasted. That tussle with Wolfe never came off. A door at the end of the room which had been standing ajar suddenly swung open, and there in its frame was a two-legged figure with shoulders almost as broad as the doorway, and I was squinting at Sergeant Purley Stebbins of Manhattan Homicide West. He moved forward, croaking, 'I'm surprised at you, Goodwin. These ladies ought to get some sleep.'

Of course I was a monkey. If it had been Stebbins who had made a monkey of me I suppose I would have leaped for a window and dived through. Hitting the pavement from a fourth-storey window should be enough to finish a monkey, and life wouldn't be worth living if I had been bamboozled by Purley Stebbins. But obviously it hadn't been him; it had been Peggy Choate or Nora Jaret, or both; Purley had merely accepted an invitation to come and listen in.

So I kept my face. To say I was jaunty would be stretching it, but I didn't scream or tear my hair. 'Greetings,' I said heartily. 'And welcome. I've been wondering why you didn't join us instead of skulking in there in the dark.'

'I'll bet you have.' He had come to arm's length and stopped. He turned. 'You can relax, ladies.' Back to me: 'You're under arrest for obstructing justice. Come along.'

'In a minute. You've got all night.' I moved my head. 'Of course Peggy and Nora knew this hero was in there, but I'd—'

'I said come along!' he barked.

'And I said in a minute. I intend to ask a couple of questions. I wouldn't dream of resisting arrest, but I've got leg cramp from kneeling too long and if you're in a hurry you'll have to carry me.' I moved my eyes. 'I'd like to know if you all knew. Did you, Miss Iacono?'

'Of course not.'

'Miss Morgan?'

'No.'

'Miss Annis?'

'No, I didn't, but I think you did.' She tossed her head and the corn silk fluttered. 'That was contemptible. Saying you wanted to help us, so we would talk, with a policeman listening.'

'And then he arrests me?'

'That's just an act.'

'I wish it were. Ask your friends Peggy and Nora if I knew—only I suppose you wouldn't believe them. *They* knew, and they didn't tell you. You'd better all think over everything you said. Okay, Sergeant, the leg cramp's gone.'

He actually started a hand for my elbow, but I was moving and it wasn't there. I opened the door to the hall. Of course he had me go first down the three flights; no cop in his senses would descend stairs in front of a dangerous criminal in custody. When we emerged to the sidewalk and he told me to turn left I asked him, 'Why not cuffs?'

'Clown if you want to,' he croaked.

He flagged a taxi on Amsterdam Avenue, and when we were in and rolling I spoke. 'I've been thinking, about laws and liberties and so on. Take false arrest, for instance. And take obstructing justice. If a man is arrested for obstructing justice and it turns out that he didn't obstruct any justice, does that make the arrest false? I wish I knew more about law. I guess I'll have to ask a lawyer. Nathaniel Parker would know.'

It was the mention of Parker, the lawyer Wolfe uses when the occasion calls for one, that got him. He had seen Parker in action. 'They heard you,' he said, 'and I heard you, and I took some notes. You interfered in a homicide investigation. You quoted the police to them. You told them what the police think, and what they're doing and are going to do. You played a game with them with those pieces of paper to show them exactly how it figures. You tried to get them to tell you things instead of telling the police, and you were going to take them to Nero Wolfe so he could pry it out of them. And you haven't even got the excuse that Wolfe is representing a client. He hasn't got a client.'

'Wrong. He has.'

'Like hell he has. Name her.'

'Not her, him. Fritz Brenner. He is seeing red because food cooked by him was poisoned and killed a man. It's convenient to have the client living right in the house. You admit that a licensed detective has a right to investigate on behalf of a client.'

'I admit nothing.'

'That's sensible,' I said approvingly. 'You shouldn't. When you're on the stand being sued for false arrest, it would be bad to have it thrown up to you, and it would be two against one because the hackie could testify. Can you hear us, driver?'

'Sure I can hear you,' he sang out. 'It's very interesting.'

'So watch your tongue,' I told Purley. 'You could get hooked for a year's pay. As for quoting the police, I merely said that they think it was one of those five, and when Cramer told Mr Wolfe that he didn't say it was confidential. As for telling them what the police think, same comment. As for playing that game with them, why not? As for trying to get them to tell me things, I won't comment on that at all because I don't want to be rude. That must have been a slip of the tongue. If you ask me why I didn't balk that at the apartment and bring up these points then and there, what was the use? You had spoiled the party. They wouldn't have come downtown with me. Also I am saving a buck of Mr Wolfe's money, since you had arrested me and therefore the taxi fare is on the city of New York. Am I still under arrest?'

'You're damn right you are.'

'That may be ill-advised. You heard him, driver?'

'Sure I heard him.'

'Good. Try to remember it.'

We were on Ninth Avenue, stopped at Forty-second Street for a light. When the light changed and we moved, Purley told the hackie to pull over to the curb, and he obeyed. At that time of night there were plenty of gaps. Purley took something from a pocket and showed it to the hackie, and said, 'Go get yourself a Coke and come back in in ten minutes,' and he climbed out and went. Purley turned his head to glare at me.

'I'll pay for the Coke,' I offered.

He ignored it. 'Lieutenant Rowcliff,' he said, 'is expecting us at Twentieth Street.'

'Fine. Even under arrest, one will get you five that I can make him start stuttering in ten minutes.'

'You're not under arrest.'

I leaned forward to look at the meter. 'Ninety cents. From here on we'll split it.'

'Damn it, quite clowning! If you think I'm crawling you're wrong. I just don't see any percentage in it. If I deliver you in custody I know damn well what you'll do. You'll clam up. We won't get a peep out of you, and in the mroning you'll make a phone call and Parker will come. What will that get us?'

I could have said, 'A suit for false arrest,' but I made it, 'Only the pleasure of my company.'

There was one point of resemblance between Purley and Carol Annis, just one: no sense of humour. 'But,' he said, 'Lieutenant Rowcliff is expecting you, and you're a material witness in a homicide case, and you were up there working on the suspects.'

'You could arrest me as a material witness,' I suggested.

He uttered a word that I was glad the hackie wasn't there to hear, and added, 'You'd clam up and in the morning you'd be out on bail. I know it's after midnight, but the lieutenant is expecting you.'

He's a proud man, Purley is, and I wouldn't go so far as to say that he has nothing to be proud of. He's not a bad cop, as cops go. It was a temptation to keep him dangling for a while, to see how long it would take him to bring himself to the point of coming right out and asking for it, but it was late and I needed some sleep.

'You realise,' I said, 'that's it's a waste of time and energy. You can tell him everything we said, and if he tried to go into other aspects with me I'll only start making cracks and he'll start stuttering. It's perfectly useless.'

'Yeah, I know, but—'

'But the lieutenant expects me.'

He nodded. 'It was him Nora Jaret told about it, and he sent me. The Inspector wasn't around.'

'Okay. In the interest of justice. I'll give him an hour. That's understood? Exactly one hour.'

'It's not understood with me.' He was empathic. 'When we get there you're his and he's welcome to you. I don't know if he can stand you for an hour.'

At noon the next day, Thursday, Fritz stood at the end of Wolfe's desk, consulting with him on a major point of policy: whether to switch to another source of supply for watercress. The quality had been below par, which for them means perfection, for nearly a week. I was at my desk, yawning. It had been after two o'clock when I got home from my chat with Lieutenant Rowcliff, and with nine hours' sleep in two nights I was way behind.

The hour since Wolfe had come down at eleven o'clock from his morning session with the orchids had been spent, most of it, by me reporting and Wolfe listening. My visit with Rowcliff needed only a couple of sentences, since the only detail of any importance was that it had taken me eight minutes to get him stuttering, but Wolfe wanted my conversation with the girls verbatim, and also my impressions and conclusions. I told him my basic conclusion was that the only way she could be nailed, barring a stroke of luck, would be by a few dozen men sticking to the routine—her getting the poison and her connection with Pyle.

'And,' I added, 'her connection with Pyle may be hopeless. In fact, it probably is. If it's Helen Iacono, what she told us is no help. If what she told us is true she had no reason to kill him, and if it isn't true how are you going to prove it? If it's one of the others she is certainly no halfwit, and there may be absolutely nothing to link her up. Being very careful with visitors to your penthouse is fine as long as you're alive, but it has its drawbacks if one of them feeds you arsenic. It may save her neck.'

He was regarding me without enthusiasm. 'You are saying in effect that it must be left to the police. I don't have a few dozen men. I can expose her only by a stroke of luck.'

'Right. Or a stroke of genius. That's your department. I make no conclusions about genius.'

'Then why the devil were you going to bring them to me at midnight? Don't answer. I know. To badger me.'

'No, sir. I told you. I had got nowhere with them. I had got them looking at each other out of the corners of their eyes, but that was all. I kept on talking, and suddenly I heard myself inviting them to come home with me. I was giving them the excuse that I wanted them to discuss it with you, but that may have been just a cover for certain instincts that a man is entitled to. They are very attractive girls—all but one.'

'Which one?'

'That's what we're working on.'

He probably would have harped on it if Fritz hadn't entered to present the watercress problem. As they wrestled with it, dealing with it from all angles, I swivelled my back to them so I could do my yawning in private. Finally they got it settled, deciding to give the present source one more week and then switch if the quality didn't improve; and then I heard Fritz say, 'There's another matter, sir. Felix phoned me this morning. He and Zoltan would like an appointment with you after lunch, and I would like to be present. They suggested half-past two, if that will suit your convenience.'

'What is it?' Wolfe demanded. 'Something wrong at the restaurant?'

'No, sir. Concerning the misfortune of Tuesday evening.'

'What about it?'

'It would be better for them to tell you. It is their concern.'

I swivelled for a view of Fritz's face. Had Felix and Zoltan been holding out on us? Fritz's expression didn't tell me, but it did tell Wolfe something: that it would be unwise for him to insist on knowing the nature of Felix's and Zoltan's concern because Fritz had said all he intended to. There is no one more obliging than Fritz, but also there is no one more immovable when he has taken a stand. So Wolfe merely said that half-past two would be convenient. When Fritz had left I offered to go to the kitchen and see if I could pry it out of him, but Wolfe said no, apparently it wasn't urgent.

As it turned out, it wasn't. Wolfe and I were still in the dining room, with coffee, when the doorbell rang at 2:25 and Fritz answered it, and when we crossed the hall to the office Felix was in the red leather chair, Zoltan was in one of the yellow ones, and Fritz was standing. Fritz had removed his apron and put on a jacket, which was quite proper. People do not attend business conferences in aprons.

When we had exchanged greetings, and Fritz had been told to sit down and had done so, and Wolfe and I had gone to our desks, Felix spoke. 'You won't mind, Mr Wolfe, if I ask a question? Before I say why we requested an appointment?'

Wolfe told him no, go ahead.

'Because,' Felix said, 'we would like to know this first. We are under the impression that the police are making no progress. They haven't said so, they tell us nothing, but we have the impression. Is it true?'

'It was true at two o'clock this morning, twelve hours ago. They may have learned something by now, but I doubt it.'

'Do you think they will soon make progress? That they will soon be successful?'

'I don't know. I can only conjecture. Archie thinks that unless they have a stroke of luck the inquiry will be long and laborious, and even then may fail. I'm inclined to agree with him.'

Felix nodded. 'That is what we fear—Zoltan and I and others at the restaurant. It is causing a most regrettable atmosphere. A few of our most desirable patrons make jokes, but most of them do not, and some of them do not come. We do not blame them. For the maître d'hôtel and one of our chefs to assist at a dinner where a guest is served poison—that is not pleasant. If the—'

'Confound it, Felix! I have avowed my responsibility. I have apologised. Are you here for the gloomy satisfaction of reproaching me?'

'No, sir.' He was shocked. 'Of course not. We came to say that if the poisoner is not soon discovered, and then the affair will be forgotten, the effect on the restaurant may be serious. And if the

police are making no progress that may happen, so we appeal to
you. We wish to engage your professional services. We know that
with you there would be no question. You would solve it quickly
and completely. We know it wouldn't be proper to pay you from
restaurant funds, since you are the trustee, so we'll pay you with
our own money. There was a meeting of the staff last night, and all
will contribute, in a proper ration. We appeal to you.'

Zoltan stretched out a hand, arm's length. 'We appeal to you,' he
said.

'Pfui,' Wolfe grunted.

He had my sympathy. Not only was their matter-of-fact confidence in his prowess highly flattering, but also their appealing
instead of demanding, since he had got them into it, was extremely
touching. But a man with a long-standing reputation for being
hard and blunt simply can't afford the softer feelings, no matter
what the provocation. It called for great self-control.

Felix and Zoltan exchanged looks. 'He said "pfui,"' Zoltan told
Felix.

'I heard him,' Felix snapped, 'I have ears.'

Fritz spoke. 'I wished to be present,' he said, 'so I could add my
appeal to theirs. I offered to contribute, but they said no.'

Wolfe took them in, his eyes going right to left and back again.
'This is preposterous,' he declared. 'I said "pfui" not in disgust but
in astonishment. I am solely to blame for this mess, but you offer to
pay me to clean it up. Preposterous! You should know that I have
already bestirred myself. Archie?'

'Yes, sir. At least you have bestirred me.'

He skipped it. 'And,' he told them, 'your coming is opportune.
Before lunch I was sitting here considering the situation, and I
concluded that the only way to manage the affair with dispatch is
to get the wretch to betray herself; and I conceived a plan. For it I
need your cooperation. Yours, Zoltan. Your help is essential. Will
you give it? I appeal to you.'

Zoltan upturned his palms and raised his shoulders. 'But yes!
But how?'

'It is complicated. Also it will require great dexterity and aplomb.
How are you on the telephone? Some people are not themselves,
not entirely at ease, when they are phoning. A few are even
discomfited. Are you?'

'No.' He reflected. 'I don't think so. No.'

'If you are it won't work. The plan requires that you telephone
five of those women this afternoon. You will first call Miss Iacono,
tell her who are, and ask her to meet you somewhere—in some
obscure restaurant. You will say that on Tuesday evening, when

you told me that you had not seen one of them return for a second plate, you were upset and flustered by what had happened, and later, when the police questioned you, you were afraid to contradict yourself and tell the truth. But now that the notoriety is harming the restaurant you feel that you may have to reveal the fact that you did see her return for a second plate, but that before—'

'But I didn't!' Zoltan cried. 'I told—'

'*Tais-toi!*' Felix snapped at him.

Wolfe resumed. '—but that before you do so you wish to discuss it with her. You will say that one reason you have kept silent is that you have been unable to believe that anyone as attractive and charming as she is could be guilty of such a crime. A parenthesis. I should have said at the beginning that you must not try to parrot my words. I am giving you only the substance; the words must be your own, those you would naturally use. You understand that?'

'Yes, sir.' Zoltan's hands were clasped tight.

'So don't try to memorise my words. Your purpose is to get her to agree to meet you. She will of course assume that you intend to blackmail her, but you will not say so. You will try to give her the impression, in everything you say and in your tone of voice, that you will not demand money from her, but expect her favours. In short, that you desire her. I can't tell you how to convey that impression; I must leave that to you. The only requisite is that she must be convinced that if she refuses to meet you, you will go at once to the police and tell them the truth.'

'Then you know,' Zoltan said. 'Then she is guilty.'

'Not at all. I haven't the slightest idea who is guilty. When you have finished with her you will phone the other four and repeat the performance—Miss Choate, Miss Annis, Miss—'

'My God, Mr Wolfe! That's impossible!'

'Not impossible, merely difficult. You alone can do it, for they know your voice. I considered having Archie do it, imitating your voice, but it would be too risky. You said you would help, but there's no use trying it if the bare idea appals you. Will you undertake it?'

'I don't . . . I would . . .'

'He will,' Felix said. 'He is like that. He only needs to swallow it. He will do it well. But I must ask, can he be expected to get them all to agree to meet him? The guilty one, yes, but the others?'

'Certainly not. There is much to discuss and arrange. The innocent ones will react variously according to their tempers. One or more of them will probably inform the police, and I must provide for that contingency with Mr Cramer.' To Zoltan: 'Since it is possible that one of the innocent ones will agree to meet you, for some unimaginable reason, you will have to give them different hours for the appointments. There are many details to settle, but that is mere routine. The key is you. You must of course rehearse, and into a telephone transmitter. There are several stations on the house phone. You will go to Archie's room and speak from there. We will listen at the other stations: Archie in the plant rooms, I in my room, Fritz in the kitchen, and Felix here. Archie will handle the other end of the conversation; he is much better qualified than I to improvise the responses of young women.

'Do you want me to repeat the substance of what you are to say before rehearsal?'

Zoltan opened his mouth and closed it again.

'Yes,' he said.

Sergeant Purley Stebbins shifted his fanny for the nth time in two hours. 'She's not coming,' he muttered. 'It's nearly eight o'clock.' His chair was about half big enough for his personal dimensions.

We were squeezed in a corner of the kitchen of John Piotti's little restaurant on 14th Street between Second and Third Avenues. On the midget table between us were two notebooks, his and mine, and a small metal case. Of the three cords extending from the case, the two in front went to the earphones we had on, and the one at the back ran down the wall, through the floor, along the basement ceiling toward the front, back up through the floor, and on through a table top, where it was connected to a microphone hidden in a bowl of artificial flowers. The installation, a rush order, had cost Wolfe $191.67. Permission to have it made had cost him nothing because he had once got John Piotti out of a difficulty and hadn't soaked him beyond reason.

'We'll have to hang on,' I said. 'You never can tell with a redhead.'

The exposed page of my notebook was blank, but Purley had written on his. As follows:

Helen Iacono	6.00 p.m.
Peggy Choate	7.30 p.m.
Carol Annis	9.00 p.m.
Lucy Morgan	10.30 p.m.
Nora Jaret	12.00 p.m.

It was in my head. If I had had to write it down I would certainly have made one 'p.m.' do, but policemen are trained to do things right.

'Anyhow,' Purley said, 'we know damn well who it is.'

'Don't count your poisoners,' I said, 'before they're hatched.' It was pretty feeble, but I was tired and still short on sleep.

I hoped to heaven he was right, since otherwise the operation was a flop. So far everything had been fine. After half an hour of rehearsing, Zoltan had been wonderful. He had made the five calls from the extension in my room, and when he was through I told him his name should be in lights on a Broadway marquee. The toughest job had been getting Inspector Cramer to agree to Wolfe's terms, but he had no good answer to Wolfe's argument that if he insisted on changing the rules Zoltan wouldn't play. So Purley was in the kitchen with me, Cramer was with Wolfe in the office, prepared to stay for dinner, Zoltan was at the restaurant table with the hidden mike, and two homicide dicks, one male and one female, were at another table twenty feet away. One of the most elaborate charades Nero Wolfe had ever staged.

Purley was right when he said we knew who it was, but I was right too—she hadn't been hatched yet. The reactions to Zoltan's calls had settled it. Helen Iacono had been indignant and after a couple of minutes had hung up on him, and had immediately phoned the District Attorney's office. Peggy Choate had let him finish his spiel and then called him a liar, but she had not said definitely that she wouldn't meet him, and the DA or police hadn't heard from her. Carol Annis, after he had spoken his lines, had used only ten words: 'Where can I meet you?' and, after he had told her where and when: 'All right, I'll be there.' Lucy Morgan had coaxed him along, trying to get him to fill it all in on the phone, had finally said she would keep the appointment, and then had rushed downtown and rung our doorbell, told me her tale, demanded that I accompany her to the rendezvous, and insisted on seeing Wolfe. I had to promise to go to get rid of her. Nora Jaret had called him assorted names, from liar on up, or on down, and had told him she had a friend listening in on an extension, which was almost certainly a lie. Neither we nor the law had had a peep from her.

So it was Carol Annis with the corn-silk hair, that was plain enough, but there was no salt on her tail. If she was really smart and really tough she might decide to sit tight and not come, figuring that when they came at her with Zoltan's story she would say he was either mistaken or lying, and we would be up a stump. If she was dumb and only fairly tough she might scram. Of course they would find her and haul her back, but if she said Zoltan was lying and she had run because she thought she was being framed, again we would be up a stump. But if she was both smart and tough but not quite enough of either, she would turn up at nine o'clock and join Zoltan. From there on it would be up to him, but

that had been rehearsed too, and after his performance on the
phone I thought he would deliver.

At half-past eight Purley said, 'She's not coming,' and removed
his earphone.

'I never thought she would,' I said. The 'she' was of course
Peggy Choate, whose hour had been 7.30. 'I said you never can tell
with a redhead merely to make conversation.'

Purley signalled to Piotti, who had been hovering around most
of the time, and he brought us a pot of coffee and two fresh cups.
The minutes were snails, barely moving. When we had emptied
the cups I poured more. At 8.48 Purley put his earphone back on.
At 8.56 I asked, 'Shall I do a countdown?'

'You'd clown in the hot seat,' he muttered, so hoarse that it was
barely words. He always gets hoarser as the tension grows; that's
the only sign.

It was four minutes past nine when the phone brought me the
sound of a chair scraping, then faintly Zoltan's voice saying good
evening, and then a female voice, but I couldn't get the words.

'Not loud enough,' Purley whispered hoarsely.

'Shut up.' I had my pen out. 'They're standing up.'

There came the sound of chairs scraping, and other little sounds,
and then:

Zoltan: Will you have a drink?

Carol: No. I don't want anything.

Zoltan: Won't you eat something?

Carol: I don't feel . . . maybe I will.

Purley and I exchanged glances. That was promising. That
sounded as if we might get more than conversation.

Another female voice, belonging to Mrs Piotti: We have good Osso
Buco, madame. Very good. A speciality.

Carol: No, not meat.

Zoltan: A sweet perhaps?

Carol: No.

Zoltan: It is more friendly if we eat. The spaghetti with anchovy
sauce is excellent. I had some.

Carol: You had some?

I bit my lip, but he handled it fine.

Zoltan: I've been here half an hour, I wanted so much to see you.
I thought I should order something, and I tried that. I might even
eat another portion.

Carol: You should know good food. All right.

Mrs Piotti: Two spaghetti anchovy. Wine? A very good Chianti?

Carol: No. Coffee.

Pause.

Zoltan: You are more lovely without a veil, but the veil is good too. It makes me want to see behind it. Of course I—

Carol: You have seen behind it, Mr Mahany.

Zoltan: Ah! You know my name?

Carol: It was in the paper.

Zoltan: I am not sorry that you know it, I want you to know my name, but it will be nicer if you call me Zoltan.

Carol: I might some day. It will depend. I certainly won't call you Zoltan if you go on thinking what you said on the phone. You're mistaken, Mr Mahany. You didn't see me go back for another plate, because I didn't. I can't believe you would tell a vicious lie about me, so I just think you're mistaken.

Mrs Piotti, in the kitchen for the spaghetti, came to the corner to stoop and whisper into my free ear, 'She's wearing a veil.'

Zoltan: I am not mistaken, my dear. That is useless. I know. How could I be mistaken when the first moment I saw you I felt . . . but I will not try to tell you how I felt. If any of the others had come and taken another plate I would have stopped her, but not you. Before you I was dumb. So it is useless.

Needing only one hand for my pen, I used the free one to blow a kiss to Purley.

Carol: I see. So you're sure.

Zoltan: I am, my dear. Very sure.

Carol: But you haven't told the police.

Zoltan: Of course not.

Carol: Have you told Nero Wolfe or Archie Goodwin?

Zoltan: I have told no one. How could I tell anyone? Mr Wolfe is sure that the one who returned for another plate is the one who killed that man, gave him poison, and Mr Wolfe is always right. So it is terrible for me. Could I tell anyone that I know you killed a man? You? How could I? That is why I had to see you, to talk with you. If you weren't wearing that veil I could look into your beautiful eyes. I think I know what I would see there. I would see suffering and sorrow. I saw that in your eyes Tuesday evening. I know he made you suffer. I know you wouldn't kill a man unless you had to. That is why—

The voice stopped. That was understandable, since Mrs Piotti had gone through the door with the spaghetti and coffee and had had time to reach their table. Assorted sounds came as she served them.

Purley muttered, 'He's overdoing it,' and I muttered back, 'No. He's perfect.' Piotti came over and stood looking down at my notebook. It wasn't until after Mrs Piotti was back in the kitchen that Carol's voice came.

Carol: That's why I am wearing the veil, Zoltan, because I know it's in my eyes. You're right. I had to. He did make me suffer. He ruined my life.

Zoltan: No, my dear. Your life is not ruined. No! No matter what he did. Was he . . . did he . . .

I was biting my lip again. Why didn't he give them the signal? The food had been served and presumably they were eating. He had been told that it would be pointless to try to get her to give him any details of her relations with Pyle, since they would almost certainly be lies. Why didn't he give the signal? Her voice was coming:

Carol: He promised to marry me. I'm only twenty-two years old, Zoltan. I didn't think I would ever let a man touch me again, but the way you . . . I don't know. I'm glad you know I killed him because it will be better now, to know that somebody knows. To know that *you* know. Yes, I had to kill him, I *had* to, because if I didn't I would have had to kill myself. Some day I may tell you what a fool I was, how I—Oh!

Zoltan: What? What's the matter?

Carol: My bag. I left it in my car. Out front. And I didn't lock the car. A blue Plymouth hardtop. Would you . . . I'll go . . .

Zoltan: I'll get it.

The sound came of his chair scraping, then faintly his footsteps, and then silence. But the silence was broken in ten seconds, whereas it would have taken him much longer to go for the purse and return. What broke it was a male voice saying, 'I'm an officer of the law, Miss Annis,' and a noise from Carol. Purley, shedding his earphone, jumped up and went, and I followed, notebook in hand.

It was quite a tableau. The male dick stood with a hand on Carol's shoulder. Carol sat stiff, her chin up, staring straight ahead. The female dick, not much older than Carol, stood facing her from across the table, holding with both hands, at breast level, a plate of spaghetti. She spoke to Purley. 'She put something in it and then stuck something in her dress. I saw her in my mirror.'

I moved in. After all, I was in charge, under the terms Cramer had agreed to. 'Thank you, Miss Annis,' I said. 'You were a help. On a signal from Zoltan they were going to start a commotion to give him an excuse to leave the table, but you saved them the trouble. I thought you'd like to know. Come on, Zoltan. All over. According to plan.'

He had entered and stopped three paces off, a blue handbag under his arm. As he moved towards us Purley put out a hand. 'I'll take that.'

Cramer was in the red leather chair. Carol Annis was in a yellow one facing Wolfe's desk, with Purley on one side of her and his female colleague on the other. The male colleague had been sent to the laboratory with the plate of spaghetti and a small roll of paper that had been fished from inside Carol's dress. Fritz, Felix, and Zolan were on the couch near the end of my desk.

'I will not pretend, Miss Annis,' Wolfe was saying. 'One reason that I persuaded Mr Cramer to have you brought here first on your way to limbo was that I needed to appease my rancour. You had injured and humiliated not only me, but also one of my most valued friends, Fritz Brenner, and two other men whom I esteem, and I had arranged the situation that gave you your opportunity; and I wished them to witness your own humiliation, contrived by me in my presence.'

'That's enough of that,' Cramer growled.

Wolfe ignored him. 'I admit the puerility of that reason, Miss Annis, but in candour I wanted to acknowledge it. A better reason was that I wished to ask you a few questions. You took such prodigious risks that it is hard to believe in your sanity, and it would give me no satisfaction to work vengeance on a madwoman. What would you have done if Felix's eyes had been on you when you entered with the plate of poison and went to Mr Pyle? Or if, when you returned to the kitchen for a second plate, Zoltan had challenged you? What would you have done?'

No answer. Apparently she was holding her gaze straight at Wolfe, but from my angle it was hard to tell because she still had the veil on. Asked by Cramer to remove it, she had refused. When the female dick had extracted the roll of paper from inside Carol's dress she had asked Cramer if she should pull the veil off and Cramer had said no. No rough stuff.

There was no question about Wolfe's gaze at her. He was forward in his chair, his palms flat on his desk. He persisted. 'Will you answer me, Miss Annis?'

She wouldn't.

'Are you a lunatic, Miss Annis?'

She wasn't saying.

Wolfe's head jerked to me. 'Is she deranged, Archie?'

That was unnecessary. When we're alone I don't particularly mind his insinuations that I presume to be an authority on women, but there was company present. I gave him a look and snapped, 'No comment.'

He returned to her. 'Then that must wait. I leave to the police such matters as your procurement of the poison and your relations with Mr Pyle, mentioning only that you cannot now deny possession of arsenic, since you used it a second time this evening. It will unquestionably be found in the spaghetti and in the roll of paper you concealed in your dress; and so, manifestly, if you are mad you are also ruthless and malevolent. You may have been intolerably provoked by Mr Pyle, but not by Zoltan. He presented himself not as a nemesis, but as a bewitched champion. He offered his homage, making no demands, and your counter-offer was death.'

'You lie,' Carol said. 'And he lied. He was going to lie about me. He didn't see me go back for a second plate, but he was going to say he did. And you lie. He did make demands. He threatened me.'

Wolfe's brows went up. 'Then you haven't been told?'

'Told what?'

'That you were overheard. That is the other question I had for you. I have no apology for contriving the trap, but you deserve to know you are in its jaws. All that you and Zoltan said was heard by two men at the other end of a wire in another room, and they recorded it—Mr Stebbins of the police, now at your left, and Mr Goodwin.'

'You lie,' she said.

'No, Miss Annis. This isn't the trap; it has already been sprung. You have it, Mr Stebbins?'

Purley nodded. He hates to answer questions from Wolfe.

'Archie?'

'Yes, sir.'

'Did Zoltan threaten her or make demands?'

'No, sir. He followed instructions.'

He returned to Carol. 'Now you know. I wanted to make sure of that. To finish, since you may have had a just and weighty grievance against Mr Pyle, I would myself prefer to see you made to account for your attempt to kill Zoltan, but that is not in my discretion. In any case, my rancour is appeased, and I hold—'

'That's enough,' Cramer blurted, leaving his chair. 'I didn't agree to let you preach at her all night. Bring her along, Sergeant.'

As Purley arose a voice came. 'May I say something?' It was Fritz. Heads turned as he left the couch and moved, detouring around Zoltan's feet and Purley's bulk to get to Carol, and turning to stand looking down at her.

'On account of what Mr Wolfe said,' he told her. 'He said you injured me, and that is true. It is also true that I wanted him to find you. I can't speak for Felix, and you tried to kill Zoltan and I can't speak for him, but I can speak for myself. I forgive you.'

'You lie,' Carol said.

LAMB TO THE SLAUGHTER

Roald Dahl

The detective in this last story, Patrick Maloney, is neither a series character nor even a recurring figure in other stories, but he, more than anyone else, gets his just deserts. The author, Roald Dahl (1916–1990), famous for his idiosyncratic tales of malice, has taken the fact that more murders are actually committed in real life over the ordinary domestic meal than in any hotel, restaurant or inn, as the theme of 'Lamb to the Slaughter'. Dahl's interest in food has come out in several of his works, not least the bizarre novel for younger readers, Charlie and the Chocolate Factory, *and the chilling short story 'Taste', about a* nouveau riche *stockbroker who is drawn into a disastrous wager with a supercilious wine expert. In the following tale, however, which I believe perfectly rounds-off this collection, it is a commonplace joint of lamb that provides the focus for a situation of mounting tension and final, delicious irony.*

The room was warm and clean, the curtains drawn, the two table lamps alight—hers and the one by the empty chair opposite. On the sideboard behind her, two tall glasses, soda water, whisky. Fresh ice cubes in the Thermos bucket.

Mary Maloney was waiting for her husband to come home from work.

Now and again she would glance up at the clock, but without anxiety, merely to please herself with the thought that each minute gone by made it nearer the time when he would come. There was a slow smiling air about her, and about everything she did. The drop of the head as she bent over her sewing was curiously tranquil. Her skin—for this was her sixth month with child—had acquired a wonderful translucent quality, the mouth was soft, and the eyes, with their new placid look, seemed larger, darker than before.

When the clock said ten minutes to five, she began to listen, and a few moments later, punctually as always, she heard the tyres on the gravel outside, and the car door slamming, the footsteps

passing the window, the key turning in the lock. She laid aside her
sewing, stood up, and went forward to kiss him as he came in.

'Hullo, darling,' she said.

'Hullo,' he answered.

She took his coat and hung it in the closet. Then she walked over
and made the drinks, a strongish one for him, a weak one for
herself; and soon she was back again in her chair with the sewing,
and he in the other, opposite, holding the tall glass with both his
hands, rocking it so the ice cubes tinkled against the side.

For her, this was always a blissful time of day. She knew he
didn't want to speak much until the first drink was finished, and
she, on her side, was content to sit quietly, enjoying his company
after the long hours alone in the house. She loved to luxuriate in
the presence of this man, and to feel—almost as a sunbather feels
the sun—that warm male glow that came out of him to her when
they were alone together. She loved him for the way he sat loosely
in a chair, for the way he came in a door, or moved slowly across
the room with long strides. She loved the intent, far look in his
eyes when they rested on her, the funny shape of the mouth,
and especially the way he remained silent about his tiredness,
sitting still with himself until the whisky had taken some of it
away.

'Tired, darling?'

'Yes,' he said. 'I'm tired.' And as he spoke, he did an unusual
thing. He lifted his glass and drained it in one swallow although
there was still half of it, at least half of it, left. She wasn't really
watching him but she knew what he had done because she heard
the ice cubes falling back against the bottom of the empty glass
when he lowered his arm. He paused a moment, leaning forward
in the chair, then he got up and went slowly over to fetch himself
another.

'I'll get it!' she cried, jumping up.

'Sit down,' he said.

When he came back, she noticed that the new drink was dark
amber with the quantity of whisky in it.

'Darling, shall I get your slippers?'

'No.'

She watched him as he began to sip the dark yellow drink, and
she could see little oily swirls in the liquid because it was so strong.

'I think it's a shame,' she said, 'that when a policeman gets to be
as senior as you, they keep him walking about on his feet all day
long.'

He didn't answer, so she bent her head again and went on with
her sewing; but each time he lifted the drink to his lips, she heard

the ice cubes clinking against the side of the glass.

'Darling,' she said. 'Would you like me to get you some cheese? I haven't made any supper because it's Thursday.'

'No,' he said.

'If you're too tired to eat out,' she went on, 'it's still not too late. There's plenty of meat and stuff in the freezer, and you can have it right here and not even move out of the chair.'

Her eyes waited on him for answer, a smile, a little nod, but he made no sign.

'Anyway,' she went on, 'I'll get you some cheese and crackers first.'

'I don't want it,' he said.

She moved uneasily in her chair, the larger eyes still watching his face. 'But you *must* have supper. I can easily do it here. I'd like to do it. We can have lamb chops. Or pork. Anything you want. Everything's in the freezer.'

'Forget it,' he said.

'But, darling, you *must* eat! I'll fix it anyway, and then you can have it or not, as you like.'

She stood up and placed her sewing on the table by the lamp.

'Sit down,' he said. 'Just for a minute, sit down.'

'It wasn't till then that she began to get frightened.

'Go on,' he said. 'Sit down.'

She lowered herself back slowly into the chair, watching him all the time with those large, bewildered eyes. He had finished the second drink and was staring down into the glass, frowning.

'Listen,' he said, 'I've got something to tell you.'

'What is it, darling? What's the matter?'

He had become absolutely motionless, and he kept his head down so that the light from the lamp beside him fell across the upper part of his face, leaving the chin and mouth in shadow. She noticed there was a little muscle moving near the corner of his left eye.

'This is going to be a bit of a shock to you, I'm afraid,' he said. 'But I've thought about it a good deal and I've decided the only thing to do is tell you right away. I hope you won't blame me too much.'

And he told her. It didn't take long, four or five minutes at most, and she sat very still through it all, watching him with a kind of dazed horror as he went further and further away from her with each word.

'So there it is,' he added. 'And I know it's kind of a bad time to be telling you, but there simply wasn't any other way. Of course I'll give you money and see you're looked after. But there needn't really be any fuss. I hope not anyway. It wouldn't be very good for my job.

Her first instinct was not to believe any of it, to reject it all. It occurred to her that perhaps he hadn't even spoken, that she herself had imagined the whole thing. Maybe, if she went about her business and acted as though she hadn't been listening, then later, when she sort of woke up again, she might find none of it had ever happened.

'I'll get the supper,' she managed to whisper, and this time he didn't stop her.

When she walked across the room she couldn't feel her feet touching the floor. She couldn't feel anything at all—except a slight nausea and a desire to vomit. Everything was automatic now—down the stairs to the cellar, the light switch, the deep freeze, the hand inside the cabinet taking hold of the first object it met. She lifted it out, and looked at it. It was wrapped in paper, so she took off the paper and looked at it again.

A leg of lamb.

All right then, they would have lamb for supper. She carried it upstairs, holding the thin bone-end of it with both her hands, and as she went through the living-room, she saw him standing over by the window with his back to her, and she stopped.

'For God's sake,' he said, hearing her, but not turning round, 'Don't make supper for me. I'm going out.'

At that point, Mary Maloney simply walked up behind him and without any pause she swung the big frozen leg of lamb high in the air and brought it down as hard as she could on the back of his head.

She might just as well have hit him with a steel club.

She stepped back a pace, waiting, and the funny thing was that he remained standing there for at least four or five seconds, gently swaying. Then he crashed to the carpet.

The violence of the crash, the noise, the small table overturning, helped bring her out of the shock. She came out slowly, feeling cold and surprised, and she stood for a while blinking at the body, still holding the ridiculous piece of meat tight with both hands.

All right, she told herself. So I've killed him.

It was extraordinary, now, how clear her mind became all of a sudden. She began thinking very fast. As the wife of a detective, she knew quite well what the penalty would be. That was fine. It made no difference to her. In fact, it would be a relief. On the other hand, what about the child? What were the laws about murderers with unborn children? Did they kill them both—mother and child? Or did they wait until the tenth month? What did they do?

Mary Maloney didn't know. And she certainly wasn't prepared to take a chance.

She carried the meat into the kitchen, placed it in a pan, turned the oven on high, and shoved it inside. Then she washed her hands and run upstairs to the bedroom. She sat down before the mirror, tidied her face, touched up her lips and face. She tried a smile. It came out rather peculiar. She tried again.

'Hullo Sam,' she said brightly, aloud.

The voice sounded peculiar too.

'I want some potatoes please, Sam. Yes, and I think a can of peas.'

That was better. Both the smile and the voice were coming out better now. She rehearsed it several times more. Then she ran downstairs, took her coat, went out the back door, down the garden, into the street.

It wasn't six o'clock yet and the lights were still on in the grocery shop.

'Hullo Sam,' she said brightly, smiling at the man behind the counter.

'Why, good evening, Mrs Maloney. How're *you*?'

'I want some potatoes please, Sam. Yes, and I think a can of peas.'

The man turned and reached up behind him on the shelf for the peas.

'Patrick's decided he's tired and doesn't want to eat out tonight,' she told him. 'We usually go out Thursdays, you know, and now he's caught me without any vegetables in the house.'

'Then how about meat, Mrs Maloney?'

'No, I've got meat, thanks. I got a nice leg of lamb, from the freezer.'

'Oh.'

'I don't much like cooking it frozen, Sam, but I'm taking a chance on it this time. You think it'll be all right?'

'Personally,' the grocer said, 'I don't believe it makes any difference. You want these Idaho potatoes?'

'Oh yes, that'll be fine. Two of those.'

'Anything else?' The grocer cocked his head on one side, looking at her pleasantly. 'How about afterwards? What you going to give him for afterwards?'

'Well—what would you suggest, Sam?'

The man glanced around his shop. 'How about a nice big slice of cheesecakes? I know he likes that.'

'Perfect,' she said. 'He loved it.'

And when it was all wrapped and she had paid, she put on her brightest smile and said, 'Thank you, Sam. Good night.'

'Good night, Mrs Maloney. And thank *you*.'

And now, she told herself as she hurried back, all she was doing now, she was returning home to her husband and he was waiting for his supper; and she must cook it good, and make it as tasty as possible because the poor man was tired; and if, when she entered the house, she happened to find anything unusual, or tragic, or terrible, then naturally it would be a shock and she'd become frantic with grief and horror. Mind you, she wasn't *expecting* to find anything. She was just going home with the vegetables. Mrs Patrick Maloney going home with the vegetables on Thursday evening to cook supper for her husband.

That's the way, she told herself. Do everything right and natural. Keep things absolutely natural and there'll be no need for any acting at all.

Therefore, when she entered the kitchen by the back door, she was humming a little tune to herself and smiling.

'Patrick!' she called. 'How are you, darling?'

She put the parcel down on the table and went through into the living-room; and when she saw him lying there on the floor with his legs doubled up and one arm twisted back underneath his body, it really was rather a shock. All the old love and longing for him welled up inside her, and she ran over to him, knelt down beside him, and began to cry her heart out. It was easy. No acting was necessary.

A few minutes later she got up and went to the phone. She knew the number of the police station, and when the man at the other end answered, she cried to him, 'Quick! Come quick! Patrick's dead!'

'Who's speaking?'

'Mrs Maloney. Mrs Patrick Maloney.'

'You mean Patrick Maloney's dead?'

'I think so,' she sobbed. 'He's lying on the floor and I think he's dead.'

'Be right over,' the man said.

The car came very quickly, and when she opened the front door, two policemen walked in. She knew them both—she knew nearly all the men at that precinct—and she fell right into Jack Noonan's arms, weeping hysterically. He put her gently into a chair, then went over to join the other one, who was called O'Malley, kneeling by the body.

'Is he dead?' she cried.

'I'm afraid he is. What happened?'

Briefly, she told her story about going out to the grocer and coming back to find him on the floor. While she was talking, crying and talking, Noonan discovered a small patch of congealed blood on the dead man's head. He showed it to O'Malley who got up at once and hurried to the phone.

Soon, other men began to come into the house. First a doctor, then two detectives, one of whom she knew by name. Later, a police photographer arrived and took pictures, and a man who knew about fingerprints. There was a great deal of whispering and muttering beside the corpse, and the detectives kept asking her a lot of questions. But they always treated her kindly. She told her story again, this time right from the beginning, when Patrick had come in, and she was sewing, and he was tired, so tired he hadn't wanted to go out for supper. She told how she'd put the meat in the oven—'it's there now, cooking'—and how she'd slipped out to the grocer for vegetables, and come back to find him lying on the floor.

'Which grocer?' one of the detectives asked.

She told him, and he turned and whispered something to the other detective who immediately went outside into the street.

In fifteen minutes he was back with a page of notes, and there was more whispering, and through her sobbing she heard a few of the whispered phrases—'. . . acted quite normal . . . very cheerful . . . wanted to give him a good supper . . . peas . . . cheesecake . . . impossible that she . . .'

After a while, the photographer and the doctor departed and two other men came in and took the corpse away on a stretcher. Then the fingerprint man went away. The two detectives remained, and so did the two policemen. They were exceptionally nice to her, and Jack Noonan asked if she wouldn't rather go somewhere else, to her sister's house perhaps, or to his own wife who would take care of her and put her up for the night.

No, she said. She didn't feel she could move even a yard at the moment. Would they mind awfully if she stayed just where she was until she felt better? She didn't feel too good at the moment, she really didn't.

Then hadn't she better lie down on the bed? Jack Noonan asked.

No, she said, she'd like to stay right where she was, in this chair. A little later perhaps, when she felt better, she would move.

So they left her there while they went about their business, searching the house. Occasionally one of the detectives asked her another question. Sometimes Jack Noonan spoke to her gently as he passed by. Her husband, he told her, had been killed by a blow on the back of the head administered with a heavy blunt instrument, almost certainly a large piece of metal. They were looking for the weapon. The murderer may have taken it with him, but on the other hand he may've thrown it away or hidden it somewhere on the premises.

'It's the old story,' he said. 'Get the weapon, and you've got the man.'

'Later, one of the detectives came up and sat beside her. Did she know, he asked, of anything in the house that could've been used as the weapon? Would she mind having a look around to see if anything was missing—a very big spanner, for example, or a heavy metal vase.

They didn't have any heavy metal vases, she said.

'Or a big spanner?'

She didn't think they had a big spanner. But there might be some things like that in the garage.

The search went on. She knew that there were other policemen in the garden all around the house. She could hear their footsteps on the gravel outside, and sometimes she saw the flash of a torch through a chink in the curtains. It began to get late, nearly nine she noticed by the clock on the mantel. The four men searching the rooms seemed to be growing weary, a trifle exasperated.

'Jack,' she said, the next time Sergeant Noonan went by. 'Would you mind giving me a drink?'

'Sure I'll give you a drink. You mean this whisky?'

'Yes, please. But just a small one. It might make me feel better.'

He handed her the glass.

'Why don't you have one yourself,' she said. 'You must be awfully tired. Please do. You've been very good to me.'

'Well,' he answered. 'It's not stictly allowed, but I might take just a drop to keep me going.'

One by one the others came in and were persuaded to take a little nip of whisky. They stood around rather awkwardly with the drinks in their hands, uncomfortable in her presence, trying to say consoling things to her. Sergeant Noonan wandered into the kitchen, came out quickly and said, 'Look, Mrs Maloney, You know that oven of yours is still on, and the meat still inside.'

'Oh *dear* me!' she cried. 'So it is!'

'I better turn it off for you, hadn't I?'

'Will you do that, Jack. Thank you so much.'

When the sergeant returned the second time, she looked at him with her large, dark, tearful eyes. 'Jack Noonan,' she said.

'Yes?'

'Would you do me a small favour—you and these others?'

'We can try, Mrs Maloney.'

'Well,' she said. 'Here you all are, and good friends of dear Patrick's too, and helping to catch the man who killed him. You must be terrible hungry by now because it's long past your supper time, and I know Patrick would never forgive me, God bless his soul, if I allowed you to remain in his house without offering you decent hospitality. Why don't you eat up that lamb that's in the oven? It'll be cooked just right by now.'

'Wouldn't dream of it,' Sergeant Noonan said.

'Please,' she begged. 'Please eat it. Personally I couldn't touch a thing, certainly not what's been in the house when he was here. But it's all right for you. It'd be a favour to me if you'd eat it up. Then you can go on with your work again afterwards.'

There was a good deal of hesitating among the four policemen, but they were clearly hungry, and in the end they were persuaded to go into the kitchen and help themselves. The woman stayed where she was, listening to them through the open door, and she could hear them speaking among themselves their voices thick and sloppy because their mouths were full of meat.

'Have some more, Charlie?'

'No. Better not finish it.'

'She *wants* us to finish it. She said so. Be doing her a favour.'

'Okay then. Give me some more.'

'That's the hell of a big club the guy must've used to hit poor Patrick,' one of them was saying. 'The doc says his skull was smashed all to pieces just like from a sledge-hammer.'

'That's why it ought to be easy to find.'

'Exactly what I say.'

'Whoever done it, they're not going to be carrying a thing like that around with them longer than they need.'

One of them belched.

'Personally, I think it's right here on the premises.'

'Probably right under our very noses. What you think, Jack?'

And in the other room, Mary Maloney began to giggle.

ACKNOWLEDGEMENTS

The editor and publishers are grateful to the following authors, publishers and agents for permission to use copyright material in this collection: Macdonald Publishing for 'The Speciality of the House' by Stanley Ellin; Random Century Ltd for 'Bribery and Corruption' by Ruth Rendell; Fleetway Publications Ltd for 'Chef d'Oeuvre' by Paul Gallico and 'Under the Hammer' by Georges Simenon; Davis Publications Inc for 'La Spécialité de M. Duclos' by Oliver La Farge and 'Poison à la Carte' by Rex Stout; Hamish Hamilton for 'Three, or Four, for Dinner' by L. P. Hartley; Constable for 'So You Won't Talk!' by Damon Runyon; Penguin Books Ltd for 'Sauce for the Goose' from *Chillers* by Patricia Highsmith; Elaine Greene Ltd for 'A Very Commonplace Murder' by P. D. James; A. M. Heath Ltd for 'A Dinner at Imola' by August Derleth and 'The Feast in the Abbey' by Robert Bloch; Chapman & Hall Ltd for 'The Man Who Couldn't Taste Pepper' by G. B. Stern; Ziff-Davis Publishing Co for 'Final Dining' by Roger Zelazny; Aitken & Stone Ltd for 'Four-and-Twenty Blackbirds' by Agatha Christie; Victor Gollancz Ltd for 'The Long Dinner' by H. C. Bailey and 'A Case for Gourmets' by Michael Gilbert; A. D. Peters Literary Agency for 'The Assassins' Club' by Nicholas Blake; The Estate of Roy Vickers for 'Dinner for Two'; Grace Publishing Co Inc for 'Rum for Dinner' by Lawrence G. Blochman; Michael Joseph Ltd for 'Lamb to the Slaughter' by Roald Dahl. While every care has been taken to clear permission for the use of the stories in this book, in the case of any accidental infringement, copyright holders are asked to write to the editor care of the publishers.